HOW SLEEP THE BRAVE

CATHERINE GAVIN

BOOK CLUB ASSOCIATES LONDON

This edition published 1980 by
Book Club Associates
by arrangement with Hodder and Stoughton Ltd

Verses from the song, 'Long ago and far away', music by Jerome
Kern, words by Ira Gershwin, © 1944 by T. B. Harms Co., are
reproduced by permission of Chappell Music Ltd.

Printed in Great Britain by
Richard Clay (The Chaucer Press) Ltd,
Bungay, Suffolk

To my husband
JOHN ASHCRAFT
Revelation 21, v. vi

THE AVENUE 1975

How sleep the brave, who sink to rest,
By all their Country's wishes blest!

There Honour comes, a Pilgrim grey,
To bless the turf that wraps their clay,
And Freedom shall a while repair
To dwell a weeping hermit there!

William Collins

When I came back from the television studio the Paris papers were on sale at the newsagents' in Shepherd Market.

I bought Le Monde and France Soir before the shop closed. Both front pages announced a government crisis. This was nothing new in France, but had a certain relevance to what I had been doing that afternoon, which was videotaping a segment of a literary chat show for TV. It would be transmitted at half past eleven that night, between a commercial for a new cat food and one for a lavatory cleanser, and I didn't think I would wait up to see it.

Not that it had been a bad afternoon. The interviewer, briefed by his researchers, spoke pleasantly about my new book, which was what I was in the studio to chat about. But he prided himself on his investigations 'in-depth', as he called it, and probed into my life and the motive force behind my writing, further than I liked. That sort of prying made good television, the floor manager reminded me by way of consolation.

This interviewer had a theory, and made it sound convincing, that I was obsessed by the dual themes of France and war, the two combining in what he called a fixation on the Avenue des Champs Elysées. Time after time I had used this splendid Paris background as a key scene in a book. In one novel I had described the Prussian victory celebrations on the avenue in 1871. In another, it was the procession of American troops on the Fourth of July, 1918. Even in the book we were discussing, he pointed out, there was a victory parade down the Avenue des Champs Elysées at the end of World War Two.

'Not in 1944,' I objected. 'The war wasn't over then. That was a military review on Armistice Day, and Winston Churchill was at the saluting base.'

'Sorry, I meant a military review. You were there yourself, weren't you?'

'In the press tribune, yes.'

'So you can speak as an eyewitness. But in your novel you make that parade sound like a triumph.'

'So it was. Just to be there in liberated Paris, after five years of war, was a triumph for all of us. And then to see Mr. Churchill back in France, and hear half a million French people cheering him and the Allied troops, and hear the Guards' band playing "The British Grenadiers", was like the long dream of victory come true. I'll never forget it. That eleventh of November was the greatest day of my whole life.'

It was the naked truth, but thirty-one years had come and gone since that great day, and the world of 1944 had passed into history. I didn't want to listen to myself talking about it on television, between the cat munching its liver-soaked titbits and the housewife gloating over her sparkling porcelain.

I read the newspapers after I got home. France Soir had a photograph of the prime minister under the headlines. He was the man threatened by the crisis, who ever since he came to power had been under fire from the Gaullists on the right of the National Assembly and from Mitterand and his allies on the left. He had to bolster up his cabinet with votes from the surviving Radicals, among whom his career had begun, and from what was left of the Christian Democrats, plus any off-beat groups which could be drawn towards his own Centre party. He had been walking a tightrope for months, but the photograph showed him relaxed and smiling, standing on the steps of the Elysée Palace with President Giscard d'Estaing. The two men had reviewed the situation, the caption said. I foresaw that after a minor cabinet reshuffle the crisis would be ended, and the prime minister, monsieur le président du conseil, would come out on top again. He was a born survivor.

I had followed his career from its beginning. I met him first in the fatal June of 1940, when more than one disaster overtook France, and I heard his war record mentioned in the Paris of the Liberation. But it wasn't until 1951 that I guessed where he was headed, when I interviewed him for an American newsmagazine, and heard his political philosophy outlined in the lucid and illuminating way in which Frenchmen of his schooling were taught to speak. As an inexperienced Deputy, he made his name in the 1951 election. That

8

was the year when Charles de Gaulle, sick of the political wilderness to which his own vanity and misjudgment had exiled him, made another bid for power. Though he had consistently reviled the party system, de Gaulle then founded a party of his own, and invited the French people to meet him after his victory on the Avenue des Champs Elysées. That the Gaullist party was defeated, and the glorious rendezvous cancelled, was largely due to the vigorous opposition and leadership of the young Deputy who eventually became the prime minister.

He never wavered in his antagonism to de Gaulle. He protested in vain against the coup d'état of 1958 and all the measures which followed it as a result of President de Gaulle's bitter animosity towards Britain and the United States. In 1969 he was one of the men who ensured defeat for de Gaulle's last referendum, and drove the old autocrat out of the Elysée into his final exile from power.

Since he emerged as a force to be reckoned with, nearly twenty-five years back, the prime minister's life had been an open book. His happy marriage was frequently described in publications like Elle and Marie Claire, while photographs of his talented children regularly appeared in Paris Match. He had been a good skier and was still a keen tennis player, which meant that winter and summer the cameras followed him in his leisure hours. But television was his medium, and the news picture repeated the image which TV had made familiar to the whole of Europe. I scanned it again, trying to find in the austerely handsome features, the grey hair and square shoulders, any resemblance to the young man I saw marching down the Champs Elysées on the day Mr. Churchill took the salute from the Allied troops.

That Armistice Day, for the future prime minister, must have marked the end of a crucial period of his life. It covered the whole of the German Occupation of France, and was the period on which he was to preserve a complete public silence. His contemporaries, churning out their memoirs, sometimes deplored his refusal to record all he had done as a member of the French Resistance. I deplored it too, but early in his career I myself came up against the stone wall of this particular reticence. I never cared for the in-depth technique, but if I had been as persistent as my TV man I might have got more out of him for the newsmagazine interview. I recalled his words when I tried to get him to open out on the

9

Resistance. He said so many brave men had died for their country, and were forgotten, that he didn't see why any risks he took should be remembered because he had the luck to be one of the survivors.

ONE

The Hotel de l'Univers et du Limousin was only five minutes' walk away from Limoges station, in a back street leading into a public market. The street was short and narrow, but heavily travelled by wagons going between the market and the freight yards, and by German army trucks transporting military personnel. The man and the girl who went to bed dog tired in the room above the front door of the hotel, half an hour after the curfew imposed by the Occupying Power, were awakened by the noise of traffic as early as half past six. They embraced, and after the girl went back to sleep the man went quietly downstairs to use the telephone he had noticed on a counter in the café, where a fifteen-year-old boy was sweeping the floor. He slept for another hour, heavily, and when he woke again it was time to shave and begin the day.

Now it was nearly nine, and he was sitting between the bed and the window, trying to read a newspaper and waiting for the breakfast he had gone back downstairs to order. The paper was a day old, bought in a darkened station during one of the halts on their long journey from Paris, and impossible to read in the blacked-out train. The light in the bedroom was not much better, for the morning was cloudy and the bedside lamp was feeble, but by straining his eyes the man was able to read what passed for news in France on March 16, 1943. Most of the meagre paper was devoted to what French journalists called 'squashed dogs', the details of stolen bicycles, traffic accidents and funerals, but the provincial editor had done his job according to the Vichy directives. He reported Allied 'atrocities' in the form of a heavy bombing attack on Naples, but there was 'encouraging' news from the Russian front, where the Germans had opened a new offensive at Kharkov, and from Burma, where the Japanese were attacking along the Mayu river. The man read it all, paying no attention to his surroundings. The room looked as if it had been pillaged by previous guests, for apart from the bed and the stained armchair by the window there was no furniture but a wooden wardrobe with a door that refused to shut and a bentwood chair with a broken cane seat. Their own new pigskin suitcases, from the *Peau de Porc* shop in Paris, struck an odd note of elegance at the foot of the bed.

Presently the man became aware of a lull in the flow of street traffic, and the end of the sound of cold running water in what the landlady had called their private bathroom. It was only a narrow area of the bedroom partitioned off with plywood, and equipped with leaking pipes, an unreliable cistern and no window. The privacy of the occupant was assured by a grimy curtain, strung across the space from which a door had been removed and used for firewood. The man threw his newspaper on the bed and looked at his watch.

'Are you nearly ready, darling?' he said, raising his voice.

'Here I am!'

The girl who pulled aside the curtain rings was fresh and glowing, with her dark hair brushed until it shone. She was not tall, but she had long legs, slim in a pair of the new nylon stockings beneath her white satin slip, and her black court shoes had high heels. The man, with an adoring glance, told her she looked like an illustration in *La Vie Parisienne*.

'Just let me get my dress on, and I'll look more respectable.' She stepped across one of the open suitcases to the wardrobe. 'Don't you think we should go downstairs to the café for breakfast? I'm dying for some coffee.'

'I told the boy to bring it up half an hour ago.'

'I think I hear him coming now.' She pulled her dress quickly over her head. '*Entrez!*'

But it was *madame la patronne* herself who opened the door, empty handed, with a look on her face which brought the man upright.

'*M'sieur-dame,*' the woman said, 'would you come down quickly, please? There's a German patrol in the house, checking identity papers.'

'All right,' said the man. 'What are they? *Feldgendarmerie? Sicherheitsdienst?*'

'They're SS men, I think.'

'We'll be down in five minutes.'

'No longer, please, monsieur, they get impatient. I called you last because you arrived so late.'

'That's fine, thank you. We'll be right down.'

He closed the door behind her and looked at the girl. This was the first real challenge since their clandestine return from England. The French and German police, working in pairs, had checked their papers on trains and at some station barriers between Rennes, Paris and Limoges, but they had not yet been questioned in a hotel, or by the professional interrogators of the SS. The girl was trying to smile.

'Don't worry, darling,' he said, 'this won't take long. It's only a matter of routine.'

'Sure.' She pulled her dress straight at the shoulders and waist and took a key ring from her pocket. 'Shall I lock the bags?' He told her yes. There was nothing of value in the luggage, for the London money was on his body and he was unarmed, but it gave her something to do, and while she piled their belongings into the suitcases he opened the window and looked down. A German sentry had been posted on each side of the front door. That accounted for the quiet in the street, of course: the French drivers would give it a wide berth when they saw the SS moving in. He gave the girl a quick kiss and said, 'Let's go.'

There were only six bedrooms in the Hotel de l'Univers, and the downstairs premises were small. The lobby at the foot of the stairs gave access, on the left, to a small café with windows on the street, and on the opposite wall a sideboard with bottles behind the zinc counter which held the telephone and a nickel-plated machine for making coffee. There was no one at the café tables, but a few silent people were picking out their luggage from a pile near the front door, under the broad wooden railing which served as a reception desk. They were supervised by the boy who appeared to be the landlady's only helper, and who had been too flustered by the arrival of the SS men to bring up the coffee.

'In here, *m'sieur-dame*,' the woman said.

The room on the right of the lobby had once been a dining room, disused since the Hotel de l'Univers went over to bed-and-breakfast terms at the beginning of the German Occupation. It faced on a courtyard containing three ashcans and a clothesline hung with dingy towels. A high wall with a black gate in it made the dining room so dark that the lights were switched on, and two forty-watt bulbs shone down from a wooden chandelier on the spruce German uniforms and the death's head of the SS on the peaked caps. What the landlady called a patrol consisted of a German captain and a lieutenant seated at two tables pushed together, with two soldiers armed with rifles standing at their backs. In front of the SS men stood a French couple with a small boy between them, the husband volubly explaining the nature of the business which had caused him to bring his family to Limoges.

'Yes, very well, your papers are in order,' the German officer said. 'You may go.'

'Merci mille fois, mon capitaine!' The Frenchman bowed obsequiously; his wife hustled the child from the room. Captain Gerhardt watched their exit with approval. Scuttling like rabbits, that was the way he liked to see them run.

'Last two,' said the lieutenant, pushing the hotel register nearer Captain Gerhardt. 'Brunel.'

'Monsieur and Madame Jacques Brunel!'

The man and the girl, waiting just inside the room, came forward to the table, not scrambling like all their predecessors, but moving with an assurance which irritated the Germans. The man addressed them as *meine Herren Offiziere*, with a sarcastic inflection in his voice, and neither Captain Gerhardt nor his lieutenant approved of sarcasm in the conquered French.

Gerhardt gave the two before him an appraising stare. The man was about his own age, in the early thirties, and tall and well groomed. His dark suit, though casually worn, was new and made of excellent material. The girl, much younger, wore a square-cut sapphire set between two diamonds above her wedding ring. Her dress of fine wool was the same colour as the sapphire, and the cut suggested to Captain Gerhardt, who prided himself on his knowledge of Paris, that it had been made by Lanvin. He decided that the Brunels were a couple of black marketeers.

He let *meine Herren Offiziere* pass, since his orders were to conduct all identity checks in French. In that language he asked for their identity cards, and when these were produced from the man's wallet and the girl's handsome black calf bag, he laid them down for the lieutenant to see, and looked from the photographs on the documents to the people they described.

'Brunel, Jacques, barrister-at-law, resident of Nice. And Madame Brunel, Pauline, born Henri, no profession, also resident of Nice. You're on your way to Nice, monsieur?'

'We are.'

'Not by the direct route. Your travel permit was issued in Paris?'

'As you see.'

Jacques Brunel was congratulating himself that since March 1 an *Ausweis*, granting permission from the Germans to travel, had taken the form of a complicated stamp on the identity card itself, and these he had obtained at the Kommandantur in Paris. The identity cards, his wife's new since their marriage, were therefore completely valid. It was a disagreeable surprise when the captain asked to see the permits they must have obtained before leaving Nice.

These cards were false even to the cardboard, having been fabricated by a part-time forger called Daniel Profetti, who owned the Bar des Sports in a Nice back street. The cardboard, the ink, the stamp, the signatures were all suspect, and as the SS man gave one *Ausweis* to the lieutenant, the Frenchman held his breath. During the long silent scrutiny the girl by his side, who had never been told of the forgeries, remained admirably calm.

'You left Nice on the eighth of January,' Captain Gerhardt said, and Brunel relaxed. So it was the date the man had been studying, and not the possibility of fraud! 'That's right,' he said, 'it was a Friday.'

'More than two months ago. Isn't that an unusually long time for a barrister to be absent from his chambers?'

'At Nice we have a long recess in the legal calendar after the New Year.'

'You went to Paris on a vacation, then?'

'We went to Paris to be married.'

The captain transferred his gaze to Madame Brunel, at whose happy and confident smile he was almost in danger of smiling back.

'You have your marriage certificate, madame?'

'And my *livret de famille*.' She took them out of her handbag, the papers which declared that Pauline Marie Henri and Jacques André Brunel, both single, had been married ten days earlier by Jules Raymond Février, *maire-adjoint*, at the *mairie* of the seventh *arrondissement* of Paris.

'So you're on your wedding journey, monsieur?'

'You could say so.'

'I could say you have an odd taste in honeymoon hotels. Was the Hotel de l'Univers your own choice, madame? Or your husband's?'

'We had no choice,' said the bride with spirit. 'This was the nearest place we could find before the curfew. It wasn't our fault the Paris express was three hours late.'

'The delay was caused by terrorists, madame. It was reported that explosives had been laid on the railway line in two places.'

'Which turned out to be two false alarms.'

'Do you take terrorist activities lightly, Madame Brunel?'

'I don't quite know what you mean,' she hedged.

'I mean the sabotage and murder attempts by the so-called French Resistance.'

'I take these very seriously indeed.'

'Good!' said Captain Gerhardt. 'I hope you'll never come closer to the terrorists than you did last night. And now, monsieur,' he went on abruptly, 'what brings you to Limoges? Legal business?'

'Family business. A visit to my sister and her husband, who live near Oradour-sur-Glâne.'

'Their names?'

'Dr. and Madame Louis Tellier.'

'Dr. Tellier!' said the captain, and this time he smiled. 'So he's your brother-in-law! I know him very well. He's an excellent doctor, and a very good friend of ours. I wish there were more like him.'

'I'll tell him you said so,' said Jacques Brunel. 'May I know the name of his appreciative friend?'

'Gerhardt,' said the captain. 'Erwin Gerhardt. You might remind him of our meetings at the officers' club. Dr. Tellier, indeed! He surely won't expect to find you at the Hotel de l'Univers et du Limousin!'

'He knows we're here,' said Pauline Brunel. 'My husband telephoned to him early this morning, before he left home. Dr. Tellier will be here to fetch us after his hospital rounds.'

'So! I wish you a pleasant visit to Oradour-sur-Glâne. *Alles in Ordnung, mein Herr,*' said Gerhardt, handing the papers back. He stood up, with a click of the heels for Pauline and a flick of his hand to the cap with the death's head badge. The four Germans marched out in cadence, through the lobby and across the café, leaving the Brunels alone in the shabby room.

'Swine,' said Pauline, and Jacques laughed.

'Never mind, Polly,' he said, 'you did well. I liked your line on terrorist activities. And now for heaven's sake let's have some coffee.'

The café was still empty, though as soon as the Germans left a few of the regulars began to appear. It was one of the days when the sale of alcohol was permitted, and the boy, who appeared to combine the jobs of barman and porter, was kept busy serving glasses of *marc* and hot grog to men who had opened their market stalls at daybreak. The coffee machine was hissing, and the landlady herself brought Jacques' and Polly's breakfast, with apologies for the delay. She said the German patrols appeared at any hour.

'Do they bother you often?' asked Jacques.

'Oftener than you might expect,' the woman said. She lowered her voice. 'They seem to think that in small establishments like mine, so near the station, they're going to unearth the Resistance boys, or lads on the run from the forced labour service. Will you require the room tonight, sir?'

'No thank you, madame. Would you get my bill ready?'

She nodded and moved away. Polly had already poured the coffee. It was made from roasted barley, but the hot milk was fresh, and so was the small pat of butter which accompanied the newly baked bread.

'This butter tastes like butter and not like axle grease,' said Polly. She was chattering to hide her consternation at what the German had said about Dr. Tellier. Jacques was vexed enough about his father, she thought, what will he do if his brother-in-law turns out to be a collaborator? Please God it's only another of their lies.

'I don't recommend the jam,' said Jacques in the same tone. He had seated his wife with her back to the window, through which he could see that the two German sentries had really gone no further than the other side of the street. Obviously they had been left to check, to see if Dr. Tellier was going to show up at the Hotel de l'Univers et du Limousin. 'You won't tell Louis about what happened this morning?' he asked.

'Not if you don't want me to. But darling, d'you know what I've been thinking? You've never told me how Louis and Marcelle met.'

'Haven't I? It wasn't as romantic as our first meeting, my love.'

'Ah, that!' They smiled at one another, and Jacques said he really didn't know much about Louis Tellier's courtship. 'I was away from home by then, and living in Nice. One day Louis appeared in Menton, out of the blue sky, and after a lot of discussion about settlements, the engagement was announced. Where did they meet? Through his sister Cécile, while Marcelle was at the Couvent des Oiseaux. His family lives near Paris, at Ville d'Avray.'

'Why didn't Louis set up in practice in Paris, then?'

'Because his grandmother left him the house at Oradour. He

wouldn't have dreamed of selling it—he's got far too keen a sense of property for that. So has my sister as a matter of fact.' He added, regretting the mild sarcasm, 'Marcelle's a born organiser, and she runs *Le Verger* very well. They were both very kind to me two years ago, when the wound I got in Norway started acting up when I was on a job in the Corrèze. I was lucky to get as far as Limoges that time.'

The girl was beginning to wonder if they were lucky to have reached Limoges this time. She knew that Jacques thought of his sister's house as a temporary shelter for herself, and she also knew that a deep tribal instinct had urged him to present his bride to his closest relative left in France. If the day begun so badly was to end in a family row about collaboration, Polly wished they had never planned this visit to Oradour-sur-Glâne. But Jacques' gratitude for the Telliers' hospitality during his two months' convalescence was reassuring, since it might obliterate the ugly picture of Dr. Tellier fraternising with the Germans. She kept the talk in this smoother channel while the men from the market came and went, and the German soldiers on duty across the street walked up and down and in and out of Jacques Brunel's line of vision.

It was well after eleven o'clock when a big Delage carrying the medical emblem came down the street and stopped in front of the hotel. The driver locked the door before he went inside, and Jacques, rising, said 'Here's Louis now', only a moment before the newcomer succeeded in wringing his hand and kissing Polly's at the same time.

'So this is the lovely bride! Well done, *mon vieux*! Heartiest congratulations to you both!' Dr. Tellier's exuberance seemed to freshen the stale air of the shabby room, and Jacques only escaped from an outburst of backslapping by helping the doctor to take off his overcoat. He sat down between them, was delighted to accept a cup of fresh coffee, and praised Pauline for being in such good looks after what must have been a wretched journey south.

Louis Tellier, at thirty-three, was shorter and stouter than Jacques, with fair hair already thinning, and grey eyes behind horn-rimmed spectacles. A faint smell of disinfectant clung to the dark suit appropriate to a rising young consultant, and his hands were reddened by innumerable scrub-ups. He looked from one to the other, smiling expansively, as he talked about the pleasant surprises: first the news of their marriage, and then the telegram announcing this unexpected visit.

18

'And how's Marcelle?' asked Jacques.

'Splendid. I left her preparing a tremendous lunch in your honour, madame.'

'Oh, please call me Polly!'

'Polly?'

'It's the "little name" for Pauline,' Jacques explained. 'Wasn't that what they called you in Baltimore, darling?'

'Just as our little girl likes to be called Margot,' said the doctor. 'She's very excited about seeing the bride. You'll be pleased with her, I think—not three years old till next month, and as reasonable as a child of seven. But listen, Jacques,' he went on more seriously, 'you'll have to make your peace with Marcelle. She thought you might have told her sooner about your marriage plans, and she was hurt because we weren't invited to the wedding.'

'Oh, I'm so sorry,' said Pauline. 'We never dreamed you would want to come all the way to Paris. And we were married very quietly, you know. Just ourselves and our witnesses.'

The doctor had been studying her as she spoke. She was a charmer, undoubtedly, though far too skinny for his taste, and he didn't like the loose hair-do. But very well turned out—of course she could afford it—and that engagement ring must have cost Jacques a pretty penny.

'Ah well,' he said, 'you know how you ladies are about weddings. But when we got your telegram, that made all the difference. She's happy that you wanted to come to us right away.'

'I'm glad,' said Jacques. 'I knew Marcelle would understand. But now tell me, have you any news of my father and mother?'

'We had a wire from them on Monday, saying they'd arrived safely at Davos.'

Jacques shook his head. 'It's an extraordinary thing,' he said. 'I never even knew he was ill. The last time I saw mother at that phoney Italian frontier, she told me he was fit and busy. And that was only last November.'

'She didn't want to worry you, I suppose. Actually he's been sick since last summer.'

'But isn't it unusual for a man to develop tuberculosis at the age of sixty-five?'

'He was badly gassed at Vimy Ridge, remember; his own doctor thinks the damage was done then. There's no doubt the right lung is affected, and he needs absolute rest and sanatorium care.'

19

'Yes, but why Davos? Considering that Menton has been a haven for consumptives for eighty years, why did he have to go to Switzerland?'

'For the mountain air and the good Swiss food. Davos is the best place for him, and if they've caught it in time he'll enjoy reasonable health for a long while yet.'

'I'm sure I hope so,' Jacques muttered. 'It must have been a fearful upset for my mother.'

'And it's a raw deal for you too.'

'In what way?'

'Being saddled with an old-fashioned law practice, on top of your own work.' The doctor spoke sympathetically, but Pauline caught the glint of annoyance in her husband's dark eyes, and rose to her feet. 'We mustn't be late at Oradour,' she said. 'I'll get my hat and coat, and ask the porter to bring down the luggage.' The men stood up as she left the café table.

'What a delightful girl,' said Louis Tellier, producing his cigar case. 'You're in luck, *mon vieux.*'

'I know it.'

'An heiress too, I understand?'

'Who told you that?'

'Her godfather, Mr. Calvert, wrote to your parents through the Red Cross, and told them the little lady was quite a dollar princess in her father's country.'

Jacques smiled. He recognised Joe Calvert's initiative for what it was: a very experienced diplomat's knowledge of the French bourgeois attitude to marriage. An unknown American girl would hardly have been acceptable to the Brunel family, but an American heiress would be welcomed with open arms.

'Pauline's not a dollar princess by American standards,' he said, 'but her late grandfather left a very comfortable sum in trust for her. She gets it when she's twenty-five.'

'Not until then?'

'Absolutely not.'

'What about the interest?'

'Her trustees are required to add it to the principal, and give her an annual account of the transaction.'

'I hope they're reliable men.'

'Well,' said Jacques, 'I haven't met Pauline's uncle, who's one of them, but I do know Mr. Calvert, the American Minister, who's the other, and I'd stake my life on his reliability.'

'Four years to wait, eh?' The doctor had taken off his spectacles to polish them, and missed his brother-in-law's gesture of impatience. 'You'll be able to set yourself up in an *étude* in Paris when the time comes, with a nice dowry like that to look forward to.'

Restraining the impulse to say 'Was it Marcelle's dowry that brought you to Menton?' Jacques got up and said that he must pay the bill.

Just as he got his receipt Pauline came downstairs. She was dressed for outdoors in a blue coat of the same colour and material as her dress, with a little cap of blue fox fur. She carried a brightly-coloured carton as well as her handbag, and a pair of black suède gloves. The boy came behind her with the pigskin bags, and they all went out to the car.

'Polly, you must sit in front beside me,' said the doctor cheerfully, 'and let me show you the sights of the Limousin.' Jacques closed the passenger's door carefully and looked up and down the street before he got in at the back. The German soldiers were no longer to be seen. They had gone back to barracks to report that Monsieur and Madame Brunel were what they claimed to be, the guests of a great friend of the German officers in Limoges.

'Have you the right time, Jacques?' the doctor asked as he started the car.

'Just on twelve.'

'Confound it, I was hoping my watch was fast,' said Louis Tellier, glancing at his wrist. 'If it's that late my secretary'll be on her way home to lunch, and there's no point in stopping at my consulting rooms. I meant to ask her to pick up some case records for me, but that'll have to wait until this afternoon.'

'Have you an office in Limoges, Louis?' said Polly in surprise. 'I thought you were the doctor at Oradour.'

'I live at Oradour, but there were two doctors there already, a father and a son in partnership, when Marcelle and I were married, so my main practice is in Limoges. I do see patients at *Le Verger* on Fridays, so as to give my colleagues a day off, but the rest of the week I drive in and out to town.'

'You never told me that, Jacques.'

'Jacques had better things to tell you,' chuckled Louis, and Polly turned round to smile at her husband. His sharply-cut features were set in a look she knew how to interpret. Six months ago I

21

didn't know he existed, and now I adore him, I share every thought he has and every anxiety. I know his inflexible patriotism, and how he despises any kind of collaboration with the Germans, let alone the sort of deal his father did to get out of France. I hope they said everything there is to say about that when I left them alone in the café.

Limoges and its porcelain factories lay behind them, and under clearing skies they took the north road to Oradour-sur-Glâne, fourteen kilometres away. A little tramway was running on a narrow gauge line along one side of the main road. It was a modern touch in a land which had been lived in and worked over for a thousand years. The farms looked prosperous and the hamlets were wrapped in the silence of the midday meal. It was a peaceful scene. But—'the war didn't quite pass us by,' said Louis Tellier, 'though you might think so. We've had a colony of Lorrainers in the village since 1940, refugees whose homes were destroyed in the German advance. Poor devils, they were in awful shape when they arrived, but they soon got organised. They brought their teacher along, and even opened their own school. Marcelle did a lot to help them settle in. Maybe that's why most of them became my patients. Or perhaps they think the doctor from Paris is just another foreigner like themselves.'

'Did they have difficulty in finding work?' asked Jacques.

'That was one of the problems, because they were nearly all factory workers, and this is a cattle-raising country. Eventually they got jobs in Limoges, and go in and out in the little tram. Now here's the Glâne, Pauline, we're nearly home.'

It was a pleasant river, bordered by willows and poplars, one of the small singing rivers of the Limousin, where from the high plateau of Millevaches flowed the waters with the singing names: Cérone, Corrèze, Vienne, Vézere and Creuse. And Oradour-sur-Glâne was a pleasant *bourg*, with its fifteenth century church, its modest hotel and its barns near the empty fairground. The Lorraine School was lively as the car passed, for a game of football was going on. Louis Tellier explained that the pupils whose parents worked in Limoges brought their own food and passed the lunch break at play. Some of them hung over the wall and waved cheerfully to the doctor and his friends. They had rosy cheeks and seemed to be well fed and clothed.

'They've settled in all right,' said Polly, waving back.

'Oh, they have,' agreed Dr. Tellier. 'The parents are a homesick lot, always talking about going back when the war—when the Occupation's over. But those kids are part of the village now. My guess is that none of them will ever leave Oradour.'

'I can see why your house is called The Orchard,' said Polly. They had driven less than two kilometres beyond the village when they came to a square granite dwelling, made imposing by a semi-circular drive and a pillared portico. A gate set in a low stone wall was standing open. The gateposts were wreathed in winter jasmine, and on one a wooden plaque carried the name of Dr. Louis Tellier in white letters, under the larger inscription of *Le Verger*. Beyond the flower-beds on each side of the drive and under the windows, where hyacinths were showing their green tips, the *verger* was everywhere, the orderly ranks of pear and apple trees stretching to the back of the house and beyond.

'It must be wonderful in June, when the blossom's out.'

'The fruit's pretty well set by June, but you'll have to come back in summer and see it all,' said the doctor, blowing a cheerful blast on his horn. At the sound two women and a little girl appeared in the doorway, and while one, a stalwart servant in a blue print dress, hovered in the background, the other woman ran up to the car before it stopped. There was no doubt about the sincerity of Marcelle Tellier's welcome. It expressed itself in hugs for Pauline and Jacques, exclamations of How marvellous and How wonderful to see you, and commands to little Margot to kiss her aunt and uncle. Marcelle and her daughter were very much alike, with smooth fair hair and rosy cheeks, and both were dressed in pink, Margot with a starched white pinafore over her velveteen dress. Marcelle was plump and pretty, and apart from the dark brown eyes Polly could see no resemblance to Jacques, and very little to their mother, in her new sister-in-law.

'This is Jeanne; she'll bring up your luggage,' said Madame Tellier, leading Polly into the warm hall. 'Louis, look after Jacques. The drinks trolley's in the salon. Pauline, let me take you to your room. Upstairs and to your left.' The hostess, in a flurry of welcome and instructions, was holding her guest's arm in a nervous grip.

The spare bedroom contained twin beds with flowered chintz

bedspreads, and the same chintz, in a pattern of lilies of the valley, had been used for the curtains and chair covers. The wallpaper was covered with family photographs, and the dressing table with so many small silver objects like pin cushions with satin padding, ring stands and hatpin holders that Polly wondered where she would find a place for her brush and comb. She began by taking off her coat, and was touched to find little Margot by her side, shyly fingering the smooth blue wool.

She knelt down and put her arms round the little girl. 'Tell me your name, *chérie*!'

'Marguerite, Rose, Marcelle, Tellier,' with a pause between each word.

'Marguerite's for my mother,' Marcelle explained, 'and Rose for her favourite cousin, Rose Verbier, and Marcelle for me. But what's the matter?' Margot had backed away from Polly and buried her face in her mother's skirt.

'What are you trying to say, you silly child?'

'Mamam, she's not a bride.'

'Margot!'

'Oh, but I am a bride,' said Polly, rising to her feet. 'Your uncle and I have only just got married.'

'Brides wear white.'

'It was too cold in Paris to wear white. This is my wedding dress I'm wearing now.'

'Oh dear, I know what she's thinking about,' said Marcelle. 'Last week Jeanne took her to a village wedding, where there was a great display of white frocks and white roses from the town; Margot was very much impressed.'

'I carried white roses at my wedding too,' said Polly to the child.

'Where are they now?'

'In a beautiful vase in a hotel in Paris,' said Pauline, improvising. 'I had to leave them behind. But I'll tell you what I didn't leave behind, except in your papa's car, and that was a present I got you at a big shop called *Le Nain Bleu*.'

'Oh please, Tante Pauline, may I have it now?'

'Now you're not to be a nuisance,' said Marcelle, but Pauline, taking off her fur cap and shaking her hair loose, said, 'Waiting for presents is no fun. Let's go and find it right away!'

The box from the famous Paris toyshop was found to contain a splendid Noah's Ark, with the paired animals in coloured suède:

25

grey elephants, tawny lions and black panthers. The ark itself was wood, striped in all the colours of the rainbow.

That Margot was delighted was evident; that she was the reasonable little girl her father claimed her to be was shown when she asked if she might take just one of the animals to play with now and keep the rest for Sunday. She chose a giraffe and put it in the pocket of her pinafore, and then she took Polly's hand and said, 'Come and see the rabbits.'

'Not just now, Margot,' said her mother.

'Isn't there time?' asked Polly.

'Well, luncheon won't be ready for half an hour, but we're going to have apéritifs first.'

'I don't think I can resist the rabbits,' said Pauline, and the three people left in the salon saw her running down the gravel drive with the child, towards a path which Jacques remembered led to the kitchen garden. Margot had got over her shyness. Her face was turned up eagerly to Pauline's.

'Margot's taken a fancy to her,' said Marcelle.

'Pauline's awfully good with little kids,' said Jacques.

'She was helping in that children's place near Menton, wasn't she, when mother met her?'

'Yes, she'd come up with some Italian kids, refugees from the Naples bombing. I see the Allies bombed Naples heavily two days ago. I'm glad Pauline's well out of that.'

'It's all so horrible, I try not to think about it. But Jacques, I couldn't make out from what mother said on the phone, if you were visiting her at the hospital, or what, when you met Pauline?'

'Actually it was when Pauline was staying with Madame Belinska at Carnolès,' said Jacques, enjoying his sister's attempts at cross-examination.

'With the Baroness Belinska!' Marcelle digested the name of a difficult old White Russian client of her father's. 'But then, is Pauline Russian herself, or is she American?'

'Her mother was Russian, but she has an American passport.' A renewed American passport, issued at the United States Embassy in London in January, during that absence from France which was to be kept secret from the inhabitants of *Le Verger*.

'There goes the surgery telephone,' said Dr. Tellier. 'Excuse me, Jacques, and help yourself to another drink.' The drinks trolley, wheeled into one corner of an overcrowded drawing room, was amply stocked, and next to the bottle of Scotch, labelled 'Very Old Highland, Made in Frankfurt', Jacques saw a brown stone jar of German schnapps. He poured vermouth into his glass.

'You're looking very well, Marcelle,' he said. 'Put on a little weight, haven't you?'

'Oh don't! I know I'm getting fat, it's terrible!'

'But you're happy?'

'Very happy, in spite of all the horrors in the world.' She went closer to her brother and put her hand on his arm. 'But Jacques dear, I was quite *un*happy when we weren't invited to your wedding. Why didn't you let us know about it before instead of after?'

'Perhaps we should have, but we decided to keep it absolutely private. Polly's an orphan, and her stepfather died not so very long ago—'

'I never knew one had to go into deep mourning for a stepfather, and an Italian stepfather at that! Couldn't you have asked some of the Verbier cousins, and the Telliers, and Cécile?'

'There's no such thing as some of the Verbiers; they're a tribe. We didn't want a party, not in times like these, so we only took our witnesses with us to the *mairie*.'

'Who were they?'

'Louis and Anne Marie Bertrand.'

'Monsieur Bertrand. I can't place him, somehow. Was he one of your friends at law school?'

'He's a theatrical agent.' Jacques, smiling down at his sister, thought that if he added 'and his wife's a cabaret girl', he would see dismay in that smooth pink face.

'I just wish you could have had a church wedding,' said Marcelle. 'But Pauline's not a Catholic, is she?'

'If she's anything, she's Russian Orthodox like her mother.'

'Oh dear!' sighed Marcelle. 'It's all so—different, isn't it? But as long as you're both happy, that's what matters. And she really is very sweet and pretty. I'm sure we wish you all the luck in the world.'

'Thank you, Marcelle.' Jacques stooped and gratefully kissed his sister's cheek.

'And I hope you and Pauline will soon have a darling baby of your own.'

'There's no hurry,' said Jacques. 'It's not much of a world to bring a kid into, these days. Now, Marcelle, tell me something. When

27

did you first know about my father's illness?'

'I can tell you exactly, it was on New Year's Day. You know how irregular the mails have been since the—the Occupation was extended to the whole of France, and to make matters worse maman took to putting just Oradour on her letters, and some of them must have gone to Oradour-sur-Vayre. You know there's often a mix-up between those two names, that's why we always write Oradour-sur-Glâne in full. So we heard nothing all through December, not until she reached us by phone on New Year's Day and told us what the doctor said. She tried to reach you too, Jacques, but there was no answer from your flat.'

'That was the day after the murder at Cimiez,' said Jacques. 'I spent most of it with the Moreaus and the Malvys, trying to prepare them to face the examining magistrate.'

'That dreadful scandal! I didn't know you'd been briefed for that!'

'I wasn't. But Pauline and I were playing bridge with all of them while the poor little boy was killed.'

'How perfectly awful!' Marcelle lowered her voice. 'Do you really think Roger Malvy killed his own son?'

'He thought Patrick wasn't his own son, that was the whole point. But the case never came to trial, so we can't pass judgment.'

'Because Roger Malvy committed suicide in prison.'

'So I read when I was in Paris.'

'And then the whole story came out at the inquest,' said Marcelle. 'Poor Chantal Malvy, what a disgrace! You used to play tennis with her when she was Chantal Moreau.'

Jacques looked out of the window. 'Don't talk about it in front of Pauline,' he said. 'She liked Chantal Malvy, and she was very fond of poor little Patrick. His death upset her very much.'

'I'm sure it's not a pleasant topic,' said Marcelle with a toss of the head.

Polly stayed outside with the child as long as she dared. She was sure the brother and sister would want to talk about their father, and felt she was better out of the way. The rabbit hutches were at the foot of the well-stocked kitchen garden, in which early lettuce had been set out between rows of winter vegetables, and the fresh country air was so warm and mild that it was a pleasure to linger, lifting up the little girl to stroke the soft velvet noses steadily moving up and down. After twenty minutes they went back to the house. Jeanne was in the portico, ready to take charge of Margot and show Polly where to wash her hands.

'All alone, darling?' she said when she returned to the salon, where Jacques was standing in front of a bright log fire.

'Marcelle went off to the kitchen, and Louis's in the surgery, I think.' He crossed the room and took her in his arms. 'They're charmed with you, Polly, and I'm so proud of you. Kiss me, my own love.'

At the feel of that little body moulding itself to his own, and those warm, parted lips, Jacques' caress flared into passion. He kissed her hair, her neck, the scented place beneath her ear, and Polly heard him whisper, 'How can I bear to leave you behind tonight?'

'Then don't leave me. Take me with you to Toulouse. Dearest, *please*!'

'You know it's safer if I go alone. Oh, Polly!'

They heard a door slam and footsteps in the hall. Polly moved away and tried to steady her voice. 'What a lot of pretty things they have,' she said, and the amusement in her husband's eyes answered her own. Besides the sofas and chairs there were no fewer than four occasional tables in the salon, as well as a lady's writing desk laden with photographs in silver frames. The walnut, mahogany and oak tops were polished to a high gloss and loaded with small silver objects, from silver cigarette boxes and bonbon dishes to Lalique glass ashtrays and figurines. The glittering array bore witness to the Telliers' sense of property.

'I was just admiring all your lovely things,' said Pauline as Louis came in.

'Wedding presents, most of 'em,' said Louis. 'Jacques, you might have given your wife an apéritif! What would you like, Pauline? Dubonnet? Vermouth?'

'White vermouth, please. Oh, here's a picture of *your* wedding! Now I see where Margot got her ideas on how a bride should look.'

Five years earlier Marcelle Brunel had been a very pretty bride, in an extravaganza of white tulle and camellias, with her four bridesmaids on her left and her gloved hand on Louis's arm. At the bridegroom's right stood four smiling ushers in white tie and tails.

'Oh Jacques, you do look smart!' said Pauline. 'And you too, Louis, of course! All of you so happy! Who's the fair-haired boy next to you, darling?'

29

'That's my cousin, Michel Marchand.'

'Is he the one in the Royal Air Force? He looks like fun.'

'Marcelle's mother had a card from him not long ago,' said Louis.

'Did she though? What did it say?'

'Oh, nothing much, just the usual Red Cross form message. But at least we know he's alive and kicking.'

'Still in the Middle East? With the same APO number?'

'Yes, I think so. It was sent from Cairo.'

Jacques looked down at Polly. 'Mike Marchand's big dream came true,' he said, 'and how I envied him, when they made him a bomber pilot in the RAF. Last year I thought he was the one with all the luck. Now I know it was me.' He lifted the hand which wore the new wedding ring, and kissed it.

'Come along, you two lovebirds,' said Marcelle at the door. 'Lunch is ready!'

The dining table was spread in honour of the newly married couple. There were white lace place mats on the polished surface, white damask table napkins, and white Limoges plates with a tiny flower pattern. There was another impressive display of silver in the monogrammed cutlery, the silver and crystal épergne on which white jasmine sprays were twisted among the fruit, and the two silver pheasants with opulent tails which faced one another from each end of the table. Jeanne was standing by the sideboard, eager for the guests' approval.

'It's perfectly beautiful!' Polly exclaimed, and smiling from her hostess to the servant. 'What a lot of trouble you've both taken!'

'No trouble at all,' said Marcelle, delighted, and her husband pulled out Polly's chair. 'Jacques and you are sitting side by side,' he said. 'We couldn't separate two newlyweds on an occasion like this.'

Jacques took his place with a smile. If they expected Polly and himself to hold hands and ply each other with titbits from their own plates, as he remembered Marcelle and Louis doing during their engaged days, the Telliers were in for a surprise.

Now, of course, the doctor and his wife were a sedate married couple, facing each other down the length of the table like the silver pheasants, and deeply concerned with the quality of the food.

'No little girl at luncheon?' asked Polly, looking at the empty side of the table.

'She's not nearly old enough for a grown-up party,' said her mother. 'Jeanne will give her something to eat in the kitchen, and then put her to bed for her nap.'

The meal began with eggs Bercy in white Limoges ramekin dishes, and proceeded to *quenelles de brochet* served with a saffron sauce. Dr. Tellier carved the leg of spring lamb which followed, and Jeanne handed potatoes and the summer green beans which Marcelle had preserved in salt. The doctor himself poured muscadet with the fish and a fine chambertin with the lamb, and beamed when Jacques praised his connoisseurship. It was a magnificent meal, such as Jacques and Polly had not eaten for many months.

Their wedding luncheon hadn't been nearly as good, said Polly, although after the wedding at the *mairie* they had taken the Bertrands to Fouquets on the Champs Elysées and enjoyed themselves very much. She chattered happily about Paris, where they had seen new plays by Giraudoux and Sartre and Claudel in the days following their wedding, and supped in the packed cafés along the boulevards. She made Paris sound like the City of Light it used to be, without any mention of the giant swastika banners draping the public buildings, or the Occupation troops roaming the streets while German army vans carried their loads of Frenchmen from Drancy or Fresnes for interrogation by the Gestapo.

Jacques listened and admired. It was Polly at her old game, of seeming to tell so much while telling nothing, and he saw that his young wife had got the measure of the Telliers. They were trying to ignore both the Occupation and the brutality of the world war, and Polly was saying exactly what they wanted to hear. Louis was playing up to her with reminiscences of his student days in Paris, of nights at the Bal Bullier and the *chansonniers* of Montmartre. Marcelle who as a schoolgirl at the Couvent des Oiseaux had seen little of Paris beyond a few heavily chaperoned visits to the Opéra and the Comédie Française, was chiefly concerned with seeing that everybody had more than enough to eat, but she was listening for every clue her new sister-in-law might drop about the time before her marriage. Born in Paris, foreign parents dead, living in Naples, staying with a White Russian baroness—it was too complicated, too exotic, for Marcelle's conventional mind. Mother told me not to pry and question, she thought, but there are some things I have a right to know about my only brother's wife! I'll get to the bottom of her, see if I don't, once we're alone together.

Jacques Brunel wondered how many similar luncheon parties were taking place that day in Occupied France. How many people, as young and prosperous as themselves, were enjoying good food and wine, smiling, dissembling, lying to one another? How many were in the Resistance? How many sworn to overthrow Philippe Pétain, the elected Chief of State, for Charles de Gaulle, the self-styled Leader of All Free Frenchmen? How many of them would die before the Allies came to rescue France?

Jeanne removed the lamb on its platter and took away the plates. For the rest of the meal, Marcelle suggested, they might help themselves, first to an assortment of cheeses, including cheese made at *Le Verger* from the milk of their own cow, and then to apples and pears from their own orchard. Louis put a decanter of port on the table.

Jacques tasted the home-made cheese, praised it, and did his best to be entertaining. He was trying to stifle an inner sense of guilt. Marcelle had made him realise that when his father's decision to leave France was taken he had not been there to give advice or help. He had, quite simply, disappeared. He had left Nice and gone to Paris: that much they knew, and in Paris he could not be found. Three years of secrecy and suspicion made it impossible for Jacques Brunel to confide in his sister. He could not say, I am the head of a Resistance network on the Côte d'Azur. I was recruited in England, in 1940, by the Special Operations Executive, and when you were all trying to find me I was in London, taken there by air and brought back to France by sea at their orders. I'm on my way back to my network now, if and provided I'm not arrested on a charge of murder.

For the dessert, Marcelle put before them delicate plates of iridescent Venetian glass, each flanked by a matching finger-bowl on a tiny lace mat.

'We bought those plates at Murano,' she said complacently, 'when we were on our honeymoon in Italy.'

'You have beautiful things,' said Polly. Marcelle made one more trip to the sideboard and lit a methylated spirit lamp beneath the coffee percolator before she sat down. 'We've been discussing what to give you for a wedding present,' she said. 'It would've been nice to have a gift all ready for you today, but we thought we'd rather wait and let you choose. We'd like to give you a dinner service. I mean, we're so near Limoges, perhaps Pauline would come to town with me tomorrow and select a pattern.' She and her husband beamed at their expressions of thanks.

'All I've got at Nice are a few of Grand'tante Marthe's Sèvres plates,' said Jacques, 'plus some odd cups and saucers I bought in the market. A dinner service would be a splendid gift, Marcelle.'

'Well then, when Pauline decides on a pattern, shall I tell the factory to pack the china and send it direct to Nice?'

'Perhaps you should ask them to hold it for a few weeks. Pauline and I haven't decided where we're going to live.'

'You're not thinking of selling the flat in the Palais Lascaris?' said Louis. 'The flat your great-aunt left you?'

'It's in a slum, Louis,' said Jacques. 'The City of Nice has slapped a compulsory purchase order on the whole place. Sooner or later I'll have to give it up, and if I'm going to keep an eye on father's business, I ought to live in Menton.'

'If only you could go back to our own old home,' sighed Marcelle. 'It does seem a shame!'

'I quite agree.'

'We knew you'd be furious about the house,' said Louis. 'After all, it'll be your own some day.'

'That doesn't follow,' said Jacques coldly. 'My father can dispose of his property as he pleases. I'm only sorry that renting it to the German commandant of Menton was the price he had to pay for his cure in Switzerland.'

'What d'you mean?'

'Oh, come on now, Marcelle! Is it possible you don't realise that not one Frenchman in ten million can leave France with the consent of the Occupying Power?' said Jacques. 'My father must have gone hat in hand to the *Militärbefehlshaber in Frankreich* to beg for his exit permit. They only grant it for a very big bribe. My father's bribe was giving up the villa to the *Standartenführer*—'

'I know it looks like that to you,' interrupted Louis Tellier. 'But think, Jacques! The Germans could have requisitioned the house at any time and never paid a penny. This way they're at least paying rent.'

'I don't see how my father could touch their dirty money.'

'They're not all brutes, you know.'

'You think not.'

It was a statement rather than a question. Polly sat silent in distress, and Marcelle jumped up to pour the coffee. It was a relief to

33

them all when the door opened gently and little Margot came into the dining room, where they had been eating and drinking for nearly two hours.

'Here she is!' 'Did you have a nice nap?' 'What a pretty jacket!' They were all glad to be interrupted by the child, who was smiling and friendly, washed and brushed by Jeanne, and wearing a dark blue knitted cardigan above her pink dress. She went right up to *la tante* Pauline, whom she clearly preferred to the grave *oncle* Jacques, and whispered, 'Oh please, *ma tante*, won't you come and see Doucette?'

'She loves to go round the place when we have visitors,' explained her mother, 'Margot, Tante Pauline might like another cup of coffee.'

'No indeed, thank you. Am I right in thinking Doucette's the cow?'

'That's what they call an educated guess,' said Jacques. He looked at his watch. 'If we're going out, I suggest we start now. Time's getting on, and I've a train to catch.'

'You're not serious about going to Toulouse?' cried his sister.

'I told you when I called this morning, Marcelle, that I'd like to drive in to Limoges with Louis this afternoon.'

'You didn't tell me *why* you had to go.'

'I've got to see a client, Mademoiselle Thibaud. I got an eviction order for her last November against a defaulting tenant in one of her properties at Nice, but she's having difficulty in getting it executed. I want to have a talk with her before I apply to the *huissier de justice*.'

'She must be a very special client,' said the doctor dryly.

'Her late father was a valued client of *my* father,' said Jacques. 'I don't intend to let the poor girl down.'

'But you'll come back tomorrow?' said his sister.

'Perhaps Pauline will come to join me in Toulouse.'

'Travel alone? In those awful trains? It's more than I would even think of doing!'

'Yes, Marcelle, but Pauline's a more experienced traveller than you are.'

Polly looked at Jacques, with a devil of mischief in her hazel eyes which lit an answering spark in his, and said demurely, 'Jacques knows best what he's got to do.'

'You're going to be a model wife, my dear!'

'*Please*, Tante Pauline!' They had forgotten Margot, standing patiently at Polly's knee, and her mother got up unwillingly, saying that if they were going to see the place they should go now, while it was still sunny and bright. It was bright but colder, and wool wraps had to be found in the hall cloakroom before the two women and the child set out across the orchard. Polly was laughing and gay. She had had her moment of weakness when she asked Jacques to take her with him to Toulouse, and now she was strong enough to give all her attention to his sister.

Marcelle, talking above her daughter's head—for the little girl was swinging on their two hands—explained that they owned one hectare of land, and that every square metre of the two and a half acres had to pay its way. A dealer from Limoges came to pick and buy all the apples, pears and soft fruits not required for the house, while the rabbits and chickens were sold at retail, live, in the Limoges market. Doucette, the cow, provided them with milk, butter and cheese, and Pauline duly admired her, standing in her little byre. She was one of the famous Rouergue breed of the Limousin, fawn-coloured with black points and as gentle as her name.

'*Le Verger* must be almost self-supporting,' Polly said. 'I can't think how you do it all.'

'Jeanne's brother gives us a day in the gardens, now and again. But he hasn't got much time to spare from his farm, and of course Louis is always busy.'

'I wasn't thinking only of the gardens, but the house, and the animals, and the selling, and looking after Margot on top of it all. But Jacques told me you were a born organiser.'

'Did he really?'—pleased. 'Where have those men got to, by the way?'

Those men were still in the dining room. 'You've seen the place often enough,' said Dr. Tellier. 'Let's have a brandy and a cigar, and we can catch up with the girls long before we need to start for Limoges. All right, Jeanne'—to the maid who came in with a tray —'give us ten minutes, and then you can clear away.'

'You've got a first-rate cellar,' said Jacques, warming the brandy goblet in his hands.

'Thanks. Look here, *mon vieux*, there's something I want to say to you, and I don't quite know how to begin.'

'That sounds ominous!'

'I've always had a great respect for you, and I don't want—I mean, I've just got to say this—'

'Out with it, then,' said Jacques, looking amused.

'You may have pulled the wool over Marcelle's eyes,' began the doctor, 'because she trusts her only brother. But you didn't fool me with that cock and bull story about your business in Toulouse. I'm no lawyer, but I'm sure the kind of business you say you have to transact with Mademoiselle Thibaud could just as well be done by letter. No man ten days married goes off alone for such a trumped-up reason, unless he's covering for something, or someone else.'

'So what's your diagnosis, doctor?'

'We never discussed politics, did we, when you were staying here two years ago?'

'You and Marcelle had come out strong for Pétain, and I hadn't; what was the use of arguing?'

'But I had a pretty good idea of what you'd been up to before you were taken ill. I guessed it as soon as I found you in the military hospital at Limoges, as thin and miserable as a scarecrow. You'd been crossing and recrossing the Demarcation Line, picking up stranded British Tommies and passing them on to other people who'd taken them further on the road to Spain. A *passeur*, isn't that the name they gave to men who did that kind of job?'

'Somebody had to do it,' said Jacques.

'Personally I believe the British let us down in '40,' said Louis, 'but if I'd found some wretched Tommy in a ditch, I wouldn't have minded giving him food and even clothing, if he needed it. But times have changed since those days. The Occupation's complete and there's nothing we can do about it.'

'There I disagree,' said Jacques. 'We can resist it.'

'Are you working for that man de Gaulle?'

'God forbid!'

'But you've as good as admitted that you carried on your—your clandestine activities after you went back to Nice? That you're now actually, completely, working for the so-called Resistance?'

'And if I am, what then?'

'Then you've thrown in your lot with a bunch of Communists, with the riff-raff of the cities, with petty criminals like those maquis- ards, as they call themselves, who've been blackmailing the farmers in the Corrèze. And if that's the case I'm asking you for your own sake, for all our sakes, to give it up.'

'If I refuse,' said Jacques, 'will you turn me in to the *Schutzstaffel*? To your pal *Hauptsturmführer* Erwin Gerhardt?'

'What the devil are you talking about?'

'Pauline and I were interrogated by Captain Gerhardt at the Hotel de l'Univers this morning,' said Jacques. 'He wasn't exactly satisfied with our papers or our story. But as soon as I named my eminent brother-in-law he was all smiles. Said you were a very good friend of the Germans, a welcome guest at their officers' club, and so on. Is it true?'

'My God!' Louis Tellier took off his spectacles and rubbed his eyes. 'Captain Gerhardt? I think I know the man you mean. About our age, tall, blond? I met him twice at the German officers' club. I've been there exactly three times in all.'

'How did you come to go there in the first place?'

'As the guest of one of the doctors at the German military hospital, after we'd been on a case together.'

'You mean you've been *working* for the Germans?'

'Listen, Jacques.' There was perspiration on the doctor's forehead, but he was not without dignity. 'I was called in the first time when one of their men, a kid of nineteen, was badly injured on a tank training course—'

'Who d'you think they'll use the tanks against?' said Jacques. 'Frenchmen, when we get back into the war.'

'I operated, and saved his life that day, and I don't regret it.'

'The life of an enemy?'

'I would have done as much for an Englishman, or an Italian, or a Japanese. I've assisted the German army doctors whenever they've asked my help. I don't regard them as my enemies. I have only one enemy—human suffering.'

'Noble,' said Jacques. 'Humanitarian. And collaborationist.'

'I've been perfectly open and above board about my visits to their hospital. But this—this adventure you're engaged in is destructive, secret, murderous! And it could end in imprisonment, you know that. Or torture. Or death.'

'Or liberty,' said Jacques.

'Will that sweet little girl you married be able to live on liberty when you're in a German concentration camp?'

'Ah, you do realise such places exist,' said Jacques. 'Don't worry about my girl,' and he smiled at last. 'She's in the Resistance with me—up to the neck.'

THREE

Toulouse at the beginning of 1943 was second only to Lyon as a stronghold of the French Resistance. It was an important railway centre, which gave men on the run from the Gestapo or the *Milice* a chance to change their route to safety, and there were a number of safe-houses in the town. The Resistance had strong supporters in the Toulouse *gendarmerie*. Although the Gestapo commander, *Rittmeister* Redzeck, was a zealous officer, the local police were always ready to give the underground an early warning of plans for house searches or arrests.

When Jacques Brunel arrived in Toulouse before ten o'clock that evening he thought it was too late to telephone Mademoiselle Thibaud and substantiate a cover story so thin it hadn't even fooled his brother-in-law. He felt safe enough as he walked the dark streets on his way to the Hotel de Paris.

The redoubtable *patronne*, Madame de Mongélard, was already a legend in the Resistance. She was sitting in her little glass cubicle in the lobby working at her accounts, with a white shawl round her shoulders and looking exactly as Jacques remembered her. She remembered him too, though it was months since his last visit, and greeted him by name.

'Good evening, Maître Brunel, you are expected. Monsieur Aletti arrived two hours ago.'

'Thank you, madame. I hope you're well?'

'Well enough, monsieur. Have you dined?'

'I'm not hungry. I hope Monsieur Aletti didn't wait for me?'

'He had some dinner in his room with the gentleman from Nice.'

'What gentleman from Nice?'

For answer she turned the hotel register round on the desk and let him read the name of Henri Froment. 'Is it all right?' she said under her breath, and Jacques told her it was perfectly all right, Monsieur Froment was an old friend. He signed the register.

Madame de Mongélard laid a heavy key before him. 'Room

Eighteen on the first floor,' she said. 'Monsieur Aletti is in Twenty-four and Monsieur Froment in Twenty-five, on the second. They said you might want some wine and something to eat later on.'

'Very likely,' said Jacques. 'I'll join them as soon as I've had a wash.'

'Joël will take up your bag,' said the *patronne*, 'and I think I'll send you a hot rum grog at the same time. You look chilled to the bone, Maître Brunel.'

There must have been a boiling kettle in the kitchen, for almost as soon as he reached his cold but comfortable room the pigskin suitcase and the hot grog in a glass with a metal lid arrived together, carried by a wheezing porter who bowed in the old-fashioned way when he received his tip. Jacques left the glass on the table and washed in cold water: when he looked at his face in the mirror above the basin he knew why Madame de Mongélard had thought he was chilled to the bone. Never ruddy, his thin face was pale and drawn, the dark eyes sunk too deeply in their sockets, as if that one day in the Limousin had obliterated the reflection of all the lovely hours with Polly. He sipped the drink. A hot rum grog had been his own prescription for clandestine arrivals in France, or for hunted men trying to get out of the country, and it seemed all wrong to be drinking alone. But it wasn't a bad idea to have a mouthful of spirits, like a man in danger, before he met the friends whose judgment could be literally a matter of life and death. In a state between fear and anticipation he ran upstairs, and knocked at the door of number Twenty-four.

'*Entrez!*' The two men waiting for him were hardly less tense, but when Jacques Brunel came in they sprang up with a show of cheerfulness. 'Glad to see you, Captain Jack!' '*Bienvenu, mon capitaine!*' The first greetings and the hearty handshakings were followed by congratulations on his marriage.

'Bravo, you've organised a fire!' said Jacques. It was a small fire, burning in an old-fashioned grate, but it took the chill off the room, and there was a handful of the thin firewood called *margotins* in the empty coal scuttle. A candle and a box of matches had been set between two ornamental vases on the mantelpiece.

'Charles managed that,' said Froment. 'He chatted up the maid, and gave her a kiss and a few francs, and she did the rest.'

'Nice work, Charles.' It was comical to see how alike the two men were. Froment, who kept a garage in the Rue Barillerie at

Nice and had served in Jacques' company in Norway, was ten years older than Lieutenant Charles Maxwell, alias Charles Aletti, seconded from the Royal Artillery to the Special Operations Executive and landed in France by submarine in the previous November. But both belonged to the same Mediterranean type, short and stocky with black curly hair, and they were dressed alike in blue suits, Maxwell's shabby and Froment's the well-brushed serge he kept for Sundays.

'Henri, this is a fine surprise,' said Jacques, sitting down by the fire. 'I didn't know you'd be coming to Toulouse.'

'I didn't know myself until yesterday, when Charles turned up at the garage and talked me into going along with him.'

'I figured Henri could put you in the Nice picture better than I could,' said Maxwell.

'Madame's not with you?' said Henri, looking at the door as if he expected Pauline to enter at any moment.

'No, I left her with my sister at Oradour-sur-Glâne.'

'I'm looking forward to meeting her,' said Maxwell. 'Henri's been singing her praises all evening. He says she came to warn you under the very noses of the Gestapo the night Malvy betrayed the Resistance meeting at Cimiez.'

'We were both too late with the warning,' said Jacques. 'But when I knifed the *milicien* in the Parc des Arènes Pauline was waiting for me with the getaway car.' He looked at his silent friends and went on roughly, 'That's what this meeting's all about, isn't it? I want to know if the heat's off, so that I can go back to Nice with some degree of safety.'

Maxwell looked mutely at Henri Froment, who said in his deliberate way, 'We think the only danger now is Pierre Orengo. Of the other men Malvy sold, Renaudon died under torture in the hands of the Gestapo, and those who were captured were taken to the camps in Germany. But Orengo was handed over to the Italians, just to keep them happy, and he landed in San Remo. He's got enough wealthy connections there to bribe the Fascist Gestapo—the OVRA—well, and my information is that Monsieur Orengo's living in a comfortable villa, under nominal house arrest.'

'Well, good for Orengo!'

'That's all very fine, Jack, but you've got to think of yourself,' said Maxwell. 'If the going gets rough, Orengo may be interrogated at the House of Torture in San Remo, and he knows you were the man who tried to get them out of the mess at Cimiez that night. If Orengo talks to save his skin and names you, it won't take the Gestapo long to tie you in with the murder in the Parc des Arènes.'

Jacques Brunel shrugged. 'I'm no more at risk now than the day poor silly Sabre lost his briefcase with all our names in it—yours and mine included, Charles! The thing that haunts me is knocking off that *milicien*. Oh, don't get me wrong! It's not a guilty haunting. That young brute shot Sabre in the back and then came after me. I killed him in self-defence and I don't lie awake about it. But when I left for Paris the papers were full of the hunt for "the third man", and when I came back from London they seemed to have dropped the story. What does that mean?'

'You knew Roger Malvy committed suicide in prison?' said Froment, and Jacques nodded with compressed lips.

'That was when the press killed the "third man" story,' Maxwell said. 'The inquest on Malvy was sensational. There was as much dirty linen washed in public as if he'd actually stood trial, wasn't there, Henri? Then there was the investigation into how Malvy got the cyanide pill, who gave it to him and when. The Criminal Brigade's too busy on that one to follow up the murder in the Parc des Arènes.'

'I hope so,' said Jacques. 'Do either of you know what happened to Malvy's girlfriend?'

'Fabienne Leroux? After she turned Malvy in to the police, and told them he'd confessed to killing the child, she packed her bags and did a moonlight flit from the Hotel Mimosa. She was coining money out of the German officers, and the story goes that she went off to Berlin with an SS colonel.'

'That I don't believe,' said Jacques decidedly. 'She was a crazy girl, but not all that crazy. She'll turn up again, and probably denounce the lot of us, but if Fabienne's out of the picture for now that seems to wrap the whole thing up.' He stubbed out his cigarette. 'All right, let's lay it on the line. What are my chances of survival if I go back to Nice?'

His friends looked at one another without speaking. A log broke and fell in sparks among the ashes before Maxwell said reluctantly, 'Fifty-fifty.'

'You, Henri?'

'I agree with Charles. Fifty-fifty.'

'That's good enough for me,' said Jacques Brunel. 'I'll go on fifty-fifty, so that's settled.' He looked at his watch. 'It's a bit too late to telephone to Oradour-sur-Glâne, but I'll call my wife first thing in the morning and tell her to come on to Toulouse. She'll be here the day after tomorrow.'

'You're not going back to Oradour to get her?' said Maxwell in surprise.

'I reserved a seat for her on the Friday morning train before I left Limoges,' said Jacques. 'She'll be all right on her own.'

'My God,' said Maxwell, 'You're a cool customer and no mistake. A train journey's no joke for a woman alone, these days.'

'You don't know Pauline,' said her husband with a smile. 'Remember the night you came ashore at Cap Martin, and I said you made a nice landing? You should have seen Polly on the beach at St. Cast, after we came over from the Helford River! The beachmaster lifted her out of the MGB, and in a couple of minutes she was streaking up the cliff path like a—a gazelle! And the next day she walked for miles, jolted in country buses for more miles, and walked again till we caught the train to Rennes, never tired, never a word of complaint! She's a wonder, that's all—'

'And this is the man,' said Maxwell to Froment with a grin, 'who used to say he didn't approve of women at war, because girls got hurt too easily ... So then you went to Paris and got married?'

'Yes, with some help from the Bertrands. You certainly picked a pair of real friends for us! They did a fine job of getting us out to London, and they never turned a hair when we showed up again in Paris a few weeks later. Polly lived with them at the Cité du Retiro while I got my residence qualification in the seventh *arrondissement*—Actually I only took a hotel room there, and went to Lyon for the big Resistance meeting.'

Maxwell nodded. His job in France was to teach sabotage, but he knew no explosive more lethal than the dissensions of the sorely divided country. The meeting at Lyon had been called in the name of unity, but he doubted if the nature of the unity had appealed to his friend Brunel.

'Jean Moulin was there,' he said, 'What did you think of him?'

'Moulin's very impressive. De Gaulle's personal representative for the whole of France, and a far bigger man than poor Alain Renaudon. He was the star of the show and he knew it. Every time he spoke he hammered home the message that there was only one leader for the French—de Gaulle.'

'Did you speak yourself?' asked Maxwell curiously.

'I put one point to the meeting. I said the British were spending one million pounds every month on de Gaulle and his movement, and one fighting division in the field after three years didn't seem to be much return for their money.'

'How do you know about the one million pounds?' asked Froment.

'An American diplomat I met in London—Joe Calvert, Pauline's godfather—had it at first hand from the Secretary of State.'

'Did *you* bring back any money?' asked Charles Maxwell.

'From de Gaulle's personal representative? Is it likely?'

'I mean from the men who recruited both of us. The SOE boys in Baker Street.'

'I brought back £1,000 in francs from Baker Street, and I'm carrying it on me now.'

'*One* thousand pounds!' said Maxwell. 'You won't get far on that.'

'You think not? The next agent is bringing you £5,000, Charles, they told me that. But I settled for a thousand, just for running expenses and black market petrol, and chiefly to reimburse old Jurac at the Col de Castillon for feeding Daniel Profetti's boy and his friends all winter.'

'The maquisards!' said Maxwell. 'Were *they* what brought you back?'

'More or less,' said Jacques. 'I feel responsible for them. It was I who encouraged young Dany to get out of Nice and up to his grandfather's farm, and the other kids followed. I want to recruit more of them, and make them into soldiers—if I can.'

'I'm with you, *chef*, the whole way, you know that,' said Henri Froment. 'But old Jurac hasn't done too badly out of his grandson and the other maquisards. The Bar des Sports has been making money lately, and I know Profetti's been keeping his father-in-law in funds. The kids are all right. Jean Dupont's been up to see them a few times in the grocery van, and he says they've all been earning wages at one job or another. Three of them got taken on as woodcutters and two found casual labour on the farms. Young Dany Profetti's got a job down at Sospel, working on the Nice to Cunéo railway line; and talking of recruits, he picked up one on the wrong side of the tracks.'

'Meaning?'

'He brought a fellow called Victor Marcati up to the Jurac farm. Marcati's a Corsican by birth, older than the rest of the bunch, and throws his weight around a bit. But Jean Dupont checked him out and seemed to think he was all right. He's on the run from the forced labour service, like the rest of them.'

'What's his record?'

'He's been done twice for poaching.'

'No, I meant his army record.'

'He served with the 173rd DBA in Champagne in 1940.'

'Good,' said Jacques. 'I'll have a look at Monsieur Marcati some time next week.'

'And you're going on to Nice on Friday?' Maxwell asked, and Jacques nodded. 'Tomorrow you and I will have a talk about weapons,' he said. 'We won't win the war with two duelling pistols and an airgun, which I believe is the extent of the armoury at Castillon. I'd like you to plan your timetable so as to spend a few days with those kids and me. I need instruction in sabotage as much as they do, because I was a company commander, not a saboteur. And about Nice and the fifty-fifty chance, I'm going to bluff it out. I made a mistake last night when I took Pauline to a rotten fleabag of a hotel in Limoges. I couldn't very well avoid it, we were nearly caught by the curfew. But when we go to Nice I'm going to take a suite at the Negresco and do the thing in style. The Boches understand that sort of act. They think any Frenchman who's throwing his money around is a collaborator or a black marketeer or both, and they leave him alone. I'm not going to crouch in my flat in the Old Town, waiting for the knock on the door. I'm going to give a reception for my bride to meet all my friends and colleagues and ask them to drink her health in champagne. Consider yourselves invited.'

'And after the Negresco?' said Maxwell, laughing.

'After the Negresco I'm going to shift my base to Menton, and go to war.'

Jacques raised his arms above his head and stretched luxuriously. He felt relieved and exhilarated at the same time, his mind clear of doubts and even of anxiety. He was back in the great, exciting, deadly game, and there was nowhere to go but forward now.

'I didn't mean to harangue you for so long,' he said. 'Let's ask them for that bottle of wine and a bite to eat. You two have given me back my appetite.'

44

A few days after Polly Brunel joined her husband at Toulouse, and travelled on to Nice with him and Henri Froment, Jean Moulin's efforts on behalf of his Leader bore fruit. The five principal Resistance groups in France agreed to accept General de Gaulle as their 'sole chief', and were amalgamated as the United Resistance Movement.

This decision was not known in Nice on the afternoon when Maître Brunel's friends and colleagues at the Nice Bar brought their wives to the Hotel Negresco to sip champagne and wish the newly married couple joy, happiness and long life. By the calendar spring had arrived, but the mistral had swooped down on Nice, bringing a cold rain with it, and the weather, rather than the Resistance, was a smoother subject of conversation for a company trying hard to put the clock back at least five years. Mingling suavely with the guests were the forger and sporting character Daniel Profetti senior, wearing one of the new zoot suits, and Henri Froment, more conservatively attired in his best blue serge. Polly herself wore a white cocktail dress which Anne Marie Bertrand, the cabaret singer, had helped her to pick out in Paris, and as all the guests brought the conventional offering of flowers there were enough white roses in the salon to satisfy little Margot Tellier's notion of what was due to a bride.

She received many compliments, and thought the most sincere came from Maître Pastorelli, the elderly bachelor who shared chambers and a law clerk with her husband. He told Polly he hoped the young Brunels would be in no hurry to give up the apartment Jacques owned in the Palais Lascaris. 'It'll take the City of Nice at least a year to clear the place,' he said. 'Most of the tenants are the sort to hang on as squatters until the police put them out, and your husband agrees with me that the City will be compelled to seek a score of eviction orders.'

'Jacques wouldn't want to be a squatter,' said Polly, 'and he thinks we ought to live in Menton for the present.'

'But where, dear lady?'

'His father owns a flat in the Rue Longue where we could have vacant possession.

'In the Old Town?' The lawyer shook his head dubiously. 'Hardly a desirable neighbourhood. I'm sorry to hear Maître Brunel talking about returning to Menton. He made a brilliant start at the Bar, and he ought to be building up his reputation in Nice with his sights set on Paris, instead of going back to a solicitor's office. But there's no future for an honest man in Occupied France, unless—'

He left the sentence unfinished, but even so it was the most forthright thing anybody said to Polly at a reception where all unpleasant topics were carefully swept under the carpet. No future for an honest man unless he pockets his honesty, licks boots at Vichy, collaborates with the Germans! 'Jacques may be lucky to have Menton to fall back on,' she said to his friend.

Next day they drove to Menton, thirty kilometres away, in Jacques' old Peugeot, which had been stored behind an iron shutter in Henri Froment's garage. The mistral had blown itself out, and in the Baie des Anges the colour of the sea was changing from an angry grey to indigo. There was next to no traffic on the Basse Corniche. It was a road which held memories for them both, and Jacques was not entirely surprised when as he drove through Monaco Polly began to talk about Fabienne Leroux. For many weeks she had avoided any mention of Fabienne, or the dreadful story of little Patrick's murder, but he knew Henri Froment had talked about it at Toulouse and told her the story of the woman's flight. Now she said,

'Has the Hotel Mimosa been standing empty since Fabienne went away?'

'Oh no. Henri says her parents came out of retirement and began to run the place all over again. They're going great guns with their German customers.'

'Do they know where she is?'

'I shouldn't think so. From what I hear they as good as threw her out on account of the scandal. It made a big sensation in Monaco when she turned her lover in to the police.'

Polly shivered. 'I don't see how she could. I think Roger Malvy was horrible, but he threw himself on Fabienne's mercy when he went to her for shelter, and she betrayed him.'

46

'She may have thought she was doing her duty to society.'

'I think she took revenge upon society,' said Polly unexpectedly. 'She always carried a big chip on her shoulder. Jacques, do you think she really went to Germany?'

'To Paris, more likely. She had friends there, I know. Fabienne's bad news, darling. She can't stay far enough away for me.'

They were silent until they reached Cap Martin, where Jacques stopped the car outside a little grocer's shop.

Jean Dupont, the owner of the shop, came out to greet them, and having hung a piece of cardboard with the crudely lettered word *Fermé* on the front door, took them into the back premises to drink their health in a fiery *marc* which made Polly cough. Dupont had been Jacques' corporal at Namsos, in the Norwegian campaign of 1940, and was the resistant in his little network whom he trusted equally with Henri Froment. He had seen Jacques and Polly together once before, and was now confident that he had been 'sure they'd make a match of it. It was great to have the *chef* back,' he continued, and as soon as he got the message from Nice he'd sent word to the boys at the Jurac farm at the Col de Castillon. 'All the lads'll be there by four o'clock,' he said. 'They'll finish off the jobs they're doing and be ready to meet you in good time.'

'What do you think of them, Jean?' said Jacques.

'They're good lads, *chef*, but they've been let run wild a bit too long. Once you take them in hand they'll soon come into line. Just keep your eyes open for Marcati.'

'That's the Corsican, isn't it? What's his trouble?'

'Well, he's seven or eight years older than the kids from Nice, see, and he's got them into the way of going down to Sospel for a night out. They've got two or three bikes at the farm now, and they use them in turns to ride down the hill and see their girls.'

'The Sospel girls got accustomed to company,' said Jacques with a laugh, 'when there were two barracks in the place. And if our kids can push their bikes back up the mountain after a night out, then good luck to them. I'll warn them that we don't want any angry fathers coming up to Castillon with shotguns.'

Dupont said 'Fine!' and waved them cheerfully away. They left Cap Martin by the old Roman road, along the shore of the Bay of Peace, to Menton under its encircling mountains. One advantage of total Occupation, as Jacques remarked, was that it had done away with that phoney frontier at Carnolès, which lay west of the town. There were no more red and white barriers across the road, no Italian guards to check their passage as they headed for the Avenue Félix Faure, where Jacques' grandfather had established his law offices soon after the war of 1870.

They left the car, after taking the usual elaborate precautions against theft, in a little square where orange trees grew, the bright fruit glowing among the dark green leaves, and walked a short distance back along the avenue to where a heavy wooden door bore the brass plate of Maître Théophile Brunel. Beside it were the plates of a doctor specialising in internal medicine and a dentist, all three much worn by time. There was no concierge, and a small door with a Yale lock set in the ancient wood opened at a push, for Jacques was expected, and Polly was surprised to find herself in a little garden with pink geraniums growing at the foot of two palm trees and mauve iris breaking into flower. The buildings, forming a square, were only two storeys high, but each had a row of attic windows beneath the red-tiled roof.

'How pretty!' said Polly. 'Does anyone live here?'

'There are flats above the main entrance, as you can see from the street, and above the doctor's and the dentist's too. The floor above our *étude, and* the attic, are used for storage: I don't believe my father, or his father before him, ever threw a document away.'

The Brunel *étude* was in the wing of the building opposite the front door, and Jacques pointed out that it had a private entrance at the back in the form of a tall gate opening on a narrow street called the Traverse Bellecour. An archway, in which the gate was set, contained several doors in what Jacques called an old-fashioned layout. On the left, one door led to the main office and another to the staircase, while on the right was Maître Brunel's private office with a washroom for the whole staff beyond. 'The apprentices used to kick at having to go out of doors whenever my father sent for them,' said Jacques, 'but he thought the clients had more privacy this way.' He opened the door of the main office and ushered Polly inside.

The main office was very large, with windows at the front and back, and divided at about one third of its length by a broad counter with a flap at the end nearest the door. The pen thus formed contained two wooden benches set at right angles, intended for callers and clients, while beyond the counter stood rows of tall desks with metal inkwells and pen rests, each with a high stool set before it. Only two of the desks were occupied, one by a little old man who changed the spectacles on his nose for a pair pushed up on the crown of his head before he recognised Jacques, and the other by a boy who climbed off his stool awkwardly and limped across the floor towards them.

'Maître Brunel?' he said. 'Please come in, monsieur. Madame.' He raised the counter flap to let them pass, and the old man seized his employer's son by the hand. 'It's good to see you, Monsieur Jacques,' he said. 'And this is the charming bride? All my sincere good wishes to you both.'

'Pauline, this is Monsieur Janot,' said Jacques. 'He's been with my father for—how long is it? Thirty-five years; and gave me my first instruction in conveyancing.'

'I had a very apt pupil, Madame Jacques,' said the old man. He looked at the girl as if he approved of her: no hat, alas, but a fresh pair of white gloves, sensible shoes, and a pretty yellow dress under a plain coat. Not a fashion-plate, to be the ruin of her husband, but a creature with plenty of spirit, he could see that.

'We've had some sad changes here, monsieur, since you were with us last,' he began, and launched into a long account of the older Brunel's illness, the renting of the villa to the German colonel (most correct in all the arrangements) and his thankfulness in hearing that the sick man had arrived safely in Davos. 'Please God we'll soon have him back with us,' he said emotionally, 'but if you could see your way to helping us out for a time, even on a temporary basis, I know it's what your father would have wished.'

'I'll do what I can,' said Jacques. 'You don't seem to be over-worked at present.'

Monsieur Janot's face fell. 'It's true,' he said. 'Business fell off badly last year, and we lost some clients to Messieurs Hervé and Furet in the Avenue Carnot. Your father wasn't equal to it, that's the truth, and of course we've had no law apprentices since 1939.'

'And who's your new clerk?' said Jacques pleasantly, turning to the lame boy standing by the counter, as if it would be wrong to get back on his stool and get on with his work. 'Do I know you? Your face seems very familiar.'

'This is Christophe Monnier,' said Monsieur Janot, 'he came to us last year, when he graduated from high school.'

'I think you know my brother, sir,' said the boy nervously. 'Julien Monnier, in the Rue Trenca.'

'Of course, there's a family resemblance. Give your brother my regards, Christophe.'

'The daybooks, ledgers and journals are ready for your examination, Monsieur Jacques,' said Monsieur Janot. 'They're all properly updated and arranged in your father's room.'

'I'm sure they are, but I'd rather not start on them until tomorrow. There must be a couple of days' work involved, and my wife and I have other engagements this afternoon. For one thing, we want to look at the flat in the Rue Longue.'

'You're not serious about living in the Old Town? I don't believe the lady would like that—'

'If it's as much fun as the Old Town of Nice, I'll love it,' said Polly. 'Just tell me, is the flat really habitable?'

'Oh perfectly, madame, but it hasn't been lived in since the last tenant died in—May, was it, Christophe? (That was old Monsieur Terno, who used to work in the post office,' he said in an aside to Jacques.) 'Your father had some repairs and painting done last summer, but he couldn't get it off his hands. People tend to fight shy of the Old Town since the bombardment.'

'That was nearly three years ago,' said Jacques. 'We'll go along and have a look at it, if you'll let me have the key. Oh, and talking of the post office, are they still renting the garage in the Traverse Bellecour?'

'No, monsieur, the garage is standing empty. The postal vans are all kept in one place now.'

When Jacques left with Polly, he had taken possession of three keys, all for Yale locks, and fitting the front and back gates of the office building, and the apartment on the Rue Longue. His only remark as they crossed the garden was 'Let's leave the car where it is, and walk. It isn't far,' and they had gone past the square with the orange trees before he said ruefully, 'Well, that wasn't much of a beginning, was it? I don't think I'll run Messieurs Hervé and Furet out of business with the help of an old age pensioner and a poor lame boy.'

'Oh, but I think the place itself has possibilities,' said Polly. 'I like the back entry, and the big empty garage.'

'So do I.'

'Is Christophe's brother Julien one of your group, darling?'

'The butcher in the Rue Trenca? Yes, he's one of the best men in the Menton group. I remember now, he once told me his kid brother was a polio victim.'

'I think the kid might be quite helpful too.'

They were walking along the Rue St. Michel, the main street of the town, which only a few years ago had been so lively with huge crowds from the northern cities, profiting by the new law of holidays with pay. Before the French trippers there had been the English *milords* and the Russian grand dukes, in the winters when Menton basked in the sunshine of the *belle époque*. Now the street was deserted and shutters were up on many shops never reopened since the exodus of 1940, while the big hotels with the evocative names, the Royal Westminster and the Balmoral, were not expecting English guests. Polly found the empty streets depressing and Jacques was silently remembering his irritation with Louis Tellier when the doctor spoke of the 'old-fashioned business' in Menton. He could have called it a moribund business and been dead right, thought the man who remembered the Brunel *étude* before the war, with four law apprentices and six articled clerks at work in the main office, and his father's confidential clerk a man who himself had earned a law degree at Paris.

'If this is the Old Town it's a whole lot livelier than the New,' said Polly. They had arrived at the Place du Cap, and could see beyond a line of palm trees to the sea. There were a lot of people about, old men sunning themselves on the low stone walls and women carrying home half empty market baskets along the steep streets which rose to the cathedral square and beyond it to the place where an ancient stronghold of the Lascaris had once stood. The Rue Longue was older than the Lascaris and the Grimaldi, for it was part of the Via Julia along which the Roman legions marched to the Ligurian shore, and at a far later date the young Bonaparte had come that way from Italy. Polly declared excitedly that it was even narrower than the Rue Droite at Nice, but it was cleaner and fresher than the Rue Droite, being more open to the sky, and intersected here and there by traverses which were flights of stone stairs leading above and below to other alleys parallel to the Rue Longue itself. One flight led up to the Cathedral of St. Michel, where the Archangel in Roman dress stood above the door with his foot on the neck of a remarkably cheerful Devil.

There was one traverse in their way which was without steps, a traverse like a gully which had been torn out of the rock by enemy action, obliterating whatever living space had been built beneath, and at the sight of it Jacques halted in dismay. 'It's worse than I realised,' he said.

'Is that the house, on the far side?'

'Yes it is. It doesn't look habitable to me.'

No rebuilding had been attempted inside the gulley gouged out by Italian shells, but a handrail had been put up for safety, and looking over the railing they could see iron struts built on the road below to shore up the pavement of the Rue Longue, and the stone-work of the house beyond was reinforced by S-shaped iron bars. It was obvious that people were still living there, because while they hesitated a heavily pregnant young woman came out guiding a toddler, and paused to speak to one of the women with the shopping baskets, plodding homeward beneath the lines of washing which hung from the windows of the tall old houses.

'It's safe enough,' said Polly. 'Do let's go in!' She was eager to see inside the house and begin what would be a new life for them both.

The gossiping women moved aside to let them enter. The lobby was small and dark, with a colonnaded staircase dating from the eighteenth century, and with what looked like a spear or lance attached to a bracket in the left-hand wall. The door with the Yale lock, to which Jacques had the key, was at the foot of the staircase, and he noted that the panels had recently been replaced by new wood. As a contrast to the modern lock there was a heavy iron bar attached to the inside of the door, ready to be slipped into an equally heavy socket.

This much they saw, in the tiny entrance hall, by the flame of Jacques' cigarette lighter, for the electricity had been cut off. But one of two doors ahead of them was ajar, and through the gap they could see sunlight lying, in the bars formed by tall louvred shutters, across a marble floor. The room was empty, the rusty hasp of the shutters opened like the window lock, and before their eyes was a scene of surpassing beauty.

They saw, across the marble balustrade of a wide balcony, the ancient bastion of Menton, sheltering the port from the west wind, and beyond the harbour wall the Bay of Garavan, with the waves breaking gently on the stony beach. To the east of the bay they could see the Porte de France, where the true Italian frontier lay, and the red rocks above it, in the clear light seeming as near to them as the palm trees fringing the beach below. Jacques had seen that great seascape a thousand times, but now he was seeing it through Polly's eyes, and he drew her close to him as she stood enchanted beside the balustrade, over which an untidy tangle of purple bougain-villaea was rioting.

'Oh, isn't it beautiful! Oh darling, we simply must live here!' she cried.

'Gently, my love; we can't live on a view,' he told her, and Polly, listening to the voice of commonsense, turned back into the flat with him. Their exploration did not take long. Next to the room they had seen was another, exactly similar: both were big rooms about five metres square, with high ceilings ornamented with carved cornices which in an earlier day would have been picked out in gold leaf. Maître Brunel's repainting had consisted of a simple coat of whitewash on walls and ceiling, which gave the two rooms a box-like appearance, and in one a fine white marble mantel-piece had had its grate removed and replaced by a small stove made of blue porcelain with a vent inside the chimney. In the other room, presumably the bedroom, there was no fireplace, but two divans with torn ticking had been left behind as not worth re-moving. The small kitchen and bathroom, opening off the hall, were as Polly said no worse than those Jacques used in the Palais Lascaris, with no hot water in the kitchen sink (where a new wooden draining board had been installed) but with a geyser in the bathroom which provided hot water for the basin and a small claw-footed tub. The floors throughout the flat were of the local marble, speckled in shades of grey, brown and terra-cotta.

'Do you really think we could make a go of it here?' said Jacques. They were standing in the bedroom, where the walls were brilliant in the light refracted from the sparkling sea.

'I think your furniture will look wonderful in these white rooms,' Polly answered obliquely, and Jacques laughed. 'There's no outlet for a telephone, nor any hope of getting a new phone put in,' he said. 'I want to be able to reach my father and mother in Davos if there's an emergency. I suppose I'll have to use the office phone.'

'Wouldn't it be better to keep in touch with them through Mar-celle? So that the monitors wouldn't register any international calls from your number?'

'You're learning fast, Pauline.'

'I've got a good teacher,' she said, and Jacques took her in his arms. 'Oh, my darling, do you really think you could be happy here? It's not the kind of home I wanted to give you—'

'But we'll be together,' she said, and put her hands round his neck.

'How many servants were there in your stepfather's house?'

'Six when I got away from Naples. A butler and five doddering old women, all equally incompetent. Nobody could make them mind, after my mother died. And goodness knows she wasn't very smart at keeping house ... Jacques?'

He was kissing her lightly, in the way she called 'nibbling', and all he said in answer to his name was 'Mm-m?'

'Jacques, I don't know much about keeping house myself.'

'I don't want a housekeeper, I want a lover.'

Polly's response was so immediate and so generous that Jacques' desire, never long dormant, flared into passion, and over her head he looked at the divan with the torn ticking and wondered if he could satisfy their love on such a dingy couch. But just as he slipped one arm beneath her knees to lift and carry her, there came a sudden pounding on the door of the flat, and a rough voice called, 'Police! Open up!'

Jacques let Polly go, and without one word of reassurance he strode across the room and pulled the door wide. 'What the devil do you want?' he said.

The policeman—he was an older man with a drooping, dragoon's moustache—said defensively, 'We've been asked to keep an eye on these premises, monsieur. And some people in the street below saw the shutters open—'

'Some people would do well to mind their own business,' said Jacques. 'I'm Maître Jacques Brunel, and the flat belongs to my father. My wife and I are thinking of coming to live here. Does that satisfy you?' He produced the Yale key from his jacket pocket.

The policeman recognised the tone of cold authority, and asked for no further identification. '*Mille pardons*, monsieur,' he said, 'I didn't recognise you. And these days, with terrorists about, we can't be too careful about premises left empty. *Mes excuses*, madame.' He touched two fingers to his képi and backed out of the little hall.

Jacques and Polly were smiling as they fastened the shutters and

54

the windows and double locked the door. But the policeman was still there when they came back down the Rue Longue, chatting idly with some of the loungers by the Porte des Logettes, above the fountain where the women had filled their pails since the days of Bonaparte, and they felt his eyes upon them as they made their way back to the car. The impression of being watched, or in a more sinister sense *gardés à vue* was so strong that even when they were driving up the Val du Carei Jacques looked in the rear mirror more than once to see if they were being followed.

But the road, running north, was empty all the way to the hamlet of Monti, except for a mule-cart coming down the steep track which led to the monastery of the Annonciade, and at Monti, where there was an inn and an old church, the only vehicle was a wood-cutter's tumbril, with the driver allowing his horse to drink at the public trough. Jacques relaxed, and answered Polly's questions: no, it was neither himself or Profetti senior who had thought of sending young Dany up to his grandfather's farm, it was the boy's mother, who wanted to get him away from bad company in Nice. The other boys had followed later. But yes, it was his own idea that they should keep an eye on Sospel, because the town was important out of all proportion to its size. 'It's easier to show you than to tell you why, darling,' he said. 'If we've time before it gets dark I'll drive on a bit further, and let you get the lie of the land.'

Polly shivered in spite of herself. The land they entered, as they left the Carëi behind, was very different from the lush valley on the outskirts of the town, where every garden had its bush of scented mimosa, its wild freesias and cyclamens. Under the limestone peaks only the *garrigue* flourished, the maze of terebinth and wild olive, of cistus and lentisk, with trees of silver broom for brightness, and here and there the blossoms of wild cherry. The shadow of the great forest of Menton fell across their path.

They came to the village of Castillon, far larger than Monti, and there they were in the cherry country proper, of which the Jurac farm was a part. There were old people at work between the rows of cherry trees, who looked suspiciously at the strange car as it passed, and the trees themselves, which would produce the famous 'pigeon's heart' cherries of the district, the sweet creamy fruit streaked with red, were showing the first pink blossoms. Among the orchards were some lemon and olive groves, planted between the stone walls of descending terraces, and on the flat table land of the Col de Castillon itself little flocks of sheep and goats were grazing in the alpine meadows.

Jacques turned the car off the road into an open space covered with grass and pine needles at the foot of the trees. 'This is where old Jurac used to load his carts for market,' he said. 'Let's leave the car here and walk up. I daren't risk my tyres on the track to the farm, it's only fit for mules.'

The mountain air was sweet and cold, and under the evergreens the maquis spread its tangles of rosemary, myrtle and rue. They could smell woodsmoke, and almost as the long low *mas* and the farm buildings came in sight they saw Dany Profetti hurrying down the track to greet them, followed by the hobbling form of his grandfather.

'*Salut*, Captain Jack! *Mes hommages*, madame!' A winter on the mountain had only increased the self-assurance of Dany-the-Terror, for whom Jacques had obtained a suspended sentence on charges of larceny and verbal menaces at Nice in the previous November. He had grown taller and broader and weather-beaten, and was now a handsome boy of nineteen, with long dark hair and dark eyes, obviously the apple of his grandfather's eye. He was a good boy, the old man said, they were all fine lads; he would be sorry when they went away.

'You've been very good to them, Monsieur Jurac,' said Jacques. 'We must have a talk about that later. But—here, Dany! Your father sent two cartons of cigarettes for the lot of you.' Dany took the package with a shout of joy, and his grandfather remarked that cigarettes were the great problem, the lads could never have enough.

'And I've got something for Madame Jurac,' said Polly, showing the parcels she had carried from the car. One contained a kilo of real coffee beans, an inestimable gift bought on the Nice black market, the other a large fruit cake baked in the kitchens of the Hotel Negresco. Dany said his grandmother would be delighted. 'She's anxious to meet you, madame,' he said, 'but I think the boys would like to see you first.'

The boys, six in number, were waiting in various degrees of embarrassment at the corner of the barn. They were dressed more or less in a paramilitary rig-out of heavy sweaters and corduroy trousers, with berets which one or two of them took off as Jacques came up, and was introduced by Dany as Captain Jack.

'*Salut, les gars*,' said Jacques. 'This is my wife, Pauline. Take a good look at her, because you'll be meeting her again, and I want you to be able to recognise her.'

There was an awkward laugh, and one low-pitched but unmistakable wolf whistle, as Dany hastily began to introduce his friends one by one. They had quite ordinary names like Georges and Eugène, but each seemed to prefer his nickname, and announced it as he shook hands with the Brunels: Jojo, Gigène, Léo, Pierrot. The most youthful, whose name was Bernard, answered to Bébé, and the tall man with flashing black eyes introduced as Victor Marcati said with a low bow to Polly, 'Totor *pour les dames*! Totor to please the ladies!'

'I know you want to talk about weapons and strategy, and all sorts of things I don't understand,' she said prettily, 'so I'll go and sit with Madame Jurac, if I may.'

The old man led her across the farmyard. Even to her inexperienced eyes it seemed to be well-kept, with a huge oil press in one corner, and all the poultry and farm animals in good condition. Polly looked back as they reached the garden gate. The young men were still outside, gathered round her husband, and Jacques in an old tweed suit looked ten years younger and more carefree, as if he had found his natural habitat in the mountain maquis. Then she turned with a smiling face to the door of the *mas*, where a little old lady in a black dress and a clean white apron, so bowed by a lifetime of toil as to be almost a hunchback, stood curtseying to her with the grave good manners of a bygone age.

Victor Marcati, the Corsican whom Froment and Dupont had mentioned, began to do the honours when the men entered the barn. He had taught the boys to call it *la chambrée*, army style, he explained; and fair enough, they slept there, didn't they? and also ate their evening meal there. At noon they ate wherever they'd been able to find casual labour, and the morning *soupe* they were allowed by *la vieille* (as he called Madame Jurac) to eat in the farm kitchen. But here Dany intervened, insisting that their sleeping quarters had been set up long before Totor joined the group, and in fact the sleeping bags were laid neatly on trusses of fresh hay. There was a long wooden table with a bench on each side in the centre of the barn, and as he sat down Jacques noted that a weapons rack had been carved in wood and held four French Army Lebel rifles and four shotguns, all very clean, and decidedly better than the duelling pistols of Jacques' prediction.

'Well, boys,' he said when they were all seated, 'it's good to see you. I wish I could have been here sooner, but I've been travelling. I see you've made yourselves very snug on the mountain, and I'm told you've worked all winter at every job you could put your hands to. Now I've got some ideas for you to think about, but first I want to ask you one question: what's the German strength down in Sospel?'

There were some murmurs, which seemed to add up to 'No strength at all, nothing to speak of' but the boy Jojo was more precise. 'The station *kontrol* was taken off at the New Year,' he said. 'There are German civilian customs officers checking the freight traffic now. Their office is at the railway station, and they're billetted at the Hotel de France and the Hotel des Etrangers.'

'That's very clear,' said Jacques. 'What about the Caserne Salel, that was turned into a concentration camp in '40?'

'It was Italian-run, *chef*, and they've moved the camp into the Hautes Alpes, at Embrun.'

'So the enemy garrison at Sospel is all Italian?' said Jacques.

'That's right,' said Dany. 'They're not a bad lot of chaps. I mean to say, they don't bother us when they see us in the town.'

'And you don't bother them, is that it?' said Jacques sharply.

'That's about it.'

'Very well,' said Jacques. 'Now let me tell you something. I was in Lyon last month, and when I was there I listened to an address by an army general—a retired army general—who was giving his views on how the Resistance should fight the enemy. He was a great believer in the redoubt theory, or the bastion theory, if you like that better.' And seeing the incomprehension in the young faces, he explained, 'By bastion he meant a high place, as it might be Fort Castillon, where the maquisards would gather in strength and wait for the enemy to attack them from the plains below.'

'As it might be Sospel,' said Dany wisely. The Corsican chimed in with 'The maquisards having no air support, Captain Jack?'

'You call me Jack,' Brunel told him. 'The other's an old nickname, out of date ... Yes, having no air support, the general hadn't thought of that. Now, I wouldn't argue with a general,' and the smile went round, 'but these are medieval tactics. That's how our ancestors fought the Saracens, holed up in the hill villages like Roquebrune and Ste. Agnès, waiting for the barbarians to come up from the sea. And that's what you boys are doing now. You're safe and snug in the Jurac bastion, and you've got to make up your minds if you're going to stay in your redoubt or come out of it, and face the enemy on his own level.'

'I thought you wanted us to overlook Sospel,' said Dany Profetti.

'But you've just told me, Sospel's out of the picture for the present. It won't always be so, because the Allies are pushing ahead in Tunisia, and it won't be long before the Germans are cleared out of North Africa. Then the next step will be the invasion of Italy, and the road and the rail northbound from Sospel to the Piedmont frontier will be as important as they were in '40. But as of now the place to fight is along the coast road and the coast railway, where we can harass the enemy on his main communications routes.'

'How are we going to do that?' said Victor Marcati. 'With the old Lebels? What we ought to have is Stens.'

'You'll get them,' said Jacques. 'I've been promised the first allocation from the next weapons container the RAF drops anywhere in this area. But now listen to me. I want you all to make up your minds *why* you're in the maquis. Is it only to dodge the draft for forced labour in Germany, which is more severe every day, or do you want to fight for France? If it's the first, there are more ways than one of getting out of trouble. Any man who doesn't want to fight here, on his home ground, has only got to go down as far as the inn at Monti, and telephone to Jean Dupont at the grocery. Dupont will come along in the van and take him as far as Nice, where Dany's father will take over. There's a good escape line to Corsica, continuing on to North Africa, and there a man on the run can join Giraud's army or get a civilian job in Algiers. I hear there are plenty of those going. Any questions?'

Nobody spoke, and Jacques went on, 'But on the other hand, if you want to fight as guerillas, in the way I've said, the same man who's promised us the Stens will be here in a few days, and he'll give us all, me included, some practical instructions in sabotage. His name?' to an interruption from Victor, 'his name's Charles and he'll be coming from Marseille.'

'Then can we blow up trains?' said Bébé hopefully.

'We'll graduate to that, never fear,' said Jacques. 'I'm here to tell you how we can make a start.'

While Jacques talked in the barn, Polly was listening to Madame Jurac in the farmhouse, which consisted of only two rooms, the second being apparently used at a store. The kitchen, which was very large, was lighted by a small window looking into the ever-greens, and by the flames of a wood fire never allowed to go out, over which a large black pot swung on an iron hinge, while a black kettle spat boiling water into the ashes. Madame Jurac was voluble, but she spoke the local dialect which owed as much to Italian as to French; it took a little time for Polly to understand her. She was delighted with the coffee, and at once produced a huge coffee mill, but her fingers were too arthritic to turn the handle, and Pauline in her yellow dress sat down on a three-legged stool by the fireside and ground enough beans to make two cups. She drank her own black, but Madame Jurac, with many gusty sighs of satisfaction, poured hers in a bowl with a lump of beet sugar, and filled it to the brim with strong goat's milk. The cake was prudently put away in a carved corner cupboard. The baker's bread Monsieur Dupont had brought, said the old lady, was quite good enough for those boys.

This was the friendly scene presented to Jacques when he entered the kitchen after a private talk with Monsieur Jurac in the store-room, at which some of the SOE money changed hands. He refused coffee, although there was still some in the pot: if they were to drive towards Sospel, he said, the sooner they were on their way the better. He would see the Juracs again in a few days.

Dany, swaggering a little, accompanied Jacques and Polly to their car. 'There's your bastion, Jack,' he said, pointing across the valley to a complex of gun turrets and outworks round a central blockhouse. 'Fort Castillon.'

'The Italians never occupied it, did they?'

'My grandfather says it's been empty since 1940.'

'Quite so. Can you drive a car, Dany?'

'No, but Victor can.'

'I'm sure,' said Jacques. 'We'll have to pick up an Italian car for you to learn on. Goodnight, Dany, we're going towards Sospel first, and then back to Nice.'

He took the first hairpin bends on the downward road with care, and then asked Polly what she thought of the boys.

'They're going to have jugged hare for supper,' Polly said.

'How d'you know?'

'That was the lovely smell from the big black pot.'

'Now they've got a poacher like Victor on the strength, they must live like fighting cocks. That fellow is too fresh by half.'

'*Totor-pour-les-dames*,' said Polly. 'D'you know, I rather liked the Corsican Ogre. But what are *you* going to do with him?'

'Follow the tried and true method with potential troublemakers. If he stays with the group I'll promote him. Make a Corsican a corporal, and he thinks he's the new Bonaparte.'

'Why shouldn't he stay with the group?'

'I warned them what they'd be in for, and gave them the chance of ducking out. They'll be discussing it tonight.'

'Honestly!' said Polly. 'That sounds like what my mother used to tell me about the *sovietski* soldiers. They held a debate on every order before they decided to obey it.'

Jacques laughed. He stopped the car and pulled her close to him. 'You've got a sensitive ear, my darling, but you didn't quite hear what Jean Dupont was telling me this afternoon. He was saying "Don't lean on them. Let them get accustomed to being told what to do before you make them do it." '

'Why didn't Dupont come right out and say so, then?'

'Because I was his officer, darling, in another kind of war than this.' He leaned across her and took a pair of powerful binoculars out of the glove drawer. 'Now take a look at the valley of the Bévéra and the town of Sospel.'

She said she couldn't see any houses, and he told her no, but she could see the smoke. If they went any nearer, they might run into an Italian patrol.

The sun was setting, and the bare limestone peaks were touched with gold. Jacques named them: Col St. Jean, the Col de Braus, the Col de Brouis, the Authion. There were farms and hamlets everywhere, now invisible: what he wanted her to look at was the roads. 'Think of it as the letter Y,' he said. 'We came up the straight leg of the Y when we drove north from Menton. At Sospel the two arms of the Y branch off. The left arm goes back to Nice by L'Escarène. The right runs parallel to the railway line and the River Roya, due north to the Italian border and to the heart of Piedmont, one hundred and seventy kilometres from Sospel to Turin.'

Pauline swept the glasses in an arc from west to east, and laid them in her lap. 'I understand now,' she said. 'Sospel is the lock to the high country, and for the past three years the Italians have held the key. How well you know it all, Jacques!'

'I should do. I was sworn in to the French Army at Sospel, and began my military service with the Bataillon des Chasseurs Alpins at the Salel barracks. I even did the four-day mountain trials, and won a *fourragère*.' He smiled. 'When you're the same age as Dany Profetti, winning a cord to wear round your shoulder seems a worthwhile thing to do.'

'I'm glad you won,' said Pauline, rubbing her cheek against his.

'Actually I had a head start over the other fellows. My cousin Mike Marchand and I used to climb the mountain tracks like goats in the school holidays.'

'You know something?' Polly said. 'You've talked more about Mike Marchand in the past ten days, since we heard of him at the Telliers', than you did in all the months since we knew each other first.'

'Have I? I've been thinking about him a lot. I wish I could get in touch with him in Cairo, and tell him you and I are married.'

Flight-Lieutenant Michel Marchand, pushing his way through the crowd surging towards the Forum of Algiers on the last Sunday of May, was carrying Jacques Brunel's laconic message in his pocket-book. Routed, for some reason, via the Cape of Good Hope, it had taken a long time to reach Cairo, and longer still to catch up with him in Tunis, soon after the celebration of the final defeat of the Axis Powers in North Africa. He read it in Tunis with some pleasure, and more envy of the man announcing his happy marriage; for well over two years he had been waiting for his own wedding to a girl six thousand miles away in Rio de Janeiro. On this torrid Sunday evening Mike Marchand was not thinking of the Brunels, or even of his own fiancée, Dina da Costa, he was merely angry at having chosen this particular moment for his first forty-eight hours' leave in Algiers.

He said as much to the two friends who were shouldering their way through the streets with him, and who merely laughed, and said why the hell should he care if old de Gaulle had condescended to turn up in Algiers at last? Considering that old Churchill was in the city too, with the Combined Chiefs of Staff and all the top brass, it was a wonder they were free to get around the way they did, but then the Algiers security was nearly as slack as Cairo. If Marchand didn't want to see the de Gaulle circus, neither did they. The form was to have a few drinks at the Regina before dinner, and then pick up some of those French popsies and take them off for a big night in the Casbah.

'You're thinking of *Pépe le Moko*,' said Mike ill-naturedly. 'Who the hell wants to get mugged in the Casbah?'

'Take it easy, Mike,' said one of the Englishmen. It wasn't like Marchand to fail to see a joke: a very good pilot, he was also regarded as a very good type, easygoing for a Frenchman, and quite unlike the British image of a Frenchman in his height and his blond, blunt-featured, pleasant looks. He was scowling now, oblivious of the provocative glances they were getting from some of the girls who had volunteered to serve in the new French Army as secretaries, drivers and interpreters. They were sporting American WAC uniforms with French insignia, and also the garrison caps instead of WAC caps with visors which had sparked off one of the major rows of spring in Algiers.

'Take that damned rubbish away,' said Mike to a dark-eyed Algerian girl wearing a white dress with a tricolour sash, and offering a tray of badges and a collecting box. His English friend said, 'Sorry, lovey, no can do,' and waved away the Cross of Lorraine set in a lozenge of blue enamel which, in the form of a brooch, was being sold everywhere in Algiers that day. The Gaullist emblem had been mass-produced for the general's arrival, and Gaullist money was being freely spent on the street loafers hired to shout, '*Un seul chef, de Gaulle!*' as the general's motorcade passed on the way to the Forum, where he was to lay a wreath at the World War I memorial. The publicity had been organised by the Algiers branch of the French Resistance network 'Combat', and the organisers had had ample time to draw up their programme, since their hero had been sulking in his London stronghold since the end of January.

It was then that President Roosevelt had described de Gaulle as the bride at a shotgun wedding, the bridegroom being General Giraud, who had taken over from the murdered Admiral Darlan as the French commander-in-chief in North Africa. But the bride had resented the American deal with Darlan, and later with Giraud, so that the marriage remained unconsummated until some sort of compromise could be worked out, such as a committee over which the two men should preside with equal powers. It was this equality which the slogan of 'One Leader only, de Gaulle' was intended to destroy.

The rivalry between the two men had kept Algiers in a frenzy of rows, rumours and riots since the time of the Allied invasion of North Africa in November 1942. General Eisenhower, whose studies at West Point had not included a course in French intrigues, declared that Gaullist demonstrations kept the population of Algiers perpetually on edge—'The crowds were rioting,' he said, 'while in Tunisia his troops were fighting for their lives.' He might have added that Frenchmen were fighting in Tunisia too, but not side by side, Leclerc's Free French command being refused permission to march with General Juin's men in the Tunis victory parade. But besides the Gaullists and the Giraudists, Algiers was seething with international hangers-on, from the pimps and drug peddlars of the Casbah to the black marketeers and currency speculators and including the members of the various delegations 'accredited to' the headquarters and missions and official bodies which proliferated in the city. It was a place to make money and to make contacts which would be useful in the future, but it was not a place for fighting. The fighting was being done elsewhere.

In public, Mr. Churchill took the credit for arranging the May meeting between de Gaulle and Giraud, and it was not a coincidence that he arrived in Algiers one day ahead of his troublesome protégé. What was not revealed was that he had very nearly succeeded in ridding himself for good of the Frenchman whom he had too impulsively accepted as a Leader in 1940, and had only been thwarted by Anthony Eden, the Foreign Secretary, and other members of his cabinet. For Mr. Churchill had not travelled directly to Algiers from London. He had been in Washington, the guest of the President, and had been exposed day and night to the argument of Mr. Roosevelt that de Gaulle was 'interested far more in political machinations than in the prosecution of the war, machinations carried on without their knowledge and to the detriment of their military interests'. The President was backed up by his Secretary of State, Cordell Hull, who said that wherever a Gaullist representative went he kept everything in an uproar. It was no wonder Churchill thought the time had come to chuck de Gaulle.

But there were men, even in Churchill's cabinet, who thought it would be wrong to throw de Gaulle over at this stage of the war. The money advanced by Britain and lavishly spent on Gaullist propaganda had done its work well, even as men like Jean Moulin had done theirs, and the British public had been told so often that all the people of Occupied France supported the Leader in London that they had come to believe it. American newspapermen in England added their romantic quota to the Gaullist legend, following the tradition that any illusionist who appeared to be making a stand for independence should be hailed by the American press as a new George Washington. Irving Greenbaum of the Chicago *Clarion* was the first London correspondent to compare Charles de Gaulle to General Washington.

Mr. Greenbaum and his colleagues were crowding round the bar of the Hotel Regina, the war correspondents' press camp, when Mike Marchand and his friends arrived on the scene. Each of the newsmen had filed a colour story on de Gaulle's triumphal entry, and also, to cover themselves with their editors, a 'speculative' on the discussions at General Eisenhower's villa, where Mr. Churchill and General George C. Marshall were meeting the Combined Chiefs of Staff. So far there had only been one session, on which no communiqué was issued. While de Gaulle drove through the streets of Algiers and was cheered at a rally in the Majestic Cinema, Mr. Churchill was working on his background notes for the talks to be resumed on Monday. The momentous topics were the immediate capture of Sicily, the invasion of Italy, and the timing of the cross-Channel invasion for the summer of 1944.

The Scotch had run out at the Regina bar before the RAF men from Tunis arrived, and so had the ice, but the American supplies were plentiful, and Mike Marchand drank a rye highball while he surveyed the crowded room. It was too early for anybody to be high or quarrelsome; on the contrary, there was the euphoric good-fellowship he remembered in Cairo after the victory of El Alamein, and had experienced recently in Tunis, with a lot of backslapping and table-hopping, and roars of laughter following the least funny jokes. He doubted if his companions would find the 'French popsies' of their dreams in the Regina bar, where the only women present were American nurses, down on leave from Tunis like themselves. There were no French girls to be seen for the moment, in or out of uniform; in fact there were no French uniforms at all, which after some incidents at Tunis Mike regarded as a blessing. In Algiers the Free French—the Fighting French they called themselves—were either hurrahing in the streets or queuing up for the rally at the Majestic, but before the night was over they would probably come to blows with Giraud's men. Mike ordered another highball. He had been in more than one punch-up with the Gaullists in the early days, and had a scar at the base of his skull to prove it, but his British uniform had kept him out of trouble since he joined the RAF, and he had no intention of getting into another punch-up in Algiers. He wondered how soon he could get his friends out of the Regina and into the little restaurant where they had been told good food was to be had. He eased himself out of the mass of humanity at the bar, and then he saw St. Exupéry.

The crowd shuffling between the tables parted for just long enough to let Mike see the one French uniform in the room—one conspicuous anywhere in a North African summer, for it was the old blue winter uniform of the French Air Force. The man who wore it with a captain's insignia was tall, portly, balding, with intense dark eyes in a face which an air crash in Guatemala had turned into something not far from a clown's face, with a twisted mouth and one eyebrow raised in a permanent question mark. He was sitting with two American officers, and appeared to be doing tricks with a pack of cards.

'My God!' said Mike, 'that's Antoine de St. Exupéry!'

'Who's he when he's at home?' said one of the RAF men.

'One of the greatest flyers of his day, that's all.'

'Never heard of him.'

Not for a world would Mike have added, in that company, that St. Exupéry was also a great writer. He himself was no great reader, but he remembered devouring *Southern Mail* and *Night Flight* as a very young airman, and when he was a ferry pilot with the RAF he had been greatly inspired by *Wind, Sand and Stars*. Saint Ex. here, doing parlour tricks to amuse two chicken colonels, while the street rabble was paid to cheer de Gaulle! 'I met him once,' he said. 'I think I'd like to say hallo to him.'

'I think it's time to be moving on,' said the Englishman. 'There's no action here, old man.'

'Here, let me buy you another drink,' said Mike. 'I'll be back before you've finished it.' He signalled to the barman, laid some money on the counter, and with a sense of putting back the clock, started off across the room towards the man who had been one of the heroes of his boyhood.

'Excuse me, sir,' he said to the older of the two American colonels, 'I wonder if I might speak to Captain de St. Exupéry. My name's Marchand, captain,' he said across the table. 'I met you five years ago in Paris, when we were both with Air France.'

The comical face crinkled into a smile, and what St. Exupéry's friends called his Mickey Mouse nose seemed to twitch with satisfaction. 'And I *saw* you once,' he said with emphasis, 'taking off from Buenos Aires, the day you won the race to Rio de Janeiro. Gentlemen, this is Mike Marchand, who broke a few flying records in his time.'

'Glad to know you, Mike,' said the senior American colonel, shaking hands, and the other man said, 'Sit down and have a drink.'

'I didn't mean to interrupt you,' Mike apologised. 'I just—I felt I had to say *bonjour*.'

'Sure,' said the American, rising. 'Look, now you've met a friend, Saint Ex., we'll be on our way. Got to hit the sack early tonight, you know! What you drinking, Mike? We'll send you over refills from the bar.'

When the Americans left St. Exupéry smiled at Mike. 'Nice kids,' he said. 'Trying to let an old crock down lightly, and doing a good job of it too. Well! Algiers is the crossroads of the world tonight. It's even brought two old South America hands together. How did you get into the RAF? The last I heard of you, Air France said you were in Bucharest.'

'I was going to ask how *you* got back into uniform,' said Mike. 'I thought you were in New York.'

'I went to New York at the end of 1940, having declined the honour of joining General de Gaulle. I'm beginning to think I stayed away too long. I've been in Algiers for three weeks, pestering General Giraud to let me fly again, and all he's done so far is send me on a tour of the desert airstrips on the same kind of PR job I did for Air France after the Aéropostale folded. My old squadron, "La Hache", is stationed at Biskra, and that's where I want to be.'

'You were with "La Hache" right up to the end in '40, weren't you?'

'Yes, with the 2/33, flying the Potez 63. Now they're telling me I'm too old to fly at all. How about you, Marchand? It must be ten years since you were flying test for Trans-Andean.'

Mike laughed. 'I'll be thirty-three in November,' he said. 'I was grounded for years because of an ear complaint that was mistaken for vertigo, and I was lucky to get into the RAF by the back door. They took me on at Takoradi when they were short of ferry pilots, and I sweated it out for over a year flying Hurricanes from Takoradi to Khartoum. Then I asked for an air crew board in Cairo, was sent on a conversion course, and posted into Bomber Command.'

St. Exupéry groaned. 'You had the luck of the devil, at thirty-two. But it's years better than forty-three, and I'll be forty-three in June. Some of the US Air Force officers I've met here think it's smart to call me "uncle".'

'The two who just left?'

'No, not those two. They only told me, in the kindest manner possible, that General Eisenhower had other things on his mind besides finding a job for the last pilot of *La Ligne*. And it's true, Marchand, I *am* the last one left of the chaps who used to fly the mail from Toulouse to Casablanca, and then from Casablanca to Dakar, and opened up the Aéropostale service with South America.'

For Mike Marchand these were evocative words. With unusual diffidence he told St. Exupéry how as a boy of eighteen, living with his uncle in Rio de Janeiro after his mother's death in Paris, he had haunted the Aéropostale offices in the Avenida Rio Branco, hoping to catch a glimpse of the chief pilots of *La Ligne*. St. Exupéry listened sympathetically. When Mike was eighteen, he was in Buenos Aires as traffic chief of the affiliated line Aeroposta Argentina, but Mike's heroes had been his own closest friends. He was glad to share his memories of Jean Mermoz, who first flew the mail between Dakar in Senegal and Natal in Brazil, and went to his death in the waters of the South Atlantic, and of Henri Guillamet, who crashed in the Andes and walked out alive, only to be killed after the fall of France, when the Farman he was piloting on a flight from Marseille was shot down in an air battle between the British and the Italians. Mike drew him out to reminisce about the days of *Courrier Sud*, when St. Exupéry and his colleagues flew the mail across two thousand kilometres of desert sand, in the single engined Bréguet 14s with the open cockpits and no radio. It was the kind of talk which Marchand found enthralling, especially when conducted in his own language by a master of words like the great Saint Ex. He thought his own desert flying, at least as a ferry pilot, had been tame by comparison, and said so modestly.

Had he had any encounters with the Gaullists in Africa, St. Exupéry wanted to know. Oh, had he not, Mike said, a proper dust-up with one brute at Freetown, but nothing to speak of since. He had kept clear of them at Fort Lamy, when the ferry convoys of bombers for Khartoum occasionally stopped to refuel in the Chad, which had declared for de Gaulle, but after he was posted to Bomber Command he had met some of the 'Metz and Nancy' squadron in the desert. They seemed to be decent chaps; but then the whole 'Lorraine' group was under British command, and unlike their Leader the Free French flyers were fighting men.

The truth was that his service in the Royal Air Force had left Marchand with little time to nurse the passions of 1940, and only his exasperation at the carefully orchestrated welcome to de Gaulle in Algiers had blown fire into the old ashes. He changed the subject by saying that he had gone back to Brazil for a short time after refusing to join de Gaulle—like St. Exupéry—and there had become

69

engaged to a girl called Dina da Costa. Knowing that Saint Ex. himself had married a South American girl, Mike was sure of his interest when he told him about Dina, a qualified pilot in her own right, who was flying passenger planes for her brother, the president of Capricorn Airways in Rio. To get her to the Middle East and marry her was impossible when the enemy was at the gates of Alexandria, but now the war in North Africa was won he thought she might soon be able to get an air priority.

'So you're going back to Cairo,' said St. Exupéry. 'Then you haven't been posted to Algiers?'

'No, thank God! I'm only here on a forty-eight. I report to Tunis tomorrow night, then back to Heliopolis.'

'The luck's still on your side, Marchand. Algiers is the damnedest crab-pot of Gaullist intrigue I've ever known, twice as bad as New York, and now de Gaulle's here himself it'll be worse than ever. General Giraud's a decent chap, he spoke very frankly about his problems when I had breakfast with him the other day, but he hasn't a clue about what he's up against in Charles de Gaulle. He'll be outsmarted at every turn, and before long he'll find himself retired and on the shelf—if he's not murdered first, like Admiral Darlan.'

'Coming, Mike?' One of the English officers, on his way back from the washroom, tapped Marchand on the shoulder.

'In a minute.' He watched the young man returning to the bar. The American newspaper group seemed larger than ever, and a few officers sporting the Cross of Lorraine were forcing their way up to the counter. Mike looked, and looked again, and then said quietly to St. Exupéry:

'You were right about Algiers being the crossroads of the world tonight. You see that fellow with the ruddy complexion? Short and thickset?'

'The air force colonel? What about him?'

'That's the man I had the big row with at Freetown.'

St. Exupéry's sad brown eyes regarded him with curiosity. 'What exactly happened? What's his name?'

'He called himself Captain Corbeau then, but when we were in Brazil before the war he was Anders Lachmann, a pilot in the Nazi-controlled Condor Syndicate. He turned up at de Gaulle's headquarters in London in the very early days with another of the Condor crowd called Schnaebel, who was executed in the Tower of London for espionage later in the year. Lachmann and I had one or two punch-ups that summer, and when I ran into him in Freetown I accused him of being a German spy. The British arrested him on my say-so.'

St. Exupéry whistled. 'Did he serve a prison term?'

'They couldn't make the charges stick. I'd called him a German national, and he could prove he was French all right, though Strasbourg was in German hands when he was born. All he drew was a suspended sentence for assault.'

'It sounds as if you'd rushed your fences. What are you going to do about him now?'

'I'm with those two RAF types, and they're waiting for me to go to dinner. I'm not going to suggest we all leave by the back door.'

'This place is packed with Americans. It mightn't be smart to start a rough-house here.'

'That wouldn't worry me,' said Mike. 'Our last fight was in the American Consulate at Freetown.'

What he didn't want to happen was a brawl in the presence of this man, whom he venerated as a flyer and who had talked with him as an equal. Mike stood up. 'Goodbye, Captain de St. Exupéry,' he said formally. 'I've enjoyed our talk. And I'd like to wish you luck, if I may. I hope you get the job you want.'

'Good luck to you too,' said St. Exupéry. 'Let's try to keep in touch, if we can.' Mike nodded and turned away. Without looking back he carried with him the image of the bulky figure in the faded winter uniform, and the compelling eyes in the sad monkey face.

Colonel Corbeau, if that was still his name, had succeeded in getting a drink, and with his glass in his hand was so deep in conversation with his friends that Marchand could easily have left the crowded room unnoticed, and without using the rear exit. He only had to go to the main door, wave to the two men from Tunis and wait for them to leave the bar with him. But the author of *Wind, Sand and Stars*, who knew men as well as he knew the desert, had summed him up accurately as a man who rushed his fences, and Mike had felt for a long time that he and his one-time enemy were bound to meet again. As well now as later, he told himself, and went without hesitation to the bar. Corbeau appeared to be haranguing his companions on *le redressement de la France*, which was the latest Gaulist slogan. Whether the general meant to straighten the country up or straighten it out was never specified: the word

71

redressement was equally insulting in either translation.

Mike's friends, grunting 'At last!' and 'Let's go!' extricated themselves from the crowd at the counter, and the men wearing the Cross of Lorraine moved slightly to let them pass. Corbeau and Marchand came face to face. The promoted colonel stood speechless for a moment, and then muttered something lost in the din of voices. Mike said, 'Well, Lachmann? Still following your Leader? What are you calling yourself tonight?'

Corbeau's hand came up, clenched in a fist. He spread the fingers into a claw, and clutched Mike by the forearm.

'Marchand!' he said thickly, 'I knew we'd meet again! You ran out of Freetown, like the coward you are, before I could settle my account with you—'

'With a cosh on the back of my head, like you did in London?' said Mike, striking his hand away. The movement, even more than the angry voices, attracted some attention at the bar. The two Englishmen understood not a word of the quick staccato speech, but some of the war correspondents had a smattering of French, and they looked inquisitively from the fat little colonel to the tall blond man in the RAF uniform. One of Corbeau's companions actually pulled him back, with a quick whisper of '*Les américains!*', and an urgent appeal to remember the general.

'You're safe enough here, and you know it,' said Corbeau, 'But I'll have it out with you yet, Marchand!'

'Any time,' said Mike, and turned on his heel. The two bewildered men from Tunis followed him down the room.

'What the hell was all that about?' said one of them, when they reached the street.

'Just a pleasant meeting with an old friend,' said Mike with a grin.

'Friend be damned. That guy looked as if he could murder you.'

72

SIX

The message of good wishes which Mike Marchand sent off to his
cousin as soon as he returned to Cairo was never delivered at Menton. It was one of the thousands of letters and telegrams which went
astray in those years, through enemy action, arbitrary censorship, or
the departure of the addressees to concentration camps. In the
general breakdown of communications the young Brunels kept only
one line open, by letter and telephone to *Le Verger*, where Marcelle
was able to give them news of the invalid in Switzerland and of her
mother.

'You mustn't quarrel with Marcelle, darling,' said Polly when
Jacques had pungently expressed his opinion of Marcelle's collabor-
ating husband. 'She's really a very kind person—and very like yourself in lots of ways.'

'I hope you don't think I'm as fond of paltry nick-nacks as my
sister is.'

'No, but you're a born organiser, which is what you once called
her. Look at the way you've transformed your father's office!'

Jacques Brunel acknowledged that he was lucky to have the
office to fall back on, as Polly had once said. There had been three
briefs, and three only, on his desk at Nice when he left for Paris,
and he found all three cases on the cause list for the spring term. He
won two and lost one, on the first day entering the Palais de Justice
with trepidation—remembering the fifty-fifty chance of survival his
friends had given him—and soon becoming aware, as the familiar
atmosphere of the law courts closed around him, that no one was
going to denounce him or produce a warrant for his arrest. But no
more briefs came his way after the third case, and his colleague
Maître Pastorelli said his desk was empty too. People were shying
away from expensive litigation in the uncertain state of affairs.

'We'll have to wait until the end of the war, *maître*,' said Jacques
grimly. 'The courts of France will be jammed for years once the
collaborationist trials begin. I wonder who'll be the Public Pro-

73

secutor, or if the judiciary will still have power in France?'

He kept his room in the Nice *étude*, of course, just as he kept the keys to the flat in the Palais Lascaris, but Jacques Brunel's life was now centred on Menton, and it soon began to move so easily that he was almost lulled into a state of confidence about his own safety. It was not difficult to adapt to the office routine. He got a carpenter in to open the window of his father's private room, which had never been opened within living memory, and to remove the hideous brown screen which deprived the room of light while adding nothing to the client's privacy. There were ample funds at his disposal, for his father had deposited a large sum to his account at the Banque Palméro, and the financial side of the practice was in excellent order, so he employed workmen to carry half the files out of the main office to the storage rooms above, and give a coat of fresh paint to the streaky walls. Soon, when he reached the office in the morning, he could hear the voices of the clients waiting to see him and lined up on the two benches in the big room. Litigation in the courts might have diminished, but at the grass-roots level there was always someone who wanted to add a codicil to a will, or lodge a complaint about a barking dog without going in person to the police, or even ask about investments. The word soon got round Menton that the young Brunel was back, and willing to listen to your story without biting your head off the way the *huissier de justice* did.

Best of all, the old age pensioner and the crippled boy were excellent assistants. The boy fresh from school was quick and clever, far above the level of an office boy, and Jacques intended to speak to his brother about having him articled. Monsieur Janot had the whole practice at his finger ends, and told the younger man so much about his father's last months at business that Jacques realised what a brave front had been put on failing health, and how real was the need for sanatorium treatment. 'He didn't quit because he'd let the practice go to blazes and wanted to get away to a neutral country,' he thought painfully. 'I'd better stick to the Bar, because I'll never be fit to be a judge.'

Monsieur Janot thought some of 'Monsieur Jacques'' innovations were peculiar, for instance the arrival of two old divans, their torn ticking covered by plain coarse blankets, and their installation in the storage rooms, and the renting of garage space for the Peugeot on the Quai Bonaparte while the garage in the Traverse Bellecour, big enough to hold a postal van, stood empty. But the great revolution was in the hours of work. From time immemorial the *étude* had been open from eight to twelve and from four to seven. Now the long hiatus for *un bon déjeuner* and a siesta was abolished and the new hours were nine to twelve and one to five: Janot was amazed at how many clients changed their habits too and turned up early in the afternoon. To cap everything, the new head of chambers did not go home for luncheon, although he lived so near; he had a light *déjeuner*, which could scarcely have been *bon*, in one of the modest restaurants which still remained open in the avenues on either side of the pretty public garden. It was the only thing the old law clerk had against young Madame Brunel, that she had failed in the first duty of every French housewife: to stupefy her husband with food at noon.

Polly had thrown herself into the rôle of housewife with her usual enthusiasm. With Henri Froment's help she arranged for the transfer of Jacques' furniture from the Palais Lascaris to the Rue Longue in the van of a man who didn't mind working after dark as long as he could get back before the curfew, and she was very effective with a tape measure, a notebook and a fountain pen when the Brunels went to the Rue Droite together to decide what to throw out and what to keep.

'There's no point in taking up the linoleum or the carpets, Jacques, they'd fall to pieces, they're so old. And we've got those marble floors in the Rue Longue.'

'Marble can be cold in winter, darling.'

'It'll soon be summer, and we can buy new scatter rugs next winter. Now the curtains, they're all frayed, so we leave them, and throw out the brocade stuff that poor swan's holding in his beak above the bed. What about the sofa? That's a bit frayed too.'

'The sofa stays here,' said Jacques with decision. He thought that as long as he owned the flat, Charles Maxwell or someone on the run might need the sofa for a bed.

The pictures were discarded, the books were packed, and so were the contents of the kitchen; the old flat, where strange painted figures of woe plunged in chariots across the ceilings, was left bare. And the morning came when Jacques awoke in a white room barer still, with only the bed standing on the icy marble floor opposite a pile of packing cases, and realised by the sounds from the dark kitchen that Polly was having trouble with the gas cooker.

It was a battered little table-top, two-burner arrangement, and the gas pressure was so erratic that now the flames were almost invisible and now they sprang up in a roar and a blaze which terrified the inexperienced cook. She tried to make toast, and the toast was burned, the coffee spurted from the old enamel pot in a jet of liquid which put out the gas. There was no milk, and Polly in her excitement dropped the precious pat of butter on the floor. It was a bad beginning, and they went from bad to worse, for the only cooking Polly had ever done in her life was as a schoolgirl in the little Paris flat she shared with her mother before she had a stepfather and a grand home in Naples. She told Jacques she could make good omelettes, but this skill was useless when there were no eggs.

Jacques loved her so much that he never complained, and he knew her so well that he never commented on the cut fingers and scald marks which showed how difficult Polly found her new job. He kissed the little blistered paws and waited, and by and by his wife learned how to prepare such food as was available, and their evening meals became appetising. About this time Monsieur Janot told Jacques that the woman who had been his mother's laundress, Madame Honorine Bensa, had called at the office to enquire if 'Madame Jacques' might care to employ her in the same way. He thought the woman was very poor and needed the money. Jacques thought they needed the woman.

He couldn't remember the laundress, for when he lived at home he took it for granted that his shirts would appear in his bedroom as if washed and ironed by invisible hands. But his mother had sometimes talked about a woman called Norine who was very reliable, and he thought this might be the same person. Madame Bensa was asked to call at the Rue Longue, and made an impressive entrance.

There was a type of physical beauty which had long existed on the Ligurian shore, although it was fast dying out, possessed by women whom old men turned to look at in the street, saying 'there go the true Mentonese.' Norine, at fifty, possessed that beauty still. She was tall, with a magnificent carriage, nobly chiselled features, and a coil of glossy black hair on which she never wore a hat. Polly took to her at once, and found her to be a tower of strength. Norine carried away the fine household linen inherited from Grand'tante Marthe to wash and dry at her little *cabanon* high above the Old Town, and brought it back ironed to perfection and smelling of mimosa and the sea. Twice a week she came for a whole morning to clean the little apartment, and helped Polly in the task she had set herself, to polish Jacques' magnificent furniture with beeswax and turpentine, and the handles with brass cream, until each piece shone and sparkled as it had done over a hundred years before.

In the living room they had the Restoration furniture, chairs and a table, Jacques' big desk with the green lamp, and the splendid secretary with the bookcase on top. In the bedroom they had a big Provençal *armoire* which held their clothes and linens, and the two pieces which were pure Louis Philippe, a dressing table with a marble top and a mirror supported by swans, and the great bed which now had fresh white muslin curtains made by Polly, and draped from the ring in another swan's beak. They moved gently in the breeze from the open window.

'You don't think the place is a bit too bare?' said Jacques, when it was all in order.

'I hate clutter.'

'You must have hated *Le Verger*, then.'

'Everyone to his taste,' said Polly. 'And how Marcelle keeps all that silver polished I'll never know.'

The Brunels had very little silver, but the Limoges dinner service had arrived safely, with an affectionate message from the Telliers. There was nothing more they needed to buy, except two deck chairs, which they found in a pathetic little shop which had sold such chairs, with beach balls, water wings and souvenirs, to the holidaymakers of the summers before the war.

After the lonely years in the Palais Lascaris, Jacques thought it was wonderful to come home to his pretty, happy girl: to drink wine and watch her over the carnations on the dinner table, and then to unfold their deck chairs on the balcony, close together, and sit with linked hands while the moon rose above the Mediterranean, and the footsteps and the voices on the *quai* below grew quieter and ceased. The May nights were so warm, the sound of the sea so gentle, that for an hour at a time they had the illusion of living in a world at peace. It was only when they lay embraced beneath the swan, and Polly held his body to hers with all her strength, that Jacques knew her awareness of danger, and of the short span of time that might be theirs.

To all appearances they were a man and a girl very much in love, and enjoying the first weeks of marriage: the new home, the restored possessions and the small successes of the kitchen. But their lives were set to the rhythm of Resistance, in a locked drawer of the secretary lay Jacques' revolver and the knife he had used to kill a man, and the first person he entertained when he lunched in a Menton restaurant was Charles Maxwell, alias Aletti.

He left the office early that afternoon and drove Maxwell up to the Jurac farm. None of the boys had taken the chance to go away, whether to Nice or to North Africa, and Jacques was glad of that, because they had made themselves into a unit during the long hard winter on the mountain. The kid they called Bébé was too young, of course. He swore he was eighteen but was probably three years younger, and therefore in no danger of the forced labour draft; Jacques knew, however, that it would break his heart to be separated from the older boys. And Bébé was intelligent, he put some good questions to 'Charles' as he was told to call the visitor, after Maxwell's short lecture on the use of explosives. He had brought a supply of plastic, which could be stuck on anywhere with Vaseline or even sticky tape, and demonstrated the use of the detonator. Plastic was all that was available, though incendiary bottles could be manufactured with petrol and sulphuric acid, if they could lay their hands on a supply of the latter.

'That won't be any problem,' said Jacques. He promised that they could plan their first attack as soon as they moved nearer to Menton and a base more easily accessible than the mountain farm. 'Pauline's working on that for you,' he said, at which of course *Totor-pour-les-dames* whistled again, and was silenced by Dany.

'Which of those two is going to be the boss?' Maxwell asked on the way back to Menton. 'Victor or Dany?'

'Dany's a good kid, but I can't depend on either of them, yet, to keep their heads in a hit. I'm going to use the Menton group first for a sure-fire success. They're all Bataillon des Chasseurs Alpins men, so I can count on them.'

'You're probably right about the BCA, but aren't you a man short at Menton?'

'I was when François lit out for Marseille, but I'll take his place myself, and Julien Monnier kept all the rest together while I was away.'

'Does it make any difference to them now you're back?'

'They say so.'

It made this difference, that all the resistants in Jacques' small network felt renewed energy and enthusiasm now they knew that

78

Captain Jack was back. He sometimes regretted having chosen his hospital nickname for his code name in the SOE: it belonged to the old days in Scotland and had nothing to do with France, but there was no doubt it had stuck. The farmers in the hills, the gas man at Carnolès, the plumber at Cabbé, the doctor at Cap Martin, took on a new lease of life because Captain Jack was back. As for the Menton group, they were delighted with his command post in the Rue Longue, which could be reached as easily by the alleys and traverses of the Old Town as by the Porte des Logettes at the foot of the Rue Longue and the Porte St. Julien at the top. They came by ones and twos after dark, the butcher from the Rue Trenca, the waiter from the restaurant outside the station, and the young science teacher whom Jacques depended on to steal enough sulphuric acid from the school lab. to manufacture their first supply of incendiary bottles.

They went into action on a dark night in early May, after the curfew, when the Italians used the deserted road to send a supply truck from their main depot at Nice to the two companies then occupying Menton. The timing and the manning of this truck had been observed over a period of ten days, and the ambush, on a lonely stretch of the highway overgrown with shrubs and Spanish broom, was completely successful. A fusillade of incendiary bottles in front of the truck brought the driver to a halt, a series of crashes and flares behind sent him and the corporal with him running to the rear: the two were quickly overpowered by six maquisards in masks, gagged and bound and left in the ditch without a shot being fired. The truck was driven rapidly to Menton and inside the big empty garage in the Traverse Bellecour, while at the back gate a happy Christophe Monnier admitted his employer, his own brother, and four other men to the Brunel offices.

'You four go up to the store rooms,' directed Jacques. 'I hope you'll get some sleep on the divans I found in the Rue Longue. The rest of us can doss down inside the truck, but remember! Nobody goes out of here until the curfew's lifted.'

With the two Monniers he spread some old rugs along the foot of the garage doors, so that no streak of light would be visible, and began to examine the spoils. They included supplies of food, flour, yeast, polenta and macaroni, a crate of cigarette cartons taken from the *tabacs* of Nice, a packing case of Government issue summer underwear and another of summer uniforms.

'Not bad for a start,' said Jacques. 'But next time they'll come out shooting. We'll have to hijack a truck of weapons first.'

Chris Monnier was making an inventory of the contents of the truck. 'The uniforms won't be much use, will they, monsieur?' he ventured. Jacques smiled. The handkerchief mask was round his neck, and he wiped the sweat off his face before he split open one of the cartons and took out a cigarette. 'I think the boys up at the Jurac farm might use them,' he said. 'I wonder if Victor Marcati can speak Italian.'

At a quarter to six next morning the two Italian soldiers were found by a gang of roadmen starting work on the hill, who after some ribald jokes consented to cut the ropes round their wrists and ankles and relieve them of their gags. The 'terrorists' had already relieved them of their sidearms, and also of their belts, so that they had to start the walk down to Menton holding up their trousers, a sight enjoyed by everyone they met. The moral effect of the tiny success was wonderful. The days of passive acceptance of defeat and Occupation were over, and someone had challenged the enemy at last.

The Italian command in Menton was thrown into operatic disarray by this mischance, and on the principle of striking the enemy when he was vulnerable Polly Brunel made the next move in the game. She allowed a day to pass for the flurry of telephone calls to and from Nice, and the scathing comments of the German allies who had only a token force in Menton at that time. Then she put on her blue wedding dress, high-heeled shoes and a great deal of scent, and went to call on the senior Italian officer with a request as pretty as her Paris hat. On the day of the 'incident' he might have refused to see her, but his lieutenant described her as a charming girl from Naples, and the harassed colonel was ready for some light relief. Polly told him that her husband's mother, now in Switzerland, had been a volunteer nurses' aide at the children's sanatorium on the road to Peille, and had been given a special allocation of petrol from the Italian authorities for that purpose. Dared she hope that a similar allowance would be made to herself? Could the signora drive a car then? Yes indeed, she drove her husband's Peugeot. Wonderful! Capable as well as kind! Did she propose to work, like her mother-in-law, at the Peille sanatorium?

This was the last thing Polly proposed to do, the Peille sanatorium being the only place near Menton where she was known as

Polly Preston, and not by the name of Henri which Jacques made her take when she first went to Nice. She said with a simper that the place was so far away, she would have to spend a whole day there at a time, and her husband wouldn't agree to that. 'We're very newly married, *signore colonello*!' she said with downcast eyes, the Italian responding with a lecherous smile. She would like to offer her services to the St. Michel holiday home, Polly went on, she heard they were short staffed there. In every respect, signora, that was unfortunately true. They needed orderlies and kitchen hands, the gardens were in a terrible state, the devoted nurses would be grateful for any kind of help. The colonel complimented the signora on her generosity. He wrote the petrol order, held her hand too long, kissed the inside of her wrist at the edge of her short white glove, and watched her go with regret.

'Now,' said Polly when Jacques came home that night, 'bring your boys down from the mountain. I've got jobs lined up for the lot of them—and a base not two miles from the railway station.'

The time had come for every man in Jacques Brunel's network to contribute something to the scheme he had in mind. Even those who were too old to take part in an armed raid, like Monsieur Ratazzi in the railway station at Nice and Dr. Lecampion at Cap Martin, were asked to make certain observations and report on them, while the farmers in the hills between the Grande and the Moyenne Corniches were asked to check times and traffic on certain stretches of the highways. Daniel Profetti heard plenty of careless talk in the Bar des Sports, and so did the Carpani brothers, whose bicycle shop at St. Roman was a centre of neighbourhood gossip. Jacques wished he could use the bottleneck at St. Roman for the interception he had in mind, because there was a network of roads just beyond St. Roman on the Monte Carlo side which could be useful for evasive action, but there was no help for it: the Moyenne Corniche was the route chosen by the Germans at Nice for the delivery of a consignment of Schmeisser machine pistols to their Italian allies at Menton.

When he attended the meeting at Lyon where General Delestraint, whom de Gaulle had designated as the leader of the Secret Army, gave his views on the 'bastion' theory—views which had the support of Jean Moulin—Jacques Brunel had told Moulin himself that he would enlist in no paramilitary organisation swearing allegiance to General de Gaulle. When a French Army, the weapon of the Republic, was formed again he would re-enlist in the 53rd Regiment of the Bataillon des Chasseurs Alpins: until then, he and his friends would exist as a *groupe franc* for the harassment of the enemy. He was quite aware that attacking the Germans might bring the *groupe franc* to a violent end, and that for every German killed the lives of ten civilian hostages might be exacted, but he had given up worrying about the hostages. He told every man in the two groups he meant to use in Operation Schmeisser that if it came to a shoot-out they were to shoot to maim and not to kill, and he added— thinking of the remarkably varied arsenal they now possessed—that they should be careful not to maim each other.

The German weapons truck came over the Moyenne Corniche very early on a fine May morning with a crew of four Bavarians, the driver and three others, who were annoyed to find their passage barred near a quarry by an excavation on one side of the road and an Italian army lorry slewed across the quarry entrance on the other. The bonnet was up, and several young Italian soldiers were looking blankly at the interior, while a tall dark man with a corporal's stripes was checking through the contents of a tool box.

'What's up, Dieter?' said a voice from the back of the German truck as the driver braked and stopped.

The driver muttered something about useless Italians as the tall corporal came up with an ingratiating smile. Totor's Corsican patois was quite near enough to Italian to be convincing to the German, although the trouble remained unexplained—something to do with the oil sump, he thought. 'I'll have to sort them out,' he said to the man beside him. 'Got to get them out of the way, even if we have to push them.' Just before he jumped down from the cab, he saw in the rear mirror a civilian van pull out from the La Turbie road and start moving slowly up behind them.

Victor Marcati knocked Dieter out with a spanner as he bent over the engine, and Dany Profetti held a gun on the second man. The two Germans at the back gave the most trouble; getting out to stretch their legs they started shooting as soon as they saw what had happened, and young Bébé, with a bullet in his thigh, was the first casualty among the boys from the Jurac farm. But the reinforcements in Julien Monnier's van, with the butcher's name painted out and false number plates for the occasion, were too many for the enemy. One had the gun shot out of his hand by Jacques Brunel, the other thought it prudent to surrender, and at gunpoint the two

82

who were unhurt carried Dieter's unconscious body into the quarry. Their weapons were added to the cases of machine pistols hastily transferred from the German to the Italian army truck, and they themselves were lightly bound. It wouldn't be long, Jacques said, before they could patch up the man with the smashed wrist, and he left them free to shout for help, which in that lonely spot might be some time in coming. Julien and one of the fishermen, who had a shallow wound in the shoulder, went off with Bébé, when both had been given first aid, to Dr. Lecampion's surgery, and Victor Marcati drove the Italian truck, loaded with men and machine pistols, to a farm high in the hills where a place was waiting for it in the barn. Jacques drove the German truck, with the science teacher beside him, to an old fairground on the outskirts of Menton, where they set it on fire and then walked into town. Jacques arrived on time at his office, and the teacher at his school.

The exploits of a small *groupe franc* in a Riviera town would scarcely have earned a mention in the 'crab-pot', as St. Exupéry had called it, of gossip and intrigue which was Algiers. Jacques and his friends were fighting the enemy with all their scanty means; Algiers was preoccupied with the infighting which began the moment General de Gaulle set foot on Algerian soil.

His aims, as usual, were purely political. First he meant to oust General Giraud from his position as High Commissioner and French commander-in-chief, and then to remove certain former Vichy administrators from the key offices they had held in North Africa since the Allied invasion. As a side-line he wished to wreak vengeance on men who had opposed him in London, like General Odic, and a ban was placed on the display and sale of books by Antoine de St. Exupéry. Over and above this bitterness, which soon earned him the nickname of 'Wormwood' among all the English speakers in Algiers, was his determination to obtain Allied recognition for himself and his movement as representing the sovereignty of France.

To this end was founded, within a few days of his arrival in Algiers, the French Committee of National Liberation, consisting of himself and General Giraud as co-presidents, and five other members drawn from the Gaullist committee in London. Mr. Churchill, with remarkable naïveté, welcomed the creation of a committee of seven, because, as he wrote to President Roosevelt, 'if de Gaulle should prove violent or unreasonable, he will be in a minority of five to two, and possibly completely isolated.' Mr. Roosevelt, who had known so many ward-heelers and Tammany bosses in his day, took the opposite view. Referring to de Gaulle as 'our mutual headache', he commentd that 'the bride evidently forgets there is still a war in progress over here.' Within a few days Churchill's hopes were dashed, and de Gaulle became 'violent and unreasonable' to the extent of demanding full control of the French forces and withdrawing from the Committee's deliberations until it was granted. It was the tactic of 'the empty chair' which he was to employ on many occasions, but this time it failed. North Africa was still under British-American military rule, and General Eisenhower was ordered to summon both the French generals and tell them that Giraud was to remain commander-in-chief, under the penalty of the cessation of American arms supplies to the new French Army he was creating.

Eisenhower's chief concern was the invasion of Sicily, timed to take place on July 10. In vain did President Roosevelt complain of the hours Eisenhower was having to waste on de Gaulle's scheming; in vain did he tell Churchill that 'we must divorce ourselves from de Gaulle. He has proven to be unreliable, uncooperative and disloyal to both our governments.' 'Wormwood' refused to be dislodged. While General Giraud, perhaps unwisely, absented himself from Algiers on the official visit to Washington which de Gaulle had long covered for himself, 'Wormwood'—in his own later words—'embarked on the next round in the game.'

If his quest for power was a game to General de Gaulle, it was a matter of life and death for some of his followers. General Delestraint was having trouble as the spring advanced. Reports were constantly reaching him that his Secret Army was being infiltrated by *Vertrauensmänner*, Frenchmen acting as the confidential agents of the Germans, and it was not easy to root them out. Jean Moulin, on the other hand, was going from strength to strength. As de Gaulle's personal representative, who had unified the major Resistance movements, he now proceeded to form the National Resistance Council. He took the chair at its first meeting in Paris on May 25, and spoke with eloquence: there were those who said that with his compelling presence, his fine record and his sincerity, Jean Moulin would make a better Leader than Charles de Gaulle.

His success was fated to be very short. On June 9 the reports about the *Vertrauensmänner* were justified: General Delestraint was caught in Paris by the Germans and later executed. On June 21 Jean Moulin attended a meeting of Resistance leaders in a doctor's villa at Caluire, a northern suburb of Lyon, and was 'given' by a traitor whose identity was a subject of debate for years. Everyone was captured and imprisoned, and Jean Moulin, de Gaulle's own man, was subjected to hideous tortures.

In less than a month, while de Gaulle importuned the Allies in Algiers, his Secret Army had collapsed and the whole system of a concerted Gaullist resistance was diclocated, if not destroyed, by the capture of Jean Moulin. A wave of arrests followed, some in the provinces but most in Paris, where men and women were taken without warning from their homes and offices to face the interrogators of the Avenue Foch and the Rue des Saussaies. The Vichy press gloated, and Radio Vichy, like Radio Paris, breathed death and threats to the 'terrorists'. In Menton Jacques and Polly listened with contempt to the collaborationist networks, when they listened at all, for Jacques swore by the neutral Swiss radio, and declined to get himself arrested for listening to the BBC. There were cryptic messages on the BBC's French service now, intended for the Resistance. 'The little frogs will croak at dusk' or 'the collie bitch has six puppies' appeared to mean that some action was to be taken, or some drop of supplies made by the RAF. Jacques said nobody in his group gave a damn for the frogs or the bitch, and he doubted if many of the listeners understood the codes anyway. His link with the outer world continued to be Maxwell, whose 'pianist', in radio contact with London, had so far managed to avoid arrest.

It was Maxwell who brought the bad news on the ninth of July. It was a very hot day, and Jacques was writing in his private room at the *étude* when he saw the British agent coming across the garden, dressed in working clothes and carrying, as he sometimes did, a carpenter's toolbag. It was the first time he had ever come to the office. Jacques let him go through the routine like everybody else, and as he sat tensed at his desk could picture Maxwell going up to the counter and giving a false name and a false errand to Monsieur Janot or Chris. He saw two clients, shown in by the boy when Jacques rang his bell, and tried to give his mind wholly to their stories, before the door opened a third time to admit Charles Maxwell, who said, 'I'm sorry about this,' without preliminaries.

'I had to see you right away,' he continued, as Jacques motioned him to a chair. 'I've brought some bad news you may want to break to your wife yourself.'

'What's up?'

'Jean Moulin died in prison yesterday.'

Jacques sighed. 'Poor devil—we expected that.'

'After all those days of torture, and he never said a word.'

'You're sure?'

'Positive. He died a hero's death, like Renaudon.'

'He could have betrayed every leader, every network, in the whole Resistance. And Renaudon only suffered four days in the prison of St. Pierre. Moulin's been in the hands of those devils for how long? Nearly three weeks.'

'Makes you think, doesn't it?' said Maxwell.

'It makes me think the men de Gaulle chooses have to know how to die.'

'I meant, it might make you think about yourself.'

'Still giving me a fifty-fifty chance?'

'Less, after your exploit with the weapons truck.'

'When am I going to get any weapons from SOE?'

'Next week, if all goes well.'

'That's good.' Jacques relaxed, and produced his cigarettes. But seeing the gravity of Maxwell's face, he laid his lighter down and said, 'There's something more. Something I've got to break to Polly. What is it?'

'Jacques, I hate to tell you, but it's happened, and it's verified. The Bertrands were arrested in Paris in that last Gestapo sweep.'

'Oh, my God! Louis and Anne Marie? Was there no hope of springing them?'

'There wasn't any time. I don't know where Bertrand was taken, but Anne Marie was seen in a convoy bound for Ravensbruck.'

Jacques put his head in his hands. 'This is going to be terrible for Polly.'

'I know. I could tell, when I met her at Toulouse, how fond she was of Anne Marie. I never knew them, Jack, but everybody said they were grand people.'

'The best,' said Jacques. 'Have you any idea how it happened? I can understand how Jean Moulin and his friends were taken: it was the Cimiez story all over again. A traitor in the camp, a meeting in a villa with only one escape route, and far too many of them in the same place at the same time.'

86

'SOE warned them again and again to decentralise.'

'Moulin didn't want to take any advice from SOE. But Bertrand! He seemed to be as harum-scarum as his show-business friends, but you could see he kept really strict security. What put the Gestapo on to *him*?'

'Too many strangers coming about his flat, it seems.'

'But he ran his business from his flat, so naturally he had a lot of visitors.'

'Too many visitors who stayed overnight, and were never seen by daytime in the Cité du Retiro. The concierge got suspicious and turned him in.'

'The poisonous bitch!' said Jacques. 'D'you know, he hinted to me once that she was inquisitive about that. Maybe he didn't tip her enough?'

'He tipped her too much, if what I hear is true. That was what started her snooping around.'

'Oh hell,' said Jacques blankly. 'Denounced by your concierge. I bet a lot of that goes on behind the scenes.'

'Well, Jack, there it is,' said Maxwell. 'I'm desperately sorry. Please give my sympathy to Pauline.'

'I will. D'you want to go along to the Bar du Soleil and have a drink?'

'Thanks, but I don't think we should be seen together. For my own sake as well as yours, Jack, you must be pretty hot these days! We'll meet in Nice next week.'

They discussed arrangements for the delivery of arms, if the drop came off as planned.

'What are we likely to get?' asked Jacques. 'The boys are clamouring for Stens.'

'Stens it is, though they're not a hundred per cent accurate. And a consignment of hand grenades. Better brush up on your first aid.'

'That's what Dr. Lecampion said, after he patched poor Bébé up. He said the man who put on the tourniquet did a rotten job.'

'It wasn't you, was it?'

'It was Victor Marcati, slapdash as usual. Must you go?'

'I'm taking the evening train to meet Roger.'

'H'm! I know he's a first-rate agent, but I wish he hadn't taken Roger for his code name. Always reminds me of poor Malvy. See you next week, then.'

Maxwell paused with his hand on the door-knob. 'Are you all

87

right for money, Jack?' he said. Jacques, who had risen from his desk, frowned slightly, and said he was. Afterwards, when he had told Monsieur Janot and Chris that he intended to work late, and would lock up when they had gone, he wondered at his own stubborn pride. He was not all right for Resistance money; the sum he had accepted from SOE before he left London was dwindling fast. Bébé had made a good recovery from his wound, but required nursing care, and that could not be had at a hospital where the admission of a patient with a gunshot wound would be reported to the police. Dr. Lecampion had put the boy in charge of a midwife who had her own arrangement with the police force, and her services had not been cheap. He was now convalescing at the Jurac farm, in the company of Victor, the one maquisard who ran the risk of being identified by Dieter, the German driver of the weapons truck, and who was forced to lie low till the great German hue and cry ended. Then in spite of Polly's optimism only three of the remaining five boys from the Col de Castillon had found employment at the St. Michel home. The other two had been taken on as gardeners at Les Colombières, a fantastic estate not far from Jacques' old home at Garavan. They were paid very little, over and above their keep, and had to be supplied with pocket money as well as lighter clothes for the hot weather.

One source from which Jacques hoped to obtain funds for his maquisards, had dried up before he could arrange anything. Allen Dulles, the western director of the American Office of Strategic Services, was stationed in Bern, and in the beginning of 1943—as Joe Calvert and his OSS friends in London told Jacques—had already channelled eight million francs to the *réseaux* of the French Resistance. Then de Gaulle and his men raised the usual hubbub, calling Dulles's enterprise 'American interference in French affairs' and by April the Gaullist 'Commissioner for the Interior' had asked the US Embassy in Bern to end the OSS contributions. 'You shouldn't have gone knocking on the Americans' door,' said the general to one Resistance man who had been in touch with Dulles. 'They welcomed you only because they believed they could circumvent de Gaulle.' He had what now amounted to persecution mania where Roosevelt and Churchill were concerned.

Jean Moulin, before his capture, had also objected to the OSS contributions, and Colonel Passy's organisation accused Allen Dulles of trying to divide the Resistance for the benefit of General Giraud.

At this point the OSS decided that the military intelligence they hoped to get from France in return for their contributions was going to be dear at the price of such friction, and the scheme was dropped.

So there was the leader of the Groupe Brunel, beginning to be strapped for money, but less concerned with that on this July night than with telling Polly what had happened to their friends. He knew that she had grown very fond of Anne Marie Bertrand; fonder than he was, although he admired the cabaret girl as a patriot and a singer. Jacques had always preferred small, slim women with lively wits to the statuesque, full-blown beauties like Anne Marie, but it was horrible to think of that magnificent body subjected to the degradations of the women's concentration camp of Ravensbruck, where the kindest fate to hope for was the bullet in the back of the neck.

He locked up and started walking home. The Menton streets were more animated, July having brought a number of French holiday-makers kept by war from the *plages* of the Channel and the Atlantic, and several shopkeepers wished good evening to Maître Brunel as he passed their doors. They had no idea that they were greeting the leading 'terrorist' of Menton, or that the quiet man in the grey flannel suit made for him in 1938, and the brown felt hat with the snap brim, was responsible for the recent series of plastic attacks on the vehicles parked at the Italian army depot. These had been effectively carried out by Jean-Pierre, the gas man, and the three resistants he had recruited in the gasworks at Carnolès. Armed with hand grenades they should be more effective still.

Jacques wished that Polly had a woman friend of her own age to share her trouble tonight. When he remembered his sister at home in the year before her marriage, she seemed to be always surrounded by a crowd of girls, going to swim, going to play tennis, chattering about summer dances and new clothes. Polly had nobody. She had been very fond of Anne Marie, and Anne Marie was in Ravensbruck. She had grown fond of Chantal Malvy, and Chantal, having lost her son and her husband in hideous circumstances, had gone to Plombières with her mother to take the cure. The friends of Jacques' parents who entertained them on their marriage belonged to the older generation, and as for the Baroness Belinska, in whose flat at the Maison Russe he had first met Polly, her health was failing fast. Jacques sent Dr. Lecampion to see her, who said there was nothing

89

much to be done. 'Old age—and malnutrition—and too much Russia,' said the doctor. 'She'll slip away quietly, one of these days.'

The Rue Longue was in lively spirits that evening, with children everywhere, skipping rope and playing hide and seek in and out of the traverses, while their mothers hung out of the windows and chatted with each other across the narrow street. Jacques let himself in at his own front door, thankful that there was no concierge getting ready to denounce him. There was nothing in the lobby but a pram and a bicycle, both chained to the newel post of the stair, and the queer old weapon on the wall. It was a Turkish lance captured at the battle of Lepanto by an ancestor of the original owners of the house. It dated back to the seventeenth century, and Lepanto, if Jacques remembered his history, was fought in 1571. With the battles of 1943 heavy on his mind he entered his flat, and heard Polly singing in the kitchen.

She came out at once to kiss him, in an exultant mood. She had bought a rabbit from Norine, who had bought it from a boy peddling poached rabbits round the hill district where she lived, and Polly had got fresh vegetables at the market, and they were going to have rabbit stew for dinner. Jacques must hurry please and wash his hands, and then they could have a glass of white wine on the balcony. It was a marvellous evening, and they would watch the sunset and see the violet crown forming above the Mediterranean.

Jacques poured wine for Polly and a *fine à l'eau* for himself, feeling that only brandy could get him through what lay ahead, and unfolded the deck chairs. Some of their neighbours were taking the air on their own balconies or at their windows, and Polly waved to them when she came out. She had a great deal to tell Jacques. A new contingent of children from Paris had arrived at the home that morning, so many more than they had room for that the director said some of them would have to go to the hostels at Albaréa and Saorge. Did Jacques whow where Saorge was?

'Of course,' said Jacques. 'It's a mountain village in the High Valley of the Roya, about as far from Sospel as Sospel is from Menton.'

'Oh, not too far away, then. The director asked if I could drive the children over.'

She said it casually, but Jacques was not deceived, and sat up at once.

'*You* drive them over! In what, please? In the Peugeot?'

'No, in the little bus. You've seen it around, with the name of the home on it, and the Red Cross.'

'Have you ever driven the bus?'

'Once or twice,' she confessed. 'Fetching and carrying the children to the station. There's nothing to it!'

'Polly, please be sensible. I know you're a good driver' (he nearly added 'for a woman') 'but there's all the difference in the world between driving in the streets of Menton and doing a hundred-kilometre round trip to Saorge. You saw what the Col de Castillon road was like; well, the road over the Col de Brouis is twice as tricky. It's one hairpin bend after another, and besides, the Roya valley road hasn't been repaired since the fighting in 1940. If it's all that important to your director, and I think he has a nerve to ask you, I'll take the kids to Saorge myself.'

'You wouldn't get past the Italian patrols in Sospel, or the German customs men.'

'Would you?'

'I've a far better chance.'

He knew that was true, and hesitated; Polly plunged ahead. 'I thought it would be a good opportunity for me to stop at the Jurac farm on the way back, and check on Victor and Bébé.'

'We get their news from Jean Dupont, and they're all right.' He rose, and took the empty glass from the girl's hand. 'Polly, I know you've got the pluck of the devil,' he said, 'you don't have to prove it to anybody, not even to yourself. Promise me you won't do anything headstrong, like going off to Saorge on your own, without giving me a chance to think it over, and to look the bus over, too. Promise?'

'Of course I promise,' she said, smiling up at him. 'Don't fuss about me, darling. Probably the kids won't be sent to Saorge at all —they were putting extra cots into the dormitories when I left tonight.'

'They'd better keep it that way,' said Jacques, and they went indoors to dinner. He had almost decided, when they were on the balcony, to suppress the news of the Bertrands' capture. Why upset her when she was so busy and happy, and looked so pretty sitting opposite him in her yellow dress, ladling out the tasty rabbit stew? But unfortunately the dish reminded her of a rabbit stew they had eaten in the forest of Compiègne on their way to England, and from that it was an easy move to talking about the Bertrands, who had passed them on to the safe-house in the forest. Polly drank the rough red wine of Provence, and talked about Anne Marie the first time they met her, singing 'Lili Marlene' at the Doge nightclub in Paris, and Anne Marie at their wedding in the *mairie*—one happily remembered detail after another until Jacques was on the point of begging her to stop. When dinner was over, and she proposed going back to the balcony to enjoy the warm summer night and the sky where the first stars were beginning to appear, he stopped her at the french window and took her in his arms. Very gently he told her that Anne Marie had been arrested, and Louis Bertrand too, but that no details were known; he couldn't bring himself to use the words 'Ravensbruck' and 'Gestapo'. He had braced himself for tears, but not for temper: the sobs were angry rather than pitiful, and Polly's first reaction was almost the same as his own. Had nobody tried to spring them? Did their friends just *sit* there and let the Bertrands be taken away, to Drancy, or Fresnes, or that horrible staging point at Royallieu? Or was Royallieu only for Jews? Had the *passeur* at La Folie farm, who sent them on to England, been arrested too? And his old father, Petit Père? Were the resistants in the north a pack of cowards?

In her anger Polly failed to see the implication which had haunted Jacques since Maxwell's visit, that if the Gestapo had raided the flat in the Cité du Retiro earlier in the year Polly herself would have been arrested with the Bertrands. He was thankful for her obtuseness as he hushed and petted her while the darkness filled the room, and before they went to bed he succeeded in calming his darling, furious Pauline. He wanted to make love to her, but even more than that he wanted her to sleep with his arms around her, quietened and safe beneath the outspread wings of the swan. But neither of them slept well that night, and when Jacques awoke, Polly in her wrapper was already sitting on the balcony, as if she found comfort in the morning light and the sound of the sea.

She came in at once when he called her and made the coffee. It was Saturday, when she didn't go to the holiday home and the *étude* Brunel closed for the weekend at midday; when Jacques came back he took her out to lunch at a black market restaurant which had recently opened on the Quai Bonaparte. They seldom went there, not so much from principle as because it was largely patronised by Italian officers, some of whom were there as usual. But the Bersaglieri seemed unusually subdued and left early, without the 'real' coffee and *grappa*, and even the cocks' feathers on their theatrical hats seemed wilted as they put them on. After they left the woman who owned the restaurant murmured something to Jacques which made him raise his eyebrows and smile. 'Probably only a rumour,' he said to Polly when he repeated the murmur, but they heard it more than once on the short walk up the Rue Longue, and as soon as they reached home Jacques switched on the wireless set. Radio Paris and Radio Vichy had substituted Wagner for their news bulletins, but as soon as Geneva came on the air they knew the truth. A British, Canadian and American force had invaded Sicily.

'So much for those gentry with the waving plumes,' said Jacques. 'Now they'll find out what it's like to have the invaders in their homeland.'

The Geneva newscaster, one of the most reliable in Europe, had more to say. General Eisenhower had broadcast to the French people, warning them not to be stampeded by the Allied invasion of Italian soil. Their eagerness to be liberated might lead them into danger. 'Do not be rash or take premature action. When the hour to act strikes we will let you know.'

The warning was repeated several times. 'Do not be rash or take premature action'—it came to have a lugubrious sound. 'Are you going to wait until General Eisenhower lets you know when to act?' Polly asked mockingly, and Jacques laughed. 'Is it likely?' he said. 'I don't think the RAF will pay much attention to *that* warning. And if they carry out their promised arms drop next week I'll go to Nice on Wednesday to take delivery of the supplies.'

'Will you come back that night?'

'I don't know.'

Most people in Menton reacted to the invasion news as Jacques Brunel had done. The French town was so near the frontier that for many years of peace there had been comings and goings, trading and intermarriages between the Mentonese and the citizens of Ventimiglia and Bordighera, so that the Italian stab in the back had caused much bitterness as well as hardship in Menton. Now the Italians were going to find out 'what it was like', and the discovery would be painful, although there were four German divisions in Sicily to stiffen resistance to the invaders. The amphibious operation, a rehearsal of things to come, had been successful; that much was known on Sunday, and on Monday Pauline Brunel made her own decision to act without waiting for the hour to strike.

She knew from the talk at the holiday home that all employers felt increasing anxiety about the Service for Forced Labour in Germany. The comb-out of men for the Wehrmacht and the Heimwehr had become more stringent since the German defeat in North Africa, and the drafting of Frenchmen to take their place in field and factory was increased to correspond. Every week a larger quota left the railway station for Marseille and the north; every man, unemployed or not, whose name was in the German card index files was liable to find himself in the quota. This was the situation which Jacques' young maquisards had left Nice to avoid, and this was the risk they ran when they left the Jurac farm to be nearer the town.

The Forced Labour office was housed in a small building near the station, which had been a bar for travellers, and it was run on six days of the week by Germans, operating with machine-like regularity. On Monday, which was the seventh day, the Italians took over—this was common knowledge, verified for the maquis by the Resistance waiter at the café in the station square. On this Monday Polly, having waited until Norine had come and gone, spent some time before the swan-supported mirror, chiefly in struggling with her hair. It was shoulder length, and awkard to put up with pins, but the result was satisfactorily dishevelled, and a sweater of Jacques' worn over an old skirt, made her as shabby as she wished to be. On this errand it would be a mistake to look chic or sexy, and as the finishing touch Polly filled her black oilcloth shopping bag, and started to walk to the station.

It was a hot afternoon, and the oleanders in the station square were dusty, but the door of the Forced Labour office was obstinately shut. Polly knocked and entered. The atmosphere inside was stifling, but the man in charge was Italian all right, a sweating sergeant in need of a shave. He spoke, in French, gruffly, but smiled when Polly answered him in Italian, and in a rush of agitated words she told him what her business was.

'Oh if you please sergeant it's about my cousin Pietro, he's disappeared from home, and we can't help thinking he's been drafted into Germany, and we're all so worried—'

'Steady on,' said the sergeant. 'Your cousin, did you say? We get a lot of cousins here. Sure he's not your husband?'—with a glance at her wedding ring.

'Oh no, sir, Pietro's married, but not to me. His wife's name's Sophia, and she's expecting a baby, so she sent me here instead, and

94

we would be so grateful, we'd remember you in our prayers, if you would tell us if poor Pietro's really been taken away ...'

'You haven't told me his name yet, young lady. And you'll have to show me your identity card.'

'Pietro Pradelli.' It gave her pleasure to use the name of a young Italian who had pursued her in Naples, and she added an entirely fictitious address in Menton. The sergeant hardly glanced at her own card.

'Pradelli. When did he leave home?'

'Last Wednesday—no Thursday, it was. He went to work and never came back, on Thursday.'

'Last week, eh? Then he should be in the last week's draft.' The sergeant got up and went to a row of filing cabinets between the window and the door. There was another bank of cabinets on the wall which faced the station, at right angles to the window, and both sets had inscriptions above them in German. Polly knew no German, but Jacques did; she memorised the words to repeat to him. But she knew exactly what the sergeant was doing. He was searching through the 'P' file of the recent draftees, and then through the files above and below it in case of a mistake, and when he drew a blank he was willing enough to look through the index of those who had not yet been called to labour in the land of the enemy. It was a most thorough search, and between heat and excitement Polly had no difficulty in panting and sobbing convincingly when the sergeant, grinning, gave it as his opinion that young Pietro had flown the coop.

'Oh poor Sophia, what on earth am I going to tell her?'

'Tell her he's joined the terrorists,' the sergeant suggested jocosely, and Polly's final sob became a laugh which she only concealed by telling the Italian he was a naughty man. In a flurry of thanks and distress she got herself out of the sinister little office, and across the public garden, and so home.

She was bathed and smiling when Jacques returned, and could hardly wait to tell him of her adventure and the useful things she had learned. But before she got very far she saw his face pale with anger such as he had never shown to her, and his voice was icy when he said,

'What was the object of the exercise?'

'I'm trying to tell you, it was to find out where they keep their card indexes. The files with the names of the men who've already

95

gone to Germany are between the window and the door, *they* can't be helped, but the names of those who haven't been called up yet are in files against the wall facing the station.'

'Well?'

'I thought when you got the hand grenades that Maxwell promised you, that wall could be destroyed, and the card indexes along with it. That would slow up the draft for a long time. Jacques, what's the matter? I thought you'd be pleased!'

'Pleased? When you've been fool enough to run a risk like that?'

'Where was the risk?'

'The risk was in the silly charade of dressing up like a poor girl, a working woman, and going weeping to that infernal office, to an Italian! What would you have done if that fellow's colonel, the man you were vamping for the petrol card, had come in to check on his sergeant, and found the elegant young lady acting another part? Don't you think he might have a few awkward questions to ask?'

'You didn't object when I went to see the colonel.'

'Don't try to side-track me, Pauline. I knew you were going to see the colonel, we planned the thing together. And I knew *where* you were going, to what they have the cheek to call their headquarters, and the exact time when you'd be there. Today you took off on your own, without a word to me, and if you hadn't come back I wouldn't have had an idea where to start looking—'

'When I asked you if you'd be coming back from Nice on Wednesday night you said you didn't know. Where do I look for you if *you* don't come back?'

'That's an entirely different matter.'

'Where's the difference?'

'Because I'm a man, and I used to be a soldier.'

'Beg your pardon, general, sir! You mean you can look after yourself and I can't?'

'Yes I do,' said Jacques, more harshly than she had ever heard him speak. 'How can I trust you after this? Only last Friday you gave me your promise not to do anything headstrong—'

'That was about driving to Saorge, I thought.'

'Don't quibble, Polly! You know what the word "anything" means, don't you? Can't you realise that we can't act independently of one another, that the success of our group means working as a team? Oh, I know you thought you were helping me,' he said more calmly, as Polly faced him down with a stare as hard as his, 'and in theory it wasn't a bad idea, to find out about the German files. Only, another time, be sure your scheme has my approval first.'

'Only, this time,' said Polly, echoing his words and manner, 'I wasn't thinking so much of helping you. I was thinking of doing something in memory of Louis Bertrand and Anne Marie.'

SEVEN

Although Mike Marchand's messages to his relatives in France were infrequent and often lost in transit, his letters to his fiancée in Brazil reached her late but regularly via Dakar and Natal. She had one in the pocket of her heavy cardigan when she came in from the dark yard where her little nephew was listening entranced to the Gauchos singing round the fire, and the boy's father, following her indoors, remarked it was time that kid was in bed.

'Try getting him away from a barbecue,' said Dina da Costa. She took off the cardigan and went to warm her hands at the great log fire in the stone fireplace. It was a Sunday, the fifteenth of August, and though it was still winter, with the south wind sweeping the pampas, her brother Tony had flown them all down to the Parana ranch from the family home in São Paulo, his sister, the boy Tonio and Tonio's governess, to give the adults a weekend holiday and the child a treat.

'Do you want a brandy to warm you up?' he said, peeling off his own turtle-neck sweater. The brother and sister were both wearing flannel shirts and jodhpurs, for they had been riding before the barbeque began, along one of the tracks which seamed the vast acres of their father's cattle ranch.

'I'd rather have *maté*,' she said, and Tony gave the order to the Indio butler who was drawing the curtains, made of a native woven fabric in barbaric colours. Dina, in her pale cream shirt and fawn jodphurs, seemed to blend into the background of vermilion and indigo, and the Brazilian woods with which the walls were panelled. She was tall and slim, and her black hair, which she had allowed to grow long, was plaited and doubled, and tied at the nape of her neck with a black silk ribbon.

The butler, bringing brandy for Tony and the hot herbal tea for Dina, said that Miss Martin had gone to bring in Master Tonio, and when Dina had only drunk a little from the silver mouthpiece, and was still cupping the *maté* gourd in her two hands, the boy came in to say goodnight. Tonio was a handsome child of nine, with black hair like his father's and blue eyes inherited from the mother who died when he was born. He had had a big day with the Gauchos, in and out of the saddle, and the grey-haired Englishwoman who was his governess said with a smile that for once he seemed quite ready to go to bed. 'Tired out,' his father said, when the door was closed.

'Me too,' said Dina. She finished the *maté*, and dug her shoulders luxuriously into the cushions of her big armchair. 'It's good to have a break, Tony.'

'You've been doing too much,' said her brother, and pulled his own armchair nearer the fire. Through the closed windows they could hear the Gaucho song beginning to die away, as if the men were thinking of the Monday morning call. It was very quiet inside the ranch house, with only the Beechcraft in its hangar to prove that they were not cut off from the outside world.

'Didn't you get a letter from Mike yesterday morning, just before we left São Paulo?' Tony asked.

'It's in my cardigan. Would you like to see it?'

'Well, yes, if I may. You didn't mention it last night—'

'Do you wonder?'

'What's that supposed to mean?'

'I've been getting letters for so long, but I can't get to *him*.'

'No progress on your air priority?'

'Absolutely none. You know we've been thinking of the Clipper route from New York to Lisbon, and then on to Cairo, but Mike says that's the worst way of all for civilians. There's a complete stop on female passengers. And yet Cairo's full of Service women now.'

'Confound the British!' Tony said. 'Just because they once had to evacuate women from Egypt to Kenya they keep their stops in operation, even though the emergency was over long ago.'

'Mike thinks there'll only be a quota restriction in a few months' time, and then I could get in via Cape Town and Khartoum. You'd better read exactly what he says.'

Dina got up and took the letter from the pocket of her cardigan. It was written on flimsy airmail paper, and she put the last sheet aside. 'This part is mostly about you,' she said, and handed Tony the first two pages.

Tony da Costa looked up at his favourite sister. She was trying to smile, but she had looked strained and unhappy for too long, even after Marchand had ceased to fly on combat missions. He swore beneath his breath and began to read Mike's letter.

'H'm,' he said. 'He thinks I'm crazy to enlist in the Brazilian Expeditionary Force. That's a great beginning.'

'He didn't know it was called the BEF when he wrote.'

'Doesn't matter. He knows Brazil declared war on the Axis Powers a year ago. He must have known that we meant to implement our declaration, ever since President Vargas met Roosevelt at Natal and asked for war matériel.'

'Read on, my dear.'

'Oh, it's my age he objects to!'

'Well, after all, you are thirty-eight.'

'Five years younger than his hero St. Exupéry, who's flying again at forty-three.'

'But you're not going to join the Brazilian Air Force, are you?'

'I'm hoping to come out of this alive,' said Tony. 'I told Marshal de Moraes in São Paulo, when he was named commander of the BEF, that I'd be glad to serve under his G4. Transport and supply, that's something I do know about. More than most of our dandy career officers.'

'Exactly, that's the point Mike makes. He says you're doing a more useful job for Brazil as the president of Capricorn Airways. He thinks nobody could take your place.'

'He doesn't know how Rinaldo's come on as traffic manager in the past three years. When the time comes, I'll bring him in from Santos Dumont airport to the city to work under me for a few weeks, and then he'll be ready to take over. Just as you've been training Senhorina Lobos to take your own place.'

'The trouble with Rinaldo is he hasn't two ideas to knock together.'

'We don't need an ideas man at present. Capricorn's been marking time since the United States entered the war. We've only been able to open one new route, Rio to Porto Alegre, and we've had to shelve the plans for an executive aircraft factory at São Paulo. Father was willing to advance the money from the cannery—*that's* booming—but we can't get the parts we need from the USA, and now we've run into fuel rationing. You know all this already, Dina,' he went on. 'All we can do is keep the Deodoros in the air until the war is over.' He walked over to the fireplace and lit one of his thin black cigars from a burning splinter of wood. 'But at least things are going better for the Allies now. Who'd have thought they could take Sicily, force Mussolini's arrest and the end of the Fascist party, all in less than a month! Marshal de Moraes is very optimistic about the invasion of Italy. He's offered me a place in his mission to General Eisenhower, and if we leave before the end of the year I'll be able to give you away at your wedding.'

Tony threw the smouldering splinter away, blew on his fingers, and saw his sister shake her head.

'Dina, sweetie, what's the matter?'

'I'm beginning to wonder if there'll *be* a wedding.'

'You're upset because this damned priority thing has dragged on so long.'

'Too long.'

'It's not Mike's fault.'

'Nor mine. But three years is too long for people in love to be apart.'

'An awful lot of women have been feeling the same, ever since the war began.'

'Oh yes, I know I'm not the only one. But Mike and I had so little of each other, such a short time together before he went away, that I can't help wondering if we'll feel the same when we do meet again.'

Tony da Costa hesitated. 'Have you any reason to think Mike's feelings for you have changed?' he asked, choosing his words with care.

'None at all, But he may find *me* changed.'

'In what way?'

'I'm three years older, Tony. And—he used to say I was beautiful.'

Tony looked at her. Beside her armchair a bowl of flowers had been placed on a low table of jacaranda wood by the servants who knew the Senhorina Divininha loved the paradise-bird blossoms, springing in flame and purple from their stiff green sheaths. Between the flowers and the firelight her face was illuminated with romantic beauty.

'Don't fish for compliments,' said Tony. 'As a mere brother I think you still look pretty good. At the vast age of twenty-seven you haven't a wrinkle anywhere, and you'll look the same for years and years to come. Our Indio blood will see to that. Come on, cheer up! You ought to be glad Mike's taken to his new job so well. Photographic Reconnaissance must be quite a change from flying Halifaxes in action—'

'He says if it's good enough for St. Exupéry, it has to be good enough for him.'

Tony laughed. 'Funny thing,' he said, 'I never thought Mike Marchand had a bomber pilot's mentality. After that career of winning air races and breaking speed records before the war, I'd have said he was a typical fighter pilot, just right for the short bursts and the quick kill. He turned out to be the exact opposite.'

'Doesn't that prove how much he's changed?'

'Developed, perhaps. I think it was the year of hard slog, ferrying war planes across Africa, with no stunt flying and no applause, that gave him the guts for the long haul in the Western Desert. And there's another thing. Couldn't you see in this letter, and in some of the others you've let me read, that Mike's far more concerned with the future of Capricorn than he was three years ago?'

'Yes, I do see,' she admitted. 'Tony, I let Mike go to Freetown when I could have held him, because I thought he was so crazy about France. He wanted to be in the war, fighting, until France was free. I always supposed he'd want to live in Paris after the war. Now it looks as if he's thinking about coming back to Brazil and joining us in Capricorn.'

'Smartest thing he could do. I wouldn't be surprised if he's thoroughly fed up with France by this time.'

'Then he's changed completely from the Mike we knew. But how can I tell?' said Dina desperately. 'Things have been happening to him that I don't know about, that I haven't shared. That's what I resent so much—the wasted years.'

'Neither one of you has wasted these three years,' said Tony. 'You've grown up, that's all.'

'It's so unfair,' said Dina, not listening to him. 'That cousin of Mike's that he used to be so fond of, Jacques Brunel—*he* fell in love with a girl and married her four months later, without doing any fighting or anything. They've been living in peace in France while Mike risked his life every day in the Desert. D'you know what I sometimes wish, Tony? I've never told anybody this before, but I can tell you. That one week Mike and I were together, when we were lovers, everything to each other—I wish I'd started a baby then. It happens to so many girls. Why couldn't it have happened to me?'

'Mike Marchand knew better than that,' said Tony gruffly. 'My God, when I remember the family row after you went with him to Africa on that proving flight, I don't think father and mother would have survived if Mike had had to apply for compassionate leave, and come back to make an honest woman of you.'

Dina laughed. 'They'd have survived all right,' she said. 'People do. And even the family row didn't last long, because they were so surprised and delighted by Ester's engagement. Poor mother thought Ester was an old maid at thirty, dedicated to her social work. And then she married a nice young doctor and had two baby girls with eleven months between them.'

'So don't lose heart at twenty-seven,' said Tony.

'I won't. I didn't mean to make a fuss, and I expect everything'll work out all right. I'm going to bed now. What time d'you want to leave for São Paulo?'

'Oh, not till the afternoon. I thought we might take the kid for one more ride on the pampas in the morning. You're off duty all day, aren't you?'

'Yes, my next flight's on Tuesday, ex São Paulo at oh-eight hundred hours, to Rio via Santos on the milk run.' Dina picked up her cardigan and slung it round her shoulders. 'Goodnight, Tony, Business as usual, as the British say.'

EIGHT

The life of Monsieur and Madame Jacques Brunel was far from being as peaceful as Dina imagined during the summer weeks when the Allies swept on to victory in Sicily. The weapons in the container dropped by the RAF at a point west of Cannes, and assigned to Jacques Brunel's *groupe franc* were collected from the dropping zone and repacked into trucks driven by Jean Dupont and Henri Froment. The smaller lot was stowed away behind the iron shutter of Froment's back premises at Nice and the other went on to Menton. There Jacques and the lame boy, Chris, had spent several evenings preparing the storerooms at the Brunel *étude* for the reception of Sten guns, 9–mm cartridges and hand grenades. The Schmeisser machine pistols were already stored in the wooden filing cabinets which dated back to 1873.

Jacques had long promised himself a grand destruction of the musty old parchments which bore witness to the French love of paperwork for paper's sake, but as long as his father lived he couldn't bring himself to a wholesale clearing-out and bonfire. What he did was pack all the papers prior to 1914 into strong cartons, which then formed a narrow partition across the back of the big garage. In the space thus acquired, which was both cool and dark, he stored the explosives, primers and detonating cord which had come from England, while the contents of each carton were identified by painted letters and figures. Chris had done this part of the work with care, and Jacques could only hope that no client would take it into his head to ask for the file copy of his grandfather's marriage contract, *an régime dotal*, drawn up in the year 1883.

On July 19 the Allies mounted a devastating air attack on Naples from their Sicilian airfields; on July 20 the airport and railway terminals in Rome were bombed. An invasion of the Italian mainland would not long be delayed, and in the south of France any number of roosters lost their tail feathers to marauding schoolboys who pinned them in their headgear in imitation of the Bersaglieri and paraded up and down in front of the furious sentries. *Giovinezza, giovinezza, primavera di bellezza!* they chanted to the men for whom Mussolini's springtime of beauty had long ago ceased to exist.

Before the end of July it was reported on the Swiss radio that Italy, through Marshal Badoglio, had opened negotiations for an armistice, and Jacques Brunel decided that before the armistice became a fact his group should strike in several different directions. There was no doubt that Polly's initiative in visiting the Forced Labour office had been rewarding, even if it was the cause of their first quarrel. They made it up before the sun went down, and her husband's cold anger, shocking at the time, left no indelible impression on light-hearted Polly. Jacques, more introspective and of course more legalistic, had been given food for more than one thought. He asked himself if he had been furious with Polly because she was so precious that it sickened him to think of her running into danger of her own accord? Or because his own authority had been challenged by her independent action? He wasn't sure. He had been far less authoritarian with the young maquisards than if they had been raw recruits on the barrack square, and he their officer. He was working alongside them rather than commanding them, because theirs was a guerilla war; he was now forced to realise that a wife deserved to be treated as fairly as a maquisard.

When she said she had planned the visit to the Forced Labour office in memory of Anne Marie, he told her that was a piece of false sentiment. Now he was not so sure. It was feminine reasoning, the personalising of a situation, but it was no less honourable as a motive than his own abstract idea of fighting to drive the enemy from France.

It was a kind of rough justice to Polly to select the Forced Labour office as the first target for the new hand grenades. Jacques picked Dany and Eugène, the two fastest runners in the group, to do the job. In the dark of the moon the two boys took the railway sentries off guard, tossed their grenades through the windows of the office, heard the crash and saw the fire spring up behind them as they raced up the public garden to the Chemin du Rosaire, once a pilgrim's way. It was a hard climb up that narrow path to the Capuchin monastery of the Annonciade, but once there they were given shelter for the night.

Polly looked like a cat presented with a bowl of cream when

Jacques told her that all the records in the Forced Labour office had been destroyed, but she was careful not to say 'I told you so!' and was ready to applaud the maquisards' successes in the night that followed. More damage was done to the Italian vehicle park, and their petrol dump was set on fire. Their food depot went next, and for the wretched Italians it was a real reign of terror. They were outrun and outbombed, night after night, by a handful of spirited and well-organised young men.

Jacques came home unexpectedly at noon one day to tell Polly that the Baroness Belinska had died in the small hours of the morning.

'Oh Jacques, I hope she didn't suffer!'

'The message from the manager said she slipped quietly away, just as Dr. Lecampion foresaw. Some of the old ladies from the Maison Russe were with her at the end. I'll have to go to the funeral, darling, because my father was her lawyer. Do you want to come too?'

'Of course,' said Polly. 'She was my mother's friend.'

'The pope from the Russian church at Carnolès has taken charge of the arrangements.'

'Those poor old souls at the Maison Russe are so lucky to have that church. When my mother died in Naples we had to send for candlebearers and a pope from Rome,' said Polly, and her young face grew old in remembered sadness. Jacques drew her close and kissed her. 'You must have been very lonely when you lost her,' he said.

'Lonely! Oh darling, if you knew how lonely I was in that great house in Naples, and how thankful I am that I met you!'

Jacques remembered that tenderly as he knelt beside her next day in the tiny Russian church. He listened to Polly joining in the Russian prayers led by the pope and so feebly echoed by a few aged men and women kneeling by the coffin, and for her sake he was prepared to go on kneeling indefinitely, though Polly had warned him that the reading from the Psalms would go on for hours. But after twenty minutes the candlebearers changed places, and one or two of the old people, helping each other with offered arms and walking sticks, got stiffly to their feet. Polly rose too, and with a grave bow towards the coffin and another to the pope, she walked ahead of Jacques out of the church.

One of the mourners was waiting for them in the garden.

'I beg your pardon, monsieur,' she said. 'Am I right in supposing you're Maître Jacques Brunel?'

'I am, madame.' Her French was idiomatic, her accent could have been anything—Russian perhaps, if Jacques had been familiar with spoken Russian. That it was English was obvious as soon as she announced her name: Miss Rachel Torrance. He introduced his wife.

'I'm glad to meet you, Madame Brunel,' said the English lady. 'Poor Natalie Belinska often spoke of you. She was a friend of your mother in the old days, I believe.'

'And of my Russian grandmamma,' said Polly. 'Do you live in the Maison Russe, Miss Torrance?' She looked as shabby-genteel as any of the old White Russians who lived near and for their church, in a well-worn black dress and shoes which had gone once too often to the cobbler, and as fragile as if the summer breeze would blow her away, but she told them proudly that she had her own house in Menton, and had walked all the way from there that morning to pay her last respects to an old friend.

'Well, you mustn't think of walking back again,' said Jacques. 'I've got my car here, so we can give you a lift.'

'How kind of you,' said Miss Torrance. 'I really ventured to address you, sir, because I used to know your dear mother. She and I were in the same working party of the Red Cross at Menton, and we made bandages together in the first winter of the war. Have you good news of her, Maître Brunel?'

'Fairly good, thank you,' said Jacques, helping Miss Torrance into the back seat of the car. 'My sister keeps in touch with them, by one means or another, and says my father's health's improving at Davos.'

'How did you come to know Madame Belinska, Miss Torrance?' Polly asked. The old lady drew herself erect; she had an almost regal manner of squaring her shoulders and giving a little bow to rebuke an abrupt question. 'I knew her in the old days in St. Petersburg,' she said. 'I was a governess in the household of—' and she repeated a once illustrious name.

'You must have had an interesting life, Miss Torrance. However did you get from St. Petersburg to Menton?'

'That's rather a long story, my dear.' She was nothing loth to tell it, leaning forward in the car. Rachel Torrance had gone to Russia as a governess about the time of the last Czar's marriage, and had remained with the same family all her working life. Prince Ivan had liberal views and was not popular at court. As early as 1915 he had foreseen the revolution, and removed his whole family, including Miss Torrance, to his French estate at Cap d'Ail. 'He left with his fortune intact and all his wife's jewels,' said Miss Torrance. 'Unfortunately Princess Anna was a confirmed invalid and seldom went into society.'

'Surely the children were grown up by then,' said Polly.

'Of course they were, but I stayed on as a—a sort of companion to the princess. Then one of the daughters, who had married an immensely wealthy Argentinian, invited them all to Buenos Aires for a long visit. The prince liked the South American way of life so much that they decided to make their home there, and the house at Cap d'Ail was sold.'

'And you were left alone,' said Polly sympathetically. 'You must have missed them very much.'

'Of course I did, because my life had been spent among them, but the dear prince was very generous. He bought a house for me in Menton, where I planned to open a tearoom, and settled a pension on me for life. It's paid to me quarterly through the Banque Palméro, where they've looked after my affairs with the greatest care—even when I was in prison.'

'In prison, Miss Torrance?' said Jacques.

'They called it the concentration camp at Sospel, monsieur. But it was prison to me, although some said the Italians weren't treating us too badly. I spent six months in the Caserne Salel, until they realised I was over seventy, and released me with some other people, too old and weak to do them any harm. Or so they thought,' said Rachel Torrance viciously. 'I must say, when I got back to Menton and found the Italian soldiers had looted and half-wrecked my poor little tearoom, simply because my sign said "The English Tea Shop", I should have liked to do a *great deal* of harm to some of them. Oh no,' in answer to a question from Polly, 'I didn't try to open it again. There were no supplies—and no more English tourists.'

'I remember the place now,' said Jacques. 'Close to the Hotel Balmoral.'

'Yes, and *so* popular with the hotel guests before the war.'

'And you live there still? The house wasn't damaged, was it?'

'Oh no, I have a roof above my head, and my pension from the dear prince. I have everything I need,' the old lady said proudly.

'Perhaps you could make something more of your property,'

Jacques suggested. 'Come and see us soon, Miss Torrance, and we'll talk it over.'

Polly told her where to find them on the Rue Longue. 'Everybody knows the House of the Lance,' she said, 'and if you tell me more about St. Petersburg I'll make you a glass of real Russian tea!'

'You're both very kind, and I have enjoyed my drive,' said the old lady. Her fluttered thanks lasted all through the short way down the promenade past the Hotel Balmoral to the door of a little house where a big boarded-up window on one side was all that was left of 'The English Tea Shop'.

'It does look dreadful,' the owner apologised, 'but I thought it would be money thrown away to have new glass put in.'

'Quite right,' said Jacques, helping her to the pavement, and holding out his hand to Polly. He looked the place over thoughtfully. 'You've got a valuable property here, Miss Torrance. Isn't there a garden at the back?'

'Yes, it runs alongside the little alley that leads to the Rue St. Michel.'

'That's what I thought. And you live here all alone?'

'Quite alone. But I'm not a nervous person, Maître Brunel!'

'I'm sure you're not. Still—this is merely a suggestion—have you never thought of renting one or two of your rooms?'

'Take paying guests, you mean? Oh, I don't think I should like that!'

'We have a friend, a young insurance agent from Marseille, who'd be glad to rent a room for his visits to Menton. He would pay on a quarterly basis, in advance.'

'I should have thought a young insurance agent would prefer to stay at one of the small hotels near the station, with a café and a billiard table,' said Miss Torrance drily.

'Charles Aletti has other interests besides selling insurance, mademoiselle. When he's not on the road, he likes to live in a quiet place. Might I ask him to call on you, when he's visiting Menton next week?'

'I don't see why not, Maître Brunel, if you'll explain my circumstances to him first. And I do hope his other interests will not include—er—young lady visitors. That I will *not* permit.'

'Of course not, nothing like that,' said Jacques hastily. 'He's really a very reserved young man. And most agreeable.'

'Then we'll leave it at that, shall we? And thank you both again for driving me home.' Miss Torrance shook hands, first with Polly and then with Jacques. Her blue eyes, so much younger than her faded face, were steady on his as she said, 'Tell your friend his interests will be safe with me.'

'You're thinking of a safe-house for Charlie Maxwell, aren't you?' said Polly after they drove away. 'Was I mistaken, or did she put a certain emphasis on the word *safe*?'

'I thought so,' said Jacques. 'She's nobody's fool, any more than the dear prince was, when he sniffed trouble brewing twice in one lifetime, and got out while the going was good.'

'Rough on Miss Torrance, though.'

'Oh, I think he treated her rather well, all things considered.'

'Considering that she was much more *his* companion at Cap d'Ail than Princess Anna's?'

'Now, Polly, you've no evidence of that,' said the lawyer.

'Only my feminine intuition,' said Polly solemnly. 'And confess, my darling, that you thought so too.'

Jacques laughed. 'Whether she was in love with the dear prince or not doesn't matter,' he said. 'What I like is that she really hates the Italians.'

Maxwell in his character of Charles Aletti, the agent of a respected Marseille insurance company, and backed up by the lavish funds of SOE, made a favourable impression on Miss Rachel Torrance. On arriving at Menton he was met at the station by Polly, or rather he was met at the news stand, for she appeared to be intent on buying magazines, and merely said, when he came quietly up beside her, that he was to go to a certain address on the promenade and then to the Rue Longue for an early dinner. He thought she looked unusually subdued, and when he reached the Brunel's flat he found out why. There was what Maxwell called a flap on, and the cause of it, predictably, was Victor Marcati.

The Corsican had tired of the company of the old Juracs and Bébé, and having grown a black moustache which he seemed to regard as a cloak of darkness covering him from any identification, he had returned to Menton on one of the irregular buses from Sospel. There, being out of cigarettes, he had replenished his stock by holding up, at gun point, the proprietor of a *tabac* near the Hanbury Fountain at Garavan, and generously shared his haul of Gitanes with the three maquisards employed at the holiday home.

'Danny Profetti came grinning and boasting to Polly about it,' said Jacques angrily. 'He seemed to think Marcati had done something clever. Polly walked the whole way to the office to warn me, and I picked up Monsieur Marcati within an hour, and gave him the bawling-out of a lifetime.'

'But nobody else had a go at picking him up, did they?'

'No, he got clean away from Garavan. I know the old boy who keeps the *tabac*, he's licensed to sell postage stamps along with postcards and soft drinks when there are any; I used to buy candy there when I was a kid. He hasn't got a phone or a car, so it was some time before *he* arrived in Menton and reported the robbery to the police.'

'Where's Marcati now?'

'Holed up in Julien's back shop in the Rue Trenca. Nice for Julien Monnier, if the police come nosing round.'

'Jacques, do give poor Charles a drink,' Polly interposed, and with a muttered apology Jacques poured brandy and water for them all. Polly took hers to the kitchen. She was in an ambitious mood, she told the guest, and intended to grill sea bass over fennel sticks for their dinner.

'How did you get on with our new friend, Miss Torrance?' Jacques remembered to enquire.

'Oh, she's a grand old girl, and the room is fine. She seems to have got it into her head that I'm running a black market operation on the side.'

'Bring her some black market coffee next time, then. And she has no idea that you're British?'

'Not the faintest. But never mind Miss Torrance, Jack, we can talk about her later. Just tell me: what the hell's the matter with Marcati?'

'God knows. I think the hit and run raid, Operation Schmeisser, went right to his head. He told me he was sick of the farm work, he joined the Resistance to blow up trains. Yes, I said, but you didn't join the Resistance to commit armed robbery, or terrorise a decent old Frenchman who might have had a heart attack and died on the spot.'

'What did he say to that?'

'Said he was sorry about the old boy, but he didn't think *this* robbery was a crime, because tobacco was a government monopoly, so all he was doing was robbing Vichy.'

'Very ingenious,' Maxwell said. 'Victor's smart all right, but I'm afraid he's becoming a liability. For a start, you'll have to get him right out of the area.'

'I thought of passing him on to Daniel Profetti in Nice, until there's a chance to ship him out to Corsica.'

'The sporting life in the Rue Paradis might be too much for *Totor-pour-les-dames*. Next off, he'll be running a string of girls, and upsetting Profetti's deal with the police. How about my taking him back to Cannes with me? We're planning a big job there, and your Corsican friend would come in handy.'

'What sort of big job?'

'Same as we're going to talk about tonight—railway sabotage.'

They discussed explosives over the refill of the brandy and water until dinner was ready. The sea bass was a trifle burned, but the sharp scent of the fennel covered all deficiencies, and there were new potatoes. A dish of stewed greengages completed a meal which the guest praised extravagantly. He found Polly out of spirits, and thought she must have got the backlash of her husband's anger at Victor's folly. But he admired the coolness of her goodnight to them both, and the absence of whimpering or entreaties to be careful. Not that there was anything particularly risky in their rendezvous for the evening.

They were going by the Rue Longue, still echoing to the cries of children at play, by the back paths behind the town hospital and finally by the olive grove of the Pian, to one of the most extraordinary domains of the French Riviera. Conceived and laid out in the Twenties by a dilettante genius, Les Colombières was intended to be the ultimate expression of Mediterranean landscape art, and in its seven hectares of grounds each classical arrangement of cypress alleys and ornamental waters flowed into the next in a style more Greek than could be truly appreciated by the French. Jacques' father, who was a friend of the owner, was critical of parterres so lacking in rose bushes and boxwood, and blind to the glimpses of the Bay of Peace when these were obtained through the arches of a colonnade not covered by rambler roses. Jacques was not sufficiently versed in aesthetics to contradict his father's judgment; he only felt, on his few visits to Les Colombières before the war, that those green spaces and perspectives broken by marble statuettes and busts had a harmony all their own.

The two maquisards who had found employment at Les Colombières as gardeners were housed some distance from the villa, in a hut, among the olive trees behind what its creator had called the Allée de Nike, where a bas-relief showed the Victory, not winged, but tying up her sandal. They ate their meals at the head gardener's cottage, but neither he nor the inhabitants of the villa enquired what they did after hours or if they found any entertainment in Menton. Their hut was easy of access, for the Menton men by way of a ravine, and for the boys at the holiday home through the paths which led from the St. Michel quarter to the olive grove, and into it the two groups, with the exception of Victor Marcati, were crowded when Jacques and Maxwell arrived from the town. They were far enough from the villa to speak in their normal voices, but their greetings were muttered rather than spoken: they had all been made aware of the *chef's* wrath at the *affaire* Marcati. Jacques' words were sharp and to the point.

'Some of you have met Charles Aletti before,' he said, 'you all know it was he who arranged for us to draw efficient weapons from a RAF drop. What you don't know is that he's a British officer. He came to France to help us towards our own liberation, and we shall take his orders as if he were an officer of our own. That's all.'

Charles Maxwell didn't know if the surprise on all the faces was a tribute to his impersonation of a man from Marseille or at hearing the word 'officer' in a guerilla camp. His accent was still Marseillais but his voice was as stern as Jacques' when he said, 'Some of you are anxious to blow up trains, I hear. My job in France is to teach you how to disrupt the enemy's road and rail communications, and the destruction of his rolling stock is of course part of that. Before we actually blow up any trains we must begin by putting the railways out of action, either by destroying the turntables at certain stations or by detonating charges set under the points. We can discount road blocks at present. You're not numerically strong enough to man a successful ambush of anything larger than a single truck, and the Stens and the machine pistols are short-range weapons. I want us to have a dry run tomorrow night at Cabbé. If it's successful, well and good; if not, there's no harm done.'

'Why Cabbé, and not Menton?' asked Julien Monnier.

'Because Menton's a bigger station, and the Germans are bringing in their own railwaymen, who carry pistols when they work. Cabbé involves the problem of transport, but I think we can lick that one.'

'Why don't we blow up the tunnel east of Menton—the tunnel into Italy?' said another. They were getting back their confidence now, and with it their passion for argument.

'That would take more dynamite than we can lay our hands on, Pierre.'

'We could get dynamite from the quarry on the Corniche road,' said Dany, and the science teacher spoke learnedly of the manufacture of nitrogen iodide.

'Far too unstable, and anyway not powerful enough,' said Maxwell firmly. 'When we're ready for tunnels we'll start with a small one first, like the one near the beach at Cap Martin. Eh, Jack?' They were both remembering the night Maxwell came ashore at the start of his mission, and the train with blinded windows which threw its yellow light on the tunnel while they hid in the undergrowth above.

'Tomorrow's Orders of the Day are for an attack on the railway east of Cabbé at twenty-one hundred hours,' said Lieutenant Charles Maxwell. 'I intend to lead the attack myself.'

The lecture which followed was as clear as anything Jacques Brunel had heard in the army, but allowing for many questions and answers it took a long time to deliver, and it was after the curfew hour when he went soft-footed down the Rue Longue. He had little fear of being picked up, for the local police and the Italian patrols were as unwilling to venture into the tunnels and traverses of the Old Town as their counterparts in the Old Town of Nice, but he knew Polly would be anxious, and as soon as he entered the flat he assured her that all was well. 'We've planned a job for tomorrow night,' he told her, 'but you don't have to worry. Maxwell's picked me to be the driver. He broke it to me on our way to the meeting that because of my advanced age and my old wound I'd be more useful at the wheel than on the railway line ... Now, darling, do let's go to bed and get some sleep.'

Next day he had a distraction for her, something which he had kept as a surprise till now: a legacy from the Baroness Belinska. Polly knew that the *étude* Brunel would have to wind up the old White Russian lady's estate, which consisted only of the annuity Jacques' father made her buy, which died with her, and her bits and pieces of personal property. Her surprise was complete when Jacques came home carrying a large, clumsily wrapped parcel, which he gave her with the words, 'You're an heiress, Polly! Congratulations!'

'An heiress? Me?'

'Baroness Belinska remembered you in something like the fiftieth codicil to her Will. "The ikon which hangs above my writing desk I give and bequeath to Pauline Mary Preston" and so on. It was dated last November, just after you stayed with her.'

Polly had the wrappings off by now and placed her legacy against the back of one of the living-room chairs. 'It's the Virgin of Kazan,' she said. 'I remember seeing this. I think it might be valuable. And don't you think it's beautiful?'

'Pretty thing,' said Jacques indifferently. The Byzantine reds and golds of the ikon made no appeal to him. 'I'll have my work cut out to distribute all her junk to the other legatees. By the way, Miss Torrance gets the samovar.'

'This isn't junk,' said Polly. 'I want to hang it in the bedroom, please.'

It was the first picture or ornament ever to be hung on their bare white walls. Fortunately a cord was attached, and Jacques fetched a hammer and nails and fastened the ikon of the Virgin of Kazan where Polly directed, on the wall opposite their bed. He had to admit, looking from the swan to the ikon, that it didn't seem out of place.

Three hours later, when the summer darkness had fallen, a plumber at Cabbé opened the door of his workshop to a group of men in dark sweaters pulled up to their mouths and dark stocking caps drawn down to their eyes. They were Maxwell, Monnier, Léo and Pierre, and Jacques Brunel was parking his car with the bonnet pushed into a clump of oleander between the workshop and the tiny railway station. Cabbé was the last whistle stop but one on the track to Menton.

The plumber, who was one of Jacques' Resistance group at Cap Martin, had been warned of their coming, and confirmed that an Italian freight train came through westbound without stopping every night at nine thirty-five. They had twenty-five minutes to do the job if they looked sharp. The maquisards had four charges ready, one and a half pounds of explosive in each charge wrapped in waterproof material, as were the primers and detonating cord. They set off up the line, walking on the ties in old rubber-soled shoes; the night was so still that every sound was magnified, and even the purring of the plumber's cat, stropping against Jacques' trouser legs, sounded like thunder to the two waiting men. Jacques offered the plumber a cigarette and lit one for himself.

'Here she comes!' The westbound freighter came out of the Cap Martin tunnel with a shrill blast of the whistle, and as the two men ran to a vantage point on the slope behind the shop they heard one or two faint explosions. The train rocked to a halt, but remained on the rails, and they saw two or three of the train crew jump down armed with lanterns. In the silence angry Italian voices were clearly heard.

'No go,' said Jacques, and 'Looks like it', agreed the plumber, and led the way back to his workshop. It seemed a long time before the maquisards came back one by one, to have their outburst of explanations sternly hushed by Jacques. 'Get into the car,' he ordered. 'For God's sake remember the curfew.' He had them back in Menton in seven minutes, dropping them off along the promenade and the Avenue Carnot to make their own way home, and then drove straight to the garage on the Traverse Bellecour. The headlamps of the Peugeot threw eerie lights on the stacked cartons and Christophe's careful lettering.

'What happened?' It was the first time Jacques had spoken since they left Cabbé, and Maxwell, the only man remaining with him, said shortly that the boys weren't quick enough, they would have to pick another team and work them up a bit.

'*A vos ordres, mon lieutenant,*' said Jacques, 'but I think the next try should be at Menton station. According to Ratazzi, our man at Nice, they despatch an eastbound freighter every night, ETA Menton twenty-two hundred hours, loaded with whatever food and drink they've scrounged from the city and the valley of the Var.'

'Okay, but I suppose you want to be in the next strike yourself?'

'If we do Menton, my old bones wouldn't be in for so much running.'

Four nights later Jacques was running as he had not run since his schooldays along an almost uninhabited road which lay below and parallel to the railway between the station and the little museum of Menton. He thought Dany and the science teacher made a better team than Léo and Pierre, although like himself they were still too slow for Maxwell, in spite of the practice they had gone through with simulated iron and steel. All they had attempted was to wedge the points on the track, which normally meant that a train going at speed would derail itself, and Maxwell's only objection to the plan was that the Italy-bound train stopping at Menton, would hardly have time to pick up speed before she hit the wedges.

They waited on the steps leading down to the back of the museum and wiped the sweat from their faces. The soot came along with it, leaving their cheeks striped and their panting mouths unnaturally red against the black. The maquisards were weird figures of the night, standing beneath the orange trees and listening in silence until their ears picked up the distant whistle and the increasing roar of the train. Then all four spoke together.

'She's not stopping!' 'She's going through!' 'With full speed up!' 'My God!' Then the crash came, the crash that to the maquisards seemed to shake the heavens, the crash that was followed by the fire and the screams of the injured and the dying.

The Italians had taken off the freighter and substituted a troop-carrying train.

That was how total war returned to Menton, and it was well for the Mentonese that Italian and not German troops were the victims of the 'terrorist' attack. If the twenty-five men killed had been Germans, the lives of one hundred Frenchmen might well have been exacted in revenge, and though the Italians did search all the houses in the vicinity of the station, and held half a dozen tenants at the guardhouse for questioning, their first task was the succouring of the many wounded men. Nobody thought of searching the house of an old governess, or the solicitor's office in a quiet garden where Dany and the science teacher spent the night. And when the medical corpsmen and the ambulances had done their work the repair gangs moved in, working all through the night and driven on by the Italian officers who knew how urgent was the need to get the main line into Italy back to full working order. Before dawn on the morning of that day the British Eighth Army had crossed the Straits of Messina, and the Italian troops were pulling out of France.

Polly heard the news of the invasion of Italy on the evening broadcast of the Swiss radio, which also mentioned an unconfirmed report that Marshal Badoglio had sent an envoy to General Eisenhower to negotiate an armistice. She switched on the set to pass the time, but when the news was over she abandoned the musical programme which followed, and went out to the darkness and warmth of the balcony. The explosion at the station, when it came, was heard in the Old Town, where it was followed by the sound of the fire engine going out, and later by the arrival of ambulances at the hospital up the hill. Polly's door remained closed, like all the doors in the Rue Longue; behind it she waited in an agony of suspense until Jacques came home. He told her what had happened, poured a drink, had a bath, took her to bed. He made love to her as violently as on the night he killed the *milicien* in the Parc des Arènes. Then Jacques slept heavily, the sleep of a man sated with death and sex, while Polly wakeful by his side wondered at his tranquillity, and gave thanks when the sky paled above the sea, and brought to light the gilt and vermilion on the ikon of the Virgin of Kazan.

That same eventful day, September 3, was marked by an escape which delighted Jacques. General de Lattre de Tassigny, a soldier whom he admired as much for his refusal to join de Gaulle as for his stand against the enemy when the whole of France was occupied, had been arrested and tried for treason because he fought the Germans in 1942. 'I tried to save the honour of the poor army,' he wrote to his wife after his arrest, but this argument did not sway his judges, who condemned him to ten years' imprisonment. He had served eight months of his sentence at Riom when his wife, his teen-age son and his Alsatian driver conspired to suborn his guards and smuggle into his cell escape tools and a rope ladder, down which the debonair general escaped in the best style of adventure fiction. Radio Vichy, next morning, bayed that his safe-house in the heart of France was known, and an arrest would soon follow. Jacques Brunel said he didn't believe it, and in high good humour agreed that since the holiday home bus had been serviced at the Citroën garage in town, Polly might if she wished drive a new contingent of Paris children to the *colonies* on the other side of the Col de Castillon.

The arrivals of July and August had been absorbed into the St. Michel home, but September had crowded the dormitories too much for comfort and health, and twelve of the newcomers were to be taken to Albaréa and Saorge. Jacques was in a hurry to join Maxwell at Miss Torrance's, and see him on his way to Cannes with the mutinous Victor Marcati; he told Polly to drive carefully, take an envelope he gave her to the Juracs on her way back, and above all to keep away from the station area, which would be cordoned off. She heard the last piece of advice with a slight shudder.

It was repeated by the director of the St. Michel home. The children had slept quietly through the terrorist attack, he said, and the staff would try to keep the news of it from them as long as possible. The quickest way to the Sospel road, by the station, was a shambles, and although the road by Les Ciappes was longer and very bad, Polly must use it, and keep the children from any disagreeable sights and sounds. The little Parisians were quite excitable enough already.

They came out in an unruly group, arguing and pushing like a Paris bus queue as they fought for the best seats in the twelve-seater bus, and the director, quite unable to cope with them, shook his head as he wished Madame Brunel the best of luck. She let them shout and sing to their hearts' content as she drove up the steep road to Castillon, where the cherry harvest had been gathered long ago, but when they crossed the plateau and began the descent to Sospel the sight of the great mountains seemed to sober them, and all down the charming valley of the Merlanson they chattered quietly about the sights so different from the Paris streets. The goatherds and the shepherds with their flocks, the children working in the fields were quite as interesting to them as the deserted Fort Castillon or the casemates and blockhouses thrown up by the French Army in the years before the war. 'A defence supposed to be as impregnable as the Maginot Line, and just as useless,' Jacques had once said of those empty fortifications.

The Albaréa *colonie de vacances* was only a few hundred metres from the highway, and this was fortunate, as the road leading to the cluster of houses on the hillside was little better than a track. The Cooperative at Sospel was where the Albarois went for their victuals and supplies, said the two pleasant women who came to meet the bus, but they kept their own cow and baked their own bread, and so Polly and the children were treated to a morning refection of hot drinks made with very little chocolate from the special ration and a lot of milk, and *tartines* of fresh bread and butter. The home was established in an old farmhouse, and the four children from Paris were soon yelling round the outbuildings with the other inmates.

Polly herded her other eight passengers together and told them to board the bus. The next stop was Sospel, and she was hoping someone from the hostel would decide to go shopping at the Cooperative, and see her past the Italian checkpoint. But no offer was made, and with the smiling goodbyes and thanks she was assured that the Italians were very friendly, and always respected vehicles from the children's homes. She told the children to behave themselves, and drove carefully into town, noting the landmarks; the railway station, a few buildings which looked like warehouses, a square planted with plane trees and the modern bridge over the Bévéra.

If there was an Italian checkpoint, this was it, as represented by three unshaven soldiers lounging against the coping of the bridge. There was no barrier or guardhouse, but the corporal flagged her down, and Polly stopped the bus with a fast-beating heart. The men didn't look friendly to her, but sullen and angry: she wondered if they had heard of the terrorist attack at Menton. The smiles broke out as soon as she stated her business up the valley of the Roya. A pretty girl speaking fluent Italian, with a cargo of what they thought of as *bambini* aboard, made a pleasant break in their guard duty, and the corporal hardly glanced at Polly's identity card. One of the men had a lump of what looked like marzipan in his pocket: he stood picking flakes of tobacco off it and rolling little grey balls of the sweetstuff to give to the children.

'May the *bambini* get out and stretch their legs?' asked Polly.

'Certainly, signora.' The corporal took a casual look at the empty seats, on which the children had left their shabby bags; each bag could have contained a hand grenade for all he knew or cared. Polly accepted a cigarette and stood chatting, asking the men how many children they had themselves, and where their homes were in Italy. She wanted a little time to study Sospel, while the children played tag in the road or hung on the bridge to watch the clear water rippling over a shallow fall. Upstream there was an ancient tollbridge with a tower, leading to the side of the river where there was a warren of tall old houses with red roofs and ramshackle balconies. The two hotels where the German *douaniers* were said to have lodged were directly opposite, and where Polly was standing road signs told her that she was at the point where the two arms of the Y, as Jacques had called it, met. 'Col de Brouis 12 Km, Tende 51 Km' said the right hand arm, and the left said 'Col de Braus 12 Km, Nice 41 Km'. Now she had her bearings and was ready to go on.

'You're taking the *bambini* to Saorge, signora?' asked the officious corporal. 'Be careful when you leave the highway at Fontan. The side road to Saorge is very bad.'

'It's the Col de Brouis I'm dreading,' she confessed, and the Italians began to praise her *coraggio*, and wondered that her *marito* let her drive the mountain roads alone. 'Just take it easy on the curves,' they said. 'We'll look out for you on your way back!'

Polly took it easy on the curves, for nothing in her driving experience had prepared her for the dizzying succession of hairpin bends which led over the watershed between the Bévéra and the High Valley of the Roya. She spoke only once on the Col de Brouis, and that was to say that if any boy started to yell he would get a thrashing, but the children, too, were scared into silence, and even when they reached the valley floor seemed to be intimidated by the menacing gorges through which the road and the railway ran alongside the grey-green waters of the Bévéra. Occasionally Polly saw some railwaymen at work, possibly on long-overdue repairs to the damage done in 1940, but except in the village of Fontan there was no other sign of human life. The cut-out to Saorge began there, and was bad but short. It had taken Polly an hour and fifteen minutes to cover the fifty kilometres from Sospel, but they had left Menton so early that it was still only half past ten when she stopped the bus in a little open space bordered with chestnut trees on the outskirts of the mountain village.

The children piled out, dragging their belongings, and ran to look over the stone wall beyond the chestnuts. Saorge lay beneath them, clinging to the side of the mountain in S-shaped concentric tiers, the houses, roofed with grey slates, divided by tiny gardens and terraces of lemon trees and olives. 'Is this where we're going to live, madame?' they cried. 'Stuck on the mountain like flies on a window-pane? Where are the shops? Where's the football pitch?'

'You're going higher up, I think,' said Pauline, 'and you'd better behave when you get there. Don't let me hear any bad reports of you! And come along, Lucienne, hurry up, Frédéric! Somebody's waiting for us at the *mairie.*'

An old fellow working on the terrace just below the wall told her where the *mairie* was, not very far away, and before they reached it they saw a middle-aged man, wearing a shooting jacket and a black beret, striding along to meet them. He ran the holiday hostel further up the mountain, he told them, shaking hands with Polly and all the children. They stared up at him rather doubtfully and the girl hoped he was going to be kind.

'I hope you're all good walkers, children,' he said. 'You've got a stiff climb ahead of you, but you'll find some nice playmates waiting when you get there.'

The children fidgeted, and one boy said there ought to be a lift, like in the Paris *métro.*

'We'll make mountaineers of you before you go back to Paris,' the director said, ignoring this sally. 'Madame Brunel, won't you come with us? My wife and I would be delighted to have your company at our midday dinner.'

'Thank you so much, but I don't feel up to a stiff climb today,' smiled Polly. 'Remember I've got to tackle the Col de Brouis again!'

'Very brave of you to tackle it at all. I don't know any other lady who could do it, certainly not my wife.' He didn't press the invitation when Polly said her husband was expecting her at home. To give conviction to her words she turned back towards the bus, looking round once or twice to wave to the children, who soon disappeared with their guide round an angle of the hilly street.

There was a rustic seat near the chestnut trees, and Polly dropped into it, more tired from the hard drive than she knew. She was in no hurry to start back to Menton. Jacques would not be home for hours—*if* he came home—if the tightrope he was walking didn't suddenly give way beneath him. And she needed an hour to herself, in different surroundings, to sort out her feelings about the terrible events of the night before.

Polly Brunel had been irrationally shocked by the derailing of the troop train. She had never been so near to sudden death, except in one or two of the early bombing raids on Naples, and the wailing of the ambulance sirens on the way to the hospital had shaken her badly. This was the reality of the Resistance, violence and killing, not the gay adventure of her imagination, and it would go on, nonstop, until the Liberation day. And Jacques was so matter-of-fact about it all! He appeared to take mass murder in his stride, almost like a news item equalled in importance by the escape of de Lattre. But then, she argued with herself, did she want him to be emotional about the way of life he had deliberately chosen? It was his cool authority that kept his maquisards together, she knew that; one weakness on his part, one display of guilt or remorse, and his group would fly apart. And this was maquisard country. The deep gorges by the Roya, the mountain forests, even the smiling valley she was gazing over, would be cover for a dozen camps of desperate men. She must try to look at it through her husband's eyes, but although in the early days of her marriage she had believed that she knew every thought and impulse of the man called Jacques Brunel, she was beginning to wonder if she knew Captain Jack.

The sound of a cracked bell, announcing eleven o'clock, roused

Polly from her reverie. She was aware of various physical needs: to get a cardigan from the bus to wear above her yellow dress, because the crystal air of the mountains had a bite after the stifling warmth of Menton; to find a washroom, to drink a cup of good coffee if such were to be found in Saorge. She wasn't hungry, and she knew she would be offered a share of whatever tasty stew was simmering in Madame Jurac's old black pot, but coffee and a cigarette she had to have before driving on. She went to the wall and spoke to the man who had directed her to the *mairie*.

'Monsieur, is there an inn or a restaurant in the village?'

He leaned upon his mattock and looked up at her. 'There used to be a good one,' he said. ' "*Aux Diables Bleus*", they called it. One went there for a glass after work, and one was comfortable. Now it's run by foreigners' (he used the expression *des gens d'extérieur*) 'and they tarted it up, and gave it a fancy name.'

'What was the matter with "*Aux Diables Bleus*"?'

'It didn't suit the Italians.' The black eyes in the wrinkled face gave Polly a look which said, And you're a foreigner too. 'Don't you know who the Blue Devils are, *ma petite dame*? You don't? That's what we call *our* battalion, our boys from hereabouts, the Chasseurs Alpins.'

'My husband never told me they were called the Blue Devils,' said Polly. 'He was in the 53rd BCA and fought at Namsos.'

The man came to the foot of the low wall and raised his arm. '*I* was in the 53rd, in the Other War,' he said. 'Shake hands, madame, you're one of us. And if you want to see what the foreigners have done to a decent *estaminet*, go past the *mairie* and the shops, and up the steps, and you'll find it.'

The streets of Saorge were a maze of stairs and alleys, but at least there was life and movement round the baker's and the grocer's, where young women with toddlers holding their skirts were buying whatever was available for the midday meal. The street, or lane, widened at the top of the last stair, and there stood the inn, with '*Aux Diables Bleus*' still visible on the fascia under the newly painted sign of '*La Vendemmia*'. The local painter's heart had not been in his work.

There was nobody in the lobby of 'The Vintage', in which a small American bar had been installed, and Polly made for a door marked *Toilette*, behind which there was a new installation of tiles and fittings. There was still nobody to be seen when she came out, although there was a smell of cooking, and she pushed open a second door marked *Restaurant*, which led to a surprisingly large and attractive room. There were a dozen tables, only three of which were laid for luncheon though all had vases of wild flowers set beside kerosene lamps. A row of small windows opened on the same breathtaking view as Polly had seen from the chestnut grove. She lit a cigarette, and stood looking down at Saorge, failing to hear the quiet step behind her, and only turning round when a voice said. *'Vous désirez, madame?'*

'Fabienne!'

It was hardly to be believed that the young woman in a plain black dress and a white embroidered apron was Fabienne Leroux. When they last met Fabienne was managing her family's hotel in Monaco and thought of Polly Preston, whom she knew as Pauline Henri, as some sort of adventuress. Now she was a servant in a mountain inn, with more than the old bitterness in her handsome face as she took Polly's impulsively outstretched hand.

'If it isn't Pauline Henri—I should say, Madame Jacques Brunel,' she said. 'What in the world brings *you* to Saorge?'

'I drove some children to the holiday home,' said Polly confusedly. 'How did you know we were married?' Fabienne laughed the sarcastic laugh which Polly well remembered, and said, 'I knew he would marry you the first time I saw you two together. And then I read it in the paper. We're not quite lost to the world here, you know! We get the *Eclaireur de Nice* from time to time. I must say I was surprised that *un pur* like Jacques should announce his wedding in a collaborationist paper.'

'There was no choice,' said Polly. 'Jacques wanted everyone to know about our marriage. But you, Fabienne? Is this your hotel now? An old man told me it was run by foreigners.'

'Foreigners from Monaco!' said Fabienne. 'Even people from Sospel are foreigners to the mountain men. I went to school with Raoul and Elise. They bought this place two years ago, and they gave me a job when I—left the Hotel Mimosa. Now, what can I get you, madame?' she went on more formally. 'It's rather early for luncheon, I'm afraid.'

'I'd like a cup of coffee, if it's quite convenient.'

'We're here to serve the public, madame,' said the mocking voice, and Pauline caught at the other girl's hand again.

'Fabienne, don't be like that!' she exclaimed. 'We've got to talk.

There's no one here to bother us, so bring us both some coffee, if it's ready, and let's sit down and talk sensibly. I want to know everything that's happened to you.'

'Oh, very well.' It was grudgingly said, but Fabienne brought the coffee quickly, with two cups and saucers, and sat down beside Polly at the window table. 'Elise is busy in the kitchen,' she said. 'We have six guests on full board, old age pensioners from Menton, who got a permit to come here for their health.'

'And you've been here since—since—'

'Ever since Roger Malvy committed suicide in prison,' said Fabienne calmly. Her tension was betrayed by her nervous fingers, rolling and unrolling the hem of her waitress's apron.

Pauline drank some coffee in silence. Then she asked, 'Why did you do it? When Roger Malvy came to you and asked for shelter, why did you give him away to the police?'

'Wouldn't you, after he'd confessed to such an abominable crime?'

'I—don't—know,' said Polly. 'What he did was unspeakable, I know, but I think he went mad, for one terrible quarter of an hour, when he realised that poor little Patrick wasn't his own child. If I loved him, and you must have loved him, I might have helped a man like that to—to cheat the guillotine.'

'Oh, but I did!' said Fabienne. 'I set him free.'

'What do you mean?' said Pauline, aghast.

'Swear you'll never tell a living soul what I'm going to tell you now.' It was melodramatic, but Fabienne Leroux had always had a taste for melodrama; she seemed almost to be enjoying the telling of her tale. When Pauline said, 'I swear,' she began rapidly:

'When Roger was in prison, awaiting trial, he asked for me to come and see him. He said he wanted to forgive me for turning him in, I'd done the right thing in the eyes of the law, and so on. So I went to Les Baumettes. And he asked me to bring him poison, any poison to kill him quickly and put an end to it all. He spoke about the cyanide pills the British agents carried, and asked me to get him one of those.'

'But how could you, Fabienne?'

'I couldn't, of course. But I went to Dr. Moreau, and he gave me what I asked.'

'His father-in-law? A doctor, sworn to preserve life, not destroy it?'

'But also Chantal Malvy's father. He wanted to finish off his rascally son-in-law before the trial, when Chantal's love affair would be brought out in court.'

'It was brought out at the inquest, anyway.'

'We weren't to know that then. And the next time I saw Roger, he asked the guard if he might kiss me. When I was in his arms, I slipped him the cyanide pill.'

There was no emotion in the stony face. If there had been tears for Roger Malvy, Fabienne had shed them long ago. The nervous fingers fumbled with the apron, and that was all. Polly sat speechless.

'Where is the lovely Chantal now?' said Fabienne with her little laugh.

'Her mother took her to Plombières, to do the cure.'

'That sounds just like them both.'

'Listen, Fabienne,' said Polly sternly, 'I don't think you quite realise that this—this terrible thing goes far beyond the Malvys and the Moreaus and you. Because you sent for the police to arrest Roger, he told the Criminal Brigade about the Resistance meeting, to save his own skin, and the meeting was raided by the Gestapo and the *Milice*. Renaudon was taken and died under torture. The man they called Sabre was shot dead, and the others are in prison because you decided to take the law into your own hands. Think of that before you sneer at poor Chantal.'

'How was I to know that fool would squeal to the police?'

'How was he to know his mistress would betray him?'

It was Fabienne's turn to be silent. Polly drank the rest of her coffee and laid some money on the table.

'How long are you going to hide up here?' she said.

'I don't regard myself as *hiding*,' said Fabienne. 'I'm *staying* here until the end of October, when '*La Vendemmia*' closes for the season. Raoul and Elise are going back to Monaco for the winter, to work in his father's restaurant, and I've got a new job lined up at the Hotel du Mont in Sospel.'

'Waiting on table?'

'Does it matter? It's food and shelter, and that's all I care about. Are you going back to Nice today?'

'We're not living in Nice, we live in Menton now. Fabienne'— and Polly hesitated, 'couldn't you come down to Menton before you start your new job?' And before you get yourself into another ghastly mess, she thought.

'Whatever for?'

'Oh, for a change, and a rest. I know an English lady who rents rooms, you could stay with her. And see people, and talk things over with Jacques—'

'No thanks,' said Fabienne with decision. 'I'm taking my medicine, Pauline, and it isn't very pleasant; I don't need an extra dose of advice from the saintly Jacques. Shall you tell him you've seen me?'

'That, and no more. He'll be glad to know you haven't run away with a German officer, as the story went in Monaco.'

'Was *that* what they said?' gasped Fabienne. 'Oh! People are vile!'

'Aren't they, though?' said Polly, getting up. 'Here come your luncheon guests, and I must go.' A group of six old people, three armed with walking sticks, came hobbling into the pretty restaurant of 'The Vintage' at a quarter to twelve.

'Mademoiselle!' 'Mademoiselle Fabienne!' The newcomers wanted immediate attention.

'One moment, please.' Fabienne followed Polly through the bar, where a youngish man, presumably Raoul, was polishing glasses for the non-existent trade. The two girls walked together to the head of the stone stair.

'I'm glad I've seen you, Pauline,' said Fabienne. 'I just want to say I'm sorry about the Resistance men. I didn't realise before how bad it was. And if ever I can do anything to make amends, I will.'

'Good luck to you,' said Polly, taking her hand. 'Good luck to all of us!'

NINE

Even before the Italian armistice, an instrument of unconditional surrender, was signed on September 28, the fruits of victory had turned sour in the mouths of the Allies. First there was the mortifying escape of Mussolini, boldly carried off by German raiders from his prison, and the setting up of his puppet 'Fascist Republic' which ensured a state of civil war in Italy. Then there was the bewilderment of British troops who had been fighting the Italians for three years, and who now were ordered, from one day to the next, to regard them as co-belligerents, if not allies—if and provided, as was not always the case, the Italians still loyal to their king wished to make a rightabout face and start fighting the Germans. Worse still, the hopes of a speedy drive north through Italy did not materialise. Hitler ordered his generals to make a stand south of Rome, and against the 'Winter Line' drawn across the peninsula from the Garigliano to the Sangro rivers the Allies were to fling themselves in vain for months.

But north of Rome, along the French border, lay Piedmont, the cradle of the House of Savoy and of Italian independence, and from Piedmont's capital, Turin, the road lay south to the Col de Tende and the High Valley of the Roya. Many men, farmers and soldiers, took that road as the autumn of 1943 closed in. Many an Italian maquis was set up in what Polly Brunel had seen as maquisard country, in the forests and ravines beyond the mountain villages. Everywhere in Italy that the German divisions stood was formed the nucleus of an Italian Resistance.

The most hopeful event of September, to the anxious Mentonese, was the liberation of Corsica, the first Department of France to be delivered from the enemy. Corsica, the land of the vendetta, provided an interesting blueprint of what metropolitan France might be like when the war was over, for some of the island's leaders were Vichy, some were for de Gaulle, and most of those who took to the maquis were Communists. The Corsicans were natural maquisards, but the Resistance was not called into action until the island was occupied in November 1942. One of the most ardent leaders of the Communist maquis was a woman, Danielle Casanova, who was taken to Germany and executed at Auschwitz in May. Her memory inspired fresh rebellion, and in July a large arms shipment was sent to the island by the combined efforts of General Giraud, the American OSS and the British SOE. When the news of the Italian surrender was received the Corsicans, not waiting to hear the terms of the armistice, rose in open revolt against the 80,000 Italian troops occupying the island. General Giraud supported them by sending massive reinforcement from Algiers, a total of 15,000 effectives plus air and naval units. With the assistance of 15,000 maquisards the whole force was needed to fight 30,000 German troops rushed in from Sardinia, and for three terrible but victorious weeks the 'Isle of Beauty' was a battlefield.

As no Allied forces were involved Corsica was an all-French victory, of great importance to morale on the mainland, but as it was not an all-Gaullist victory it was frowned on in the 'crab-pot' of Algiers. De Gaulle told Giraud he was 'chilled and displeased at the way you have acted in reference to myself and the government' —by government he meant the French Committee of National Liberation. General Giraud had acted correctly in ordering the invasion of Corsica without reference to de Gaulle, for he was still, under the Allies, the French commander-in-chief in North Africa. But he was no longer the co-president of the Committee. As Antoine de St. Exupéry had predicted, de Gaulle had easily edged him out of that position, by the simple expedient (which Mr. Churchill had not foreseen) of increasing the Committee's membership from seven to fourteen and packing it with his own men.

Being no politician, Giraud went calmly on with his preparations for a French share in driving the Germans out of Italy. Only one thousand men fighting under the French flag, and those of the 4th Moroccan 'Tabor' of native troops, had taken part in the invasion of Sicily, and while the fighting in Corsica was still going on, it was Anglo-American co-operation which had secured possession of Salerno and Naples. What was now planned was the despatch to Italy of a force of 105,000 men, the largest French force in the field since the defeat of 1940, to be known as the French Expeditionary Corps, under the command of General Juin.

Two weeks before the corps sailed another of the spectacular

Allied conferences of 1943 was held, this time at Cairo, which put the whole Middle East on security alert and reduced to blasphemy and frustration one prospective bridegroom. Flight-Lieutenant Mike Marchand was pacing up and down beneath the palm trees on the bank of the Nile on the Monday afternoon when President Roosevelt arrived in Cairo, damning the President and the British Prime Minister and General Chiang Kai-Shek and their enormous entourages under his breath, and replying in monosyllables to the remarks of the people he knew in the little crowd. They were all waiting for the flying boat from Khartoum, which as usual was late, and might not have taken off at all, while Mike was compulsively looking from his watch to the westering sun, for he was waiting for his bride. It was three years and two months since their parting at Freetown.

The flying boat appeared, a cross in the sky which grew larger, and landed on the far side of the Nile. Those on the landing stage could watch the passengers disembarking and getting into the launch, and Mike saw Dina dressed in white, whipping off her dark glasses as she waved to him. Tony da Costa was by her side, wearing a seersucker suit he must have bought in New York, and carrying a panama hat. His smile was as cheerful, his hair as glossy as ever, he seemed to have put on some weight. The launch came up to the landing stage, and Mike like everybody else was sharply told to remain on the embankment until the passengers went through the special security checks required by the presence of the Allied leaders. It was frustrating to stand there, smiling enthusiastically, while papers were scrutinised and suitcases were laid open on trestle tables for the examination of luggage already checked out at Khartoum. Tony da Costa seemed to be in trouble. The inspector called first one colleague and then another to examine the contents of one suitcase, while Dina standing aside exchanged waves of the hand with Mike, miming surprise, dismay and impatience in a series of nervous gestures quite uncharacteristic of the girl he remembered. It was ten minutes before Tony was waved on, when Mike was able to say, 'Go get the bags, George!' and send the dragoman from Shepheard's hurrying for the da Costas' luggage.

Then Dina was in his arms again, as beautiful as ever, but her grey eyes were questioning as he bent his head to kiss her, and then she laid her cheek against his with a sigh of content. Tony came up, ready with a South American embrace. Beneath the palm trees they all talked at once about the trip, the stopover at the Grand Hotel in Khartoum, the two days at Cape Town—saying the first things that came into their heads, while the dragoman made urgent signs to the drivers he had engaged, and two horse-drawn gharries came slowly alongside.

'Are we going straight to Shepheard's, Mike?'

'Yes, of course, darling, but there's something I've got to tell you first.' He looked so worried that the two Brazilians laughed, and when Mike said it was this damned conference Tony told him, 'I thought you were going to say your leave was cancelled.'

'Well no, it's not that bad, but I'm afraid some of our plans have to be altered. Your reservation of a suite at Shepheard's has been cancelled, Tony. All the suites have been requisitioned for the top conference brass.'

'Have we got rooms at all?' Tony asked.

'Only a cubbyhole for you, I'm afraid, but there's a very decent room for Dina, not too noisy, above the garden.'

'And it's only for two nights,' said Tony briskly, 'unless the top brass means to interfere with the wedding.'

'Only with the honeymoon,' said Mike miserably. 'It was all arranged for us to spend a week at Mena House. Now that's off! The conference is actually going to be *held* there, and the big shots are all in villas near the Pyramids, with five hundred anti-aircraft guns in place for their protection. Dina, I'm so terribly sorry—'

'It isn't your fault,' she said. 'We've got the flat to go to, haven't we?'

'We can do better than the flat, I think,' said Mike. 'We may be able to hitch a ride to Beirut. I'll know for sure tonight.'

'Well, fine,' said Tony da Costa, taking charge of the situation. 'Are these carriages for us? Why don't we get along to Shepheard's now, and start with baths and drinks? I've got sand in my hair, and even under my fingernails—' The dragoman indicated that all four suitcases were in one gharry.

'You two go on ahead,' said Tony. 'I'll follow with our friend here and the bags. Mike, could you explain to him that he's not to take my briefcase? I've got all your papers, and a lot of letters and stuff for you in there.'

'I'm horribly sandy too,' said Dina as their gharry drove away. 'The khamsin was blowing hard when we left Khartoum.'

'You look lovely,' said Mike. 'The white dress is pretty enough for the wedding.' The folds were crumpled and there was sand in them, but he saw that for some unfathomable reason she needed reassurance. He put his arm round Dina and took both her hands into one of his, and told her he adored her.

'Oh Mike,' she said, and he felt her relax against him, 'I can't believe I'm really here!'

'You've come a long way, my darling.'

'I think we both have,' she said, and looked out at the unfamiliar streets of Cairo. They were going down an avenue where streetcars ran, each car filled with Egyptians in shabby office suits, while men wearing the red fez and once-white *galabeyahs* clung in grape-like clusters to the steps and tried to dodge the shafts of the gharries. The city's fleet of taxis had been commandeered to supplement the army transport needed by the enormous staffs of five hundred persons which President Roosevelt and Mr. Churchill had each brought with them. The pavements were crowded with street vendors, bootblacks, trinket sellers, all importuning the slowly moving mass of men in khaki or in blue. Dina thought the man beside her, in the unfamiliar Air Force blue, was not so different from the Captain Marchand she had seen as a schoolgirl, wearing the dark blue of the Trans-Andean air line.

'Isn't it hot!' she said, taking off her white silk headscarf and shaking it free of sand.

'It's humid today, but it'll be cooler in an hour or so. You'll have to get used to the idea that November isn't summer here, Dina!' First the khamsin wind and now the humidity, he thought. We're getting married in a couple of days and all we can talk about is the weather.

But the gharry was pulling up at Shepheards, and there was the usual surge forward of child beggars, shoeshine boys and porters, the latter directed by the gigantic Nubian, who controlled the outdoor traffic of the famous old hotel. Tony, the dragoman and the bags were all on the pavement beside them, and Mike was leading the da Costas up the big staircase, across the terrace where everybody at the tea-tables studied the three of them, and into the vast Victorian hall where Tony da Costa registered for his sister and himself. Two European clerks in morning coats moved out from behind the desk to show the new arrivals to their rooms, and with two *farrashes* in white robes carrying the luggage they made an imposing procession as they started for the stairs.

Mike went to one of the telephone boxes in the lobby, talked and came out whistling. He had no idea how long the da Costas would need to take baths and change, but he made sure of a table on the terrace by going out and sitting there himself. In a remarkably short time he was joined by Tony, wearing a sharp black silk suit which caused some eyebrows to rise, and seemed to bring out the African strain in the mixed da Costa heritage. Mike jumped up to greet him with the news that it was 'all fixed up for the flight to Beirut'.

'Nice work!' said Tony. 'How about a hotel?'

'I laid on a reservation at the St. Georges after Mena House was scrubbed out. It was the flight I was worried about, but it turned out to be a piece of cake.'

'So now everything's fine. Let's drink to that!'

'Hey, George!' Mike summoned the nearest waiter and whisky was ordered for them both. After the first sip, Mike's face grew glum again, and he said, 'The hell of it is, we've got to be at Heliopolis by noon on Wednesday, or we don't fly.'

'So what?'

'I'll have to ask the priest to put the wedding forward, when Dina and I go to see him tomorrow. And alert the guests—'

'Mike,' said Tony, 'will you for God's sake relax? Will you and Dina go off by yourselves tomorrow and leave all the rest to me? I'm an old hand at this. I organised Ester's marriage for her and it was a smash hit, the best wedding even seen in São Paulo, and I'll do the same for Dina. I'll have a chat with the manager tomorrow. I think this Shepheard's is quite a place.'

The Brazilian looked around approvingly. The sun had set, and the swift Egyptian darkness had fallen, made more intense by the lights which sprang up immediately: fairy lamps in the trees on the left side of the terrace, great white lamps at the head of the steps and neon strips in the windows of the shops across the street. There was a constant movement among the tables as friends greeted one another, and each new arrival, man or woman, was appraised by experts as they came up the long stone stair. The scent of flowers, the perfumes of the women, mingled with the tainted warmth, the faintly rotten sweetness, which was the breath of Cairo.

'I hope to God Dina'll like the flat,' said Mike. 'I don't suppose she'd want to drive across the Nile and look at it tonight?'

'I'm sure she wouldn't,' said her brother. 'It's been a rough ride from Rio, Mike. She'll enjoy seeing the place far more tomorrow, when she's had a good night's sleep.'

'I don't know about enjoying it. The flat isn't up to much, I'm afraid; it isn't easy to get a short-term rental here.'

'Will you stop worrying, confound you?'

Mike Marchand tried to laugh. Then a new worry crossed his mind, and he asked anxiously what Tony had done with his brief-case.

'It's perfectly all right, locked into the hotel safe.'

'Oh! Good! But that reminds me: what was all that fuss about your luggage at the landing stage? You weren't carrying firearms, were you?'

'Only my Service revolver.' And, enjoying Mike's startled look, Tony went on, 'It was my uniform they seemed to be interested in. I don't suppose they'd ever seen a Brazilian army uniform before.'

'You brought your *uniform* with you?'

'I had to, Mike. I'll have to wear it when I join Marshal de Moraes and his mission at Algiers on the sixth of December. I'm officially on leave at present—just like you.' He was tempted to add, 'And you French haven't got the monopoly of patriotism,' but held his tongue.

'Who's the mission going to Algiers to see? Not de Gaulle?'

'God, no! General Eisenhower, of course and then on to Naples to meet General Mark Clark. Our First Expeditionary Infantry Division will fight with the Fifth Army, under his command.'

'I see. And then will you go back to Rio?'

'Not me. Not G4. We'll be staying behind at Caserta GHQ, preparing for the arrival of the Division.'

'Which will be when?'

'Can't say yet. You know Brazil well enough to understand the problems. Before the war our army was trained by a French military mission, now we've got to switch to American methods, so the American manuals have to be translated into Portuguese and dis-tributed, for a start. Then we've got to pick men able to fight in a climate and terrain they're not accustomed to, which means the first contingent will probably be small. I've got to see they're pro-perly fed and clothed when they arrive in Italy—'

'You don't think you should see them properly equipped before they sail from Rio?'

'I've a fancy to be where the action is,' said Tony da Costa.

'And good luck to you,' said Mike. 'I'm glad you'll be within shouting distance, if it turns out that Dina needs some help.'

'What sort of help?'

'If anything happens to me, I mean.'

'I thought you were in the clear, once you were in Photographic Reconnaissance.'

'Once the war in the desert was over, eh?' said Mike. 'That's what all these people think.' With a large wave of his hand he indicated the men and women on the terrace, laughing and listening to the band. 'Cairo's one gigantic funfair now, compared to what it was less than eighteen months ago. But the Germans have still got twenty-five divisions in the Near East, *with* Luftwaffe support, and flying recces in a single-seater plane, unarmed, is slightly more dangerous than what I was doing in Bomber Command. Don't say so to Dina,' he added hastily.

'Have another drink,' was Tony's rejoinder.

'Let's wait till she comes down,' said Mike. He turned round restlessly to look for Dina, then back again to Tony. 'Are you going to wear your Brazilian uniform on Wednesday?'

'I wouldn't want to take the shine out of the bridegroom,' said Tony with a grin. 'Here comes Divininha now.'

She made an entrance, it was the only word for it. Quite unintentionally, and quite unself-consciously, Dina da Costa riveted the attention of everyone who saw her as she came through the door of the hotel and hesitated for a moment, looking round for Mike and Tony. Her white cocktail dress was very simple, and her white lace wrap embroidered with red flowers was not new, but one that Mike remembered from happy evenings in Rio de Janeiro. It was her refreshed and astonishing beauty which caught the eye. Mike jumped up and went to kiss her hand. In the café society of Cairo, now at its most extravagant, there were many lovely and exotic women, some of Levantine or Coptic blood, but Dina's looks had been called Euro-Afro-Indio, and it was the blood of three races which had given her the skin like clover honey, the black silk hair, and features fit to be immortalised in bronze. Mike was aware of the sensation she created, and was flushed with pride as he led her to the table.

Dina herself was bubbling over with something to tell them both. 'Oh, do you know what happened?' she began. 'I asked the *farrash* to bring me some drinking water, and he brought it in a *whisky bottle*! So then I knew that all those empty bottles I saw in the corridor had held water, not spirits! And there was I thinking that the people staying at Shepheard's were on the greatest drinking binge of all time!'

Mike could have told her that some of them weren't doing too badly in that line, but he said they could do better than drinking water in an old whisky bottle, and motioned to the waiter to pour the champagne he had ordered before Tony joined him. It had been in an ice bucket but was not too cold, and as Dina clinked glasses with him, her face vivid with laughter, he saw that the other ice was broken, and said joyfully, 'Now we're all going to have fun!'

They did have fun, all the better fun because they made no attempt to dine alongside the 'top brass' in the old-world splendour of Shepheard's dining room, but went round the corner to a little restaurant where the food was excellent. Like every other such place in Cairo when the great conference was on, it was crowded, but they were given a table on the pavement, removed from the passers-by only by a low hedge, and Dina was amused by the street vendors who dangled amber beads and silver wire bracelets in front of her—the bargaining and the beggars and the noise reminded her of the Rua do Ouvidor at Rio, where Capricorn Airways had their offices. Having come from a brilliant capital she was not much impressed by the bright lights of Cairo, which in that district almost blinded new arrivals from the blacked-out cities of Europe, but the Arab faces and the strange language and the exotic flowers were different enough from Rio to be fascinating. Mike bought a spray of tuberoses from a brown hand held insistently over the little hedge, and helped her to pin it to her shoulder.

'They suit you, darling,' he said, for there was something in the chiselled perfection of the white petals, which seemed to personify Dina in her white dress. Tony agreed.

'She ought to carry them on Wednesday,' he said.

'It's not on,' said Mike. 'I've chosen her bridal bouquet, and it won't be tuberoses.'

'Oh, what?' Dina begged to know. 'Roses? Camellias?'

'You'll find out, my love.'

They were back at Shepheard's before ten, with 'Cairo night life just getting into its stride,' as Tony remarked wistfully, but all he was allowed to sample of night life that evening was a visit to

Shepheard's famous bar, where Mike introduced him to its equally famous drink, the Suffering Bastard. Dina went upstairs to bed. She said she was sleepy, but her first purpose was to wash her hair clean of the sand carried by the khamsin wind at Khartoum. She had been warned not to open the long window in case a late mosquito entered, but she sat down beside it with her black hair spread across her shoulders: it would dry quickly in the warm room. She could see the hotel garden quite clearly in the lights from many windows. It was quite empty, and the French maid had told her that it was nearly always so. Alas, madame could not have breakfast in the garden; the management objected to food and drink being served there, but she, the maid, would be happy to arrange madame's breakfast by the window. Madame would enjoy the early morning hour, it was the best time of the day in Cairo.

Certainly eleven o'clock that night was not the best hour, and to Dina, brushing out her hair, the night grew heavy and disquieting as it wore on. There was what she thought must be an open-air cinema in the neighbourhood, for behind the garden trees she could see the flickering of a screen and hear the amplified voices of the actors, punctuated by yells of approval or derision from the audience. The music she had found amusing outside the restaurant seemed more strident now, sometimes ululating like the muezzin, sometimes plangent; always a world away from the samba rhythms and the *fado* music Dina knew so well. Over and above the other noises came the steady barking of what sounded like a pack of pariah dogs. She took another bath and felt more comfortable. In less than thirty-six hours she and Mike would be married. She looked for his tuberoses, which she had placed in a small vase beside her bed. The petals were turning brown already, and the flowers looked more like a funeral than a wedding.

Next morning Dina had fruit and coffee in her room, watching the gardeners raking the gravel and watering the lawns in the empty garden below, while Tony in his cubbyhole struggled with Shepheard's overloaded switchboard as he called up one South American contact after another. Mike, who had spent the night in the flat which was to be his married home, did rather better with his telephone calls. He succeeded in borrowing a car for the day from a friend at the American Embassy, his own two-seater having been left at Heliopolis until the return from Beirut, and he obtained the priest's consent to an earlier hour for the wedding at St. Joseph's

Church. It was going to be a busy day. Dina was coming to see the flat later in the morning, and Mike meant to insist that Tony should come too: he had some news which he wanted both the bride and her brother to hear. The two houseboys whose services were included in the rent of the flat were told to go out and buy flowers and have everything looking nice when the lady and gentleman arrived, and to be ready to serve a decent cup of coffee.

After the visit of inspection Mike and Dina were to lunch at the Continental Hotel with his commanding officer, and from there they were to go to St. Joseph's for a talk with the priest and the completion of the formalities of their marriage.

About the time Mike was leaving to pick up the borrowed car, the great Cairo conference assembled for its first plenary session at Mena House. It was to last, from start to finish, for over a fortnight, which included a visit to Teheran for President Roosevelt and Mr. Churchill, who were to meet Stalin there. It was to discuss nearly every aspect of the global war. The topic of paramount importance was Operation Overlord, the invasion of France across the English Channel, including the selection of an Allied general as Supreme Commander of that invasion. The simultaneous invasion of France across the Mediterranean was tabled as Operation Anvil.

The defeat of the German armies in France, and the liberation of France from the long Occupation was thus discussed not only by the two great Western leaders and their Combined Chiefs of Staff, by Chiang Kai-Shek and Stalin, but also by a host of lesser luminaries. Everybody who was anybody showed up at the Cairo/Teheran conference. Lord Louis Mountbatten flew in from India. Field-Marshal Smuts arrived from South Africa. President Ismet Inönü, the successor to the great Kemal Atatürk, had a contribution to make; so had Stalin's Foreign Minister, Molotov, so had Anthony Eden. There were kings in exile in Cairo at that time, George II of Greece and Peter II of Jugoslavia, whose kingdoms had become mere battlegrounds, and whose hopes of regaining them were small. Among all these notabilities, discussing the fate of France, one man was conspicuously absent and that was the man who regarded himself as the incarnation of France, General Charles de Gaulle. His talent for mischief-making, demonstrated again in the Middle East in that very month of November, automatically debarred him from a seat at the conference table.

Not that any thoughts of the general troubled Mike and Dina as they drove from Shepheard's to the Sharia-el-Nil, with Tony in the back seat telling Mike to hurry, because he'd a luncheon date with a Brazilian export-import guy at the Mohamed Ali Club. They were both excited at visiting the place which was to be their first home, and Dina was pleased with everything, from the teeming streets to the Kasr-el-Nil bridge, and her first sight of Gezira Island.

The flat which Mike had taken furnished was in a modern building, up one flight of well-carpeted stairs. He was vague about the original owner, some old chap, he believed, who had skedaddled to South Africa in the days of the emergency and was in no hurry to come back; the flat was rented through an agency. But there had been so many sub-leases, so many changes of tenant, that a whole procession of officers from Britain and the Dominions had come and gone, for six weeks, for three months at a time, that Mike was only sure about the last of them, an Australian group-captain who had put him on to the place when Dina's arrival in Cairo became at last a certainty. He tried to see it through her eyes.

Dina praised the living room, which was spacious, and lit by two big windows on the Nile. There were flowers on the tables, of Benares brass made in Birmingham, and Ahmed and Anwar, the houseboys, came in at once with Turkish coffee on a brass tray, very neat in their clean white gowns. They bowed low to Dina, not quite sure, after a long succession of bachelor masters, how they would take to working for a married lady. Dina greeted them pleasantly, and said everything was very nice.

It was not really nice, because reckless people had held too many parties there for the good of the carpets and the upholstery, which had started out in a depressing shade of beige, and had been cleaned by the houseboys into even more depressing shades of brown and grey. A procession of ebony elephants marched across the shelf which pretended to be a mantel above the empty grate, and there were insipid water-colours of Devon lanes and Yorkshire moors which inclined Mike to think that the old chap in South Africa was an Englishman. 'Do you think you could be happy here, my darling?' he asked Dina anxiously.

'Anywhere!' she said, and as Mike kissed her Tony da Costa said, 'If ever a man was *de trop*, it's me. It's time I was on my way. I'm going to walk over to Gezira and pick up a taxi, and then I can get ahead with my arrangements for the wedding.' He had already outlined some improvements on Mike's original plans for the reception which had startled the bridegroom.

'You said you'd something to tell us. Out with it!' he commanded, as Anwar came in with fresh cups of coffee and snapped his lighter for their cigarettes.

'Thanks, Anwar; now don't come back until I ring,' said Mike. '... Okay, Tony. I want you to hear this along with Dina, because your parents have been so generous to her that I'd like you to know what my Uncle Pedro means to do—no, what he's already done—for me. Your father and mother and Ester wrote me wonderful letters, darling,' he said. 'I read them here late last night. But Uncle Pedro's took the longest time to read.'

'It was in the biggest packet, heaven knows,' said Tony. 'With your baptismal certificate, birth certificate, parents' marriage lines, the lot. He made me check them out with him before we left. I don't suppose you knew he had half that stuff in his safe.'

'I'm not that crazy,' retorted Mike. 'I put all that stuff, as you call it, into his keeping when I first went out to Rio at eighteen. Everything was there, just as I expected. It was Uncle Pedro's letter that was the big surprise.' He paused, and then said very quickly, 'He's given me his house at Alto da Boa Vista.'

'Darling! That beautiful house!' gasped Dina, and Tony chimed in with 'Now that's what I call a wedding present!' He would have said much more, but was silenced by his sister's look. She had told him a hundred times that he must not press Mike to return to Rio after the war. Much as they both hoped he would join them in Capricorn Airways, the decision must be Mike's alone, and she would do nothing to influence him—not even reveal, as now, all her joy at old Senhor Ferreira's munificent gift. So Tony only said: 'You mean he's actually made it over to you, Mike?'

'Yes. He's transferred the title to me by deed of gift, and he enclosed a letter from his lawyer, acknowledging that the papers are in the lawyer's keeping. Old Uncle Pedro! He's always been generous to me beyond words, but I never expected anything like this.'

'Alto da Boa Vista, of all places,' gloated Tony, for the beautiful mountain suburb was one of the show spots of Rio de Janeiro, 'You and Dina'll have a home to be proud of, later on.'

'But where's he going to live himself?' asked Dina quickly.

'Right there, for the time being,' Mike smiled at her. 'Rather than leave the house standing empty, he'll go on living there with his Italian servants, but he wanted to secure the property to me.'

'And what about Heitor and Ruy? His sons—will they mind?' said Dina. 'They've been very nice to me, and they're fond of you, I know, but still—'

'The letter says he talked it over with them both and they absolutely agreed. Heitor and Ruy Ferreira are rich men in their own right, he says, and their homes and businesses are in the State of Minas Gerais, not in Rio. What Uncle Pedro wants is to move into a much smaller house near theirs in Ouro Preto, so that he can play with his grandchildren every day.'

'Poor old darling, I think he was lonely, all by himself in that big house,' said Dina. 'It's a splendid wedding present, Mike. Congratulations!'

'Your Uncle Pedro turned up trumps, Mike!' said Tony.

'I only wish he could be here tomorrow.'

'So do I,' said Dina.

When Tony da Costa took his sister to St. Joseph's Church next morning in a limousine he had contrived to hire, there were many people he could have wished to be there. His parents, his little boy, his sister and her husband should all have been there with Dina and Mike, and as he was by nature given to display he was depressed by the smallness of the company Mike had invited to be present. Tony remembered the splendours of the nuptial mass in the Cathedral of São Paulo when Ester married Dr. Roberto da Silva, and the series of parties given by his parents in their joy that the plain daughter, the devoted social worker who had earned the title of 'the saint of the *favelas*', was making such a happy and suitable marriage. The beautiful daughter had not even a bridesmaid to attend her, for she had declined to be followed up the aisle by a stranger, and Mike, instead of a best man, had asked two of his brother officers, both Catholics, to be the witnesses. 'You can't double in brass, *mon vieux* Tony,' he had said. 'You can't stand in for your father *and* be the best man too! The only other guy I'd like to have for my best man is my cousin, Jacques Brunel, and I haven't heard from him for the past six months.'

'He's in France, isn't he?'

'Yes.'

Whatever Tony da Costa thought, the bride and the bridegroom seemed to miss nobody, and had eyes only for each other. Mike Marchand's blond good looks had never appeared to better advantage than when he wore Air Force blue, with a strip of mauve and silver ribbon on his tunic, and as for Dina— 'he was right about the tuberoses,' Tony thought, as he watched his sister's rapt face. The waxy white flowers would have been wrong with her white satin dress, and Mike's bouquet, obtained after long hunting through hothouses, was a sheaf of the royal orange lilies which best suited Maria da Gloria Divininha on her triumphant wedding day.

There were flowers all around her when she stood with her husband to greet their wedding guests. By what amount of bribery and corruption Tony had prevailed upon the manager of Shepheard's to transfer the reception from the salon Mike had reserved to his sacred garden, where not so much as breakfast might be served, was never known. 'The bride's family gives the party!' Tony said, and in this case it could have been added that the bride's family made the party, for it was Tony in his character of millionaire playboy who brought two very different groups of guests together. The champagne helped, for it was poured lavishly, and so did the equally lavish buffet spread beneath the trees, but it was the bride's brother who in his own words 'got the show on the road'. Some of the RAF types muttered that he seemed a funny sort of fellow, and one WAAF officer was heard to say, 'My dear, who *is* that extraordinary little man?' but the South American guests whom, thanks to his innumerable contacts, he had rallied by telephone, responded at once to Tony's gaiety. He congratulated himself. Instead of twenty 'dreary Britishers', as he thought of them, standing around drinking sherry in a dark room and grousing about the heat, he had assembled over a hundred lively people for whom the wedding of Senhor Ferreira's nephew and Senhor da Costa's daughter was a great South American occasion. The ladies were beautifully dressed, and if their high spiked heels dug holes in the hotel manager's cherished turf, that only meant another item on Tony's colossal bill. The beautiful bride was praised and kissed, the bridegroom's hand wrung by total strangers, the string band played with a verve increased by frequent gulps of champagne. A guest from the British Embassy said unsmilingly that he'd never seen anything like it since King Farouk's own wedding.

It was over all too soon, for the bride had to change her dress before they caught their plane to Beirut, and still carrying her sheaf of orange lilies, Dina waved goodbye to all the lively company. A kiss and thanks for Tony, a 'Bless you both!' from him, and in a flurry of rose petals Mike and Dina got into the limousine, to be driven through the crowded streets to Heliopolis. Soon after that they were borne above the crowds, and were together again in their natural element—the air.

TEN

An early morning take-off was the general rule for planes leaving Heliopolis, before the sun burned through the thin air of the desert and deprived it of whatever lift it could provide. It was perhaps lucky for Mike and Dina that the Lockheed Lodestar used for the courier flight to Beirut left at noon, when only a token force of the ground staff remained on duty, and the flight despatcher turned a tactfully blind eye on the woman passenger. The pilot greeted her laconically, hailed Mike with the 'thumbs-up' sign, and took off without delay.

Their flight path ran up the Nile Delta to Alexandria, and beneath the Lockheed's wings lay an intensely cultivated country, its vivid green seamed with lakes and irrigation ditches on either side of the blue line which was the Suez Canal. Over the great port Mike pointed out King Farouk's summer palace, Montaza, a pale pink cube in a eucalyptus grove, and then two sights in striking contrast: the concentration of force at the airfield, where five RAF squadrons were posted to protect the great men at the Cairo conference, and in the harbour the French naval squadron immobilised since the surrender of 1940. 'Admiral Godefroy and his crews get their pay and food from the British,' Mike told Dina, 'since the admiral decided not to make a fight for it like Gensoul at Mers-el-Kebir.'

The next leg of the flight lay over the desert, empty of everything but camel tracks, and then northward over the ancient settlements of Palestine. The pilot intimated that he wasn't going in to Lydda; they left the Holy Land behind them at Haifa, and were over Lebanese territory at Tyre and Sidon. Then, about two hours after leaving Heliopolis, they saw the blue mountains of the Lebanon, and the double crescent of white houses which was Beirut.

Mike and Dina were lucky again in the timing of their arrival, and also in the fact that Mike was wearing British uniform. For ten days there had been a fierce anti-French movement in the city, which had only just subsided, but even the most violent of the demonstrators, at two o'clock in the afternoon on the twenty-fourth of November, were sleeping it off in a long siesta. The only inconvenience the Marchands had to suffer was the pestering of a mob of ragged children, who never slept, offering to guide them to this or that hotel, and even the children were shaken off once the taxi driver accelerated outside the perimeter of the airfield. They arrived in style at the Hotel St. Georges.

'Le Saint-Georges' had been as far as luxury and gourmandise were concerned the symbol of the French presence in the Eastern Mediterranean since the end of World War I. The Second World War had left its scars, but the place had been well maintained and was still attractive, and the suite reserved by Mike had a magnificent view over the Mediterranean. The reception clerk and the servants bustled about, one man opening the shutters for the breeze and another closing them against the strong sunlight, while a sleepy maid stumbled between the big bedroom and the bathroom. Mike urged them gently out and locked the door. This was their hour, his and Dina's, long awaited, and at last in the frantic fusion of lips and bodies they were united.

Mike awoke after the sun had set, when the evening breeze began to ruffle the net curtains. He tried to kiss Dina awake, but she only murmured 'Sleepy! I'm so sleepy!' and buried her forehead in his neck. After a few minutes, while he held her closer, she raised her head and looked at him disbelievingly. 'It wasn't a dream! It's true!' he heard her say.

'Did you dream of me, my darling? As often as I dreamed of you? Like this?' And then the dream became reality again.

Presently they were bathed and dressing, Mike in a dark civilian suit when Dina had only got as far as her white wrapper of Swiss lawn and *broderie anglaise*, the frills falling back over her slender arms as she brushed her hair high and coiled it behind her head. She had laid out a low-cut dress of flame-coloured chiffon, the nearest match, she said seriously, to the tiger lilies which the maid had arranged in a crystal vase on the dressing table.

'Would you like me to order drinks up here?' asked Mike, watching her in the glass.

'If you want to, darling.' She spoke as lazily as he did. There was no hurry, they had all the time in the world before them.

'I want to show you off in the bar, my love. It's the place to see and be seen in Beirut, at this hour of the evening.'

'I'll hurry,' she said. 'You've been in Beirut before, then?'

'Not to stay at the St. Georges, but on leave. Beirut was one vast leave camp before the row this month.'

'What row was that?' But Dina was lifting her dress over her head, and when she emerged she went on inconsequently, 'If you know Beirut I expect you know where the best shops are, or if there are any.'

'There used to be some nice boutiques. What d'you want to buy, Dina?'

'Clothes, of course.' And when he laughed his wife explained quite reasonably that she and Tony had only been allowed to take two suitcases each on their long journey, and her wedding dress had to be packed so carefully there wasn't room for many other clothes. She would need a lot of things to get her through the winter.

'Well, I know nothing about it,' said Mike, 'but there must be some good dressmakers in Cairo, and there certainly are wonderful silks in the shop windows.' He studied the flame dress. 'You look lovely, darling. I suppose you don't want to wear your wedding gown tonight?'

'People would stare.'

People did stare, of course, at Madame Michel Marchand, as strangers always stared at Dina da Costa, and from the appraising eyes in the bar they went out to a battery of eyes on the marble terrace above the sea, where tables with pink-shaded lights were set for dinner. In November it was still warm enough in Beirut to dine out of doors, and also to dance, for a string band appeared at nine o'clock and played the Paris tunes of before the war. They had learned a few of the movie hits, like 'As Time Goes By' but time had stood still on the terrace of the Hotel St. Georges. Mike noted with malicious interest that there was not a French uniform to be seen. They'd be smart to wear civvies in Beirut tonight, he thought. He took care to speak English to the waiters, and to Dina in Portuguese.

As for themselves, he told her, they might as well have put a sign saying 'Newly Married' on their table, for she didn't need white satin to proclaim that she was a bride. Dina glowed beneath his gaze, and the *sommelier* smiled sympathetically as he filled and refilled their glasses with the vintage burgundy which Mike much preferred to champagne, and of which, the man said enigmatically, a few fine bottles still remained in the cellars. It was worthy of the fine food, and although neither one would have admitted it, they were

146

very hungry. They had had nothing all day but a few canapés from the Shepheard's buffet, which they had no recollection of eating.

They danced together, as they had danced at the Hungaria in London and the Copacabana in Rio: they were dancing their way across the world, said Dina dreamily, dancing cheek to cheek with all the old perfection. Mike's hand was hot on her waist. It burned through the flame-coloured chiffon, until without a word spoken they walked off the marble floor and went back to the bedroom where there was nothing but cool darkness and the sound of the sea.

Next day they hardly left the neighbourhood of the Hotel St. Georges, except for an early stroll round the streets of the European quarter and the twin crescents by the bay. That district of Beirut was full of youth and colour, for as Mike said it was a great leave centre, from the Church of England hostel for ATS girls to the famous 181 Leave and Transit Camp. They saw WRNS officers, smart in their white uniforms and tricorne hats, coming out of the Normandie Hotel, and Circassians from their barracks on the edge of town, wearing astrakhan caps, baggy tunics and breeches, and riding boots. They saw black soldiers from the Basuto Pioneer Corps. Beirut was a melting-pot of Allied troops and colours, where the shopkeepers were doing a roaring trade and nobody seemed to be taking the war too seriously, since last week's emergency was over.

Two years earlier it was a different story. Since the fall of the Ottoman Empire Syria, and with it the Lebanon, had been a French mandated territory, which remained loyal to Vichy after the disaster of 1940. This loyalty became a threat to the British in May 1941, when the danger of their position in the Middle East was increased by a Vichy promise to grant the Luftwaffe landing facilities in Syria. General de Gaulle, impatient to fight his own countrymen, was clamouring for an attack on the Vichy troops by the Free French alone, but after his fiasco at Dakar this was not acceptable, and his six battalions, of course led not by himself but by General Legentil-homme, had to be augmented by a considerable force of British and Dominion troops which could ill be spared from the fighting in Crete. Even although de Gaulle promised independence to Syria and the Lebanon as two separate states the fighting dragged on for weeks, and it was not until the middle of July that General Dentz and the Army of the Levant surrendered. They declined, not surprisingly, to join de Gaulle, and were repatriated to France.

The war in Syria was not extensively reported in Brazil, and Dina had forgotten what little she knew about it. She and Mike were too lazy on their first morning to do anything more energetic than buying swimming gear, changing in their room and establishing themselves on the sand beside the bay. Mike spoke about renting a car through the hotel management, and exploring the Lebanon as far as Baalbek and the famous Cedars, but after they had swum in the clear blue sea and dried in the sun he fell asleep, while Dina gently spread cream on his tanned but fair skin, and put a towel round his shoulders. She did not sleep herself, and her skin had pigments which needed no lotions; the clover honey colour would turn to heather honey if she stayed long by the sea, and that was all. She lay on her towel, dazed with love and happiness, and thought how much more beautiful was this deserted Mediterranean beach in the shelter of the mountains than the famous Copacabana. She had never been a beach girl at Rio, thinking the beach life a waste of time when swimming in the rollers of the South Atlantic was nearly impossible, and sunbathers were at constant risk from the yelling gangs of footballers who raced all over the sands. Here at Beirut there was nobody on the little beach but themselves and a few young mothers with babies or toddlers; Mike had said the leave men got passes to swim at what was still called the *Bain Militaire*.

Now and again Dina raised her head and studied her husband. She had a feeling that this morning sleep was the beginning of a long process of catching up with the exhausting years behind him. As a bomber pilot he had flown fifty operational sorties in the Western Desert without a wound or a mishap, but Dina as a flyer herself knew that the damage was not always visible, or even understood by the victim. The nervous strain Mike had suffered, which he concealed so well awake, was revealed when he slept by his incessant tiny movements, the twitching hands, the turning of his head with a sudden jerk, and the occasional muttered words. He woke of his own accord, to her relief, and they had another swim before going up to lunch.

After his morning sleep on the beach Mike's siesta was short, and by mid-afternoon they were lounging in deck chairs on the balcony, sipping long drinks made from fresh oranges and lemons and watching the Lebanon change colour as the soft full light moved towards sunset, and the mountain range changed its hues through opal to crimson and purple. It was then Mike began to talk about his part in the desert fighting. He had never written about it to Dina, and since they met in Cairo had spoken only—and casually at that—of his new posting to Photographic Reconnaissance. He had caught the trick of understatement from the 'RAF types' who were his comrades in arms, and 'I was so damned lucky' was his most extreme comment on his service in Bomber Command.

There Dina had always known that her imagination could not follow him. At the beginning of their long separation, when he was a ferry pilot, she had tried to identify with him as he flew across Nigeria through the *haboob* with its swirling columns of red dust, to land in searing heat on the dangerously short runway of El Fasher in the Sudan. She succeeded because she was flying too. At the controls of her Beechcraft, carrying Capricorn's passengers on the much shorter hauls between Rio and São Paulo, São Paulo and Santos, south to Porto Alegre and north to Belo Horizonte, Dina had coped with her own problems of wind and weather and monotony. She had made more than one forced landing on a primitive airstrip, lost her bearings, and flown through the jagged lightning of a tropical storm. But she could not envisage war.

Now Mike was beginning to tell her, as the smoke from his cigarette curled grey against the violet crown appearing over the sea, what it was like to be at the controls of a bomber when the flak was coming up and the Luftwaffe fighters were coming in to intercept, and when at the command 'Bombs away!' death exploded in flame, flesh and metal among the Germans and their armour on the desert sands below. She kept still, saying nothing but holding tightly to Mike's hand, until he pulled her to her feet and said, 'That's quite enough of that!' before he kissed her.

Some atavistic wisdom told Dina that it was not enough, it was only the beginning of a process as healing as sleep, but she went indoors willingly from the dark balcony, and put on the white satin dress to please him. 'We didn't fool anybody yesterday evening, so wear your wedding dress tonight!' he told her, and Mike was rewarded when he saw the sensation his wife's slim figure in the unadorned white, with no jewels but her new wedding ring, caused among the fat little Lebanese women in their elaborate black cocktail dresses, hung with baroque jewellery like so many Christmas trees. That evening was a repetition of their first. They ate and drank, they danced by candlelight to the old tunes, they lingered again over the details of their wedding from the church to the garden party. In their room, before they went to bed, there were no words spoken except for Dina's 'I'm glad we came to Beirut—I love the sea,' and Mike's 'And I love you, my darling; if it had only been for today, those three years of waiting would have been worth while.'

Next morning they swam before breakfast, and over coffee discussed where to go on an excursion now made possible by the delivery of a venerable Ford sedan. Mike, who had seen the car in the hotel garage, and had firmly told the man who delivered it that the last thing he needed was an Arab driver, said they wouldn't go very far in that rattletrap. 'We needn't plan on getting to Baalbek,' he said, 'and anyway over there we might run into some hotheads from the Mountain Warfare School, and spend the day in a guard-house. We'll do better to go up the Lebanon, and have lunch in one of the mountain inns.'

'I'd love that,' said Dina. 'The maid says Aley's a pretty place.'

'It used to be quite a show place, but it's probably off limits, as the Yanks say, now. The British Headquarters are at Aley, under GHQ Middle East, and it's also the official residence of General Sir Edward Spears, British Minister to the Republics of Syria and the Lebanon.'

'Oh dear,' said Dina, 'that sounds very pompous. Don't let's go to Aley.'

'I know,' said Mike. 'Beit Mery. There won't be any sentries or saluting there.'

One of the charms of Beirut was that the great mountain range was so close, and so easily accessible, that in winter it was said to be possible to swim in the Mediterranean and ski on the Lebanon in one and the same day. Dina and Mike attempted nothing so heroic; the Ford, said Mike, would provide adventure enough, and they were about to drive away amid fumes from the exhaust when one of the hotel pages came running up to the car with a telegram.

'What the hell—' said Mike angrily. He had jumped to the conclusion that his leave was cancelled. But the message was from Tony da Costa, and economically crouched in hard cablese:

'Algierswarding thirtieth stop when lovebirds returning query tony,' it ran, and Dina asked at once, 'But when's the thirtieth?'

'Tuesday,' said Mike. 'That's all right. My leave's up on the first, so we'll be "cairowarding" ourselves on Tuesday.'

'So soon?'

' 'Fraid so, darling,' said Mike gently. 'If I can lay on transport first thing on Tuesday morning we'll be able to see Tony before he goes. We'll send him a wire when we come back this afternoon. But I thought he wasn't due in Algiers until the sixth.'

Dina looked wise. 'I imagine Tony wants to get there ahead of the mission and see General Eisenhower first if he can. He's afraid General Dutra, the War Minister, will try something underhand with the Allies. He got a lot of publicity at home for being the man behind the BEF, and he just might use it for a *coup d'état* against President Vargas. And you know Tony is a Vargas man.'

'Sure,' said Mike. 'Skulduggery, publicity and a *coup d'état*. Good old Tony! That's the language they understand in Algiers. "The hate mill," as Saint Ex. calls it . . . Now let's get going, or those damned kids will strip the car. Look out, you little devils!' The child beggars dropped off screaming with laughter as the Ford gathered speed.

Beit Mery was an enchanting place to visit, as long as they kept away from the solitary inn. It was built in a forest, on one of the high escarpments of rock looking west over the Mediterranean, and from the straggling village street paths wandered away beneath the pines, paths which ended in glimpses of the sea, very blue under that day's strong sun, or of the handsome villas of the rich Lebanese. One long vista ended in the sight of a Maronite Christian church, another in the Orthodox cross above a Greek monastery, and far below, among the orchards, they could see the whitewashed houses of the Arab farmers. Mike and Dina walked for an hour under the evergreens, enjoying the pine-scented solitude, walking first above and then below the highway until they came full circle, and returned to the centre of the village.

The inn at Beit Mery served lunch indoors and out, but the cool dark interior tables were all occupied, and the Marchands were given a table for two on the terrace, which was warm and crowded. Their immediate neighbours were three war correspondents, who had invited three local girls to help them spend the expense money they were stretching for a few days' leisure after the emergency, and four Australian NCOs who had brought up four ATS girls in an army lorry. The inn, for the time being, was an extension of the leave camps of Beirut, noisy, matey, relaxed, and the Arab waiters drafted from the village were far from professional in their service. The Marchands sat over lunch only until Mike's watch told him the telegraph office would be open, for the Australians had begun to sing 'Waltzing Matilda', competing strongly with a radio playing Arab music inside the inn. To a combined disharmony of bawling and static Mike paid the bill, and they walked back to the car.

'Do you suppose it gets quiet up here at night?' asked Dina, while Mike swore at the sluggish ignition.

'I wouldn't know. But I could use a swim after that,' he said.

'After we've wired to Tony. Do you know where the telegraph office is?'

'Somewhere in the Arab quarter, I believe.'

But Mike lost his way in the Arab quarter, with its network of narrow streets, and the British redcap on patrol could only give him a vague idea of the direction. Turn left, turn right, turn left again, going very slowly between the narrow pavements where suspicious Arabs, in army-surplus or army-stolen jackets worn over white skirts or baggy western trousers, scowled at them from the open cafés. At last they came to a crossroads where there were taller, more official buildings, and before he could stop her Dina leaned out of the passenger's window and called to a well-dressed passer-by:

'Pardon, monsieur! Où se trouve le bureau des PTT, s'il vous plaît?'

The man stopped dead, his face convulsed with rage, and he spat out something in Arabic which neither Mike nor Dina understood. At once the Ford was surrounded by a yelling gang of youths, and by older men in gown and fez, shaking their fists at the man and the girl in the car. A stone whizzed along the dilapidated bonnet and bounced off the windscreen.

'Imshi!' shouted Mike *'Imshi*, you bastards! Get away!' he took a chance on knocking someone down, and drove forward as fast as he could while the crowd scattered. He missed an oncoming tram by mounting the pavement, hit an empty barrel, and straightened out as he saw familiar landmarks up ahead. He recognised a big Arab café, standing high where the two crescents met, and then the way was clear round their own quiet beach to the garage of the Hotel St. Georges.

'Dina, are you all right?'

She was too proud to show her fright, but she was shaking when he helped her out of the car. 'Mike, what happened? What made them all so angry?' she said.

'It was my fault, I should never have taken you down there. Here, George,' he said to the Arab garage hand who came out of the office, 'put the Ford away. I'll come back and have a look-see later on ... Now, Dina! I'm going to do what I should have done hours ago: ask the concierge to get off a telegram to Tony. You go on up to the room.'

When she was gone he scribbled a long message to his brother-in-law, saying that the plane to Algiers never left as scheduled, and they would join him at Shepheard's not later than Tuesday afternoon. Then Mike saw the manager, told him the rented Ford was unserviceable and must be replaced by a better vehicle in the morning. The manager agreed as soon as he had gone with Mike to the garage and heard the mechanic's report on the engine. He was a Greek by birth and anxious to please a British officer. 'All these demonstrations, sir, are very bad for business!' he said plaintively, and Mike agreed with him. The incident of the afternoon made him think the French were washed up in the Levant, and further, that there was an underswell of violence in the Arab quarter which might turn to murder and arson when the French had gone. He ran upstairs three at a time.

Dina had got over her fright, and reached the stage of being angry with herself for being frightened. Angry and defiant too, her first words to Mike showed that.

'What did I do wrong?'

'Darling, you spoke to that man in French.'

'What's the matter with French? I've been talking French all the time to the servants and the waiters here!'

'Yes, here in the hotel, that's all right, but—calm down, darling, and let me try to explain.' She shrugged her shoulders, but she sat down and lit a cigarette. 'That's better,' said Mike. 'Now listen, it was all my fault. I ought to have warned you to speak English out of doors. Or Portuguese. But not French. Because the people here are furious with the French ... You must have read *something* about it!'

'I'm sorry, darling, when I'm flying I sometimes don't see a newspaper for days together.'

Nothing she said could have disarmed him more than that 'when I'm flying'. Mike said simply, 'I understand. It's been the same with me. But you do know the French were fighting each other in the Levant two years ago?'

'Yes.'

'At that time de Gaulle needed the support of the Syrians and the Lebanese, so he told them (which of course he'd no right to do) that he would grant them independence and allow them to hold free elections to decide on their constitutions as separate states.'

'Well?'

'He broke his promises. The elections were never held until quite recently, when the Nationalists took the law into their own hands in both countries. The Lebanese government decided to end the French presence in the republic. With the result that de Gaulle sent his delegate from Algiers, a man called Helleu, to arrest the Lebanese President and some of his ministers and throw them in prison. They were only released, under pressure from the Allies, a few days ago.'

'I do remember hearing about the arrests when we were in New York.'

She was taking the rotten story lightly, *bon Dieu*! Mike had to remind himself that de Gaulle's outrageous action, which had shocked the West, would not make the same impression on a girl from Brazil, where a *coup d'état* was a normal political weapon, and where President Vargas, her brother Tony's powerful friend, had ruled as a dictator for the past eight years. But Dina was not dismissing it, for she asked, after a reflective silence, if there had been fighting before the prisoners were released. 'There was a good deal of bloodshed in Beirut,' said Mike.

'I see.' Dina stubbed out her cigarette and began to unfasten her dress. 'Then I don't blame those people for not liking the sound of French ... I feel dirty, Mike, let's change and have a swim. And for the future we'd better stick to Portuguese.'

It was all very well, but when Mike made love he thought in French, and the Portuguese endearments he knew were vulgar enough to make Dina giggle, and ask him where he picked them up. So their third night as man and wife began differently from the two nights which went before, with a kind of teasing hostility quite unlike the romantic passion of their beginnings. Mike felt the marvellous body in his arms sliding away from him, denying, with clenched knees; listened to Dina's whisper of *'Amigo de coracão!'* from lips that refused to part beneath his own, and heard a stifled laugh instead of a moan of ecstasy. He exerted all his strength then, and mastered her, taking in Dina's body his revenge for the Arab insults of the streets, and when he gasped, *'En français! Dis-le-moi en français!'* he held back almost beyond his power to hold back until she cried out, conquered and begging, *'Je t'aime, Michel! Je t'aime!'*

The next day, Saturday, was the day when Mr. Churchill and President Roosevelt flew to Teheran to meet Stalin for a discussion of the invasion of Europe. Mr. Churchill did not record that any time was given to the troubles in Lebanon, supposed to be ended with the release of the ministers, but he did note that 'everywhere people would say "What kind of France is this which, while itself subjugated by the enemy, seeks to subjugate others?"'

De Gaulle's defence was that the British minister, Sir Edward Spears, was to blame for the whole fracas. There was a time when General Spears had been de Gaulle's great champion, the man originally responsible for his public relations campaign, and more than that: the man who brought him to Britain in the first place. Now de Gaulle had quarrelled with his first benefactor. He resented the whole British presence in the Levant. However, it was not Spears but Mr. Churchill who, while the Lebanese ministers were still in prison, had instructed the British Commander Middle East to prepare to re-establish order in Lebanon.

'We wouldn't have minded a dust-up with the Wogs,' said a cheerful young Englishman to Mike Marchand, who answered drily that they might have had a dust-up with the Frogs instead.

'Wogs or Frogs, anything for a spot of action,' said the Englishman, who had introduced himself as Major Jack Wood, Indian Army, seconded to British Troops North Levant. 'My chaps are getting restless, stuck up there at Markab.'

'They're Dogra troops, you said?'

'Best in India, and don't talk to me about the Gurkhas,' said Major Wood, draining his glass of beer. He had begun talking to Mike and Dina on the grounds of having seen them the night before at the St. Georges, when Mike remembered there had been an unusually large crowd on the terrace. Now they were in an even more crowded spot called George's Bar, much favoured by young officers on leave and homesick for an English pub; Mike had thought it might amuse Dina. She was talking with animation to another young major (promotion seemed to come quickly in BTNL) and showed no disposition to move on to the Bar Russe or the *'Chat Botté'*.

Markab, said Major Wood, accepting a beer from Mike, was the backside of creation. It was on the coast between Tripoli and Latakia, on the north road into Turkey, and was nothing but a hamlet built round a castle the Crusaders had taken three years to reduce. BTNL had been there since the fighting in '41, without a day's home leave, and most of the officers were completely round the bend. He, Wood, had been saved from insanity by his current three-day pass to Beirut, and a taste of the flesh-pots after the horrors of the Casino at Markab.

'There's a casino, is there? That doesn't sound too bad.'

'The Casino Hotel, I mean, gambling strictly prohibited. Our cantonments were built as a leave camp for Allenby's army, back in 1918, so you can imagine we're not living in luxury. You flyers have the best of it—'

'Sometimes,' said Mike amiably. He hadn't met any Indian Army officers before, but this was a pleasant chap, tall and fair like himself, a typical Englishman. He caught a glimpse of his own face in the clouded mirror behind the bar, and thought as far as looks went he was a typical Englishman himself.

He put his arm round Dina's waist, for the place was overcrowded, and the customers were pushing up to the bar to be served. Jack Wood introduced a few of the newcomers, though with the gramophone belting out 'Sweet and Lovely' at full pitch the names were lost in the din. Everybody was talking at once, but Mike remembered later that it was Wood who first mentioned the Pigeon Rocks.

'Bit of a scrum in here,' he remarked, as the frantic Arab boy who was helping George to serve the drinks upset a bottle of soda water across the zinc counter. George, a perspiring Greek, flung a dishcloth at his head, and one or two Lebanese girls shrieked as the splashes of washing-up water hit their dresses. Two couples were trying to dance in a corner of the bar.

'Had enough?' asked Major Wood sympathetically. 'How about coming along with Bob and me for a spot of dinner at the Officers' Club?'

'Thanks, but no,' said Mike, 'I'm planning to take my wife to the *"Chat Botté"* tonight.'

'Very nice,' said the Englishman, 'but far beyond the means of the Markab Musketeers. Maybe we'll bump into you tomorrow. Mrs. Marchand!' he said, raising his voice above the din.

'That's you, darling,' said Mike, pulling her closer to him.

156

'You're Mrs. Marchand now, remember?'

'Am I likely to forget?' she said beneath her breath. 'Yes, what is it, Major Wood?'

'You must get your husband to take you to the Pigeon Rocks tomorrow night. The Wogs have a big *tamasha* there on Sundays, you'd enjoy it.'

'What's the Pigeon Rocks?' asked Dina.

'A restaurant with a bad reputation,' said Mike.

'And the most beautiful location in Beirut,' said Wood. 'You shouldn't miss it. There'll be a firework display tomorrow, to celebrate the release of the ministers.'

'No *brasileira* can resist fireworks,' teased Mike, as they drove to the '*Chat Botté*'. 'I can see we'll be dining at the Pigeon Rocks tomorrow.'

'Is it really an awful place?'

'Not really. Local businessmen take their girlfriends there, that's all. And the food used to be good.'

'I hope it's as nice as George's Bar,' said Dina. 'I liked that.'

'Why?'

'It reminded me of the crew quarters at one of our way stations.'

Exactly! A place where young men enlisted in the same Service gathered to talk shop, compare notes, check their briefings ... He had been in the Capricorn crew room at Santos Dumont airport, when Dina in her flying kit was the only girl in the game and as good a pilot as any of the men. No wonder she was 'in her plate' in the ambience of George's Bar! No wonder she didn't answer—yet —to 'Mrs. Marchand'!

The Citroën unwillingly supplied by the car rental agency was not much better than the Ford. It had got them to the foothills of the Lebanon on Saturday, for a picnic lunch among the olive groves, but Mike abandoned the idea of any further exploration. On Sunday night it took them as far as the Pigeon Rocks on the highway not far out of town, climbing an easy slope so sluggishly that Mike finished the trip in first gear. He was annoyed to see that there was no attendant in the dusty parking-lot.

'What a fantastic place!' said Dina, as they went through an opening in the hedge of oleanders, and entered the wide terrace among the rocks where the restaurant tables had been set. It was on a cliff high above the sea, dark now, though there had been a

157

crescent moon earlier in the evening, and while acetylene lamps were burning in the kitchens and service rooms, there were only candles on the tables. The faces of the diners seemed to hang, disembodied, above vases of flowers and bowls of fruit.

'All the tables are taken,' said Dina. 'I hope they didn't forget to telephone from the hotel.' All the tables for two were certainly occupied, and groups of up to ten persons were gathered round the rest. By candlelight it was impossible to distinguish one party from another.

'We'll be all right,' said Mike. 'Here comes the *maître d'hôtel*.' The Greek headwaiter came up, bowing, and begged to know Mike's name.

'Marchand,' said Mike. 'From the St. Georges.'

'Ah, certainly, sir. Reception telephoned for a reservation. We have a very nice private room for you—'

'I asked for a table for two.'

'Unfortunately,' with another bow and a shrug, 'it is impossible tonight. You will find the accommodation most attractive—'

'But we want to see the fireworks!' protested Dina.

'Madame will have a perfect view of the fireworks. Please, sir, follow me!'

Mike made way for Dina, and followed with a smile. He knew the layout of the Pigeon Rocks very well, and wondered how often a man had shared one of the *cabinets particuliers* with his own wife. There were ten of them, partitioned and roofed with reeds, down a path at right angles to the outdoor restaurant, and those nearest the kitchens were occupied, as the clink of dishes and the sound of voices proved.

'Does this please madame?' said the *maître d'hôtel*, opening a door.

'It's charming,' said Dina, without conviction.

'The fireworks will be let off from that boat down below.'

'Oh yes, I see.'

'I'll send the waiter and the *sommelier*, sir.'

'We don't have to stay if you don't like it, darling,' said Mike when the door was closed. 'Would you rather go back to the St. Georges?'

'Oh no, let's stay, now we're here.' She wasn't quite sure of the place, though, he could tell by the way she looked around. It was both simple and suspect, with a fine rug on the floor and a beautifully set table with a lighted paraffin lamp instead of candles, and bowls containing fruit and flowers. There were two dining chairs, and a divan along one side of the room—a broad divan, with an embroidered Arab cover. Mike hoped the sea air coming through the big window had dissipated all the odours of scent and sex which must inevitably cling to that divan. He joined Dina at the window.

'Don't lean too far out, darling,' he warned.

Beneath the windows, all along the line of rooms, there ran a rim of soil, not to be called a path and not half a metre broad, along the top of the cliff. From there it was a sheer drop to the sea, where men could be seen moving about on the deck of a boat moored to a landing jetty. While Mike and Dina watched, a single star-shell soared up from the boat and exploded in a shower of pink and gold.

'We really have got front row seats,' exulted Dina, and Mike agreed. If the service was good they would do very well in their *cabinet particulier*, and the service was better than good, for a waiter was there already with the menu, another with the wine list, while a third was setting out, unasked, glass dishes of cheese, olives, pine kernels, peppers in oil and a flask of *arak* in a bowl of ice. He poured the anise spirit into two chilled glasses.

Fireworks came up in golden rains from the sea while dinner was ordered, with a bottle of the obligatory champagne.

They drank each other's health in *arak* as soon as they were alone, laughing and well pleased with the Pigeon Rocks. Mike thought they'd got the best of both worlds. A good dinner in one of the most beautiful settings in Beirut, and at the same time they were well out of the crowd. He knew that the plain-clothes police kept a sharp eye on the Pigeon Rocks, but a small detachment might not be able to control an excitable mob if a gala evening in honour of the ministers should turn into a nationalist demonstration. In which case he intended that he and Dina should leave quietly; beyond the last of the private rooms it would be no distance to the parking lot.

Meantime there was nothing to be heard but applause, as Catherine wheels and Roman candles sprang from the deck of the fireworks boat to explode against the sky. Nothing but 'Oh's' and 'Ah's' of admiration from the diners on the terrace, and closer at hand the little throaty laughs and the deeper tones of endearments which were celebrations of another sort. The private rooms on each side of their own were not occupied, although the red-shaded paraffin lamps were lighted; they could be seen through the reed walls which were not the most discreet part of the Pigeon Rocks' arrangements.

The service, at least, was impeccable. The *mezze* tray was removed and with smiling courtesy the food was served, the champagne poured, and the bottle left in an ice bucket. Presumably this was the moment when the diners in the private rooms demanded privacy.

Mike and Dina dined with their chairs turned to face the sea. The men in the boat were prolonging their display: there were tantalising intervals of darkness, during which a band played on the terrace, and then the show began again. Dina was absorbed in the bouquets of gold and silver flowers springing from a fiery basket, when Mike heard the sound of a door closing and a key turning in the lock.

He jumped up at once. It was their own door, which had been left slightly ajar, and the lock was a heavy mortice, by no means as flimsy as the walls. He rattled the door, which was also solid, resisting both hand and shoulder. 'Hey!' he called out, 'what's going on! Somebody open this door!'

'Somebody's coming, I think,' said Dina at the window. 'Mike, what is it?'

He heard the quiet footsteps as well as she did. But the steps stopped at the door before their own, the door between their room and the terrace restaurant, and through the reed partition Mike could see a dark shape bending over the lamp. Then the red glass was broken, the lamp lay on its side, and a tongue of flame and oil licked the tablecloth.

Mike knocked their own table over as he jumped for the window. 'Dina,' he said, 'do exactly what I tell you. Get out of the window and don't look down. Keep close to the wall and start moving to your right. I'll be behind you and I won't let you fall.'

The trail of oil and fire was spreading in the next room and in a moment would be devouring the reeds and leaping to the roof. Dina gave him one terrified look and stepped out of the window, Mike helping her and blessing the pilot's reflexes which sent her off along that narrow ledge, with no handhold but the reed walls of the two remaining rooms, and no support but his own hand on her waist.

He had ordered her not to look down, and long as it was since Mike Marchand had suffered an attack of vertigo he dared not look down that sheer drop to where the waves of the Mediterranean were curling softly round the rocks. The rockets were bursting half a dozen at a time, and the applause was mounting; he thought that if there was a marksman in the fireboat he had the perfect target in Dina's white dress against the dark reed walls. It wouldn't take a marksman, if the narrow ridge of soil began to crumble they were both done for, and there was a terrible heat at his back and the flames had leaped the roofs.

But the soil was packed firm and they beat the fire; he had Dina by the hand and was hurrying her headlong towards the opening in the oleander hedge.

'Mike, the car!' gasped Dina. 'The car's that way!'

'Never mind it. Down to the road!' He pulled her across the parking-lot, through the gate and on to the verge of the highway. The noise from the Pigeon Rocks was not applause but screaming, and one or two cars slowed down as they went by, but failed to stop. The headlights showed Mike and Dina to each other, both panting, with scratched hands and shoes. Mike had no jacket, and Dina had a long tear in her dusty dress. Then a bigger vehicle came down the road to Beirut, and Mike ran out holding up his RAF identification.

The army lorry with the insignia of the Royal Electrical and Mechanical Engineers came to a halt, and a lined suspicious face looked out of the cab.

'What's the trouble, sir?' said a flat Midlands voice.

'My car's broken down,' said Mike. 'Could you give my wife and me a lift into the city, sergeant?'

'I daresay I could,' said the sergeant. 'Thomson' (to his mate) 'move over and make room for the lady.'

'It's very good of you,' said Mike. He lifted Dina over the wheel and made a place for himself between her and the driver's mate. The REME sergeant, a middle-aged man, looked them both over by the dashboard light.

'Some trouble back there, sir?' he said as he started his lorry.

'The place seemed to be on fire when we left,' said Mike.

' "Lo, the smoke of the country went up as the smoke of a furnace," ' said the sergeant. ' "And God destroyed the cities of the plain." That's your Beirut for you, Thomson! Sodom and Gomorrah! If the Pigeon Rocks burns down tonight, it'll be the judgment of the Lord.'

ELEVEN

Mike Marchand had been too optimistic about the Tuesday flights. He admitted as much to Dina when they landed at El Maza airfield instead of Heliopolis early in the evening, after a long wait for a plane at Beirut, and learned in a hasty telephone call to Shepheard's that the flight to Algiers with Captain Antonio da Costa on the passenger list had gone out on time at three o'clock in the morning.

'It's too bad,' he said, as he came back from the telephone in what served as the airport lounge at El Maza. 'I was really hoping we could see the old boy before he left.'

'Oh, so was I! I wanted to thank him again for our wedding party.'

'Well, it can't be helped,' said Mike. 'Maybe we'll meet up with him at Naples, you never know. I called the flat. Ahmed said they'd been waiting for us all day, and he'll have dinner ready. Thank God we've got a telephone!'

'We couldn't get on without it. Here's our porter, Mike, I told him to fetch a taxi.'

'Trust you to get everything organised.' She had taken the tiresome wait at Beirut in her stride, bless her. Dina had been on too many holdovers as a pilot to worry about a delayed flight as a passenger.

Mike wasn't really sorry to have missed Tony da Costa. Tony's enquiries about the fire at the Pigeon Rocks would have been very probing. Their names had appeared in *L'Orient* that morning as two of the people who had reserved a table at the restaurant and (like all the other guests) had escaped unharmed, and the Beirut paper's stringer in Cairo would certainly have sold the story to the *Egyptian Mail*. And Tony would have had more searching questions to ask than the Lebanese police when they came to see the Marchands at the Hotel St. Georges, accompanied by an agitated man from the car rental agency, who found the Citroën in the parking lot with its tyres slashed. The police, who had had their orders, were passing off the whole episode as an anti-government demonstration. What else could have disrupted a gala held in honour of the ministers imprisoned by the French?

So Mike sat contentedly in the taxi with his arm round Dina, a man too accustomed to danger and the split-second difference between life and death to dwell for long on the terrible minutes when they edged their way along that narrow ledge above the sea. The Cairo streets were raucous with the clanging of trams and the braying of donkeys, while their driver kept his hand on the car horn all the way from El Maza to the Sharia-el-Nil. It was pleasant to reach the palm-lined street with the view over the Nile to the polo grounds of Gezira. The houseboys had been watching for the taxi, and had the door of the apartment open in readiness. Mike swept Dina up in his arms and carried her over the threshold.

'Félicitations, madame, monsieur!' said Ahmed, touching his heart, lips and brow, while Anwar bowed from the waist and said, 'Ladyship, sir, many happy returns!' The living room was full of flowers which Ahmed said had arrived that day. He had left the cards in the bouquets sent by many of the guests at the wedding reception.

'You'll have a lot of thank-you notes to write, darling, and a lot of invitations to answer,' said Mike. There was a pile of stiff cards on the gimcrack writing desk, inviting Flight-Lieutenant and Mrs. Marchand to cocktails, buffet luncheons and even a dance in aid of RAF charities. 'They must think I'm grounded,' said Mike with a laugh. 'Ahmed, call me at half past five tomorrow and have a gharry here at six.'

'But dinner first, monsieur?'

'Certainly dinner first.'

Dinner was served on a folding table opened out in the centre of the living room, and consisted of tinned soup, underdone grilled lamb, and a flan which had obviously been made with goat's milk. 'Hardly up to the St. Georges' standard,' commented Mike. 'You'll have to take the boys in hand, darling. Otherwise they'll think they can get away with murder.'

Dina opened her eyes wide at the last word, but said nothing, for Ahmed was coming in with the coffee tray. 'Oh for a Brazilian cafézinho!' said Mike, tasting his coffee cautiously. 'Remember how Belinda used to keep them coming up, like on a conveyor belt, out at Santos Dumont?'

Dina nodded. What she wanted was a gourd of *maté*, drunk by a Gaucho fire. 'I think I'll begin unpacking,' she said, getting up. 'You've got an early start tomorrow.'

'You're right,' said Mike. 'It's been a long day.' He moved to an armchair by the fake fireplace, so that the boys could clear the table and fold it back in place against the wall, and stretched out his long legs. He wasn't sorry to be back in Cairo, ready for the early morning call. Dina was an angel, and they'd had a wonderful time in Beirut, until he'd been conned into heading for that trap at the Pigeon Rocks. He wondered if a search of the records at 'Grey Pillars', as GHQ Middle East was known, would turn up the name of Major Jack Wood, British Troops North Levant, stationed at Markab. Major Wood, or his paymaster, had certainly written *finis* to the honeymoon.

He was smoking a cigarette and thinking luxuriously about bed when Dina came back. She had unpinned her hair, which lay in black silk locks over the white *broderie anglaise* wrapper he liked so much, and Mike held out his arms to her with love. But she hadn't come to be petted. She asked if it was all right to open the windows.

'Yes, why not?'

'Mosquitoes.'

'Not this late in November. I'll do that!'

But Dina had pulled the windows open already, and instead of the smell of fatty lamb and cigarette smoke in the room there seeped in the rank odour of the Nile.

'Mike, we have to talk.'

'Sweetie, it's getting late—'

'Not all that late.'

'I'm flying tomorrow.'

'I haven't forgotten that. But listen, Mike! All the time we were hanging about at Beirut airport, I was thinking about what happened at the Pigeon Rocks.'

'Oh, for God's sake, Dina! Didn't we talk it into the ground, all day yesterday?'

'Except for one thing.' She left the window and sat down in the chair opposite Mike. 'Did you ever find out what became of that man Lachmann?'

Taken completely by surprise, Mike blurted out, 'Whatever put Lachmann into your head?'

'The fact that someone tried to kill us both on Sunday night,' she said. 'What happened to Lachmann, after he was released from prison in Freetown? I know he followed de Gaulle to Brazzaville, but then?'

Mike said reluctantly, 'I met him in Algiers last May. Still in the Air Force, still calling himself Corbeau. Colonel Corbeau now.'

'What happened when you met?'

'It was in public, and we didn't come to blows. That's about all.'

'You never told me!'

'It's not the sort of thing you can put in a letter that has to pass the censors. Though I must say St. Exupéry has no such inhibitions.'

'The great Saint Ex.! How does he come into it?'

'I was with him when I ran into Corbeau in Algiers, and he's written to me once or twice since the Americans posted him to his old squadron, "La Hache". He said Corbeau was still flying sorties, but was known to be one of de Gaulle's hatchet men, sort of an air force ADC. Which means he's still with the great Leader in Algiers.'

'I wonder,' said Dina. 'I think he's dangerous. I wish I'd never told you I knew him when he was flying for Condor in Brazil. Or better still, that we'd both stayed at Freetown till his trial, after we accused him of espionage.'

'Don't be silly, darling, you couldn't possibly have stayed in Africa. How would you have got back to Brazil, if not on that Pan Am proving flight? And I'd have lost my only chance to join the RAF if I hadn't gone on to Takoradi. Remember, the Crown was satisfied with our sworn statements, but even though Neil Grant was flown out from England to back them up, the charge of espionage wouldn't hold up in court. You can't think our being there ourselves would have made any difference?'

'I don't know,' said Dina. 'You move on from things so fast. You flew back to Brazil as soon as you had that row with Lachmann in London, and you left for Takoradi after the row at Freetown. And you certainly didn't hang around at Beirut, did you?'

'Are you saying I'm afraid of Lachmann and his bully-boys?'

'No, I don't think you're afraid. I know you're a brave man, darling. But I think you're impatient. You don't like being bothered with any sort of trouble for very long.'

'You should have married my cousin, Jacques Brunel. He's the one for staying put.'

'What a mean thing to say!'

It was, and Mike was instantly remorseful. He jumped up and knelt beside Dina's chair. 'Forgive me, sweetheart. I've been on edge ever since you were in danger at that rotten place, and all because of me.'

'Are we any safer here?'

'Of course we are!' He did his best to soothe her. He tried to make her see the humorous side of the affair. The revivalist REME sergeant, who sang gospel hymns all the way to Beirut; the pickle they would have been in if he hadn't been carrying his wallet in his hip pocket instead of in his jacket, and so on. He even succeeded in keeping her off the car with the slashed tyres—when he sheered away from it in the parking lot he had been afraid of something quite other than slashed tyres, say interference with the steering or the brakes. Eventually he coaxed her to bed, and having no confidence in Ahmed, set a cheap alarm clock for half past five. But Ahmed, on his mettle for the first morning, called him at five o'clock and Mike got up with silent curses and went to report for duty at Heliopolis.

He was gone long before Dina awoke, still early enough for a blue morning mist to be above the Nile, with the palms grey instead of green, when Anwar brought her breakfast tray to a card table by the bedroom window. She watched the feluccas moving gracefully between the Sharia-el-Nil and the island where the Gezira Sporting Club was the hub of Cairo's social activities, and prepared to face a new day and a new way of life. Dina wasn't sorry, since they had kissed and made up before they slept, that she had spoken her mind the night before. It had cleared the air, and of all their sharp exchanges the only words which stuck in Dina's memory were Mike's 'I'm flying tomorrow'. She envied him.

She was left with no idea when or if he would return for dinner. He had said he would telephone from Heliopolis, so when she was dressed Dina decided to make some provisional arrangements with Ahmed, who resourcefully suggested tinned soup, grilled lamb and goat's milk cheese. Anwar said he would go to the shops in the Muski and get some real bargains for Ladyship.

It was unfortunate that Dina, who had been making out the

manifests and bills of lading for Capricorn Airways for years, had no idea of how to draw up a shopping list for a household of four people. The great house in São Paulo where she spent her childhood was superlatively well run by her mother, and since she became Tony's assistant at Capricorn they had shared a hotel suite in the Copacabana Hotel. At the Parana ranch there was a housekeeper, a butler and a staff of Indian servants. It was no wonder that she was baffled by Ahmed's request for an egg-beater and a pot-scourer, never even having seen such utensils in use.

It took the two houseboys less than twenty-four hours to realise that Ladyship was the softest touch they had ever known in all their years of Foreign service. She could count in cruzeiros but not in piastres. She didn't mind how many relatives and friends they entertained at her expense in the back premises, and she allowed them to play Arab music on the kitchen radio all day long. That is, until the neighbours complained, for in Rio Dina was accustomed to hear music blaring constantly from the open windows of the Rua do Ouvidor, and was impervious to the noise. But a lady from Berkhampsted, married to an RASC major and occupying the flat above the Marchands', came down in a rage a few days after they set up house, and asked to see the bride. 'I told her to her face that this was a high-class building,' fumed the Englishwoman to her husband, 'and we weren't accustomed to crowds of natives on the back stairs, or their dreadful music screeching night and day! Really, Mrs. Merchant, I said, if that's your name, we might as well be in the Muski!'

'What did she say to that?' asked the major, bored.

'She said she was sorry, she hadn't been to the Muski yet, but she believed it was very interesting.'

'Sounds as if she wasn't quite all there.'

'Oh, she's not *mental*, if that's what you mean, but I don't think she understands English very well. If you ask me there's a lick of the tarbrush there.'

'Good God! You mean she's a Gyppo?'

'I don't know what she is, but she's a chee-chee girl.'

Dina had been quite serious about the Muski. She wanted to go to that ancient bazaar quarter, seamed with lanes barely a metre broad, and see the food stalls Anwar patronised as well as the silversmiths and carpet weavers sitting cross-legged at their trade. She had been told that the Catholic Church of the Assumption in the Muski was more beautiful than St. Joseph's, and she wanted to know if it was true. She especially wanted to buy scent from the perfumer who mixed his scents to match his clients, and had his stall next to the vendor of the richest Damascus brocades in Cairo. But Mike put his foot down on the Muski, part of which was off limits to British troops, unless both the houseboys escorted her. Dina felt she was part of a procession when they all set out, and she was sure that the boys were getting a cut on the purchases she made. But she enjoyed the perfumer, who bowed and salaamed between keen glances at her from below his fez, and even took her hand like a palmist and followed the lines intently before he mixed his liquids in a little phial. The scent evolved was heavy and aphrodisiac, so much so that Mike said 'Good God, what are you wearing?' when he came home that night. Then he put his nostrils and afterwards his lips to the pulses she had touched with the new scent, and said, 'Tiger Lily! That old chap knew what he was about, my love!'

It was the only success of the visit to the Muski, for unluckily Dina, who enjoyed the luscious fruits of Brazil, asked Anwar to carry home a basket of melons, pomegranates, dates and bananas, and ate some unwashed at her solitary breakfast and lunch next day. The result was an attack of 'Gyppy tummy' which laid her low for a week and caused a doctor to be called in.

'I can't think of anything less romantic than a bride with diarrhoea,' she said weakly to her husband, when the doctor's remedies had taken effect and Dina had progressed to a diet of charcoal biscuits.

'Poor darling!' said Mike. 'It happens to most of us sooner or later. I should have warned you about the fruit.'

'I'm sorry we're missing some nice parties.'

'I am too, but people will ask us again.'

Better than any party to Dina was the sound of Mike's homeward progress down the Sharia-el-Nil. Six months earlier he had bought an old MG with its bonnet tied up with a leather strap, and before Dina's arrival had it repainted yellow like the Duesenberg they had driven in Rio de Janeiro. The MG with a souped-up engine made as much noise as the Duesenberg ever did, and the sound of its approach made Dina sigh with thankfulness that Mike had completed one more flight in safety. She now knew that Photographic Reconnaissance was not the 'piece of cake' the pilots called it. Mike had been on courses in mapping as well as photography since his commanding officer reported on him for reconnaissance out of Cairo, but Dina knew it was his skill as a flyer which counted for most. There were substantial Luftwaffe formations in Bulgaria, covering neutral Turkey, others in Rhodes and the Dodecanese, still others in Crete and Greece. On all his missions to photograph the German strength in these areas, where the Germans must at all costs be pinned down and not permitted to reinforce their armies in Italy, Mike had to take evasive action against the Luftwaffe, and that in an unarmed plane. He was quite willing to talk about his sorties in the approved nonchalant way, but his nerves betrayed him when the nightmares rode his sleep.

The 'circus', as Mr. Churchill called it, came back from Teheran before Dina fell a victim to the fruits of the Muski, and by the time she was better the second round of the Cairo conference was over. The protective air squadrons were withdrawn from Alexandria and the Luftwaffe grew bolder, sending their own reconnaissance planes on daring surveys of northern Syria. This had no effect on the gaieties of Cairo, which increased as Christmas drew near. Apart from the uniforms in the street, the only sign of war was the British tanks massed round Kasr-el-Nil barracks. Mena House, where the conference had taken place, became once again a resort hotel with a swimming pool and charming gardens, and golfers appeared on the nine-hole course near the Pyramids of Giza.

Dina was not quite the success Mike had anticipated at the Service parties they attended. The senior wives found it impossible to condescend to her, and thought her much too striking and much too assured for the wife of a mere flight-lieutenant. Women nearer her own age were jealous of her beauty and her clothes. She got on best with the Service girls, who seemed to have some purpose in life, although she was never quite certain what it was. She knew it involved much to-ing and fro-ing at Grey Pillars with cardboard folders and important faces, and that the young women officers were contributing to the defeat of the enemy. The men fought shy of her. She was 'different', they said, and Mike made the difference more apparent by his eager introduction of her:

'My wife's a flyer herself, you know.'

'Really? Where'd you do your flying, Mrs. Marchand?'

'In Brazil. My brother—'

'Oh, Brazil!'

'I'm sure they don't know Brazil from Bolivia,' she would say to Mike. What she really meant was that they didn't take her seriously, a woman with nearly two thousand flying hours on her logbook, and when their duty was done, their *acte de présence* made, as Mike called it, the Marchands would slip out to where the MG waited under the guard of a 'George' waiting for his tip, and drive to a night club. The top spot was the *'Auberge des Pyramides'*, only opened in August, where it was possible to dance, have supper, and watch the King of Egypt watching the belly-dancers when the floor show began. King Farouk at thirty-three was grossly fat and indolent. His friends said his life was ruined on the day the British tanks surrounded the royal palace to keep him faithful to the treaty with Britain when Rommel seemed to be on the way to victory.

It was fun to roar out to the *'Auberge'* in the MG, past the flocks of goats and camel teams which entered Cairo by night, with a red hurricane lamp tied to the tail of the last camel. Fun to move from the Biblical simplicity of the animals to the sophistication of the *'Auberge des Pyramides'*, to eat a light supper out of doors, and move in to the dance floor when the big band began. There was a new movie theme song, just out, which they both loved, and which Mike said was as much 'their' song as 'We'll Meet Again' had been in 1940:

> Long ago and far away
> I dreamed a dream one day
> And now that dream is here beside me,
> Long the skies were overcast
> But now the clouds have passed
> You're here at last!

The music swelled triumphantly, and Mike held Dina very close.

> Chills run up and down my spine
> Aladdin's lamp is mine.
> The dream I dreamed was not denied me,
> Just one look, and then I knew
> That all I longed for long ago was you

Sometimes they danced on the terrace, among the flowers, and when the band played 'Long Ago and Far Away' they escaped into their private world. Dina forgot how often she expected to see

Lachmann skulking beneath the palms of the Sharia-el-Nil—not the Corbeau of Freetown and Algiers, but the Anders Lachmann of the Nazi-controlled Condor air line, whom she had first met in an air pageant in Brazil. And Mike forgot that tomorrow might be the day when death caught up with him above the desert where death had been stalking him for years. It was still tonight, and their dream was there beside them under the Egyptian stars.

Sometimes at the *'Auberge des Pyramides'* they joined friends for drinks. Those friends were no more than casual acquaintances made in the shifting world of wartime Cairo, but they were always young men of the same sort as Mike Marchand, except that they saw war as an adventure rather than a cause. His uniform was always correct, but the young men of Raiding Forces Mediterranean and Special Boat Services, whose mission by sea was the same as his by air, were much given to unorthodox attire. General Montgomery with his berets and his badges had started the trend, and the suède shoes, corduroy trousers and scarves worn by the trendiest of the Marchands' friends had earned them the title of The Groppi Grenadiers. Not that any of them were seen in Groppi's famous tearoom, where ladies went for morning coffee and light luncheons after shopping at Cicurel's the Harrods of Cairo, or a session of sewing and knitting for the troops.

'Mrs. Marchand can't cast on a sock, let alone turn the heel!' said one censorious lady to another, on Dina's first and only appearance at a knitting party, where she was reduced to holding a skein of wool on her hands while another girl wound it. 'Mrs. Marchand can't hem a simple seam on a hospital nightshirt!' they said at the sewing party, and the tea volunteers, none of them under fifty, said Mrs. Marchand wasn't perhaps *quite* the right person to serve tea to the dear soldiers at the YMCA. Very attractive, of course, but perhaps *too* exotic!—They had heard the wolf whistles which greeted Dina when she took her place at the tea urn.

'My dear, what did you *do* with yourself before you were married?' said one 'voluntary worker' when Dina made a conspicuous failure of tying up book parcels for the military hospital at Ismailia. 'Really, your fingers are all thumbs!'

'Not when I'm flying,' said Dina, and that was the real problem. She was grounded, as surely as Mike Marchand had been grounded until a Jewish doctor in Rio de Janeiro cured the ear ailment which had given him vertigo, but unlike her husband Dina Marchand had no hope of flying again. At least not in Egypt, and while she was more than willing to do war work it seemed that apart from sewing and knitting every niche was filled, and jealously guarded by the 'old hands' who had been in Egypt since the palmy days between the wars. They were as intent on preserving their way of life as their opposite numbers of the British Raj in India.

'Well, darling, why don't you go oftener to the Sporting Club? There's always plenty going on there,' suggested Mike, when he realised how difficult Dina found it to fill her days. 'Get up a tennis four, or take a golf lesson, or something.'

'I haven't played tennis since I was at boarding-school.'

'Start again then, you might be quite good. And there's always the pool—'

'I don't care for swimming in fresh water.' Mike's exasperated sigh was stifled in their bedroom wardrobe, where he was rummaging for what he called his lucky muffler. It was one of the silk scarves printed with maps, issued to pilots in case of baling out over enemy territory, and Mike delighted in it because the pre-World War I name of Montenegro appeared in place of Albania. Dina found it for him.

'You're right, I ought to swim oftener,' she said. 'Will you pick me up at the pool when you come off duty?'

'Of course I will, darling. Kiss me, and look after yourself.'

In a few minutes she heard the roar of the supercharger as the MG started for Heliopolis, and Dina smiled. It would be worth spending the afternoon at Gezira to see the women clustering round Flight-Lieutenant Marchand as soon as he arrived.

She had never been able to adapt herself to the tempo of life in Cairo. Since her first night at Shepheard's, when the outdoor cinema and the barking of pariah dogs had kept her awake for hours, Dina had slept uneasily, for even in the residential quarter where they lived there was always the sound of dogs and of mysterious wailing. At daybreak there was the call of the muezzin and the song of the boatmen on the Nile, mingled with Ahmed's knocking and the ringing of Mike's alarm clock on flying mornings, and Dina's fitful sleep was over for the night. If she could have slept in the afternoon all might have been well, but accustomed to working through the busy afternoons at home in Rio, Dina could not compose her body for the long siesta which even in midwinter closed every shop and office in Cairo from one o'clock to half past five. It was miserable to stay in the flat, tossing hot and wakeful on her rumpled bed. It was less miserable, but still boring, to cross the bridge to Gezira Island, and lie in a deck chair in a shaded corner of the club lawns.

Dina could not know that the days of British Gezira were numbered as surely as the days of King Farouk. She thought the Sporting Club was a pretty place, with the Nile flowing round the island, and the nannies watching over the English babies asleep in their prams, and often wondered why so many of the women she met were so disagreeable. Born into a multi-racial country and working with the happy-go-luck Cariocas of Rio de Janeiro, Dina had no idea of the petty jealousies which tormented so many of the women of the Gezira Club. They were all enjoying a degree of luxury and leisure which few of them had known in Britain, and they were hanging on to their privileges with all their might. Like barnyard hens they spread their wings against the bird of paradise, and Mrs. Marchand was that bird, the challenger. Her skin, which never flushed or freckled, was the wrong colour. Her hair, which never frizzed in humid weather, was too black. ('D'you suppose she dyes it?') Her cheek-bones, well, my dear, they made her look like a Red Indian. Where did poor Mr. Marchand pick her up? Of course he's French himself (sniff) although he *looks* all right, and my husband quite likes him. For the critics of Gezira, Dina might as well have been born in Bengal as in Brazil, for she was known to all comers by the name the RASC major's wife had given her, and was called 'the chee-chee girl'.

The weather was more humid in February, and Dina grew more limp and less inclined to storm the closed world of Gezira. The Club was more like a British cantonment, prepared to face the mutinous sepoys of ninety years before, than a sports and social meeting-place as the bad news of February 1943 accumulated. The Allies were coping with two major set-backs in Italy, the siege of Monte Cassino and the unsuccessful landing at Anzio, while nearer Cairo there were predictions of a Communist *coup d'état* in Greece. What was not spoken of at Gezira but known in the inner circles— just as the decisions of the Cairo/Teheran conference were known —was that a new trial was preparing for battered England in the form of a secret weapon which Hitler was planning to launch from sites on the Channel coast. Mike Marchand often picked up such fragments of information if he came off duty early and dropped in for a glass of Stella beer at 'The Cock and Bull' which bore enough resemblance to an English pub to attract the editors of the British army newspaper, who were full of news the censor wouldn't pass.

Dina was only mildly interested in the secret weapon. She was moody these days, and Ahmed and Anwar were the first to suffer. Now that Ladyship had learned to count in Egyptian currency every akka was questioned, and she had started complaining about cooking smells. For Dina felt queasy enough to dread another attack of 'Gyppy tummy' and had put herself back on a régime of charcoal biscuits.

More than the two houseboys, her husband suffered from Dina's moods. It was a grievance that he had never once allowed her to be at Heliopolis when he took off on a reconnaissance mission, nor to watch him return with his mission accomplished. She had never even seen Heliopolis, except on that one occasion when they flew to Beirut! In vain Mike explained that that had been a special privilege, winked at by authority but never to be repeated; that Heliopolis was a military airfield with strict security rules, and that as for his landings, these were always followed by a long debriefing. He wouldn't want to keep her hanging around. At this point Dina burst into tears.

She hadn't treated *him* like that, she said between sobs, when he was grounded in Brazil. She'd found a doctor for him, she'd let him fly her Puss Moth, she'd made Tony give him a chance on the Beechcrafts—everything! And now he wouldn't even talk to her about his recces! Mike then made the mistake of being funny, and asked her if she wanted to take up a Halifax bomber and fly an operational sortie over Crete.

At least it made her angry enough to stop crying. She went to bed in all the indulgence of being misunderstood. It was true that Mike Marchand had never fully understood how closely Dina's vocation as a flyer parallelled his own. Because her experience as a pilot was necessarily more limited than his, he supposed it to be less deep, which was not the case. If she never rose to Mike's emotional and indeed mystical approach to flying—an attitude copied from his early heroes—Dina had set herself to be a commercial airline pilot from her schooldays, and had made herself a good one. Cut off from the world she knew best, she had begun to feel herself rejected by the one she loved the most.

But Dina's reminder of the days when he flew her Puss Moth out of Santos Dumont airport had made its mark on Mike. He knew that without Dina's faith there would have been no come-back for Michel Marchand, no RAF, no war. He went off to Heliopolis before she was awake next morning, wondering how he could make it up to her. By three o'clock he was back in the Sharia-el-Nil, rousing Ahmed from his siesta in the pantry. He learned that Ladyship had gone to Gezira, went on foot over the bridge to the island, and hunted across the Club lawns until he saw her sitting beside two other women near the pool. She jumped up when she saw Mike and came running, looking her lovely eager self again, so that he caught her in his arms to the great satisfaction of a nanny walking a toddler along the path. Ever so nice they looked, the tall, fair RAF officer and the girl in the white dress, just like a picture in a magazine! The two women Dina had been trying to talk to thought otherwise. The Sporting Club was going to the dogs, their glances said, when a Frenchman could stand there in broad daylight, kissing a chee-chee girl.

'You're back, darling, how marvellous!' exulted Dina. 'Didn't you fly today?'

'Not me, I was in a briefing session all the morning. I've got some wonderful news for you, Dina!'

'Oh, what?'

Mike took her arm and drew her out of earshot. Then he said, 'Pack your bags, darling! We're going back to France.'

He repented of his teasing when he saw his wife's bewilderment. 'To France? But I thought—How can we be?' she stammered, and Mike had to tell her he wasn't posted to metropolitan France exactly, but to Corsica.

'I thought Corsica was an island!'

'So it is, but it's also a French Department, and the Corsicans themselves liberated it nearly six months ago. Think, Dina! It's not much more than an hour's flight from Nice, and an hour and a half from Naples.'

'When do we leave?' asked Dina fearfully.

'I report at Bastia on the fifth of March, that's a week from today. We'll try to get you out to Naples a day or two earlier, to see what Tony can fix up for you.'

As soon as she understood that she was not to be left behind in Cairo, the fate she had secretly dreaded, Dina's excitement matched

Mike's own. She was bubbling over with plans as they walked back to the flat where Ahmed and Anwar, scenting change, had polished the electro-plated tea service that was seldom used, and were prepared to serve tea to the best employers, meaning the easiest to cheat, they were likely to have while the British remained in Egypt.

Not all the inhabitants of Corsica regarded themselves as French citizens, nor wished the *Ile de Beauté* to continue as a Department of the French Republic, but when he landed at Bastia on March 5 Mike Marchand was happy to think that he was back in France. He heard French spoken all around him. He met French colleagues in the newly-formed Photographic Reconnaissance Flight, bunked with them in the crew quarters at the Borga airfield, and lined up for Spam with them in the American mess. By dint of keeping quiet and not arguing, he soon got a better idea than he could ever have in Cairo of the latest intrigues in the 'crab-pot' of Algiers.

Corsica had contributed largely to the downfall of General Giraud. His action, as commander-in-chief, in despatching French troops from North Africa to assist in the liberation of the island without consulting de Gaulle, had brought swift punishment from General 'Wormwood'. On October 1, three days before Corsica was completely liberated, he persuaded the augmented French Committee of National Liberation to vote for a single President to whom the French commander-in-chief would be subordinate. Of course they voted for de Gaulle, from whom Giraud must henceforth take his orders; it was well for the conduct of the war that the French Expeditionary Corps had already been organised by Giraud and equipped by the Americans. The first units of this Corps arrived in Italy on December 8, and were fighting alongside the US Fifth Army.

The French Committee met regularly in a girls' high school in Algiers, on the same lines as the original committee had met in London. The members were permitted to state their views on the subject under discussion, but not to vote. 'Wormwood' had the right to sum up, and then the committee adjourned. They had been supplemented since September by what de Gaulle called the Consultative Assembly, a much larger body of eighty-seven members, no fewer than thirty-five of whom were former legislators, as if the Third Republic had been told it was dead but refused to lie down and die.

176

Any fool could see that in the French Committee and the Consultative Assembly Charles de Gaulle was setting up what he hoped would be the future government and parliament of post-war France. Yet although the Frenchmen Mike Marchand met in Corsica were no fools they were not primarily interested in these manoeuvres. What was most often discussed in the mess was the beginning of the purge which might be expected to follow in France as de Gaulle began his revenge upon his adversaries.

These adversaries were French, not German. It was General Juin's men who were fighting the Germans in the desperate battles against Hitler's Winter Line. De Gaulle, in Algiers, had imprisoned three Frenchmen who had fallen into his power: Pierre Flandin, who for a time had been the Vichy Foreign Minister, Marcel Peyrouton, Pétain's former Minister of the Interior whom Admiral Darlan had appointed Governor-General of Algiers, and an elderly man called Boisson, in 'Wormwood's' eyes the chief of the three criminals.

Boisson had been the Governor of French West Africa when de Gaulle made his abortive attempt to land at Dakar in September 1940. With the sturdy words, 'France has entrusted me with Dakar. I will defend Dakar to the death,' he had fought off the attack by the British and elements of the Free French, and put de Gaulle to flight. Two years later, after the Allied landings in North Africa, Boisson had brought over the whole of his territory to the Allied side without bloodshed. He had been powerful in Algeria, and survived for a few months after 'Wormwood' came to Algiers, but he was at the mercy of an elephantine memory, one which never forgot a slight or even a criticism, and on December 21 Boisson, who had lost a leg at Verdun in the defence of France, was thrown into an Algerian prison. It took Allied disapproval, Mr. Churchill's scolding and above all President Roosevelt's fury, to set him free.

That was an indication of the wrath to come, and Michel Marchand was not the only Frenchman in the Allied air pool in the Mediterranean theatre of war to feel a cold wind from the future. Meantime he was excited by the great upsurge of activity in Corsica, which was being turned into a vast aircraft carrier for the duration of the war.

The airfield of Borga, where he reported for duty, lay twenty-five kilometres south of Bastia, protected from the sea by a narrow spit of land enclosing a lagoon called the Etang de Biguglia. It was only one, although the most important, of the seventeen airfields being laid out on the eastern side of the island, from which the Allied air forces were bombarding northern Italy, Austria and Germany, and preparing to support Operation Anvil, the landing in the south of France planned to coincide with the cross-Channel invasion. Mike had only to overfly Bastia harbour, or even look out across the lagoon or the Golo River, to see shipping building up in the Tyrrhenian Sea for the landing in Provence.

He spent a week at Borga before he flew a reconnaissance mission, getting used to the twin-engined Lightning P38 with the six fuel tanks of which two were jettisoned en route to lighten the plane for the return. There was a good deal of map work to be done, what was called 'ploughing the area', to combine a mapping mission with aerial photography, and then he was ordered to overfly a very familiar coast. He had expected to be moved when he flew over the soil of France again, but when the moment came he was too intent on dodging the flak to have time for sentiment. Intelligence reports stated that Field-Marshal Kesselring, the German C-in-C in Italy, expected the invasion to take place between Menton and Imperia on the Italian Riviera, and Mike's orders were to bring back photographs of the fortifications along that part of the coast. It was strange to look down on Menton and remember going home for the holidays with his cousin Jacques when they were both at the Ecole des Roches. He wondered if Jacques were down there now, plodding away at his law books. There was no sign of enemy activities across the mountains, and Mike took pictures of Fort Castillon, where the swastika was flying, and the blockhouses and casemates round Sospel.

When he landed at Borga, cut his engines and pushed up the Plexiglass cover of his aircraft, one of the ground staff came running across the tarmac. 'Signal for you, sir,' he said. 'Thought you'd like to see it before you go for your debriefing.' He watched sympathetically as Mike read the message and gave a whoop of joy. 'My wife's coming in from Naples the day after tomorrow,' he said. 'My God, I was beginning to think she wasn't going to make it!' For even Tony da Costa, that accomplished fixer, had not found it easy to get Dina on a flight from Naples/Pomigliano to Bastia.

'What's the chance of a ride into town?' asked Mike when he was on the ground. A supply truck going up in an hour? Fine, he should be able to manage that. The MG had been sold before he left

Cairo, and one of Mike's problems was how to get hold of transportation for Dina and himself. Dina's trip all set! His high spirits lasted through his session with the Interrogation Officer, and the half-hour ride in the truck taking parcels of American food to the hungry citizens of Bastia.

The day of Dina's arrival was a Monday, and Mike spent the morning on a mission west of Cannes, nearer the true target area of the invasion, recording the blockhouses and antitank walls which the Germans were strengthening along the coast. He returned late, and spent a long time with the Interrogation Officer, so that the midday meal had ended before he was free. He broke out a pack of C-rations from his locker and ate the contents of it philosophically. Tonight he and Dina would have a black market dinner down in the Vieux Port, just to celebrate her arrival, and thank God he'd been able to borrow a jeep from the car pool.

The sun was shining from a sky of lapis-lazuli blue, the Tyrrhenian Sea gave back the colour, and the met. report was excellent. There was no reason at all why the damned Dakota should be late, unless the Yanks at Naples had taken it into their heads to cancel the courier run. Mike was as keyed up as he had been four months ago, when he was waiting for Dina and Tony to arrive from Khartoum, and after a good deal of kidding his American friends were sympathetic enough to let him watch the radar screen when the Dakota came in across Cap Corse and flew steadily south over Bastia.

'Here she comes!' They were talking about the aircraft, but he was thinking about Dina, and hoping she'd be the first off the plane. She was not. There was a rush of young GIs in heavy kapok jackets who he guessed had hitched a ride as well as Dina, and then she appeared herself, with a wave and a word for somebody behind her, and she was wearing a flying suit.

'What the devil are you dressed up like that for?' He had hardly kissed her when he blurted it out.

'The pilot thought I might be cold.'

'You little liar,' said her husband fondly. 'He let you take the controls, didn't he?'

'Only for ten minutes,' said Dina. 'I told him I was qualified.'

'Qualified!' said Mike. 'Suppose you'd had a Messerschmitt on your tail?'

'Oh, don't scold me, darling!' she pleaded. 'It was wonderful!'

'Yes, I know,' said Mike. 'But where you're going to change out of that outfit, I don't know.' There was no such thing as a women's washroom at the rudimentary American airfield.

'It's all right,' said Dina, 'I'm wearing slacks underneath.' With complete unconcern she unzipped the flying suit and stepped out of it, handing the garment to a hypnotised mechanic.

'Where'd you get the slacks?' The whole thing was getting to be like a replay of one of their old days at Santos Dumont. Dina was tall enough and slim enough to look well in black slacks, and as in the old days she was wearing a black sweater and a white leather helmet.

'Tony bought them for me at the PX in Naples.'

'Good idea, slacks,' said Mike, walking her towards the gate. 'We're going in to Bastia in a jeep.'

'I've been jeeping round Naples for the last ten days.' There was a group of men round the jeep, and some eager beaver had put Dina's two suitcases in the back.

'This is Tom, and this is Jean-Paul, and this is Greg, and this English type is Basil,' said Mike, with a circular wave of his hand. 'And this is my wife. Come and have a drink with us tomorrow night, you chaps. Right now we want to get into town.'

Dina was laughing as she said 'Hallo! Goodbye! See you soon!' to the admiring airmen. But her laughter died as they turned into the pock-marked highway, where the rubble of what had once been homes showed how fiercely the Germans had defended the way to Bastia. 'Is it bad in the town, darling?' she hazarded.

'Pretty bad. Bastia was harder hit than any other place in Corsica; Ajaccio got off scot free by comparison. But it's all relative, Dina—how about Naples?'

'Naples was unbelievable,' she said slowly. 'Between the bombing and the shelling, I don't see how they can ever build it up again. And the people are in rags, Mike, ready to steal the shirt off your back if they think they can get away with it, and all the time so cheerful—I don't understand.'

He glanced at her sideways as she sat beside him in the jeep, and it seemed to Mike Marchand that there was a change in his wife's face, which perhaps came of looking for the first time into the unmasked face of war.

'And how's Tony?' he asked.

'Tony is very uncomfortable, perishing with cold, in a very grand room at the Palace of Caserta. He's beginning to think he made a bad mistake in not going back to Rio with Marshal de Moraes.'

'Because of the cold?'

'No, because he thinks he could have done a better job there than here. Too much politicking in Rio, just as he feared.'

'They must be learning fast in Rio,' said Mike drily. 'Did you stay at Caserta too?'

'Yes, in a medical centre. An American army nurse let me share her room while I was there. Tony had a jeep, of course, and we went into Naples for our meals—you know the sort.'

'You and I are going to have one of that sort in a couple of hours, in that little bistro by the harbour.' He pointed down from the high road of the Terra Vecchia to the old harbour, with the fishing boats of the Vieux Port at their moorings, and the Cathedral of St. John the Baptist rising protectively above. Round a half moon of shell-damaged buildings they drove into the Place St. Nicholas.

'I got us a room at the Cyrnos Palace,' he said. 'It's hardly the Hotel St. Georges, but there's nothing better to be had. Mind—don't trip—the carpet's torn.'

'Oh, I like this place,' Dina told Mike twenty minutes later, coming to lean beside him on the windowsill. Dina had washed, and was wearing a dark wool dress with the little white Brazilian shawl he liked tied round her shoulders. The sun had warmed the room all day, and now the cool evening air was coming fresh off the sea through the window Mike had opened wide.

'It's big enough,' said Mike, 'and it seems to be quite clean.' He looked round critically at the huge old-fashioned bedroom, which like everything else in Bastia seemed to date from the Second Empire, when Napoleon III was trying to revive his uncle's Corsican legend.

'Oh, I didn't mean the room!' said Dina. 'I meant I like to be near the sea, but high up, and able to see the people in that lovely square—' She pointed down at the Place St. Nicholas, where a statue of the great Bonaparte stood near a bandstand placed in the centre of the square. The citizens of Bastia, hungry but victorious, were starting their evening promenade under the budding trees.

'You like it better than Cairo, do you?'

'Well—it's more like *us*, isn't it?' Mike nodded. He knew what she meant. It was European, not African; humanly speaking, it was the ancestor of Brazil. His clasp tightened on her waist.

'Did you miss me, darling?' 'Yes.' 'Terribly?' 'Terribly—' 'Like this?' She put her hand over his, where it lay on her breast.

'Mike, wait—listen! I want to tell you something. I—when I was at Caserta I got that American nurse I told you about, to take me to see a doctor.'

'A doctor! Dina, were you sick?'

'No, I'd stopped feeling sick by that time.'

'Dina!'

'We're going to have a baby, Mike.'

While he was kissing her, and telling her how glad he was, how proud, how much he loved her, more than ever now, it came to Mike Marchand with absolute conviction that he would survive the war and live to see his son.

TWELVE.

While so many people enjoyed the winter in Egypt, very few enjoyed the winter in the south of France. It was the hardest winter of the war, with rations cut to a minimum, new restrictions everywhere, and the hand of German oppression heavy on the land. For some of those who had already taken to the maquis it was also the last winter. Between October 1943 and the first of May twelve hundred maquisards died victims of the ruthless German hunters.

They were tracked through the forests by police dogs, and if they were wounded dragged helpless from the wards of such hospitals as dared to take them in. If they ambushed and killed a few unwary German soldiers the men of a whole village might be taken hostages and shot. As well as their own lives they risked the lives of their wives and children, who could be picked up in a raid and bundled into the cattle trucks for Auschwitz. But the Resistance had taken hold in France, and it survived.

The Gestapo had a headquarters in Menton now, though no one would admit to knowing where. '*La Geste*', as the boys of Jacques Brunel's group had jokingly called it, now ceased to be a joke, and the boys themselves were keeping out of sight. Their future was a problem, for as all forms of charity but their own were despised by the Germans, orders had been given for homes for the aged and children's holiday colonies to be closed down. 'Let the brats go back to Paris, or wherever they came from,' said the commandant. 'The buildings at the St. Michel home will be requisitioned for a *Soldatenheim*, and used for our own convalescents. Give the French three days to clear the post and cordon off the area.'

'Polly, what are we going to do?' said Jacques, when Polly brought home the news of this development. She had never known him to be so despondent, or so much at a loss. 'Here's Dany and the other two boys back on our hands, and what about Léo and Pierre at Les Colombières? They can't stay in that unheated hut much longer. If it was summer they could take to the forest, but not with winter coming on.' He sketched a hopeless gesture with one hand.

'I asked the director if I could fetch the children from Albaréa, or half of them, in the bus, but he said no,' said Polly. 'A German truck's going to bring them all here tomorrow and round the whole lot up for Paris.'

'Please God they won't be rounded up for Germany.'

Polly sighed. 'I thought I might get Dany in the bus as well, and drop him off at the Col de Castillon,' she said. 'Don't you think they'll all have to go back to the Jurac farm?'

'Only if old Jurac agrees. Have we enough petrol to get up there tomorrow, darling?'

'Plenty, in the little garage,' she said, meaning their own lock-up on the Quai Bonaparte. 'But we've seen the end of the extra petrol, I'm afraid.'

'We'll have to liberate some more.'

Jacques had said 'Have *we* enough?' but he didn't mean to take Polly up the mountain. He sent her on an errand to Miss Torrance, and told her to keep her eyes open at the St. Michel home. It would be interesting to know what happened to that handy little bus with the Red Cross painted on its sides. And on being stopped by a German patrol at Monti (they were everywhere, damn them!) Maître Brunel with his impeccable I/D and his excellent German easily convinced the sergeant that he was on a legitimate journey to make the Will of an ailing old man.

Monsieur Jurac cackled when he heard the story. 'Draw me up a Will if you like, monsieur,' he said, 'it'll be something to show if the Boches take it into their heads to search the house. Everything to Dany, he's my only grandchild, and I'm proud of the way he's turned out. I was wild when my daughter went to the bad and had to marry that gangster Profetti, and the boy was spoiled rotten between the two of them. But last winter did him a power of good. I want to be sure the land'll belong to him when I'm dead and gone.'

'All right, Monsieur Jurac, I'll see to it, but can you face another winter with six boys to feed, and the Boches on your doorstep? You'll be well paid for their keep, of course—'

Jacques was glad to be able to say that. The money he brought from London was all spent, but his father had sent him an impressive sun through the Swiss bank Lombard and Odier, who had ways and means of distributing money to various towns in France, and Jacques had received his (earmarked, of course, for the *étude* Brunel) through the Banque Palméro at Menton. It made Jacques happy to think that the money his father got for renting his house to the Germans was being ploughed back into the French Resistance.

He shared a magnificent dish of pheasant with the Juracs and Bébé, who had shot the brace of birds himself, and old Madame Jurac told him to bring *la petite dame* to see her soon. It was a cheerful meal, and Jacques knew that two years back he would have missed it, for then he would have talked to Jurac in the sunny yard, bowed distantly to his wife, and gone on his way. It was Polly with her quick friendliness who had broken down his reserve and taught him to be friendly too.

Dany, Jojo and Gigène left the St. Michel home even before the children did, and spent a couple of nights under Miss Torrance's roof. If that lady thought her occasional lodger, Monsieur Aletti, had some oddly assorted friends, she never said so, and why should she? Monsieur Aletti paid for his accommodation in advance. When the first three had gone, driven up to the Col de Castillon under the canvas cover of Jean Dupont's grocery van, she welcomed Pierre and Léo until they could travel in the same way. They were just in time, for a week later the Germans closed the mountain road at Monti, saying there was too much traffic between Menton and Sospel. The mountain farmers could go to Sospel for their rations, if they were so fond of baker's bread.

Jacques Brunel went up to the farm with Pierre and Léo and spent the night on the hills, going over the old tracks behind Fort Castillon which he and Mike Marchand had known as boys, and tested his half-forgotten woodcraft by returning through the great Ubac Foran, the forest of Menton. He lost his way once or twice, for the night was dark, and when the rain began to fall he was soaked to the skin. Polly scolded when he came home after the curfew was lifted, dripping and chilled. She predicted a bad cold, which developed by the next day, and turned into a sharp bout of influenza.

Jacques rather enjoyed a few days in bed, being nursed by three capable women. Norine made him hot lemon drinks with fruit from her own garden, and Polly stood in line at the fish stall outside the market for a morsel of sole to tempt his appetite. Miss Torrance used all her ration of flour to make some Russian cakes, as enjoyed by the dear prince and all the princely family, and as made by their chef when they all lived in St. Petersburg. On the first day he was too feverish to talk long to Miss Torrance, but when dusk fell he liked to look at the candle burning in the little *lampadka* she had given Polly to put underneath the ikon of the Virgin of Kazan.

'You're doing too much, darling,' Jacques told Polly when he was up and dressed and sitting by the stove in the living room. It was fairly warm there compared with the big bedroom, where the only heat they had came from a 200-watt one-bar radiator which worked off a lighting point and gave as much warmth as a box of matches.

'What, carrying in a few logs?' said Polly. 'Norine built them up very neatly in the lobby, and I don't even have to go down a cellar stair to fetch them.'

'I sometimes wish we had a cellar. How's the wine situation?'

'Good enough to make you hot mulled wine at bedtime.'

'Just like a ski-ing holiday,' said Jacques, and Polly giggled. She was sitting on a little rug in front of the blue porcelain stove, through the red mica window of which a heartening glow was seen.

'I wonder why people are always so surprised here when the weather's bad or the mistral blows,' she said. 'It was just the same at Naples. My stepfather used to treat bad weather as a personal affront. Naples was supposed to be all "*O Sole Mio*" and "*Santa Lucia*" according to him. I wonder what it's like in Naples now,' she finished, with her eyes on the mica glow.

Jacques stroked the brown hair. Not as silky as it used to be, not as bright. Polly might say she wasn't tired, wasn't doing too much, but her pallor and her dull hair showed not the lack of cosmetics— those were still obtainable, even outside Paris—but of fats and proteins and all the proper food which gave good health and energy. There were millions of Frenchwomen in the same condition.

'You know Marcelle and Louis want you to visit them after the New Year,' he said, and she looked up with sudden interest.

'They asked us both,' she said. 'If we got a railway permit, could you go too?'

'Hardly.'

'What makes you think I'd want to go alone?'

'You'd get a rest, and some decent food for a change. I'm sure Marcelle's pantry shelves will be crammed with good things for the holidays.'

'Pooh,' said Polly. 'I don't need a rest. I've hardly been busy at all since the St. Michel home closed down. And as for goodies, just wait till you see what Norine and I have planned for Christmas!'

'Oh, Polly,' he said, and turned her face up to his, 'you really are a darling. We'll keep our first Christmas alone, just the two of us —and our first New Year.'

'But no celebrations,' she said. 'I don't want to remember last New Year's Eve, and poor little Patrick Malvy's death. We'll wait until it's daylight on New Year's Day, and then we'll drink a toast to 1944—the year of Liberation!'

It was a nice thought. But Jacques, as soon as he was back at his office, decided it would be a pity not to see the Old Year out in style. So he made his plans accordingly, and when midnight struck the Germans, like the Italians before them, found their biggest petrol dump in flames, and a blaze lighting up the night sky which could be seen in Nice.

'Good show,' said Maxwell, when he came to Menton a few days later. 'How about punishment?'

'They sent the officer on guard at the dump and his platoon to the Russian front, and stopped the whole town's rations for a week. Sometimes you'd really think they're simpletons. As if most people didn't have emergency supplies to last ten days! But the gas we blew was going to their tanks in Italy, so we may have done the Allies a bit of good.'

'How d'you know?'

'About the gas? The German commandant told me, when he came in to arrange about the transfer of my father's villa. He's got to report to Berlin, so it looks as if he's had it too, but the lease covers his successors for the duration of the war. I asked him his successor's name. He said he didn't know.'

'He'll be heard of hanging from a meat-hook next, the way he's let the Menton terrorists get out of hand. But I thought your clerk handled the Villa Mon Bijou problem for you.'

'Janot sees that the rent's paid—and it *is* paid on the dot—but the fellow asked to see me personally, and I thought why not? He wanted to apologise to me for taking the name "Mon Bijou" off the gate post, as being unsuitable for military occupation. I said his action was a fine example of the famous German good taste, that I'd always disliked the name myself, and they could call it "Haus Hitler" for all I cared.'

'What did he say to that?'

'He was very gratified, and begged me to use my influence in the town for the maintenance of law and order. Have a cigarette?'

Maxwell struck a match for them both. 'You're a cool hand, Jack, as I've said before, but you'd better lie low for a bit till you see how the new man turns out. Any word about Orengo?'

'Nothing. I hoped he'd be released, if he's still alive, at the time of the Italian armistice, but not a word. His wife and family are with her parents in Lyon ... Charles, when do we get some useful weapons? I daren't risk a shoot-out with machine pistols and Stens.'

'You're not to risk a shoot-out at any time, till London gives the word. I've brought you a couple of two-inch mortars and ammo. They're handy little weapons—'

'For producing smoke, maybe.'

'Jack, I don't think you quite understand the position. The RAF ran one hundred and thirty dropping operations in December, and only two of them succeeded. There just isn't the matériel to go round. And—I know this doesn't apply to your group—there've been too many complaints of misuse of the containers. Stuff left to rust on the ground, or sold on the black market, or worse, sold to the *Milice*. You have to face it, there's been some pretty serious infiltration of the Resistance.'

'It doesn't take an infiltrator,' said Jacques bitterly. 'What do you think of General de Lattre going over to de Gaulle?'

'It's not my business to think,' said Maxwell. He knew the facts. General de Lattre de Tassigny, who had refused to join de Gaulle in 1940, had been flown to London after his spectacular escape from Riom prison in September, and after a spell of recuperation in the Middlesex Hospital had arrived in Algiers just before Christmas. There he was offered the command of 'Army B'—'Army A', otherwise the French Expeditionary Corps, being on active service in Italy.

'It's none of my business,' Maxwell repeated, after a look at the handsome sullen face before him, 'but if it comes to a landing in the south of France de Lattre might be the very man to lead your troops in battle. And he'd be fighting under an Allied commander, don't forget that.'

'And with the authority of the *Chef des Armées*, General de Gaulle,' said Jacques. ' "*Chef des Armées*" indeed! De Gaulle hasn't heard a shot fired in anger since Dakar.'

'Jack, does it never occur to you that you may be wrong?'

'About General de Gaulle?'

'No, not if de Gaulle's all you say he is, but about the men who've accepted him and what he stands for. They can't *all* be villains! Juin and Béthouart and de Lattre are good soldiers. You said yourself there were good men, like Georges Bidault, at that meeting with Jean Moulin at Lyon. And surely there must be some decent chaps in this new Assembly at Algiers.'

'Time will tell,' said Jacques, and so they left it. Only Polly knew the depth of her husband's disillusion with the men who had 'climbed on the bandwagon'—an American expression she herself had taught him. Only Polly knew how weary he was of the pettifogging details of daily life in a solicitor's office. He visited his chambers in Nice from time to time, and usually looked in at his empty flat, although his appearance at the Palais Lascaris was the signal for most of the other tenants to pour out on to the painted staircase with shrill demands for his help in securing their squatters' rights. The City of Nice, as had been foreseen, was having great trouble in obtaining the eviction orders.

It was ironical that Maître Brunel had obtained three eviction orders for clients in Menton, pleading in the Cour de Petite Instance where his father had pled so many times before him. It was not pleasant to enter the Palais de Justice through a door over which the swastika flew under a banner with the usual boast, 'Germany Victorious on All Fronts!' But he had to do it, not only for the sake of the future but as a means of keeping in touch with the group of resistants in Nice which included Paul, a policeman at the law courts, and Edouard, a valuable clerk in the Préfecture de Police. And pleading a case, however trifling, made up for the long hours spent in his Menton office, patiently listening to the clients who shuffled forward one by one, or more often as married couples, to tell their tale of woe to Maître Brunel.

In spite of the Occupation, life went on. There was always a marriage contract to be drawn up or a Will to be changed, or the purchase of a property *en viager*, which meant that the owners gave up their title to a third party in exchange for a fund to be enjoyed during their lifetime. '*Deux têtes, 83 et 79 ans*', was how a *viager* was advertised in the local paper, and Jacques often felt a pang of pity, quite misplaced, as the owners of the two white heads were led into his private room by Christophe Monnier.

These were not trivial matters, but Jacques felt he had sunk very low when he was consulted on *disputes entre voisins* which, as he tried to explain, should be referred to the police station. He reached a low point on the April afternoon when he had to cope with two 'quarrels between neighbours'. One good lady desired to issue a summons against the people next door, who kept a cockerel which woke her up at three o'clock every morning. She was followed by a married couple who wanted to 'pursue in justice' *their* next door neighbours, who were throwing garbage into their personal dustbin. Jacques knew in theory that *les poubelles* were the top cause of annoyance in the town, taking precedence even over music after ten o'clock at night, but he had never been consulted on the rubbish bins before, and he went home that night dejected. Polly, who knew that he had not completely recovered from his bout of 'flu, threw a log in the stove and brought him a restorative brandy and water. It was late April, and the sun had been shining, but when evening came the big room grew chilly, and Polly was bundled into a heavy sweater and a cardigan.

'Darling, it sounds like an awful bore,' she said when he described his afternoon. 'Crowing cocks and garbage, no wonder you were mad. But just think how it'll pay off in the end.'

'I won't be able to buy you diamonds with the money I made this afternoon, sweet.'

'I wasn't thinking about diamonds, I was thinking about something else. When we came to live here first you used to tell me you once hoped to be the mayor of Menton and a Deputy for the Alpes Maritimes.'

'That was kid stuff, Polly.'

'Only kid stuff? Don't you still care about it? I think you do.'

'To be mayor of Menton, mayor and Deputy? That's a forlorn hope, my dear.'

'No it's not. Everybody knows you now and everybody trusts you. When the time comes they'll all vote for the man who sweated out the Occupation with them in Menton.'

'They're more likely to vote for some hero who sat out the war in London with de Gaulle.'

'But promise me you'll try, Jacques!'

'*Ma pauvre chérie,*' said her husband, kissing her, 'I believe you think I could be the President of the Republic.'

'I'll settle for prime minister,' Polly said, and Jacques shouted with laughter. By which she knew that she had pulled him out of his depression, and when she heard him whistling in the bathroom she wished fervently that she could complete the process by giving him a satisfying dinner. It was a long time since Julien Monnier had been able to sell her a juicy steak, or even a slice of liver. There was nothing to eat but some artichokes, the small tender ones called *les violets*, and a local dish called *le tian*. It consisted chiefly of baked tomatoes, courgettes and potatoes, but even on that scanty fare Jacques' good spirits persisted, and the next day brought another bit of cheer. It was a letter from Mike Marchand, saying he had been posted to Bastia, and was with his wife at the Cyrnos Palace Hotel.

'Maybe we'll all be meeting soon!' said Polly. 'I feel I know your cousin Mike already. I wonder what Dina'll be like! ... What's the matter, Jacques?' He was studying the crumpled envelope.

'This letter's postmarked Nice,' he said.

'What of it? Mike got somebody to post it for him.'

'Which means the felucca line's begun operating again. I'll check with Henri Froment next time I go to Nice.'

'When will that be?'

'Some time next week.'

It turned out to be some time next day. About ten o'clock next morning the phone in Jacques' private office rang, and the familiar voice of Maxwell, with the accent more 'Marseille' than any Marseillais, said *'Bonjour maître*! A client of yours has been arrested, and would like to consult you as soon as possible.'

'A regular client? Have I acted for him before?'

'Yes, in that matter of the tobacco control.'

'Where are you calling from?'

'Nice central post office. I don't want to hang around here—'

'You've got the spare key to my flat?'

'Of course.'

'Wait there for me. There's a train at eleven. I'll be with you about half past twelve.'

'A bientôt.'

Jacques hung up the phone and stared unseeingly at an enlarged sepia photograph of his grandfather above the filing cabinets on the opposite wall. He was thinking of Victor Marcati doing the cigarette hold-up at Garavan, and arguing that tobacco was government controlled. Yes, but that time Totor had got away with it, now he'd actually been arrested, and what did that mean? It was too risky to prolong a call from a public phone, but Jacques would have liked to know what the charge was. Theft or terrorism? Was he in a cell at the prison of Les Baumettes, or held at some police station? If the latter, was *Totor-pour-les-dames* 'singing his head off' as they'd said of Roger Malvy when he was arrested for the murder of the child? Jacques scribbled a note to Polly, telling her he had been called to Nice, and asked Chris Monnier to deliver it on his way home to the Rue Trenca for midday dinner.

It was twenty minutes past midday when he let himself into his old flat in the Palais Lascaris. A smell of cigarette smoke told him Maxwell was in the living room, now denuded of all furniture but two old chairs and the big sofa, on which Maxwell had put a japanned tray and some oddments of plates and glasses which Polly had not thought worth taking to Menton. A litre of *vin ordinaire* and some bread and cheese in paper bags completed the luncheon preparations.

'*Salut*, Jack,' said Maxwell, getting up. 'I brought some provisions. I knew you wouldn't have time to lunch.'

'Thanks, Charles,' said Jacques. 'That's a big help, and I'm hungry.' He splashed some wine into the cheap tumbler, and cut himself a hunk of bread and black market cheese. 'Well, go ahead,' he said, 'Tell me the worst.'

'It's pretty bad.' He told the story. Victor Marcati had been taken into one of the Cannes Resistance groups and got a job on the railway, doing the same maintenance work as he'd been doing when Dany Profetti first met him at Sospel. The head of his group thought of him as a steady sort of chap, until the whole group, six in number, had been ordered to raid a *Ravitaillement* centre in Cannes and take the month's supply of ration cards and tickets to distribute to a large maquis up in the hills. It hadn't been a difficult operation, because the clerks in the rationing centre were secretly sympathetic to the maquisards, and no one was hurt in any way. But it had been too much for the Corsican, who had gambled away his wages from the railway, and he had taken the train to Nice to raid a suburban post office. Before he could get away with the money the postmaster buzzed an alarm, whereupon Marcati shot and wounded him, using the butt of his revolver to knock out the clerk who went to the postmaster's rescue. But the alarm had sounded and the police were on their way. Passers-by hindered Marcati's flight and he was captured at the end of a short chase through the streets. 'Then they threw the book at him,' concluded Maxwell. 'He was taken before the examining magistrate on two counts, armed robbery and grievous bodily harm, and was committed for trial at the next assizes.'

'At Aix-en-Provence.' Jacques drew a long breath. 'Where is he now?'

'In Les Baumettes ... I'm damned sorry, Jack. I ought to have kept a closer eye on him, especially after his exploit at Garavan, but he seemed to be doing all right with his new group—'

'You can't be everywhere,' said Jacques. 'The problem is, what are we going to do now? It's six weeks to the assizes, which means Totor can "give" two networks, the Cannes circuit *and* mine, if he wants to do a deal with the police. Hell and damnation! The man's a criminal. If it wasn't for the threat to us, I'd let him rot his guts out in the Baumettes prison. As it is—'

'You don't think we can spring him, do you?'

'I think we'll have to have a try. The Prosecutor is Vichyiste to the fingertips,' he went on, obviously thinking aloud. 'He'd be delighted to think a bunch of terrorists could be turned in—for a consideration. If he'd agree to talk to Marcati—no, that wouldn't do. I'll have to see Froment first.'

'Froment knows about all this,' said Maxwell. 'The story was in the morning paper.'

'You see the problem is not only how to spring Marcati before he gives us all away, but what to do with him when we've got him.'

'The right place for him is back in Corsica.'

'It's certainly more suited to his talents. I could start a vendetta with Marcati myself, damn him.'

'You don't feel like taking a gamble that Marcati *won't* talk? So far the police have nothing to connect him with the Resistance.'

'He's such a blowhard he'll tell them of his own accord, unless he's stopped. Charles, I've lived for over a year with the threat of Orengo hanging over me. Sometimes I can forget it for days together—how Orengo might be driven to tell, at last, who brought them the warning that night at Cimiez, and by inference who was the third man in the Parc des Arènes. I don't propose to be put on the rack again on account of *Totor-pour-les-dames*.' Jacques finished his second glass of wine. 'I'm going to the Palais de Justice now to have a look at the charges against Marcati and find out if he asked for legal aid. Then I'm going to see Profetti and Froment, and get them to come here at six o'clock. Can you hang about and let them in?'

'Sure.' It was a comfort to have Maxwell on the job. Jacques set off through the warren of the Old Town, making first for the Rue de la Préfecture where he walked slowly, looking up at the official buildings as he passed, and then round the corner into the law courts, where he spent nearly an hour. On the way into the new part of the town he passed the door of his Nice office, on which his name and the words *'Avocat au Barreau de Nice'* were displayed on a brass plate. Jacques Brunel hesitated here. He thought of going up to greet Maître Pastorelli, but those words held him back. He was going to do the Nice Bar proud, if his plan worked out.

He had a coffee standing at the counter of the Bar des Sports in the Rue Paradis, talking quietly to Daniel Profetti while Dany's father swabbed down the *zinc* and nodded, and then retraced his steps to Henri Froment's garage. There he made his longest stay, for if the task he meant to set himself was the hardest, Froment would run as great a risk, and Froment was not convinced that *ce gangster de Marcati* was worth the trouble. Characteristically, it was his former captain whom he worried about rather than himself, and when they all assembled at the Palais Lascaris it was Froment who said, 'After we've got Marcati out we may have to spring *you, mon capitaine.*'

Polly saw the problem differently. When Jacques told her the whole story late that night she only nodded, and said, 'Yes, I see why you have to get him out, and the sooner the better. Friday would be the best day, don't you think?'

'If Froment can square the seamen, and I can square the Prosecutor's office, but it's terribly short notice, Polly. It only gives me one half hour's interview tomorrow with my esteemed client, to tell him what *he* has to do—'

'His is the easy bit,' said Polly. 'If it all works out on Friday night, then you could go to Corsica yourself.'

'*Me* go to Corsica? Do you know what you're saying, Polly?'

'Yes, perfectly. You'd make absolutely sure that Totor's out of the country—and he's quite capable of giving you all the slip once he's got as far as the docks at Nice—and you could see your cousin, and come back again on Sunday night.'

He looked at his young wife, sitting on the edge of their bed beneath the swan and taking her stockings off as calmly as if she weren't suggesting something as dangerous as unexpected. 'They aren't running weekend trips to Bastia, you know,' he said. 'And where am I supposed to be in the meantime, please? And doing what?'

'Oh Jacques darling, you'll be in hospital licking your wounds,' said Polly with a giggle. 'I'm sure Victor Marcati packs a terrific punch.'

'I'll talk it over with the other men tomorrow,' said Jacques. He opened the balcony door wide, for the nights were growing warmer, and saw the lights of torches on the few fishing-boats allowed to put to sea. He got into bed and took Polly in his arms. 'You wouldn't be nervous alone, if I went—over there—for a couple of days?' he whispered, and Polly said sleepily, 'I would pray for you, my darling. Goodnight now.' He kissed her, and waited while she settled in her favourite place, with her face buried in his shoulder and her arm uncomfortably tight across his throat. After she was asleep Jacques detached the arm and pulled the bedclothes over Polly. The silent town was asleep too. It was the dark of the moon, which made the idea of a night passage to Corsica all the more realistic, and now that Polly had put it into his head he was eager to see Mike Marchand again. The candle in that lamp thing of Miss Torrance's was flickering in the night air. He liked to think of Polly saying a prayer for him before the ikon of the Virgin of Kazan.

Jacques Brunel was back in Nice early the next morning, going through the formalities required for an interview with a prisoner awaiting trial, who—in Jacques' opinion quite rightly—had not been allowed bail. He did not express this opinion to the prison governor, but set himself to obtain the privilege of talking to his client alone in his cell, with the warder no nearer than the corridor, and when this was granted Maître Brunel spoke to the prisoner in terms not often used in Les Baumettes:

'Don't waste my time with your excuses, you damned fool! You're as guilty as sin, and you know it! Now listen to me, and be prepared to do as I tell you—'

The hours of Thursday went by in interviews. The governor was unwilling to let the prisoner go into Nice, even to see the Prosecutor, even under guard; the Prosecutor played hard to get, and said he might, no more than might, be represented by a deputy; the Resistance man, Edouard, at the Préfecture had to be seen along with the policeman, Paul. Finally there was an interview with the skipper of a felucca called *L'Aiglon*, of Corsican registry, which slipped in and out of a small harbour in the Lazaret quarter of Nice. Jacques was committed then, and ready to go through with Operation Totor, and the only comment he made to Polly, when he went through the plan again with her, was:

'You realise that if I'm found guilty of conspiring to defeat the due processes of law I'll be finished at the Bar, and may even have to serve a prison term myself?'

'You'll get away with it,' she said confidently. 'You always do.'

'Even if I do, I'll have to live with the knowledge that I've touched rock-bottom, and gone even lower than the rubbish bins?'

'Oh darling, don't worry so,' said Polly, and her vivid face was all compassion. 'You were only in the nice safe middle before. Maybe you've got to go lower than the low, before you can rise to the very top.'

Jacques tried to think of that as he entered the Rue de la Préfecture at Nice next day. The narrow street was full of German soldiers, as if they scented something in the wind, but one of their vehicles pulled out, at the orders of the military police, to make way for the prison van from Les Baumettes. Victor Marcati came out with his usual swagger, but in handcuffs, and went through the doorway which in normal times led to the Bureau des Etrangers, where Jacques was waiting to greet him with a nod. The policeman, Paul, was on duty, and led the way to a small conference room above the street. Jacques glanced up at the window and saw that Paul had taken off the latch. He looked down at the street, and made sure that Henri Froment's repair truck, with the plain canvas top and the name painted out, was in the proper place.

The deputy Prosecutor came in, a younger and more vigorous man than Jacques cared to see, but encumbered by his heavy robe. He motioned to Jacques to take a chair in front of his desk, and surveyed the prisoner. Marcati was playing the part up to the hilt, of course. The swagger was gone, and he drooped between his warders, apparently held up only by the irons on his wrists.

'Maître Brunel, I don't think we have met before,' said the man behind the desk.

'I haven't had the honour, Maître Chauchat.' said Jacques. There was twenty years' difference in age between them.

'Take off this man's handcuffs,' said Maître Chauchat, and the senior warder protested.

'With respect, *monsieur le procureur-adjoint*,' said the warder, 'this fellow's dangerous. The governor said we was to keep him in irons—'

'Take the handcuffs off and let the man sit down,' said Maître Chauchat, raising his voice, and Victor collapsed into a chair beside Jacques, taking a folded sheet of paper from his pocket as soon as his hands were free. 'Now, Maître Brunel, what have you to say?'

'Monsieur, I represent Victor Marcati, a French citizen here present,' said Jacques. 'He has been committed for trial at the next assizes on charges of armed robbery and grievous bodily harm. My plea, when the case comes to trial, will be mitigating circumstances, and I now plead before you that this case is too delicate to go to the assizes, and should be heard *in camera* here in Nice.'

'You may explain further, *maître*.'

'Victor Marcati was never in metropolitan France until he was mobilised with his regiment, the 173rd DBA, at the outbreak of war. He did well during the action in Champagne. In 1940, rather than go back to an impoverished home in Corsica, he found employment as a labourer, a *cheminot*, on the railway. Unfortunately he fell in with a gang of terrorists, who accustomed him to the idea of violence, and under whose orders he carried out single-handed the raid on the post office in the *quartier* St. Philippe. He is now prepared, *in camera* and for a measure of clemency, to reveal the names of the leaders of the gang.'

'Maître Brunel, you are a young man,' said Maître Chauchat patronisingly, 'but I imagine not such a novice that you don't know the *parquet* looks with disfavour on the presentation of a bargaining plea.'

'In this case the bargain is an important one, monsieur. The Justice Ministry itself would be glad to have the names Marcati is prepared to surrender.'

'Well, well, let us hear the names, my man.'

'I'm naming no names with this lot breathing down my neck,' said Victor, speaking for the first time.

'I submit, monsieur,' said Jacques, 'that my client is entitled to secrecy before he submits the list of names to you.'

'Yes, well, you have a point,' said Maître Chauchat graciously. 'The warders will withdraw.'

'I tell you, monsieur, this fellow's dangerous—'

'He doesn't look very dangerous to me, and we have a policeman

197

present'—with a glance at Paul, standing at ease near the door. 'Clear the room.' As soon as the sullen warders had gone out, the deputy Prosecutor said to Victor Marcati:

'You understand, I promise you nothing. The *parquet* does not bargain with an individual sent for trial. But I can say that you'll receive special consideration in view of your willingness to denounce the terrorists whose lives are a blot on the fair fame of France. Will you read those names aloud or give your list to me?'

'I'd rather give it to you, sir,' and Jacques saw the hand come out from under the robe and stretch like an unsheathed claw across the desk. The little rat, he thought, it's not the Justice Ministry he wants to give that list to, it's the Gestapo.

'I don't know if you can read my writing, sir,' said Victor Marcati. He got up, while Jacques tensed his muscles, and walked round the desk to lay the paper before the deputy.

'Can you read *this* name, sir?' said Victor innocently. The lawyer gasped, as well he might, for the first name among the local terrorists was that of Charles de Gaulle, followed by the Bishop of the diocese and the mayor of Nice. Totor had enjoyed making up the list, but it was too long for the occasion. At that moment he knocked the deputy backwards off his chair, kicked the man's robe over his face, leaped for the window and flung it open.

Jacques, as in duty bound, cried *'Halte-là!'* and made to stop him, while Paul rushed forward from the door. Jacques received a blow to the jaw which sent him to his knees. Through a haze of pain he saw Marcati, on the windowsill, swinging a kick at Paul's chest, and Paul staggering backwards, tripping over a chair and falling, just as the Corsican steadied himself on the narrow ledge with one hand on the bracket of the street lamp above. Then he jumped, graceful as a cat, down to the roof of Froment's van waiting in the street below. The wooden struts groaned but the canvas held, and in an instant Marcati had rolled off, hit the pavement and was in the passenger's seat beside Froment. The truck took off at high speed, past the German vehicles, past a group of *miliciens*, one of whom fired at the tyres and missed, past the sentries outside the Old Préfecture, and so up the narrow street ahead and into the trackless warren of the Old Town. The law could hunt there for a month and never find its prey.

Jacques Brunel got unsteadily to his feet. The room was full of men, the stampede led by the two furious prison warders, and one of them was helping the deputy Prosecutor to get up. Paul, the policeman, was standing up too, and panting, but he hadn't lost his place in the scenario. 'Are you all right, Maître Brunel?' he came in on cue, and Jacques, improvising but truthful, said he thought his jaw was broken. Then he remembered his lines, and managed to say, 'Somebody send for a doctor!' before he clapped his handkerchief to his bleeding mouth.

In the end, after a great deal of shouting and telephoning, they were all taken in an ambulance to the St. Roch hospital, where even under Occupation conditions traffic injuries were so common that the staff refused to take seriously any patient not requiring major surgery. The elderly lawyer was treated for shock, and taken to a private room. Paul was found to have a bruised rib, which was strapped up, and Jacques had contusions but not a broken jaw. 'Shouldn't wonder if he loosened a few teeth for you,' said the intern on duty. 'Better see your dentist in the morning.' All three were assured that 'their days were not in danger', that favourite St. Roch formula, but a senior house-surgeon, hearing that not one but two luminaries of the Bar were in Casualty, ordered Jacques to be given a sedative and taken to a cubicle curtained off at the back of the reception area where there was a cot and a pile of rugs. 'Strip down to your shirt and trousers and wrap up well,' said the doctor. 'After a good sleep you'll be a different man, monsieur. Though I must say you were a fool to tangle with a young thug like that. You'd have been wiser to leave him to the police.'

'I quite agree,' said Jacques. His jaw was aching and his head was throbbing. The last thing he remembered before the sedative took hold was Polly saying she thought Victor would pack a terrific punch.

Jacques must have been heavily sedated, for he slept until nine o'clock and woke with his headache gone. Someone had been in the cubicle, for the glass of water had been put on the table beside the cot, and he drank it greedily. There was one hour to wait before his plan required Daniel Profetti to arrive at the St. Roch hospital.

Punctually at ten o'clock the young intern appeared and switched on a light. 'Awake? That's good,' he said. 'A friend of yours has come to take you home, but let's have a look at you first.' He took Jacques' pulse, sounded his heart and flashed a pencil torch into his eyes. 'No concussion,' he said. 'Okay, you can be discharged. By the way, you gave your home address as Menton. I hope you're not planning to go that far tonight?'

'No, I'm staying in the city,' said Jacques. He pushed aside the weight of blankets and sat up. His head was perfectly clear. 'Where's my jacket? Did I have a hat?'

'No hat,' said the intern. 'Here's your jacket and your tie. And here's your friend.' They were in a hurry to use the cot for another patient, of course; through the parted curtains new emergency cases were being helped into Casualty.

'*Salut*, Daniel,' said Jacques. 'Kind of you to come and fetch me.'

'Are you all right?' said Dan Profetti anxiously. 'What a terrible thing to happen!' He looked like an undertaker in his respectable black overcoat, black homburg and white silk scarf. 'I brought you something warm to wear,' he said. 'It's a chilly night.'

'Very thoughtful,' said Jacques. 'I'll change in the washroom. But tell me first, have they caught that wretched fellow?'

'Not yet, but the police are following several clues,' said Profetti solemnly, and the young doctor showed Jacques the way to the men's washroom. He told him *ce monsieur* had paid the bill, shook hands and left him.

There was no one in the washroom. Jacques tore open the brown paper parcel Profetti had brought, took off his jacket and pulled on a heavy black wool sweater. The black wool cap and shaving tackle which the parcel also contained he put in each of his jacket pockets. As he washed he saw that the left side of his face was badly swollen.

'I've got a car waiting at the side entrance,' said Profetti, appearing at the door. 'Better hurry up.'

The car, an old Renault, was driven by Edouard, the Resistance man at the Préfecture, who whistled when he saw Jacques Brunel's bruised face. 'Are you all right, *chef*?'—it was going to be a catchword for the next few days.

'Right as rain,' said Jacques, getting into the car. 'Where is he?'

'On his way to the docks with Charles. Don't worry, he wasn't seen at the Palais Lascaris, and everything went like a breeze. Except that you and Paul got the worst of it.'

'The bastard!' said Jacques, 'he did it on purpose.' He felt his jaw again. 'What about Froment?'

'Froment's having supper with his sister-in-law, and the truck's in his friend's garage in the Place Garibaldi, getting new number plates and a fast repaint. You should know. You planned the whole thing yourself.'

'So I did.'

'Do you think you're fit for the night run to Corsica?'

'Dan, I want to make sure we've seen the last of Marcati. The thought of spending the next twelve hours in his company makes me want to throw up, but I started all this and I'm going to see it through.'

No more was said until they reached the dock gates, where a guard asked to see their passes and accepted money instead. Not far from the gates a shadow detached itself from deeper shadows, and Charles Maxwell asked Jacques if he felt all right.

'I'll survive,' said Jacques. 'Is he aboard?'

'Aboard, and very subdued.'

'Are you going back to the Palais Lascaris tonight?'

'I think I'd better try another hideout, just in case the police come round. And I won't be here when you get back from Corsica, Jack. I've been ordered north to Grenoble for a week or so.'

'See you when you come back, then,' said Jacques. 'And thanks for everything.'

He and Profetti had to walk over grass-grown cobbles along the last stretch of the way, for the *Aiglon* was berthed in a long-disused section of the old docks. When they reached her they were challenged in a whisper, and in a whisper Jacques replied. He went aboard with a word of thanks to Profetti, and no words at all for the muffled figure who sat for'ard with averted face.

The *Aiglon*, rated as a felucca, was unlike the feluccas Dina had seen daily on the Nile in being power driven, but the skipper went out under sail and ran before a favouring wind for nearly an hour before he switched on his engines. There was some movement on the deck, but Jacques obeyed the skipper's order of silence and sat still, glad of the heavy sweater, sometimes dozing, sometimes awake and tense until he woke from a deeper sleep to find a sailor offering him a mug of coffee, and a nacreous dawn breaking over a splendid promontory.

'*Le Cap Corse!*' said the sailor in his normal voice. 'You want anything to eat, monsieur?' There was a powerful smell of frying fish.

'Just a bit of bread, thanks.' The coffee was strong and good, the distant mountains indigo against the rising sun. A scent half resinous and half flowery was borne on the off-shore wind.

'*Ça va, chef?*'

It was Victor Marcati who brought the bread, a couple of slices on a tin plate, with a lump of the Corsican cheese called *brocciu* and a bone-handled knife. Victor had been fighting off sea-sickness, and looked it. His black curly hair was damp with sweat, and on his pallid face the dark stubble made him look more like the Corsican Ogre than ever. He stood before Jacques humbly, swaying with the motion of the boat.

'*Ça va!*' repeated Jacques. 'You've got your nerve, Marcati. I'm alive, and they tell me the postmaster you shot is out of danger too.'

Victor shuffled and clutched the rail, muttering something about not meaning to hurt anybody, anyway.

'Shut up,' said Jacques. 'You can go and get me some more coffee.'

He had his eyes on the blue mountains; there was a wildness to them, different from the Maritime Alps he knew so well. The felucca was close enough inshore for red-tiled roofs and white walls to be visible, and from the villages the smell of woodsmoke mingled with the scent of the maquis.

'The skipper says he'll berth at St. Florent in an hour,' said Victor. Being sent on an errand had given him back some of his brash self-confidence, and his next observation was that those bastards had taken away his cigarettes in prison. Could the *chef* by any chance spare him a Gauloise?

Jacques, with resignation, shook out a crumpled pack. 'What'll you do when we get to St. Florent, Marcati?' he enquired.

'Well, my home's at the Ile Rousse, see, the birthplace of Paoli,' bragged the Corsican. 'There's a good road west from St. Florent, and I'll be able to hitch a lift. Maybe I'll get back my old job on the Corsican railroad, *chef*, that's to say if I'm lucky.

'You don't call me *chef* any more,' said Jacques, 'and you've had the luck of the devil so far. You'll find plenty of jobs going with the Americans, but don't try any funny stuff with them, because their MPs won't be as easy to cheat as the cops in Nice.' He left Marcati and went to find the skipper. Five o'clock on Sunday afternoon was the *Aiglon*'s sailing time, the man said, which meant they would berth at Nice well before daylight. He asked no questions of his passenger, and answered the only one Jacques put to him. Bastia, he said, was twenty-five kilometres from St. Florent, by a road across the foot of the peninsula which led north to Cap Corse.

It seemed as if the whole population of St. Florent, eight hundred strong, had turned out to see the *Aiglon* enter the little port. *Totor-pour-les-dames*, now his jaunty self again, might well have lingered in the crowd, but with Jacques' eye upon him he thought it wiser to start at once down the road to the Ile Rousse. He did come up first to say '*Au revoir, monsieur*' and mumble another apology, whereupon Jacques against his better judgment gave him twenty francs to see him on his way.

Jacques turned away from the sea and looked towards the little old town. The houses clustered round an ancient Genoese fort, and in their fresh whitewash they looked clean and welcoming. The Tricolore was flying above the police station. No swastikas here! It was the first time for nearly four years that Jacques Brunel had set foot on liberated territory, and his spirits rose with every step he took. He went into the post office, which had just opened, and put in a call to Bastia.

'*Hotel Cyrnos Palace, je vous écoute,*' said a girl's voice from the hotel switchboard. He had no idea what his cousin's Royal Air Force rank was now, so he asked for him by the old rank of Mike's record-breaking days:

'*Le capitaine Marchand, s'il vous plaît.*'

THIRTEEN

Michel Marchand and his wife Dina were living the happiest days of their lives in Corsica. Mike was doing the job for which his life had been a preparation, completed by Dina's love and the coming child, while Dina had entered a new state of tranquillity. She was in splendid health. The malaise of early pregnancy and the tensions of Cairo were behind her, and she felt completely at home in their shabby rooms in the Cyrnos Palace. In Brazil Dina had been accustomed to two extremes, the luxury of her homes and the austerity of the transit hotels and crew quarters she shared as a Pan Am stewardess and a Capricorn pilot. She had grown to dislike the middle-class flat on the Sharia-el-Nil and the slovenly service of Ahmed and Anwar. Here there were cheerful little Corsican girls to keep the bedroom and the bathroom tidy, and that was quite enough domesticity for Dina.

Mike began by being anxious about Dina's condition. It was his first experience of becoming a father, and he had lived too long in an all-male society to know how to set about it. He had a vague idea that women should keep their feet up, drink a lot of milk and sew tiny garments, and above all they should consult their doctors regularly. He wondered aloud if the American army doctor who had confirmed Dina's pregnancy had much experience of midwifery on a battlefront. He wondered if a Corsican medico would be as skilful as the great event deserved?

Dina reassured him. 'The Corsican doctors get a lot of practice,' she said. 'Every female in Bastia between eighteen and forty-five seems to be pregnant, and the babies are lovely. If we're still here in October I'm sure some local obstetrician will see me through.'

'You ought to be at home with your mother to look after you, darling.'

'Mother would worry me to death, Mike. She fussed and fretted dreadfully over both of Ester's babies, only Ester likes fussing, and I don't. And if you think you can ship me back to Brazil to have the baby, I'm not going.'

Well no, not Brazil. Mike conceded that the journey was too long, and perhaps too hard, but why not Portugal? Why not plan on going to that neutral country, say in August, and having the baby at Cascaís? Wouldn't those cousins of her father's, or whatever they were, be glad to have her as their guest?

'Those three old tabby cats? They'd fuss me more than mother,' said Dina bluntly. 'No, darling, we're staying together. We're not going to be parted again.'

So that was settled, and though letters were written to São Paulo and Rio with the good news it was long before any answers could be expected. As for Captain Antonio da Costa, much closer at hand in the Palace of Caserta, he merely sent a laconic telegram saying *I thought so*. Mike and Dina were alone together, with no one to interfere or give advice, and while an older woman might have lamented that wild rides in a jeep over the pot-holed and shell-pitted Corsican roads were injudicious in the third month of pregnancy, they did no damage to Dina's superb body and a great deal of good to her spirits. The miasma of the Delta was forgotten, and so were the snubs of the Gezira Sporting Club—not that Dina ever realised she was being snubbed, she only thought 'those funny little women' were as hopelessly middle-class as her furnished flat. In Bastia they were part of a young, congenial group of flyers who had no Gezira, no Turf Club, no Mena House swimming pool, but who were perfectly happy in their off-duty hours to gather round a beat-up piano and sing popular songs.

When Mike was free they usually had dinner in the hotel, or in one of the little restaurants of the Vieux Port, but sometimes they liked to have a picnic in the room, eating off a table in the window and listening to the hum of the evening promenade in the Place St. Nicholas. And since there was no wise woman to tell Dina that the broken cobbles of the Boulevard Paoli, which seemed hardly to have been repaired since it was planned by the Emperor Napoleon III, were as dangerous to a pregnancy as jeeping round the roads, she shopped there in tranquillity for a bottle of red Patrimonio wine, new bread and cheese, and an assortment of the cold sausages with a chestnut flavour which she and Mike enjoyed.

Those were good evenings, and there were also good days at the airfield, when Dina went down in the jeep with Mike and drove back with whoever happened to be going into Bastia. The airfield —they were beginning to call it Poretta now—was an American base, without any of the restrictions of Heliopolis, and at a certain distance Dina could watch take-offs and landings to her heart's content. The first day Mike took her there the station commander invited her to have a cup of coffee with him, and showed her the met. office and the radar screen, talking to her as one pilot to another, and telling her, when she asked, that the body of water due east of the airfield was called the Etang di Biguglia.

'I saw it when I came in from Naples. I thought it was land-locked.'

'No ma'am, it's not landlocked, there's a narrow channel to the sea on the north. The folks have big plans for cultivating the area after the war.'

'It reminded me of the Lago do Bomfim, outside Natal in Brazil,' said Dina, and Mike smiled at her. She was faithful to the memory of their first night as lovers, and to the lagoon remembered by both of them for the fifty-three take-offs of Jean Mermoz.

Nobody discussed politics at Poretta, nor was there much talk about the war during the rowdy get-together evenings at the Cyrnos Palace or the Voyageurs. The war was there, a gigantic, inescapable fact, and there was no point in dwelling on it, especially since the Luftwaffe, flying after bigger game in Italy, had eased up on the bombardment of Corsica. The double invasion of France would be the next step, and the young flyers taking off from Poretta could see the invasion build-up going on all around them. Jacques Brunel could have seen it for himself if *L'Aiglon* had approached Bastia instead of sailing west of Cap Corse and into port by the peaceful waters of the Golfe de St. Florent.

When Mike took his telephone call in the lobby on that Saturday morning, the first of May, he ran upstairs in a hurry to tell Dina the great news.

'My cousin Jacques is here!'

'Oh Mike! Here in the hotel?' cried Dina, beginning to get out of bed.

'No, no, darling, take your time! He came across from Nice last night in the *Aiglon*, and he's at St. Florent. I'm going over in the jeep to fetch him right away. Where's my lucky scarf? What did I do with the keys?'

'The jeep keys are on the dressing table where you left them,' said Dina, amused. 'What luck it isn't a flying day!'

'Isn't it though?' Mike drained the tepid coffee remaining in his breakfast cup. 'Old Jacques, what do you know? I couldn't believe it when I heard his voice. Now Dina, take it easy and don't get in a flap.'

'*I'm* not the one who's flapping! I'm going to make myself look pretty for your cousin Jacques, and I'll order something very nice for luncheon—'

'Bless you!' He kissed her and was gone. Dina in her silk night-dress went to the window and looked down into the Place St. Nicholas. It was as noisy as only a Corsican square could be on a Saturday morning, and the jeep had not the decibel power of the supercharged MG, but Mike had a talent for noise, and the jeep took off with the thrust of a Lockheed Lightning. He was in St. Florent in three quarters of an hour, having been detained first by a bullock cart and then by a string of pack mules, and found his cousin eating a supplementary breakfast outside a seashore inn.

'*Bonjour Michel!*' '*Eh bien, mon vieux Jacques!*' They weren't South Americans, so they did not embrace but shook hands vigorously, and Mike's characteristic greeting was, 'What the hell have you done to your face?'

'Spot of trouble yesterday in Nice.'

'Are you on the run from the police, by any chance? You look like it.'

'Sorry if I'm not presentable. I tried to be, at least I shaved at this place after I'd ordered coffee—'

'You need a good brush down. Jacques, it's great to see you! How long has it been? Four years or thereabouts?'

'It was at that hospital in Scotland,' said Jacques. 'Four years ago next month. Sit down and have a cup of coffee. I've got a lot to hear.'

'And a lot to tell, by the look of you.' Jacques thought by the look of Mike he was just the same. The blue eyes were bloodshot from long hours of strain, and there were white lines of wrinkles where a flyer's goggles pressed, but the blunt features weren't blurred and the cheerful grin hadn't changed since their schooldays. There hadn't been much to smile at, the last time they met.

Four years ago, and before that they hadn't met since Marcelle's wedding. Before *that*—there had been too many gaps since the days at the Ecole des Roches for Jacques to remember. But they were talking now as if they had met the day before, the way they'd always done, and Jacques was glad he had come to Corsica.

'If you came over on the *Aiglon* I take it you left Nice in a hurry,' Mike was saying. 'It wasn't possible to bring Pauline with you?'

'Not this time,' said Jacques. 'I'm going back tomorrow afternoon. Say, that note with your address—did you send it to Nice by *L'Aiglon*?'

'No, the skipper of the *Rio de Rome* took charge of it. We're very Bonapartist here in Corsica! Well, if you're ready, Jacques, let's go. Dina's excited about meeting you.'

The return trip was accomplished in thirty-five minutes, nothing more delaying than a few goats having been encountered on the way. Mike slowed down on the slope above Bastia to give Jacques a view of the harbour.

'My God!' was all Jacques could say. The argosy before them seemed to stretch halfway to Elba.

'Looks as if it won't be long till the invasion.'

'How long?' said Jacques. 'This month? May, I mean, or June?'

'Not later than June.'

'We can hold out all summer if we have to.'

Mike said no more. He drove straight to the Place St. Nicholas, parked and locked the jeep, and took his cousin to the hotel cloakroom, where Jacques was able to remove his heavy sweater and brush the dust from what had been a good dark suit. When he came out Dina was waiting with Mike in the lobby, and Jacques was as he later said 'knocked endways' at the first sight of her exotic beauty. He kissed her hand and wished her every happiness.

He was the first relative of her husband whom Dina had met in Europe, and for Mike's sake Dina had dressed in her best. She wore a favourite white dress with a barbaric necklace, of solid gold links set with cubes and prisms of rough rose-quartz and yellow tourmaline, such as Jacques had never seen in his life. But he saw beyond the grandeur to Dina's real simplicity, and soon they were the best of friends, all three talking the morning away and presently enjoying an excellent lunch.

'Must you really go back so soon, Jacques?' said Dina when they had finished.

'I've *got* to go back aboard the *Aiglon*, Dina. This is a kind of holiday for me. I only wish Pauline could share it.'

'Have you got a photograph of her to show us? The American flyers always have a lot of snapshots in their wallets.'

'I haven't, I'm afraid, and I don't think any snap would do her justice. Pauline's a little bit of a girl, not like you; with her it's all in the colouring, brown hair and hazel eyes, and the expression, all fire and spirit—'

'Go on,' said Mike, laughing. 'You've become a poet, *mon vieux* Jacques!'

'You'll understand when you meet her.'

'Well,' said Dina, rising, 'you two must have a lot to talk about. I'm going upstairs for a bit, and then I have to plan for tonight's party.'

'I didn't mean to crash a party,' said Jacques when she had gone.

'It's only a few of the boys from Poretta, they like a sing-song on a Saturday night. Jacques, I'm awfully glad you're here. There's a bit of business I want to discuss with you.'

'I don't seem able to get away from business,' said Jacques, looking amused. 'But I'm at your service, Mike.'

'Then let's get out of here. It's not too hot for a stroll down to the Vieux Port.'

Bastia lay somnolent beneath the afternoon sun. The two men walked across the empty square into the Terra Vecchia and down to the waterfront, where the bars and *bistrots* had lowered their awnings against the brilliant light.

'Here's a good one, the "Paoli",' said Mike. 'Let's have a glass of wine, Jacques. It's too hot for brandy.'

The proprietor folded his newspaper and came to take their order. He filled two glasses with cool *vin rosé* and left the bottle on the table. Mike turned it round so that Jacques could read the label, *Fleur du Maquis*.

'Like the name?'

'The name's all right, and so's the wine,' said Jacques.

'You came here on maquis business, didn't you?'

'I doubt if you'd call the fellow I was escorting back to Corsica a flower of the maquis.'

'Like that, was it?' They had always been able to talk in this way, fast and elliptically. Talking shorthand, Mike had called it when they were at school. But now he began to talk 'longhand', slowly and very seriously, looking at the Jetée du Dragon on the other side of the fishing boat harbour. The proprietor of the Bar Paoli was half asleep over his paper, and the only other patrons were an old man who had drunk too much *pastis* and a couple whose arms and legs were so completely intertwined that it was obvious they would soon rise and go elsewhere.

'Jacques, I want you to draw up my Will.'

'For God's sake, man, haven't you *made* a Will?'

'Only on a Field Service form, after I joined the RAF.'

'You should have made a new one on your marriage.'

'I didn't think about it at the time. But now—I've got a lot more to leave, and there's the kid.'

'You mean Dina's expecting a child?'

'Yes, didn't you guess?'

Jacques thought of the slender body and the graceful movements, and said he didn't. 'When?' he wanted to know.

'About the middle of October.'

'Well, congratulations, *vieux*,' said Jacques awkwardly. He was as little used to the idea of fatherhood as Mike himself.

'So if anything happens to me, I want to make sure the kid's all right,' said Mike, and his cousin, well used to incoherent clients, took him patiently through facts which he was obviously putting into words for the first time. The da Costas were immensely rich, so Dina would be all right whatever happened, and of course the kid too, but Mike Marchand wanted to leave his son something of his own. Jacques remembered how generous his uncle, Pedro Ferreira, had always been to him? Had settled a lump sum on him when he was twenty-one? Mike had hardly touched the principal, it was all there in a Rio bank. And then there was the house at Alto da Boa Vista. Uncle Pedro had made the title deeds over to his nephew on his marriage. What Mike wanted was to have all his property in Brazil, now considerable, left in trust to Dina for his child.

'Or children,' said Jacques. 'Dina may give birth to twins.'

'For God's sake!' said Mike blandly, 'you think of everything, don't you?'

'It's my job.' And I'll never be finished with executries, he thought, as he listened to Mike's urgent request that he would draw up the Will immediately, naming himself as the executor and the principal trustee. 'There's nobody in the world I trust more than you,' said Mike so earnestly that it was almost cruel to tell him the Will should be drawn up by a solicitor in Bastia, where it could be validated as the testament of a French citizen on French territory, and this could certainly not be done at short notice on a Saturday afternoon. 'As for me,' said Jacques, 'I'll accept the executry with pleasure, but I ought to have another French citizen to act with me.'

'Why?'

'Because something might happen to me too,' said Jacques dryly, and poured himself another glass of the *Fleur du Maquis*. He suggested Monsieur Palméro, of the Banque Palméro at Menton, as an older and reliable man. 'As regards the trust,' he said, 'I don't think I can take that on, since your estate's all in Brazil. What about Dina's father?'

'Or her brother Tony. That's Captain Antonio da Costa, Brazilian Expeditionary Force, at Caserta.' For Jacques was making notes on the paper tablecloth.

'Somebody on your side?'

'Oh—well, say my elder cousin, Heitor Ferreira. He's a very decent guy.'

'Right. Now here's what you do.' Jacques wrote down the name of a Bastia solicitor with whom his father had had many dealings, and whose *étude* was no distance from the Cyrnos, in the Rue Sébastiani. 'You can look up the number in the phone book,' he said, 'and go to see him some time on Monday.'

'I'm flying on Monday.'

'Well, Tuesday, then. Leave the signed original with Maître Vatel, and have him send copies, also signed by you, to Captain da Costa, Senhor Heitor Ferreira, Monsieur Palméro and myself. Though when Palméro and I get ours is anybody's guess.'

'I knew you'd know what to do,' said Mike Marchand gratefully. 'That's a load off my mind, Jacques.'

'It'll be a short Will,' said the lawyer with regret, 'but it'll take care of your estate until the baby's born. You may want to alter it when you're living in France again, and have other children.'

'I don't expect to live in France after the war,' said Mike.

'You mean your wife wants you to go back to Brazil?'

'She never said so!' Mike exclaimed. 'I made up my own mind, as soon as we knew the kid was coming. Listen, Jacques! I don't know how you feel about it now, but I was anti-de Gaulle "from the first hour", from the moment I heard that megalomaniac claim to speak for France, and I haven't changed in the past four years. Every time there was a row I hoped the British would see the light, and throw him over, but they never have the guts to do it, and now we're saddled with him, it may be for life. He's built his caricature of a government and a parliament on the weaknesses of other men, and above all on the weakness of a divided France. When he comes to power there'll be no place in his France for a man like me.'

'Some of us may have to put up with it,' said Jacques. 'But I agree with you that de Gaulle has got the whip hand in Algiers.'

'Antoine de Saint Exupéry writes to me about it,' said Mike, not without pride. ' "The hate, muck and slander factory they call the *redressement*", that's what he calls de Gaulle's campaign. He doesn't want any part of it, and nor do I.'

'De Gaulle knows how to play both ends against the middle,' said Jacques Brunel. He was watching the smoke from his cigarette spiralling upwards, gold instead of grey in the amber light reflected from the terra-cotta awning above their heads. 'The BBC tells the French what a great man the British think he is, and the Resistance spokesmen tell the British he's the saviour of France, and each side knows it isn't telling the truth.'

'I blame Churchill for more than half of it,' said Mike. 'I was in London when the whole thing began, and I know how Mr. Churchill got carried away by some romantic notion of de Gaulle as the Constable of France. Yes, I know it's enough to make a dog vomit,' he added, seeing Jacques' disgusted face, 'but that's what he called him.'

'Isn't it a queer thing,' said Jacques, 'that all the Constable of France rot came about because of the man's height and his own name? Charles de Gaulle—Charlemagne—Gaul—it was made to order for his publicity! If he'd been a fat little guy with a joke name like Tartarin de Morpion he wouldn't have got far with the romantic Englishmen.'

'Marshal Foch was a fat little guy.'

'Marshal Foch was a great soldier.'

'Well, if you think that way what are *you* going to do about de Gaulle?' said Mike argumentatively.

'In law there isn't much I can do,' said the barrister. 'He's already been condemned to death for desertion by a military court, of course *in absentia*. In the civil courts he could be found guilty on three clauses of the Penal Code. Clause 166, he "violated and betrayed the duties entrusted to him" when he fled to England. Clause 86, he "abandoned the national territory", that's the same thing. Clause 84—I've got the order wrong, but it doesn't matter—he "led an enterprise to demoralise the nation", which is a very good description of the Gaullist movement.'

Mike laughed, and poured the last of the *Fleur du Maquis* into their glasses.

'D'you think you'll ever get a chance to prosecute him on these counts?' he said.

'No, nor will anybody else. But I'll tell you what I can do, Michel. I can fight the man and what he stands for at every election in France,' said Jacques, with unusual violence, 'and by God I'm going to do it if it takes me the rest of my life.'

Mike shook his head. 'That's too big a take-on for me.'

'Because you've always gone out for the fast rewards—at least until you joined the RAF.'

'What are you getting at?'

'There couldn't be a much bigger take-on than what you're doing now.' Jacques smiled. 'I can't wait for you to meet Pauline. You and she have a lot in common. She's another one who likes to keep moving on.'

Mike finished his wine. 'Are you trying to tell me I'm wrong to plan on moving back to Brazil?'

'Oh no, I think it makes a lot of sense. You worked there for years before the war, and now you've got a stake in the country. A big stake,' repeated Jacques.

'Dina's grandfather was French,' said Mike defensively. 'He went to Brazil after the war of 1870 and had a grand life there; I don't see why I shouldn't do the same. If my son grows up to be a good *brasileiro*, that's all I ask.'

'He'll have a fine inheritance, and I don't mean only money,' said Jacques. '... D'you think Dina will be wondering where we are?'

'Yes, let's get back and keep her company,' said Mike, rising. 'She'll be downstairs again by now. She's supposed to have a nap in the afternoons, but the devil himself couldn't keep her in bed longer than an hour. She's too restless!'

And that makes two of you, said Jacques, but not aloud. When they returned to the hotel they found Dina as much refreshed by her short rest as her husband seemed to be at having begun the arrangements for his Will, and no serious thoughts troubled either of them as they met the boys from Poretta who came in later for beer and music. They brought girls with them, of course: some American army nurses and a few pretty Corsicans among whom Mike and Dina seemed to be in their element. Not that Dina neglected her husband's cousin. Early in the evening she sat with him for a while, and talked about his parents and his sister in a way which showed Mike had told her a good deal about them all.

'But your mother and Mike's mother were not sisters, no?' she said.

'They were first cousins, Dina. My mother was very fond of Michel's when they were girls in Paris. In fact my own sister called her little girl after both of them. Marguerite Rose.'

'How sweet! How old is she?'

'Four last month.'

'And do they live at Menton?'

'The Telliers? They live at Oradour-sur-Glâne.'

'If our baby is a little girl Mike wants to call her Rose.'

'And if he's a boy?'

'Pedro Miguel.'

Very tactful! Mike looked at the Brazilian girl, and still couldn't quite believe in her perfectly concealed baby as she got up to greet some late arrivals. They were in a room which in peacetime had been a writing and reading room for the Cyrnos Palace residents, the only survival of that time being an upright piano on which an American airman was pounding out the latest tunes. The boys from Poretta were all in one uproarious bunch, British and Americans mixed up together, along with the two French pilots from Mike's own Flight. It was a foretaste of what a Liberation party in Paris might be like, and Jacques, walking across the room to join the group, felt guilty and resentful because Polly was missing this. When Dina stopped beside him again and asked him if he cared to dance, he thanked her and shook his head. 'I haven't danced for years,' he said. 'You'd be better off with Mike.' Come to think of it, he had never danced with Polly. He didn't even know if she liked dancing. She didn't have many amusements, and at present her idea of a big time was having poor old Miss Torrance to lunch and listening to her stories about St. Petersburg.

He had given Dina the right advice, because when they danced together she and Mike Marchand were something to see. The other couples knew it, and left the floor one by one. The pianist knew it, and slid into a tune Jacques had never heard before.

> Long ago and far away
> I dreamed a dream one day,
> And now that dream is here beside me

The fair head was bent over the silky dark one and Mike whispered something to Dina which made her smile.

> Just one look, and then I knew
> That all I longed for long ago was you

I'm glad they're both so happy, Jacques thought, but my God! I wish I had my own girl here tonight.

The party broke up early, because some of the men were flying in the morning. It seemed strange to Jacques to have no curfew, and be able to go out with Mike for a final cigarette in the Place St. Nicholas.

Mike had an exuberant plan to go to Sunday lunch at Erbalunga, so at midday they all piled into the jeep, Mike and Dina in front and Jacques in the back seat for the ride of ten kilometres on the Corniche road which ran up the west side of the Cap Corse peninsula. It was a beautiful highway, a miniature version of the three Corniches between Nice and Menton. The sea was on the right hand, the shore line broken by steep rocky *calanques* and tiny sandy bays, with here and there a fisherman's inn or a rowboat jetty. On the left of the road the maquis was coming into flower, with a dizzying scent of rose laurel, juniper and strawberry trees. Above the maquis towered the great crags and peaks, with a farmhouse or a chapel perched on the skyline. Erbalunga itself was a picturesque fishing village, with one good inn and an old Genoese fort on a promontory above the sea.

'Erbalunga's a great place,' said Mike, when they were all settled on the balcony of the inn with glasses in their hands. Mike's contained only mineral water. He was flying next morning, and he had always been ultra-disciplined about having nothing to drink, not so much as a beer, before he flew a mission. 'I want Dina to come out here for July and August. She doesn't realise how stifling hot it's going to be in town.'

'It's a lovely place, but wouldn't you be lonely?' said Jacques to Dina.

'I don't think so. It's so close to Bastia, I could see all our friends just as often as I do there, and Mike's planning to go fishing on his off-days.'

'What, like those old chaps down there?' jeered Jacques looking at a row of elderly men in straw hats and shirt sleeves, who were perched on the rocks with fishing lines dangling in the water. 'I'll believe that when I see it, Mike.'

'There's good fish to be caught at Erbalunga.' This was proved at the luncheon table, where they had a big tureen of *aziminu*, the Corsican *bouillabaisse*, and a platter of cheese and fruit. The inn at Erbalunga seemed as much a rallying point for the Allied air forces at Sunday lunch as the Cyrnos Palace was on Saturday night, and a new group of friends surrounded Mike and Dina and their visitor when it was time for coffee to be served on the flower-hung balcony. The hour passed quickly, and Dina protested when her husband insisted on taking her back to Bastia for her rest.

'But it's nearly four o'clock, darling, and I've been resting,' she said. 'I'd like to go to St. Florent with Jacques. I've never even *seen* St. Florent—'

'And you're not going to see it today,' her husband assured her. 'The road to St. Florent is where you draw the line, madame!'

'But must we go just yet?'

'I don't want to miss the boat, Dina,' said Jacques.

'That's the way he is, darling,' said Mike. 'The most punctual chap I ever knew.'

'It *is* one hell of a a road,' said Jacques half an hour later, when he had said goodbye to Dina outside the hotel in Bastia and was being driven at speed along the road they came the day before. New gaps and potholes seemed to have appeared overnight, and the passenger was flung from side to side as the jeep bucked its way over the ruts. Jacques sighed with relief when they saw the houses of St. Florent, and the *Aiglon* at her moorings in the little harbour.

'I got you here on time, anyway,' said Mike.

'You did, and I can see the skipper waving. I think he wants to leave on time too. So don't hang around, Mike. I know you want to drive on to Poretta.'

'I think I'd better. There wasn't any message when I checked at the hotel, but I'd like to look in at the airfield to make sure.'

'And you'll be sure to see Maître Vatel on Tuesday?'

' "Don't fuss", as Dina's always telling me. I'll be at his office first thing in the morning. Don't forget your sweater!'

'I've got it right here.'

'You'll need it at sea tonight.'

They were standing by the jeep, not far from the quay, not sure of what to say: goodbye, or good luck, or *à bientôt*. 'It's been great to see you!' was what in the end they both said together, while Mike added 'Give our love to Pauline!' and Jacques replied 'Here's to all four of us at the next celebration!' as the skipper waved again. Jacques said, 'I must go,' and then in English 'Happy landings!' The airman said 'You too!'

Twenty-five kilometres to Bastia, on through the town, and then down the long tree-lined road to Borga/Poretta. The Lightnings were in their hangars and there were two Dakotas on the ground. There was the usual evening activity in the different ops. rooms and the anti-aircraft guns were in position on the perimeter. Everything was normal in the world Mike knew best, everything that was the reverse of the underground world Jacques Brunel had chosen for his own. Mike swore as he got out of the jeep. It made his hackles rise to think of a great guy like Jacques thrown away in the maquis, where no man could be trusted and no sacrifice would ever be honoured. He went into the duty officer's Nissen hut.

'Anything for me?' he asked.

'Hi, Mike, nothing new till tomorrow morning's briefing. Oh, say!'—as Mike was turning to go—'the courier plane from Algiers came in at one o'clock. There was a letter in the pouch for you. Marked personal. Here you are!'

'Thanks a lot.' Mike picked up the letter and went outside. The sun was no longer shining and a heavy cloud ceiling had come down. He thought of the *Aiglon*, clear of the shelter of Cap Corse, and facing the buffets of the open sea.

He opened the envelope with his thumb. He knew the hand-writing, of course, it belonged to one of the men he most admired, and he was always proud to think that a great writer was willing to write to him. The letter said what he hoped it would. Antoine de St. Exupéry, grounded for some time as the result of an accident, had been reinstated by General Eaker, USAAF, in the 2/33 'La Hache' squadron, and expected to be posted to Poretta in the course of the next few weeks.

Saint Ex. coming to Poretta! It was the best news Mike Marchand had had since Dina told him about the baby. He looked round the expanding base where the Stars and Stripes was flying and wanted to tell everybody, from the station commander down to the mess cooks, that one of the great aviators of all time was on his way. He was so pleased that he almost missed the postscript to the letter.

'Your friend Lachmann, alias Colonel Corbeau, is back from the Middle East and has been posted to Ajaccio, effective June 6.'

As if a flash of lightning had rent open the dark sky, Mike knew that destiny had caught up with him, and that the sixth of June would be a day to remember.

FOURTEEN

When Jacques Brunel returned to the House of the Lance on Monday evening he announced his arrival by a heavy crash which brought Polly running out of the living room, to find him leaning against the kitchen door and rubbing his ankle. A bicycle with whirring wheels lay upside down upon the floor.

'What the hell's all this?' he said, and Polly, trying not to giggle, said it was her new bike, the bike he'd ordered for her, which one of the Carpani brothers had brought over from St. Roman in the afternoon.

'Why didn't you chain it up in the outer hall?' said her injured husband.

'Because I haven't *got* a chain, and I'm going to keep it on the balcony. Norine's got some sort of tarpaulin cover at her place, and she's bringing it down tomorrow.'

'Well, all right,' said Jacques, setting the bicycle upright. 'Come here and kiss me.'

'So you got away with it again!' she exulted in his arms. 'Didn't I say you would?'

She drew him into the living room and gasped when she saw his face. The swelling had gone down, but his cheek was much discoloured.

'Darling, what happened?'

'*Souvenir de Marcati,*' said Jacques with a laugh. 'I was furious on Friday night, but I thought my face was my fortune when the police turned up in the Place du Palais this morning.'

'At your *étude*? Oh Jacques, what did they say?'

'Just give me a minute,' said Jacques, 'I've been talking all day long. Is the geyser working? Then I'll have a quick bath and tell you the whole story.'

He told her, from the first word to the last, sitting at the table in a clean shirt and slacks, and lighting one cigarette from the stub of another. The police had arrived at the Nice *étude*, he said, at nine o'clock in the morning, just when the old clerk he shared with Maître Pastorelli was sorting out the mail, and they found Maître Brunel at his desk, ready to assist them with their enquiries. Where had he been since his discharge from hospital? Why, in his own apartment at the Palais Lascaris, recovering from the attack that brute had made on him. Had they found the brute? Not yet, monsieur, but it was only a matter of time. 'Our friend Paul gave them a tip to hunt in the St. François quarter and kept them clear of the Rue Droite,' he said. 'They hadn't been near the Palais Lascaris. They were decent chaps. I know them both by sight, so they condoled with me on my bruises and took off.'

'They sound better than the men who came here on Saturday night.'

Jacques stared at her. 'The Menton police?'

'That fat sergeant from the central police station, and another cop. There was a plain-clothes man with them too. He spoke French, but I don't think he was French. I think he was a German.'

'What did they want?'

'To talk to you, of course. You gave the Menton address at St. Roch, so they came looking for you here. I said I'd no idea where you were. I snivelled a bit, and let them think you were spending the weekend with your mistress.'

'My God, Polly! Did they believe you?' Polly said she didn't know, but they went away. It was ten o'clock at night, she said—as if that made any difference to the plain-clothes man from the Gestapo.

Ten o'clock on Saturday night—just when the boys in Air Force blue and khaki had been at their liveliest round the piano in the Cyrnos Palace. 'Bless them all, bless them all/The long and the short and the tall'—the catchy tune had been ringing in his head ever since. 'Oh darling,' he said, 'I do feel a swine. Leaving you to cope alone—'

'Why not? It seems to have turned out all right.' Except, Polly knew, and Jacques knew too, that after this episode they would be 'kept in sight' by the police favourable to Vichy—if Vichy were going to last much longer.

'You haven't told me nearly enough about the Marchands,' she said. 'Was Michel very glad to see you?'

'I think he was, and he seemed glad to be able to show off Dina.'

'Is she very pretty?'

'She's a beautiful creature. Tall and slim, and carries herself like an Aztec princess.'

'The Aztecs lived in Mexico,' objected Polly.

'Talking of South America,' said Jacques, whose ignorance of the sub-continent was total, 'the latest bee in Michel's bonnet is to live in Brazil after the war, I thought she might have put him up to that, but he says no. Mind you, if he were still a bachelor I'd give him about a year in Brazil before he pushed off to some other place, but now he's married I think he'll stick to the job her brother's got waiting for him in Capricorn Airways. Dina's expecting a baby in October.'

'Oh.' It was such a dry little sound that Jacques dropped the subject of the Marchands and asked Polly coaxingly what she'd been doing with herself. Had the boys been looking after her? Oh yes, Jean Dupont had stopped by on Saturday morning, and Dr. Lecampion in the afternoon when he was on his rounds in Menton, and Julien Monnier had brought an ox kidney which they were going to have for dinner. And after Chris brought the phone message saying when *le patron* would be back, she had her first ride on the new bike.

'How did it go?'

'Well, I was a bit wobbly at first, because I hadn't ridden a bike for years, and this is one of the new ones from the Peugeot people with wooden handgrips instead of rubber, and some sort of synthetic stuff on the pedals. But I got on all right. I went as far as Garavan, and came home past your old house. I knew it because you can see the marks where "Mon Bijou" was on the gate post.'

Jacques grunted. 'How does it look?'

'The villa? All right,' said Polly cautiously. In fact the Germans had given the exterior a new coat of paint, and the terraced gardens, as far as she could see from the road, were in good order. 'There were two sentries on the gate, in German uniforms I didn't know. Not like the ones you see around the town.'

'Had they the death's head badges in their caps?'

'No, so it wasn't the *Schutzstaffel*, like Limoges. Of course I couldn't stop to look.' Polly stood up and sniffed. 'I think the kidney stew's ready to eat now,' she said, 'and I'm sure you're famished.'

He was, and it was soon clear that what he guiltily persisted in calling his 'holiday' in Corsica had given Jacques Brunel a new access of energy. The sight of the huge reserves of American matériel in the island, the preparations for invasion both by air and sea, had convinced him that the liberation of the south of France must soon take place. He summoned Julien Monnier and Jean Dupont to meet him in Dupont's grocery after hours, and discussed with them a long-formed plan to move the maquis, or rather the new men Monnier had recruited in the town, to the forest of Menton. There was a kiosk in the woods not far above the path which entered the forest north of Monti which they all thought might be the first shelter in a future encampment. Dany Profetti, who was the liaison officer between the Jurac farm and the town of Sospel, reported that the Garage Rey, which ran the bus service, was feeding a large group of maquisards in the forest of the Monte Grosso. There were Italian partisans in the buildings at Albaréa where the children's holiday home had been, and Dany said they were being fed by a woman. Some of the Sospel *gendarmes*, who had come out for the Resistance, were taking food and supplies to other maquis in the forests of Segra and Ongra, and all the high country was coming alive in the hope of liberation.

Elsewhere in France such groups were being organised on Gaullist lines. Although de Gaulle's so-called Secret Army had perished with the death of General Delestraint, a new organisation had come into being under the command of de Gaulle's nominee, General Koenig. It was called the French Forces of the Interior. De Gaulle refused to recognise any Resistance movement he did not control, but this did not disturb the maquisards encamped in the High Valley of the Roya. Their purpose was to give what help they could to the Allies when the invasion started, and to eliminate the enemy from Sospel to the Italian frontier.

None of these free groups made the mistake of barricading themselves into a position from which retreat would be impossible. Already an awful example of the danger of the 'bastion' theory advanced by Delestraint and Moulin had been given on a high plateau near Annecy in the Haute Savoie. There the Glières maquisards had established themselves, 1,500 metres above sea level and, less than five hundred strong, had been attacked by one thousand German troops. Betrayed by *miliciens* in the valley and battered by Stuka dive bombers, the men of Glières were fortunate in having an escape route through a snowbound pass, and many of them got away to safety. The others died, leaving behind them a heroic name and a blue-print for another and greater tragedy of the same sort.

On May 20 General Eisenhower, now the Supreme Commander of the Allied Forces in Europe, made a radio broadcast to the French. At the time of the Sicily invasion he had warned them against premature action. Now he gave them specific orders to store up information which might be valuable when the invasion began. Watch the enemy's formations, vehicles, despatch riders, officers and NCOs. Keep your eyes on road and rail bridges, and the key points of gas, water and electricity. Know where he has located his supply dumps, petrol and ammunition. This was easier said than done in the area between Nice and Menton, where after repeated raids the enemy was nervous enough to shoot at any loiterers, but everyone from school children to old age pensioners entered with zest into the other sort of observation. The old men sunning themselves on the stone seats near the fountain by the Porte des Logettes, the children playing tag round the little innocent stone figure of a girl holding flowers in the Place des Herbes, could have told General Eisenhower the rank and regiment of every German who appeared on the Rue St. Michel at Menton, or drove his truck along the Quai Bonaparte to the frontier. As for the maquisard named Jean-Pierre, he held the Carnolès gasworks in his hand, and like Lenin in the October Revolution, was merely waiting for the hour to strike.

General de Gaulle, too, was impatient for his hour and power. He had dismissed General Giraud with an empty title and since May 26 his Committee had been known as the Provisional Government of the French Republic.

President Roosevelt, always sceptical, said he couldn't see 'how this would save the lives of any of our men', and as de Gaulle had been kept out of every top-level consultation since Dakar, it was perhaps injudicious of Mr. Churchill to fetch him from Algiers on the eve of the invasion of France. The visit only made more bad blood between the general and the Allies. Four thousand invasion vessels were already at sea with one hundred and fifty thousand men aboard for the first assault wave, and as Mr. Churchill reminded de Gaulle, these men were about to risk their lives for the liberation of France. De Gaulle chose this moment to refuse to give General Eisenhower precedence in a broadcast to the French people, or to allow French liaison officers to accompany Allied troops to France until the future administration of the country was settled.

In this impasse Winston Churchill complained to Mr. Roosevelt that de Gaulle had 'not a single soldier in the great battle now developing'. This was not exactly true. On D-Day the United States had twenty divisions in Britain, ready for the strike, the United Kingdom had fourteen, including imperial troops, and Canada had three. General de Gaulle had one, General Leclerc's 2nd Armoured Division, but it was in Yorkshire waiting for the arrival of its Sherman tanks. The solitary force owing allegiance to the Leader of All Free Frenchmen which actually took part in the attack on the beaches on D-Day was one battalion of marine commandoes.

The question of the broadcast was a silly obstruction at the last minute, but finally de Gaulle accepted the bait of an invitation to visit President Roosevelt, for which he had long been angling. He returned to his old and favourite battleground, the studios of the BBC. There, in equivocal terms, he made yet another broadcast to France.

Polly Brunel listened to very few broadcasts during the run-up to the invasion, in the last two weeks of May. From the wireless set which they kept tuned to Radio Vichy she learned that the German installations in Northern France were being bombarded day and night. On some nights in April there had even been heavy Allied bombing of the capital, which took Marshal Pétain to Paris for the first time in four years to attend a memorial service for the dead in Notre Dame. The people of Menton were despondent. If this was the prelude to a cross-Channel invasion, what would happen to their town when the Allies crossed the Mediterranean? Polly, without much conviction, tried to cheer up such anxious friends as Miss Torrance, Madame Honorine, and the girl upstairs who had given birth to two babies, by two different fathers, since the Brunels went to live at the House of the Lance. They were all of the opinion that liberation meant a new bombardment of the town, and for the townsfolk it would be 1940 over again.

Polly had other anxieties, much nearer home. The police had come back to question Jacques, this time without a plain-clothes man of whatever nationality, but represented by the chief inspector of Menton himself. He was a burly individual who had always been on good terms with the Brunels, father and son, and who was usually to be seen about in a pre-war tweed suit of excellent material and cut. It was disturbing that he was wearing full uniform for his call on the Brunels. He was accompanied by a policeman who was also a shorthand clerk and made a record of the questions and replies.

Deprecating the need to put those questions which, he said, had been forwarded by the Brigade Criminelle at Nice (just to save Maître Brunel the trouble of visiting their office himself, you understand) the *commissaire* asked how Victor Marcati, now a fugitive from justice, had employed Maître Brunel as his counsel in so delicate a matter as plea bargaining? Because in the normal way, *monsieur le commissaire*, if those tactics had failed he would have represented Marcati at the Aix assizes. He believed the records showed that he had had some success at Aix as a defender. Undoubtedly; and in his first and only interview with the prisoner at Les Baumettes he had been so impressed by the man's tale of terrorist influence as to open a *démarche* with the Public Prosecutor? Yes, he had. And had Maître Brunel seen that absurd list of names which Marcati had left behind him when he escaped through the window? No, but he had been shown it since. Was not the ex-general de Gaulle considered in some quarters, say at Vichy, to be a leading terrorist—though quite unlikely to be known to the man Marcati? The *commissaire* abandoned that line of questioning and asked Jacques why he had not let his wife know that he intended to stay in his flat in Nice after his discharge from hospital? He thought he had left a message at St. Roch, but frankly, *monsieur le commissaire*, he was so confused after that fellow's assault that he might have forgotten to do so.

'Madame gave the police another reason for your absence from home,' said the inspector, and Polly came forward, drooping and tearful, to say she thought she had some reason to be jealous, but now, now—with a hand on her husband's sleeve—she knew that she'd been wrong. The *commissaire*, swayed like all Frenchmen by the hint of an illicit passion, broke off his interrogation there and said they would probably hear no more about it.

But in spite of this assurance Jacques was summoned to the office of the Brigade Criminelle three days later and interrogated again, this time in the presence of a silent man in plain clothes. This time, too, he was asked to identify the kind friend who had taken him away from the St. Roch hospital by car. He warned Profetti, of course, by telephone, and Profetti was involved in too many rackets with the police to be in great danger, but the next step might lead to Edouard, and the next step to Froment, and they were all in jeopardy over the *affaire* Marcati.

'We'll have to take to the maquis before long, Polly,' he said in an attempt to be cheerful when he got back from Nice.

'Or take a trip to Oradour-sur-Glâne,' she said.

'What put that in your head?'

'A letter from Marcelle. It took nearly two weeks to get here!'

'I'm not surprised. What's new at *Le Verger*?'

'Read it and see.'

Madame Tellier's letter breathed a happy self-importance. Louis and Margot were well, and papa's health, they learned from Davos, was steadily improving. And now for the great news! Marcelle was expecting a baby in December. Of course she and Louis hoped it would be a son this time, and Margot had specially ordered a baby brother from Father Christmas.

'I am suffering quite dreadfully from morning sickness,' the letter went on, 'just as I did before Margot was born. Alas, dear maman can't be with me as she was then, keeping house for Louis and looking after me, but Cécile Tellier has promised to come down from Ville d'Avray next week, so I shall be well taken care of. Fortunately I saved all Margot's baby clothes, as one can't buy things of such quality at present.'

'What a bore my sister is,' said Jacques. 'You'd think the Germans had occupied France just to prevent her from buying baby-linen.'

'She must have been glad to have your mother with her last time,' Polly said.

'I suppose she was. I remember maman was at Oradour when war was declared, that's probably the time she means.'

'You'll notice Marcelle didn't ask *me* to go and help out,' said Polly in a muffled voice. 'She asked her other sister-in-law instead.'

'Well, but—my dear girl, of course she did! Cécile's got nothing else to do, and besides, she's had some nursing training. You don't know a thing about babies—'

'And if I don't, whose fault is that?' cried Polly. 'Do you think I like hearing about Dina Marchand's baby, and now Marcelle's baby, and never—never mine!'

'Polly! Now listen, my darling!' But Polly was weeping hysterically, too wrought up by all her anxieties to listen to him calmly. Jacques had to take her in his arms and rock her as if she were a baby herself before her sobs steadied down to an occasional sniff.

'Polly, do you remember that night you came to me at St. Mawes in Cornwall and we had a long talk before we sailed next evening from the Helford River? We had no idea what our lives in France would be like. We didn't even know then about my father's —illness. But we both agreed that it would be too difficult, and even too dangerous, to start a family right away—'

'Oh, don't be so logical!' she said, and took up the lock of black hair which sometimes fell across her husband's brow, twisting it round her fingers in a way he disliked.

'Don't *curl* it!' he said. 'I must be logical, my love! Or be practical, at least! Here we are, expecting the invasion from one day to another. What would you do if you'd a little helpless baby to take care of now?'

'I'd get by,' said Polly, and gave the curl a vicious tweak. 'Other women do.'

'I don't want you to have to get by in that way,' said Jacques. 'And you know what we agreed, Pauline.'

'But we weren't married then!' she said. 'I feel quite differently now!'

There was feminine logic for you! Jacques released her with a sigh. Polly went off at once to the kitchen, and as he watched her retreat Jacques remembered a Latin tag from his schooldays. 'You can drive out Nature with a pitchfork,' it ran, 'but she keeps on coming back.' He was beginning to understand what it meant.

Marcelle Tellier, as June came in, was basking in the fulfilment of Nature and a steadily more prosperous pregnancy. She was still plagued by nausea, but it was not of the pernicious sort, and with her sister-in-law to bring her a light breakfast in bed and get Margot started for the day Marcelle was on foot by ten o'clock and ready to take charge of her household. Cécile Tellier was a great help. She was a plain, down-to-earth girl, short-sighted like her brother, and would have made a good doctor like him but for her father's prejudice against what he called bluestockings. She had been a good student and a devout Child of Mary when she and Marcelle Brunel attended the Couvent des Oiseaux. Now her rôle in life seemed to be that of a universal stopgap, making herself useful wherever one of her relations needed her.

The news of the Allied invasion of northern France hardly disturbed the peace of Oradour-sur-Glâne, where the only excitement was the anticipated visit of a travelling circus famous for its performing dogs. Cécile Tellier was anxious about her parents, who at Ville d'Avray outside Paris were a good deal nearer to the Normandy beaches than the Telliers in the Haute Vienne. Marcelle, wrapped in the euphoria of her condition, predicted that the invaders would get nowhere near Paris. There would be fighting, certainly—the radio said there was fierce fighting—and then the two sides would come to some sort of a compromise and sign a peace treaty. They might even become allies and fight against the Russians!

Dr. Tellier did not encourage his wife in her fantasies. He was not such a fool as to wish for a German victory, but he dreaded the conflagration which might spread all over France before the Allies won. Above all he dreaded the excesses of the maquisards, or the French Forces of the Interior as they styled themselves now. Thank god there was no maquis in Oradour-sur-Glâne.

Since Jacques Brunel's visit to *Le Verger*, and his cutting words about the doctor's fraternising with the Germans, Louis Tellier had found excuses for declining any invitation to the German officers' club. He assisted their doctors when it was absolutely necessary, but his assistance ended at the door of the military hospital, and he refused to listen to the Limoges rumours about what went on in the Gestapo headquarters. There were other premises under German direction, like a *manège* which had once been the riding-school of the 21st Chasseurs, where captured maquisards were gathered at a staging point for the concentration camps, but Dr. Tellier had never been asked to visit such places and so could truthfully say he knew nothing about them. He thought the FFI probably deserved all they got. Like many of the French bourgeoisie, he went in terror of communism, and believed implicitly that the FFI, especially in the neighbouring Department of the Corrèze, was infiltrated by Communists. To protect himself and his family and his beautiful property of *Le Verger* from the ravages of communism had become one of the doctor's aims in life.

Dr. Tellier was less than fair to the French Resistance, because its members, whether in the FFI or as *groupes francs*, were except for the marines the only Frenchmen fighting *in France* when the Allied invasion took place. There were 30,000 Resistance men in Normandy who eventually gave valuable support in the long-drawn-

228

out battle. They were the lucky ones, for they had their Allies beside them and the enemy in front; the unlucky ones were those who rose to challenge the more fluid elements of the German army which were ordered north from other regions of France to bar the path of the invaders. Such an element was the 'Das Reich' SS Division, commanded by General Heinz Lammerding, which was making its way north by Brives and Limoges when it encountered the Resistance in the charming town of Tulle.

Tulle was a quiet place of streets and squares, and long *quais* along the River Corrèze, shallow and peaceful in the sunny days of June. The fighting which started there on the day after the invasion was at first an affair between Frenchmen, as the resistants (mostly Communist *France-Tireurs et Partisans*) attacked the Vichy French forces responsible for keeping order in the area, and the FTP took the town. Then the German armour appeared on the scene. General Lammerding had been attacked by the FFI along his whole line of march, first at the crossing of the Dordogne, then on June 7 at Souillac, on June 8 at Noailles, but he got his revenge in the town of Tulle. The maquisards were defeated in a pitched battle. The dead were thrown into a common grave. More than four hundred hostages were taken, and of those one hundred and twenty were hanged, by groups of ten, from the lamp posts and balconies of Tulle.

Although Limoges, where Dr. Tellier had his practice, was only ninety kilometres from the town where this massacre took place, no news from Tulle had reached Limoges by Friday evening, June 9. Nobody telephoned from the hospital where he was a consultant to give Louis any indication of trouble in the area on the Saturday morning when he regretfully told Marcelle that she couldn't possibly drive into town with him.

'Oh Louis, you know how I depend on the Saturday shopping,' said Marcelle, with her handkerchief at her mouth. She had tried to get up, and had fallen back on her pillows in a fresh access of nausea.

'I know, darling,' said Louis, 'but you're really not fit to drag round the shops today. Give Cécile your shopping list and she'll get you everything you want.'

'Or as much as she can get,' said Marcelle. 'Louis, isn't this horrible sickness going on too long? After all, it *is* the fourteenth week—'

229

'You'll be better soon, dear; remember how it was with Margot. Shall I tell Jeanne to bring you some weak tea and toast? I think you'll be able to keep that down.'

'Some *dry* toast, please. Louis, I'm sure I'll be all right in an hour or so!'

'Yes, but I can't wait that long, I've got to get to town. Here comes Cécile with her notebook and her pencil.'

With Cécile Tellier came Margot, who climbed on her mother's bed to play with her doll, and was told not to shake the bed and bounce about.

'Don't you want to come in to Limoges with papa and Aunt Cécile?' coaxed Mademoiselle Tellier.

'I want to stay at home with Jeanne and maman,' declared the child.

'Well, here comes Jeanne now. Off with you to the kitchen and play with her!'

When they left her alone Marcelle drank the weak tea, nibbled the dry toast and began to feel better. It was ridiculous to lie in bed on such a beautiful June day! She got up and took a tepid bath, very slowly, and having brushed her fair hair with a hundred strokes and buffed her nails, felt refreshed and fit for anything. It was always the way, after the disabling sickness she felt as if she could clean the house from attic to cellar—not that she intended to do any such thing. She went to the kitchen and told Jeanne, who had a half holiday on Saturdays, about the cold chicken and salad to be left ready for dinner. With Margot dancing alongside she inspected the kitchen garden. Under their netting the strawberries were coming on nicely and would be ready for the table in another week. The green fruit was setting on the orchard trees. Everything at *Le Verger* was fecund, was fruitful; it made Marcelle Tellier happy to be part of the ripening year.

'Don't you go stooping and stretching and doing too much,' said Jeanne, appearing at the back door. 'What do you want for lunch?'

'Very little, Jeanne. A boiled egg and some more toast, perhaps.'

'I think that hash we had last night upset you,' said Jeanne. 'Mademoiselle Cécile put in too much salt.'

'I can't bear salty things just now,' admitted Marcelle. 'But mademoiselle does like to try her hand at cooking—'

At least they didn't quarrel in the kitchen, Jeanne and Mademoiselle Cécile, though they were rivals for the preference of Margot. Marcelle called the little girl to her and gave her a duster which the child had partly hemmed herself. They would dust papa's surgery, she said. It wasn't at all too soon to teach Margot methodical ways.

Margot dusted the books, because books were easy, and Marcelle dusted and polished her husband's carefully ordered desk. There! He'd gone away without the tonic for the boy at the Ferme Lacloche, something special he'd brought out from Limoges late last night, and meant to deliver on his way into town. I worried him and he forgot all about it, she thought remorsefully. And the tickets for the new tobacco ration too. How very annoying—Louis does so enjoy his cigar.

They all ate lunch in the kitchen, bowls of thick country soup for Jeanne and Margot, with a large plate of the salty hash and mashed potatoes for Jeanne, the boiled egg and toast for Madame Tellier, and stewed pears for them all. Marcelle, as she had predicted, now felt wonderfully well.

'I think I'll walk into the village, Jeanne,' she said when lunch was over. 'It's the first day of the new tobacco ration, and the doctor forgot his tickets. If I don't go to the *tabac* today, the cigars will be all sold out.'

'The *tabac* won't be open yet.'

'No, but it will be when I come back from the Ferme Lacloche. I might as well go and ask for the Fabert boy, the doctor wants him to start taking a new tonic.'

'Is that the refugee who broke his leg?' said Jeanne, clearing the table with speed. She was always in a hurry to get home on Saturdays. It was the day when people from Limoges came out on the little tram to scour the countryside for black market food, and Jeanne's brother did a thriving if illicit trade in poultry.

'Yes, Claude Fabert,' said Marcelle. 'He fell through a trapdoor in the barn, poor boy.'

'Poor fool,' said Jeanne, without heat. The local people had accepted the Lorrainers long ago, but there was always the feeling that they weren't up to country ways. Claude Fabert's parents were employed at one of the china works in Limoges, but the boy had taken to the farming life and was a young cattleman at the Lacloche farm.

'Sure it won't be too far for *her*?' said Jeanne, with a sideways jerk of her head at the little girl.

231

'Oh no, it's just the other side of the village. Come on, sweetie, and get tidied up.'

Jeanne was ready to leave before they were. Her home lay in the opposite direction, on the banks of the Glâne, so they parted at the gate, after making sure that all the doors were locked. *Le Verger* was at its most attractive, for though the fruit blossom was over the roses were in bloom, and Marcelle looked back approvingly at the property—house, gardens, orchards—as she closed the gate. She and the child were just out of earshot when the telephone began to ring.

Cécile was in a draper's shop trying to obtain the fabrics and sewing materials on Marcelle's list, and Dr. Tellier was leaving the hospital when ten German army trucks began rolling through the streets of Limoges from the direction of Tulle. The canvas screens were down and the occupants could not be seen, except for two German soldiers who stood in the rear holding machine pistols, but the length of the convoy was ominous and so was its destination, the former *manège* of the 21st Chasseurs. A few Frenchmen daring enough to approach the *manège* saw manacled men, some with their shirts in shreds, being driven inside like cattle.

Half an hour later Dr. Tellier was sent for by the German officer in charge of the riding-school, *Sturmbannfüher* Erwin Gerhardt.

Major Gerhardt had been promoted since the days of their social meetings at the officers' club, but he had not forgotten the amenable young doctor, who was still, his informers said, willing to help the Germans in any humanitarian cause.

'Ah, Herr Doktor!' he said, with a flick of the crop he carried to his death's head cap, 'how good of you to come so quickly. We have an emergency here, and I believe you can be of some assistance to your countrymen. Our own doctors are rather overworked at present.'

'In Normandy?' said Louis Tellier. The sarcasm was out of character, and the German raised his eyebrows.

'Come this way, Dr. Tellier.'

It was such a sight as Louis had never seen before. Mobilised in the *Service de Santé* in 1939, he had spent the war in the military hospital in Limoges, where wounded men were cared for in clean beds and orderly wards. The men before him in the badly lit riding-school were not wounded, though most of them bore the marks of blows and had blood on their garments; they were simply lying on

232

the musty tanbark as they had been spilt out of the trucks, trying to pull themselves upright by each other's arms and shoulders. Some of them were asking for a drink of water.

'Where have these men come from?' asked Louis Tellier.

'They spent last night under guard at Tulle,' said Gerhardt. 'They're very lucky to be alive. These are terrorists, Herr Doktor! They attacked our troops in Tulle at daybreak yesterday, killing forty, for each of which the lives of three of these so-called resistants was exacted.'

They had been speaking German, which Louis Tellier knew quite well. Now he turned to the nearest prisoners and said in French, 'Is it true what this man says? Have one hundred and twenty men been executed in Tulle?'

'Yes, it's true!' 'My God, it's true!' 'They hanged them from the balconies, ten at a time!' 'My brothers were among them!' The yells broke out from every corner of the shadowy hall.

'Silence!' cried Gerhardt. He spoke a word to the German corporal who stood behind him, who fired a pistol shot into the air. 'One word more, and nobody goes free!' said the major. 'Remember, there are balconies in Limoges as well.'

'What is it you want me to do, Major Gerhardt?' said Louis. 'How many prisoners have you here?'

The major consulted a list in his gloved hand. 'Three hundred— no, three hundred and one,' he said. 'Now, sir! Six nurses are on their way here from our own hospital. You will have ample help; all we want you to do is give first aid to those who require it, and then submit a report on the number who are fit to travel.'

'Travel to where?' said Louis.

'I don't think you quite understand, Herr Doktor; these are the orders of General Lammerding. Some of these men declared, while they were being held as hostages at Tulle, that they had never been members of the *Francs-Tireurs et Partisans*. Others swore that at the moment the attack on our troops was perpetrated they were at work in the local factory which is producing arms for Germany. If they can prove their innocence they'll be set free. The others will be sent to the staging point at Royallieu, and from there to the labour camps in Germany.'

'I see,' said Louis. 'And they'll all receive a fair trial?'

'Of course.'

'But first, I do the weeding out? I decide who is fit to travel and who is not? If a man is fit to travel he goes to Royallieu whether his innocence is proved or not? On the decision of a French doctor who can later be accused of sending Frenchmen to the gas ovens? Very clever, Major Gerhardt, but it won't work. I'm not under the orders of the man who hanged his hostages from the balconies of Tulle. Get one of your own doctors to do your dirty work.'

The German army nurses who had arrived at the riding-school stood petrified by what they heard. The Frenchmen nearest the two men, who understood nothing, but saw Louis pick up the bag he had set down on a trestle, began to say, 'Doctor, don't leave us! Doctor, we need help!' He turned to them at once and said, 'I'm going to the German military hospital to complain to the head surgeon of the treatment you're receiving here. After that, if I have to, I'll go to the Kommandantur.'

Louis Tellier didn't know if any of it would work. He found his way barred by Major Gerhardt.

'You know that I could arrest you for disobeying an order given by the Occupying Power?'

'I deny your right to issue such an order,' said Louis. 'Let me pass.'

A crowd had gathered in the street, and in reply to their questions Dr. Tellier told them what he knew of the Tulle tragedy. He heard the rising sound of anger behind him as he walked first to the German hospital and then to the Kommandantur to lodge his useless protest. It was long past the hour when he was to meet Cécile for lunch, but knowing her good sense he was sure she would go to his consulting rooms and she was there, sitting in his private office with his anxious secretary.

'Oh Louis, there you are!' 'Oh, doctor, we heard you'd been arrested!' they exclaimed together.

Louis wasted no time in talking about himself. In a few words he described the calamity at Tulle, and the arrival of three hundred men at Limoges en route for the concentration camps. 'A German division has run amok in the Corrèze,' he said. 'They may be in the Haute Vienne by now. In which case the maquisards will rise and the whole countryside will be a battlefield. And Marcelle and Margot are alone at *Le Verger*.'

'What are you going to do?' said Cécile fearfully, as he reached for the telephone.

'Tell them to take the tram and come right in to Limoges.

There's safety in numbers, and we can all go to a hotel for the night. If Lammerding and his men by-pass Limoges we'll be all right. Damn! She must be in the garden.'

'No reply?' said his sister. 'No.' Louis put down the phone. 'I wonder if I should take the car and run out to Oradour?'

'Doctor, your surgery,' said the secretary. 'It's two o'clock and there are several patients in the waiting room already.'

'I'll go to *Le Verger* if you like,' said Cécile Tellier. The three of them looked at each other, irresolute, undecided, like so many French people for so many years.

'No, you stay by the phone, Cécile,' said her brother. 'Keep calling, and the moment you've got Marcelle send mademoiselle into the surgery to tell me. Try again in ten minutes. She can't be far away.'

She was passing the first houses of Oradour-sur-Glâne at that very moment, with Margot, who at four years old was a sturdy walker, stepping out bravely beside her. The tobacconist was shut, as Marcelle had expected, but the Restaurant Avril and the Hotel Milord were doing a big trade, their outdoor tables filled with the people who had come out from Limoges for the day. They were not all black market buyers, for many people came out to Oradour-sur-Glâne on a fine Saturday, to fish, to see the children they had sent to friends for a short holiday, or just to eat a good plain country meal and enjoy a glass of wine in the sunshine. Marcelle waved to several acquaintances, and stopped to speak to others. Margot was more interested in the small boys and girls galloping past her up the street, afraid of being late for afternoon school. She dragged on her mother's hand as they passed the fairground, asking when they were going to see the performing dogs.

The Lacloche farm was at the far end of the village, on the opposite side of the road from the church but nearer the river. Lacloche was a prosperous farmer who had been a childless widower for ten years before his remarriage, and his sons were little boys of four and five. Marcelle knew that Claude Fabert was very well treated at the farm, almost like an older son, and she was not surprised to find him propped up with cushions on the wooden settle in the kitchen with his leg in its plaster cast stuck out in front of him.

'But you're still at table. I didn't mean to interrupt!' she said when Madame Lacloche drew her into the farmhouse kitchen. The farmer said he was taking an extra half-hour, it was such a hot day, and Madame Lacloche, flattered by a call from the doctor's wife, insisted on pouring a glass of raspberry syrup for the little girl, and a thimbleful of home-made plum brandy which Marcelle hardly dared to touch. The boy from Lorraine was silent, nursing his bottle of tonic, but it was he who asked if they couldn't hear a lot of carts on the road.

'I don't know who'd be moving carts at this hour of the day,' said the farmer, and Margot said hopefully that it might be the performing dogs.

'They're not coming till next week, silly,' said the older Lacloche boy, and his little brother, who had run to the foot of the garden, came back to say that it *was* the circus, there were men with funny coloured clothes in the wagons. Nobody in Oradour had ever seen the green and yellow camouflage denims worn by the *Waffen SS*.

'And the good doctor's keeping well, madame?' said Madame Lacloche conversationally. 'Mademoiselle Tellier's spending a little holiday with you?' Everybody in the village knew about the expected baby, for Jeanne had spread the news around, but unless Madame Tellier mentioned it herself it was not Madame Lacloche's place to do so.

'Isn't that the town crier's drum?' said Marcelle abruptly. Everyone stopped talking to listen. The drum beat came nearer. The farmer opened the back door to hear better. The drummer was past the church and near the hedge between the farm and the road.

'Hear ye, hear ye! All citizens, men, women and children to assemble forthwith in the fairground of Oradour-sur-Glâne! All to be provided with their papers of identity! A check is ordered by the Occupying Power!'

They heard the drum beat fading, the voice less audible. 'All citizens, men, women ... in the fairground ... by order of the Occupying Power!'

'What an extraordinary thing!' said Madame Lacloche, getting heavily to her feet. 'The Occupying Power indeed! I thought there were no German troops nearer than Limoges.'

'There was a company at St. Julien last night, I heard,' said her husband. 'Come on, old girl. The sooner our papers are checked the sooner I can get back to work. Claude, boy, stay where you are. I'll take your card along and explain that you're a cripple.'

The boy with the broken leg said nothing. But his eyes grew

wide with fear, and as Marcelle took Margot's hand and prepared to follow the Lacloche family, he made a sudden clutch at her skirt.

'Madame Tellier, don't go away! I know the Germans—I saw them in Lorraine—I'm sure this is a trap! I'll help you to hide from them—'

'But Claude, you heard the town crier. Everybody has to go to the square, or the fairground, or whatever you like to call it. The mayor will be there to talk to their commander and everything will be all right! It's a silly waste of time, but we have to do it—'

'Please, madame, for your little girl's sake, hide from the Germans! They'll go crazy now the Allies have landed, they won't care what they do or who they kill. You and your baby too!'

When Claude Fabert said *bébé* he meant little Margot, but the mother with a sudden primitive fear thought of the unborn child. She clutched the living child and said 'Tell me where to go.'

'I'll show you.' The boy started to drag himself off the settle.

'Claude, your leg! You mustn't move. You can't!'

'I walked today, madame. I can walk now, if you'll give me my crutch—'

It was a clumsy thing which Lacloche had made for him, and when Claude limped from his room, across a passage, to share in the family dinner, he had had the farmer's strong arm for support. He was a big boy, and Marcelle stumbled beneath his weight.

'But where are we going?' she said, bracing her arm round his waist. Claude told her down the well would be the safest place.

'I couldn't possibly climb down a well, nor could my little girl.'

'Then the rabbit hutches, madame, that's all I can think of. And hurry, in case Madame Lacloche comes back to look for you.'

But the farmer's wife was thinking of her own children. They'd been playing out of doors all morning, and their little shirts were dusty. Imagine not having time to put clean shirts on them, and wash their faces before other people saw them! She fumed her way to the fairground, where she saw the senior Dr. Desourteaux, who was also the mayor, talking to the young German officer. The doctor seemed to be angry about something. He'd been out the whole morning at a confinement, and was probably annoyed at being taken away from a belated dinner. It was a comfort to see that the old doctor's suit was dusty too.

The Germans were not making the slightest attempt to check identity cards. As the empty ground filled up, they moved in behind the people with their rifles in their hands, and all the exits seemed to be blocked by machine gun crews. Very few of those who had been hunted out of their houses, and none of the children, nearly two hundred in number, whom their teachers had marshalled from the schools, could read the insignia on the camouflage denims the Germans wore. But everybody could see that they were very young, some as young as seventeen, none older than twenty-five, and that they were in the grip of a rapidly mounting excitement which flushed their cheeks and made their fingers tremble on the triggers. They were two hundred strong, soldiers of the 3rd 'Der Führer' company of General Lammerding's 'Das Reich' Division.

The mayor, who had brought so many of the villagers into the world, turned to face them, and they were quiet at once to hear what he had to say. 'Citizens of Oradour-sur-Glâne!' ...

'Where are we going, maman? Is it a new game?' said Margot, as the three of them made their slow way through the vegetable garden.

'We're going to see Claude's rabbits, darling, you'll like that.'

The rabbit hutches, in rows four cages wide, were built against the granite wall of a cow byre, empty at this season when the animals were in the fields, with a covered space between the wall and the back of the cages used for cleaning out the trays. The rabbits, mostly Dutch in neat black and white, moved expectantly in their cages, hoping to be fed. There were three white Himalayans with pink eyes, a breed Margot had never seen before.

'Oh look, maman, how pretty!' But all maman said was 'Hush!' and Claude leaned exhausted against the door of the byre.

'Look through the hedge, madame, but carefully. I think there's someone there.'

Kneeling with her hands on the ground and her head only slightly raised, Marcelle saw two German soldiers setting up a machine gun in the middle of the highroad to Limoges. Then a cold wave of terror shook her from head to foot, and she knew all Claude had said was true. He saw it in her face as she turned towards him.

'In here, madame, and lie down. Make Margot lie down too.' He pushed them both into the space behind the hutches and pulled a sack down over the gap. 'Don't move if you hear them coming. Don't move for your life!'

... 'Citizens of Oradour-sur-Glâne,' the mayor was saying. 'We are the innocent victims of a great mistake. The German officer says we have given shelter to the maquisards. We all know that's not true. He says his men have found a stock of arms and explosives stored beneath the church. We know this is impossible.'

'Get on with it, Herr Bürgermeister,' said the German. 'We haven't got all day.'

'This man has ordered me to choose thirty hostages,' said the mayor steadily, 'whose lives will be security for us all. This I have refused to do. I have offered my own life, and the lives of my four sons, instead.'

There was a long breath, hardly a moan, of incomprehension and disbelief. It couldn't be happening—not here in peaceful Oradour, under the blue sky, with the luncheon tables on the terrace of the Hotel Milord, and the school children standing so good and bewildered, in such orderly rows! And the old doctor and the young doctor standing side by side—could you believe it—with the three other Desourteaux shoulder to shoulder with their father and brother—could you believe that all of them had made up their minds to die? But the German officer, who spoke horrible French, shouted loud enough so that everybody understood, 'Enough of this play-acting! Women and children to the church, and men into the barns! Complete your house searches, soldiers, and report to me!'

They had searched the houses pretty well already. They hadn't found any maquisards, or any hidden arms, but they had marked down a number of valuables to be looted later, and they ran back to the square at the double. The Lacloche farm was the furthest from the village southward, and therefore the last to be searched. Marcelle Tellier heard two voices shouting. *'Raus! Alles 'raus!'* from inside the farmhouse before the heavy boots came pounding through the yard.

Claude Fabert had fallen twice on his way to the well. His leg, under the plaster cast, was not equal to what he had asked of it. And Farmer Lacloche, thinking of his little boys, kept a wooden cover on the old well, with two heavy granite stones on the top, and to remove all that took the lame lad many minutes of sweating effort. He knew it was no good when the two soldiers came raging past the beehives, and one of them cried out, *'Ein Terrorist!'* He made one last involuntary movement, as if to dive head-first into the black water far below, at the foot of the steps in the brick work which might have meant his safety, and then the shots hit him between the shoulder-blades, and Claude slumped down on his knees with his arms spread out along the moss on the well coping.

Inside the rough and ready shelter with Margot in her arms, one hand over Margot's mouth and her cheek pressed to the hard soil covered with ends of straw and rabbits' droppings, Marcelle Tellier lay motionless. She had heard the shot and Claude's last cry. Now she saw the army boots coming up at the level of her eyes, through the wire netting of a cage in which one of the Dutch rabbits crouched in fear. She heard without understanding what the rough voices said.

'How about a juicy rabbit, Hans? Make a good supper, with a bottle of their wine?'

'Plenty of time for supper, mate. Wasn't nobody here but the terrorist they was hiding. Let's get back to the square and not miss any of the fun. There goes the whistle now!'

When Marcelle dared to take her hand from her child's mouth, her first thought was that the little girl had suffocated. Her face was blue, her eyes rolled backward in her head. But when her mother clasped her in an agony of fear, she moved and licked her lips, and then said piteously, 'Have I been bad?'

'No, no, my darling,' the poor woman said, 'but bad men have hurt poor Claude, and we must stay here very quietly till papa comes to fetch us, and not talk—'

'When's papa coming?'

Marcelle twisted her watch round on her wrist. It was a gold Swiss watch on a gold bracelet, one of Louis Tellier's engagement presents, and had always kept excellent time. Now she thought it must have stopped, for it marked only three o'clock, not much more than an hour since she locked the doors of *Le Verger* and set out for Oradour-sur-Glâne. Louis would be in the middle of his afternoon surgery. She tried to make Margot more comfortable and told her to close her eyes. Then she raised herself to the level of the cage above, looked past the rabbit and the wire netting, and saw the body of Claude Fabert.

The sickness which overpowered her then had nothing in common with the cold nausea of the mornings when Jeanne brought tea and toast and Cécile brought eau de cologne, and everyone was kind and considerate. It was the sickness of absolute physical revulsion, of retching that became dribbles of salt liquid oozing down her chin and the front of her pretty dress. Marcelle Tellier slipped a long way down the ladder of civilisation in that half hour. It was not a woman but an animal which lay in the dirt clasping its young one, listening to the shots and screams, smelling the burning buildings and the roasting flesh.

The men who were herded into the barns of Oradour died by bullets and hand grenades, if they were lucky. The less fortunate, who were only wounded, were burned alive. The women and children were all burned—all but one, who escaped through a high window, just as a few men escaped from the barns and one boy escaped from the Lorraine School. The other Lorrainers, as Dr. Tellier had once predicted, never left Oradour-sur-Glâne. Their calcinated bodies were found in the ruins of the church, along with the infants, the young mothers, and the old women who died at the hands of the war-crazed boys of 'Das Reich', while the blue sky grew dark with the smoke from their funeral pyre and the word went out across the Limousin that Oradour was on fire.

Louis Tellier, with Cécile by his side, was one of those who drove like madmen from Limoges, to be stopped before they could approach Oradour by armed Germans who shouted, '*Alles kaput! Alles kaput!*' and shot down any man who tried to force his way across the cordon. One or two of the Germans, whether from compassion or cruelty, spread the rumour that the women and children had been sent to safety in the woods. Many men, Louis Tellier among them, spent the rest of the day threshing wildly from thicket to thicket, path to path, in the woodlands of that countryside.

It was not until seven o'clock that the last shots were heard in Oradour. Then the village, all but a few houses, lay in smoking ruins, and bodies which looked like statues of melted lead were lying in the streets. Marcelle Tellier and her daughter lay in their fouled garments, within a few paces of the dead body of the boy who had saved them, and all Margot's gift for being reasonable, all her mother's sense of property were reviving into an urgent will to live.

Marcelle had stopped thinking about Louis. He was a man, and could look after himself. She was the guardian of two lives, the child in her arms and the child she meant to bring to birth. They were now all that mattered. The house and all that it contained, all the possessions of which she had been so proud, were of no importance compared with the need to hold on to those two precious lives. As the sound of shooting died away and the noise of singing and merriment began she was planning, with an animal's cunning, a way to escape from the enemy.

The village lay between her and her home. The machine gun emplacement guarded the highway. But if she could slip out of the vegetable garden, through the farmstead and down the poplar thickets where the honeysuckle grew she would reach the Glâne, and the river, she knew, curled in a long loop round the fields and pastures until it passed the farm where Jeanne's family lived. If she could get that far, her life and her children's would be saved.

It was hard to make Margot understand what they were going to do. The child was in a state of shock so deep that she was beyond even whispered speech, but at last she crept out of the shelter and let her mother lift her in her arms. Putting one hand over the child's eyes, she carried her past Claude's body and the drying blood on the stones where he had fallen. She almost lost her nerve in the pasture nearest the farm, for the cattle had come to the gate and were mooing. It was the hour when they were accustomed to be milked. But the Germans on the gun, if they were still there, paid no attention, and Marcelle, still carrying the child, arrived at the river bank.

She tore off a breadth of her petticoat, dabbled it in the water, and wiped Margot's face and her own. Then she fetched water in her cupped hands and made the child drink. Margot looked more sensible then and spoke a few words, but the 'reasonable little girl' had relapsed into baby talk, saying 'me tired' and 'maman carry Baby' as if walking was beyond an infant's power. Marcelle lifted her up and began the long way through the willows, but she staggered under the dead weight, and the thought came to her that if she strained herself in carrying the living child she might lose her baby. She sat down then with Margot in her lap, and wept. In the summer sunset she could still see the smoke of Oradour-sur-Glâne, and in the reflection of that agony the little river seemed so clear and cool, the water so inviting with its fringe of forget-me-nots and grasses, that the temptation to slip into it with Margot in her arms and be borne away with the tide, was very great. But the dominant urge of possession refused to be denied; she struggled to her feet and forced the child to stumble on. At last she came on some familiar landmarks, a picnic place, a red-tiled roof in the distance and a meadow bright with cowslips. She made a final effort, pulled Margot up the steep slope of a hilly pasture, and as Jeanne and her brother came running across the fields towards them Marcelle Tellier took the last steps to safety.

FIFTEEN

As soon as the Allied invasion began, the quiet watchers at Menton saw considerable movement among the Occupation troops. There was nothing as spectacular as the departure of the 'Das Reich' Division for the Normandy front, but whole companies were entrained after dark for Marseille en route for the north. At Nice the members of the new Resistance network which had taken the place of Pierre Orengo's 'Knife' circuit held up the troop movements successfully by sabotaging points and turn-tables outside the main station, and the heavy Allied bombing raids on Marseille did further damage to the railway yards. At Menton it was thought that the Germans would not dare leave the garrison under their full strength for long, in expectation of the invasion from Corsica and North Africa which could only be delayed for a few days.

The Resistance waiter at the station café, who had a room at the top of a tenement overlooking the station, was better placed than most to report on the movements of the Occupation troops. He described a new development, which was the passage at one o'clock each morning of a train made up of two coaches only, coming out of Italy and travelling west, which sometimes, but not always, stopped to pick up passengers at Menton. These passengers were brought to the station in an armoured car, and the waiter believed that they were prisoners of the Gestapo, on their way from the secret headquarters in Menton to the Villa Lynwood at Nice.

The Villa Lynwood, which once belonged to an English owner, had been requisitioned at the beginning of the Italian Occupation, and used as a prison and place of torture by the OVRA. After the Italian surrender it had been taken over by the Gestapo, who used it for 'specials' whose interrogation might lead to the arrest of terrorists. If a train was running regularly out of Italy carrying human freight for the Villa Lynwood, it could only mean that the Gestapo was casting its net far and wide north of the Winter Line, and holding Italians as well as the French at the Villa. Ratazzi,

Jacques' elderly resistant at the Nice station, confirmed that Italians had been seen clambering down from the two-coach train in the small hours of the morning.

One good result of the Germans' partial withdrawal was the end of the road block on the Sospel road at Monti. The bus was able to come through occasionally, and what was more important to Jacques, he was able to double the shifts of Julien Monnier's maquisards working on the new encampment in the forest of Menton. He took extra men in the Peugeot, using stolen German petrol, right up to the gates through which hikers and trippers had entered Ubac Foran in the days of peace, with weapons from the store of the *étude* Brunel in the boot of the car. The old refreshment kiosk and the empty cottage of the forest ranger, with a clear kilometre of woodland between them, were to be two separate bases for mobile camps of the wigwam sort, with straw for flooring and tree branches cut into timbers for the roofs.

On the same day as the calamity at Oradour-sur-Glâne Jacques delivered more weapons and ammunition to the new maquis, which already numbered twenty young men, and drove on to the Col de Castillon. It was the first time he had been there for weeks. The only boy on the premises was Dany Profetti, the liaison officer, who had a good deal to report on the situation at Sospel.

'You may think the Germans are leaving Menton,' he said in his agressive way, 'but they haven't all gone west. A whole column of them came over the Col on Thursday, with guns and weapons-carriers, and the boys in the Albaréa maquis say as many more came over the Col de Tende from Italy, down the valley of the Roya. Looks as if the Boches mean to stand and fight at Sospel, Jack.'

'I always thought they would,' said Jacques. 'It's a natural strong point for them when the invasion starts.'

'*If* it starts,' said Dany. 'I thought the Allies were meant to hit the Côte d'Azur this week.'

'So did we all,' said Jacques. 'How do you know about the Albaréa maquis, Dan?'

'I've been up there half a dozen times. They're in the old kids' holiday place, not far from the bridge, and they're a pretty good lot —for Italians, that is.'

'No Frenchmen among them?'

'Four, and the girl from the Hotel du Mont, she's French.'

'You mean they have a woman with them? Living at Albaréa?'

'No, she doesn't live there, she just brings food up from the hotel. She's a great girl,' said Dany, 'the boys are crazy about her.'

'Is her name Fabienne, by any chance?'

'Why, do you know her?'—surprised. 'I wouldn't've thought she was your sort, Jack.'

'She used to work for the Resistance when she lived in Monaco.'

'Oh, she's from Monaco? I thought she came from Saorge.'

'She gets around,' said Jacques. 'Watch your step there, Dany. Fabienne Leroux is not a very stable character. Also if she's stealing food from the Hotel du Mont she might land you all in trouble.'

'Not a chance,' said Dany. 'Everybody in Sospel's working for the Resistance.'

'All right, I'm glad to hear it. Tell the other boys I want them all in the forest by six o'clock on Tuesday evening. When we've thirty men we can start invasion training.'

'But not me,' said Dany jealously.

'No, you can stay up here and liaise. Now let me speak to your grandfather—' He was glad to get away to the Juracs without being asked what had happened to Victor Marcati. Luckily the boy was too taken up with his Albaréa maquis—and with Fabienne Leroux, confound her! to be concerned about the Corsican.

Jacques finished a satisfactory weekend with a raid on the *Soldatenheim*, formerly the St. Michael children's home. It was organised in the hit-or-miss way he hated, but which sometimes worked quite well. A woman who did washing for the men brought back from the Italian front for rest and recuperation told Madame Honorine, as she hung out the Brunels' laundry on the same hillside, that the *Soldatenheim* would be empty for a day or two, all the inmates having been ordered back to Italy. This was enough for Jacques Brunel, who had long had designs on the twelve-seater bus with the Red Cross markings. It had never been seen in Menton since the children were sent home, so most probably it was still in the garage which Polly had once described to him, and which he made her carefully describe again. After that it was child's play to approach the *Soldatenheim* through the woods with Julien Monnier, overpower, gag and bind two eighteen-year-old sentries, force an entrance, and drive the bus away. As Julien remarked while they went to the Traverse Bellecour, the damned kids were lucky to escape with their lives. The bus was left in the big garage, and the Carpani brothers who ran the bicycle shop at St. Roman set to work on the manufacture of false number plates, in which they specialised.

It was possible that if Jacques Brunel had known on Sunday night of the carnage at Oradour-sur-Glâne, the German sentries at the *Soldatenheim* might have been strangled instead of gagged. But it was not until Monday morning that Radio Vichy broadcast the news of a tragedy too monstrous for even Radio Vichy to exonerate. Jacques tried again and again to reach *Le Verger* by telephone, only to be told that all communications with the Haute Vienne were suspended, and it was not until late in the afternoon that the reliable Cécile Tellier herself reached him from Limoges. His sister was safe, she told him at once, and Margot too. They were both recovering from shock in a private nursing home in Limoges, and Marcelle was in no danger of suffering a miscarriage. But they were among the less than a score of survivors of a catastrophe in which hundreds had perished—how many, it was still impossible to tell.

'The Germans are calling it a regrettable mistake,' said the voice of Cécile Tellier, sounding tinny and remote on long-distance. 'They say their men may have confused Oradour-sur-Glâne with Oradour-sur-Vayre, where there may have been a maquis group; we don't know. Louis doesn't believe it. He says those men went berserk, like the Germans at Tulle, as much maddened by war as any lunatics. He hunted for Marcelle and the child all night on Saturday, Jacques. It wasn't until Sunday morning that Jeanne's brother found me, and told me they were safe.'

'But where were you, Cécile? Not at *Le Verger*, surely?'

'I drove back to Limoges and slept on the sofa in Louis' office. I—I couldn't go back to *Le Verger* yesterday, or even today. It won't be habitable for some time to come.'

'You don't mean to say they burned it down too?'

'No, the walls and the roof are intact, but the brutes looted the place thoroughly. They stole all the silver, and anything too big to carry they destroyed.'

'My God, Cécile! Marcelle and Louis were so proud of their home—'

'Marcelle hasn't been told about it yet, and Louis says he doesn't give a damn as long as she's safe, and Margot.'

'What's going on in Limoges?'

'The RAF came over, hurrah! Louis is doctoring the FFI.'

'That's a switch,' commented Jacques Brunel to his wife, when he told her the story that night. 'Louis Tellier as a maquisard is something I would like to see. And Cécile exulting in a bombardment by the Royal Air Force, that's every bit as good.'

'Between the RAF and the FFI, the Limogeois will liberate themselves,' said Polly enviously, and it turned out to be true. Among those killed in the fighting was Major Erwin Gerhardt, and with him other German officers and men of the SS, who got no nearer the fighting in Normandy than the banks of the Vienne. But the 'Das Reich' Division marched on, fighting a war of attrition all the way, until the day came when General Heinz Lammerding was killed in action, never to be brought to human justice for the atrocities of Oradour-sur-Glâne.

It was comforting to Jacques to think that the excellent Cécile had got a message of reassurance through to the Brunel parents at Davos. 'I offered to go to Limoges myself,' he said, 'but Cécile said there was nothing I could do. I felt so useless, Polly!'

'Darling, you're doing all you can.' It was cold consolation, as cold as the quarter moon shining above the Mediterranean. Oh when would deliverance come? There was no sign of an Allied ship upon the tranquil sea.

Jacques and Polly sat up too late that night, discussing the Oradour tragedy in all its aspects, and Polly saw that in spite of his sarcasms at Louis Tellier's expense Jacques was genuinely shocked at the thought of what his sister must have suffered. 'I always knew she had a lot of guts,' he said more than once, and again, 'Poor little Margot, she must have been scared silly!' Polly agreed with everything in her thankfulness that a man of such reserve should reveal his real affection for his sister and his niece. She only drew away from Jacques when he spoke of the coming child, asking her awkwardly if she thought the new baby would be born, well, all *right*; he meant, not—disfigured in any way? She controlled the desire to answer him with the words which had wounded her, that she 'didn't know a thing about babies'—he was too much hurt himself for such a cheap revenge. She only said the doctors must know best, and it was a mercy Marcelle could be taken to a nursing home. She was young and strong and she would soon recover. So Jacques was soothed by Polly's attempt at comfort, and before the early grey of dawn appeared above the sea he found his best consolation in her arms.

They were late in the morning, and Jacques was in a hurry. He wanted to spend a couple of hours at his *étude* before going to Nice, where a solicitor who sometimes put briefs in his way had asked him to prepare a written opinion on a piece of impending litigation. He had enough of his petrol ration for June left to allow him to drive over, and Polly seeing his haste volunteered to walk to the Quai Bonaparte with him and lock the garage after he had left. 'It'll save you a couple of minutes, maybe,' she said.

'Is Norine coming in today?' asked Jacques, pulling on his jacket and riffling through the contents of his briefcase.

'Only to bring the laundry back. Why?'

'Nothing. I thought if you weren't going to be too busy in the house you might walk along and see Miss Torrance. I'd like to know if she's heard from Charles Maxwell lately. I haven't seen him since the Marcati row was on.'

'That's true,' said Polly. 'I'll go and see Miss Torrance right away. But he doesn't usually let her know his movements, does he?'

'I suppose not. He sometimes sends a postcard saying when he means to arrive, and by that she knows he'll turn up at three o'clock in the morning, via the alley wall. He doesn't like her to be scared.'

'He's probably busy in Marseille,' said Polly, as they walked together down the Rue Longue. The children were in school, the women at the market, and the narrow street was very quiet.

'He did tell me he might be going to Grenoble for a bit. The new man from London's up there now.'

'I thought Grenoble was right off his beat.' The vague uneasiness about Maxwell added itself to the troubles of the day, and Polly was not smiling when she kissed Jacques goodbye. He waved as he drove away, but later on he remembered how still she stood, with the padlock of the garage in one hand, and the other raised in a grave salute. It was a very hot day, with no breath of wind stirring, but it seemed to Jacques as if Polly were leaning forward, like a runner facing into a gale.

When Jacques was out of sight Polly walked straight along the *quai* in the direction of the promenade until she came to the little house with the boarded-up tearoom window and was admitted to Miss Torrance's living room.

Miss Torrance was *so* sorry, but she had no news of dear Monsieur Aletti—who seemed to have taken the place of the dear prince in her tender heart. *Last* time he was here he had actually paid the rent of his room until the end of the year, instead of a quarter in advance as he usually did. Didn't that look as if he meant to be away from Menton for some time? Miss Torrance and Polly played the game seriously, telling each other how busy the life of an insurance salesman must be in these troubled times, and the cliché took them straight to Oradour-sur-Glâne. Polly escaped from Miss Torrance's twitters by inviting her to tea that afternoon to hear the whole story of Marcelle Tellier's ordeal. She then stood twenty minutes in line outside a bakery to buy a few macaroons for the occasion, and walked home by way of the covered market.

Jacques got to Nice before lunch, and to save time had a cup of coffee and a roll at the counter of a café on the Rue de la Préfecture. From where he stood he could see the window, with the ledge beneath and the street lamp above, where the Corsican had stood poised for his jump to freedom—'Marcati's Leap', the *Eclaireur de Nice* had taken to calling it, with the comment, wrong as usual, that Marcati was probably still holed up in the safety of the Old Town. He could see it still from his own window when he reached his chambers, which rather surprisingly were empty. His fellow tenant must have gone to court and taken his clerk with him, and when the court rose they would go to their respective homes for lunch. Jacques looked forward to a few hours without interruption, studying an interesting case. It was the usual thing: a rich old man marries a skittish young woman and dies of it, and his heirs-at-law sue the widow for what they consider their rightful share of the spoils. Jacques saw that the lady had taken certain precautions to ensure her inheritance, but were they enough? He took off his jacket and pulled several law books from the bookcase—his own professor's interpretation of the Code Napoléon, more up-to-date by far than the volumes in his father's room at Menton. He unscrewed his fountain pen and set to work. He was making notes of an important precedent when the door of his room opened to admit Monsieur Bosio, the elderly clerk he shared with Maître Pastorelli.

'*Bonjour, Maître Brunell!*' The old fellow had been hurrying, and was out of breath. 'I saw your car in the square when we came out of court. I thought I'd better come right up and repeat the message.'

Jacques looked over the cluttered papers on his desk. 'Have I missed a written message, Monsieur Bosio?'

'No, sir, no, I thought it best to leave nothing in writing, the man appeared to be so agitated. I mean Monsieur Profetti, senior of course. You remember we got off the young Profetti in '42: robbery, verbal menaces and resisting the police.'

'Of course I remember, Monsieur Bosio.' Jacques spoke sharply. 'His son's not in trouble again, is he?'

'It's more likely to be the man himself. He called here about eleven, very anxious to see you, begs you to call at the Bar des Sports in the Rue Paradis at your earliest convenience.'

Monsieur Bosio's expression as he said the name and address of Profetti's bar indicated just what he thought of a young barrister who frequented a sporting bar in a street with a bad reputation.

'Thanks, Monsieur Bosio,' said Jacques. 'I'm busy at present, but I'll see what Profetti wants by and by. Don't let me keep you from your lunch. *Bon appétit!*'

When the clerk had gone he went to the open window and watched him cross the Place du Palais. The midday heat was intense, but although he was a child of the Midi and revelled in the sun, Jacques Brunel felt a chill at the thought of Daniel Profetti disturbed enough to leave his bar and hurry through the city to bring him some kind of warning. He must have telephoned the *étude* and heard I'd left for Nice, Jacques thought, which means the hue and cry has only been up since about eleven o'clock. And Dan was free to move around, so he hasn't been arrested for complicity in the *affaire* Marcati. But the story of Marcati's Leap was building up, and the police might be able to write *finis* to it before nightfall. Jacques put his jacket on, locked the legal papers in a drawer, and went to get his car from the Place du Palais.

It only took a few minutes to drive to the Bar des Sports in the narrow street near the great Masséna square. Dany Profetti's father was behind the counter, attending to the needs of his lunchtime regulars, who were punishing the *pastis* as usual. He motioned Jacques Brunel into the private room behind the bar and poured a glass of armagnac for each of them.

'What's up, Daniel?'

'Pierre Orengo's in custody at the Villa Lynwood.'

It was so unexpected that Jacques' right hand jerked convulsively, and a little of the liqueur spilled over the rim of the glass. He said 'Are you sure?' and cursed himself for the fatuous question. In matters concerning the police the forger was always sure.

'Oh, there's no doubt about it,' said Profetti sulkily. 'He was seen with his guards at the station two mornings ago, and they were pushing him into the Villa Lynwood van. One of my squealers out there—' he indicated the *pastis* drinkers in the bar—'says the Boches mounted a big drag-net operation in San Remo over the weekend, to round up men like Orengo who'd been able to pay for their protection. They got some little fish who didn't matter, but the biggest catch was our old friend Orengo, alias 'Couteau', ex-boss of the defunct 'Knife' circuit. So they brought him back across the border, and gave him the Villa Lynwood treatment. He didn't last very long.'

'You mean he's dead?'

'I wish to God he were. No, I mean he talked. Among other revelations, he told them Charles Aletti was the British agent in place, who supplied 'Knife' with English money, and Jacques Brunel was the man who tried to get him and his friends to scatter on the night that Malvy sang.'

'Very interesting,' said Jacques. He had himself under control now, and raised the glass to his lips with a steady hand. 'Any more?'

'Plenty. After they'd had another go at Orengo, he told them the last he saw of Brunel he was climbing over the wall of the Parc des Arènes with the late lamented Sabre.'

'That does it,' said Jacques. 'I wonder why they didn't pick me up this morning.'

'Maybe they thought they could get something more out of Orengo, and pick the lot of us up,' said Profetti grimly.

'You're right, Dan,' said Jacques. He knew what the man was thinking. Profetti had no reason to suppose that Captain Jack, under torture, would be any braver than Orengo. 'It's the damnedest thing,' he went on, 'I can't realise it, somehow. Here I've been thinking for a month that fool Marcati would bring me down, and it turns out to be Orengo. My God, it's eighteen months since that night at Cimiez. I thought it was all forgotten ... Well, thanks for the warning. I'd better be on my way. Lucky I've got the car here, isn't it?'

'Where do you think you're going?' The forger was on his feet. He was twenty years older than Jacques Brunel and in poor condition; at that moment he looked menacing.

'I'm going back to Menton to pick up my wife, tell her what's happened, and drive her to the Jurac farm.'

'You wouldn't get past the first checkpoint outside Nice.' Profetti let that sink in, and said persuasively, 'There's a safe-house near Grasse that Aletti sometimes uses. You could hide out there for a day or two until the Gestapo makes the next move.'

'Which will be what? No, Dan, I'm not going to Grasse.' In Profetti's stifling room he seemed to feel walls closing in on him. Go to the old flat at the Palais Lascaris? There was sure to be a German stake-out there. Hide in Profetti's cellar, or Froment's garage until darkness fell, and then go back to Polly? 'The first thing to do is get the car out of the Rue Paradis,' he said, and saw the quick look of relief on Profetti's face. The man's nerve had broken since the police questioned him about his visit to the Hôpital St. Roch. 'And then I'm going to phone my office and tell them to take a message to my wife.'

'Your office phone is sure to be tapped.'

He had to admit that Daniel was right. By the time that Maître Brunel was merely one of the crowd of loafers who were whiling away the Occupation in one of the huge cafés in the Avenue Félix Faure he was beginning to lose his sense of his own identity. He was unarmed and cut off from help, and for the first time in all his years in the Resistance Jacques Brunel felt himself to be defenceless.

It was a little later in the afternoon when his young wife's own defences fell. Miss Torrance's visit had been fixed for four o'clock, and she was always punctual, so Polly arranged the tea things and the plate of macaroons in good time. It was too hot to set the table on the balcony, because they had no awning, and in any case Miss Torrance preferred to have her tea indoors. Dear Princess Anna had always served tea in once of her reception rooms, even when the princely family had followed the imperial court to Livadia; the princess and the governess had belonged to the generation when outdoor pleasures were meant for children only.

The first knock fell on the door when she was in the kitchen lighting the gas under the tea kettle, and Polly called *'J'arrive!'* as she blew out the match. But the second knock fell too loudly on the panels for the frail hand of Rachel Torrance, and Polly in the little hall said, 'Who is it?' before she lifted the iron bar out of its socket.

'Gestapo! Open up!'

She had no time to be afraid. She pulled the bar clear and turned the door knob to admit four men, two of them with guns in their hands, who pushed past her and ran into the empty, sunlit rooms.

The other two seized Polly by the arms, holding her firmly above the elbows, and propelling her forward into the living room.

'You are Pauline Brunel, born Preston?' said one of the armed men, after a quick inspection of the balcony.

'What do you want with me?'

'Answer the sergeant,' said one of her captors, gripping her arm painfully.

'I'm Madame Brunel.'

'Where's your husband?'

'Isn't he at his office?'

The sergeant pointed at the table set for two. 'You expect him home?'

'He doesn't drink tea,' said Polly, and the sergeant, whose French was strictly limited, swore at her in German, and told his men to search the flat. They threw the clothes and linens from the *armoire* on the floor, and hunted through the writing desk without finding anything but one or two letters from Marcelle. When they had destroyed the Brunels' few possessions as far as possible, the sergeant told Polly she was under arrest and would be taken to headquarters.

'Let me take my coat, then, and my handbag.'

'You won't need a coat, and we'll take the handbag. *'Raus!'*

They walked down the narrow street with the sergeant ahead, the two men still gripping Polly's arms in the middle, and another man in the rear. The gossiping women and the toddlers had disappeared as by a miracle from the doorsteps, and there was no one in the Rue Longue except Miss Rachel Torrance, trotting happily along to her tea party, who froze at the sight of Polly and her escort. Polly looked straight ahead, and Miss Torrance, too, made no sign of recognition. She had heard enough stories of the Russian Revolution to know not to approach a prisoner under arrest.

But she waited, leaning on the guard rail and apparently interested only in the gap left by the Italian bombardment, until she heard the sound, shocking in the absolute silence, when the Gestapo car started up and drove out of the Place du Cap. Then she began walking back by the way she had come, through the Porte des Logettes and down the Rue St. Michel, stumbling painfully on the cobbles and feeling her heart struggling in her breast as she tried to hurry. She was so dizzy that as she passed the alley leading to her own house—the dear prince's gift, a thank-offering for the days when Rachel Torrance was young and pretty, and he her only lover—it was a temptation to go in for a moment and sit down. But she wasn't going to yield to the stifling heat, any more than she had shown the white feather to those cowardly Italians (and she was so confused now that she had to remind herself that dear little Pauline was in the hands of the Gestapo and not the OVRA); she was going straight to Maître Brunel to tell him what happened. The blood surging up in her thin body turned her walk into a lurch, so that it was only a compassionate hand that saved her from being run down by a mule cart in the Place St. Roch, and she stumbled repeatedly as she went on, too slowly, to the *étude* Brunel. Chris Monnier saw her coming down the garden path, with her head shaking from side to side, and limped out to give her his arm. No, Maître Brunel was not in Menton, he said, 'Can I help you, madame? What do you say?' (for her voice was indistinct) 'In private? In here?' The boy opened the door of Jacques' room and tried to help her to a chair. But Miss Torrance could go no further. She slid from the protecting arm down to the ground. She saw a kind young face bent over her own, and murmured an endearing word in Russian. Then in a last moment of lucidity she realised she must speak French, and raised herself on Christophe's arm to say, 'Madame Brunel is in the hands of the Gestapo!' She saw by his shocked face that he understood her, and began to tell him that he must find her husband. But at that moment the hammer of blood which had been beating in her brain began striking faster, and killed Rachel Torrance with its final stroke.

About a quarter of an hour after Polly's arrest, while the Rue Longue was still deserted, Madame Honorine Bensa arrived from the opposite direction, carrying on her head a wicker basket containing the Brunels' laundry. She walked superbly, with the carriage that made the pensioners sunning themselves in the Place St. Julien, below the city hospital, smile and say, 'There goes one of the old originals!' Norine was aware of the admiration, and enjoyed it; she was smiling as she knocked on Polly's door for politeness before she used her key. 'Madame?' One of the two gas jets was burning in the kitchen, and Norine turned it out before she went into the living room. That room told its own story, with the un-used tea table and the books and papers strewn across the floor. The bedroom was in the same disorder. Norine put down her basket, closed the balcony doors and bolted them, and went out to the lobby which held the lance from the Battle of Lepanto. She knocked at the door of the other flat entered from the lobby. It was opened, slowly, with the chain still up, and a neighbour's face peered out. '*Bonjour madame*, do you happen to have seen Madame Brunel this afternoon?' '*Non!*' The door was slammed. But the young woman who had had too many babies by too many different men was leaning over the banister. '*Psst! Ma'ame Norine!*' she whispered, and with a nod at Polly's door drew her hand quickly across her throat. '*La Geste!*' and she vanished up the creaking stair.

The old men in the Place St. Julien saw Madame Honorine going past again, without a smile in their direction. It had not occurred to Norine to hurry to Maître Brunel's office with her story. Thanks to the freemasonry of the washerwomen who used the hillside for their work, Norine had a much better idea than most people in Menton of where to find the Gestapo headquarters. First she wanted to know if 'her young lady' had actually been taken there. Once she knew that, it would be time to go to Polly's husband, and tell him what he ought to have found out for himself six months ago.

It was only a short way by car from the Rue Longue to the Gestapo headquarters. For the first part of the journey, along the familiar Quai Bonaparte where she had waved goodbye to Jacques in the morning, Polly could think of only one thing. The German sergeant had called her 'Pauline Brunel, born Preston', and Pauline Henri was the maiden name on her identity card. If they knew her father's name then they also knew where she had been known by it: if they knew her as Polly Preston they knew a good deal more. It gave her a hint of what her interrogation would be like.

As yet she could scarcely believe in her arrest. The long period of safety, the many risks Jacques had taken and survived, had given her the habit of security, and the sea, the road, the houses she knew so well all made her feel as if the car was moving through a montage more of the cinema than of real life. They were coming up to the Hanbury Fountain, and there Polly began to wonder if she was to be taken across the border to some Gestapo prison in Italy, for they were within half a kilometre of the Porte de France. It was only a fancy, because in a moment the army car swung left and turned back towards Menton along the Boulevard de Garavan.

'*'Raus!*' said the German sergeant. 'Get out, you!' A sentry posted at the gate—*what gate*? pulled the door open and seized Polly's arm as she scrambled out of the car. She stood still while her guards again took up their positions, looking at the gate post. As she had seen from her bicycle a month before, traces of the words 'Villa Mon Bijou' were still visible on the stonework.

They took her into a handsome entrance hall with a black and white tiled floor, and handed her over to a young lieutenant with a muttered explanation which Polly could not follow, except that it seemed to end with the words 'for Captain Eckhardstein'. The officer told her to sit down, and went away. Polly sat on an oak chair, the kind of chair concealing a chest for rugs and scarves and not meant for comfort, and the two soldiers stood behind her for a half hour that seemed endless. The officer had gone, possibly to alert Captain Eckhardstein: the idea, Polly guessed, was to break down her control by subjecting her to silence and fearful anticipation. At that all her courage, the courage too often expressed by a love of danger for danger's sake, stiffened into opposition. She was in the home of her husband's youth, brought as a prisoner where she might have been welcomed as a bride, and for his sake and the sake of her own pride Polly Preston would be brave as long as courage lasted in the clutches of the Gestapo.

The single window in the entrance hall faced north, and Polly was not prepared for the brilliant light which filled the room into which she was at last taken. She guessed that it had been Jacques' mother's drawing room, with its pretty rosy wallpaper and delicate flower paintings. Only the carpet had been taken up—could it be to avoid bloodstains?—and the marble floor of the local stone was bare. Everything else was as Madame Brunel had left it, the piano, the Louis XV chairs, the flower-filled stands on each side of the bay window, and the gilt-fronted bookcase with leather-bound volumes of Racine and Molière. It was more terrifying to find a Gestapo office installed in this ambience of feminine charm and culture than if there had been instruments of torture on the table and a row of meat-hooks on the wall.

There was nothing immediately terrifying about the man who sat behind the writing table. He was a German officer of the same age and type as Erwin Gerhardt at Limoges, and his voice, when he spoke to her in French, was pleasant. 'Sit down, Madame Brunel,' he said, 'I have some serious news for you. Your husband, Jacques Brunel, was arrested today in the city of Nice.'

'On what charge?' Polly forced herself to say.

'He is accused of the murder of Bastien Léquipe, a French citizen, in the Parc des Arènes at Cimiez on January 5, 1943.'

'I never heard of Bastien Léquipe in my life.'

'Not by name, perhaps, madame.'

'Of course there's been a terrible mistake,' said Polly, taking courage from the sound of her own voice. 'My husband's duty is to administer the law, not to break it. You say this man Léquipe was a citizen. I take it my husband was arrested—wrongfully—by the civil power?'

Captain Eckhardstein smiled. So she was one of the smart ones, who often broke faster than the others in the end. He said. 'Bastien Léquipe was a member of the *Milice*, madame, and subject to our military law. Your husband was arrested by the Gestapo.'

'Will he be tried by military law? Will he be represented by counsel at this trial?' said Polly.

'That will depend on his willingness to assist us, Madame Brunel, and yours too.'

'Mine? How do I come into it?'

'Because we have an interesting dossier on you as well as on your husband. We know from the records of the Peille sanatorium, where you worked for a short time in November 1942, that you are an American citizen, that your name is Pauline Mary Preston, and that you changed your name to Henri before your marriage to Jacques Brunel. We know you resided in Paris with Anne Marie Bertrand, arrested for terrorist activities and executed in Ravensbruck, and we also know that you were seen in a motor car at the gate of the Parc des Arènes on the night Léquipe was murdered. The car was a Peugeot, and a policeman on duty in the Avenue Jean Jaurès saw a woman in Brunel's Peugeot, driven by him, about half an hour after the arrests at Cimiez.'

Polly licked her lips. They had come terribly near the truth, and if they could produce witnesses—! She remembered the policeman very well.

The German was watching her keenly. 'Make no mistake, Madame Brunel,' he said, 'we can bring this crime home to your husband, and to yourself as an accessory after the fact, unless'—he paused for emphasis '*unless* you both supply us with the names of your husband's accomplices in his terrorist activities. We want to know the British agents operating on the Côte d'Azur, the places used for Royal Air Force drops of arms and supplies, and the safe houses operated in the area.'

'And make no mistake,' said Polly with spirit, 'I don't know what you're talking about, and I know nothing about anybody's terrorist activities. I used to do volunteer work among deprived children, until you people sent them all away. Now I'm just a housewife, and I wouldn't recognise a terrorist if I met one in the middle of the Rue Longue.'

Captain Eckhardstein sighed. 'I was afraid you were going to say that,' he said. 'It's all part of the terrorist script, isn't it? Believe me, madame, we shall gratify your taste for melodrama. I can see by the way you're looking behind you every time the door creaks that you expect a masked man to come in and tear off your finger-nails, or mark your pretty face with a burning cigarette. That won't happen here. I shall have to send you on to Villa Lynwood, where they have complete facilities for interrogation.' He touched a bell. 'Take the prisoner downstairs.'

'When shall I see my husband?' Polly cried as the guards pulled her to her feet, and Captain Eckhardstein smiled. 'Probably at the Villa Lynwood,' he said. 'I hope you'll be able to recognise each other.'

They marched her down two flights of back stairs to what Polly supposed was a second basement, and pushed her into a room which might have been a servant's bedroom. It now contained no furniture but a pallet and a chair, with an electric light fixture high up in the ceiling, and a lavatory in a small closet ventilated by a grating in the outside wall. The window in the room with the pallet was large and opened easily, but as in many similar houses on the Côte d'Azur it had an ornamental Spanish grating with thick bars only one hundred centimetres apart. When Polly looked out she saw the sea, as if she were on the balcony at the House of the Lance, and well-kept gardens falling in three terraces to the back wall of another house below. The first time she looked out there was a woman on the path between the terraces lugging a heavy bale of what looked like washing, but she only glanced once in Polly's direction before she was out of sight.

Polly sat down on the pallet, a prisoner for the first time in her life. In spite of what lay before her she felt all was not lost. 'I don't believe they've arrested Jacques,' she thought. 'That sergeant gave the game away when he asked me where my husband was. They know a lot, but they're only trying to make me betray Jacques, and that I'll never do until he and the boys come to wherever I am and find me. I'm not going to sit here and weep about it.' For Polly, who cried for Anne Marie in Ravensbruck, and wept with jealousy of another woman's coming child, had no tears to shed for herself. She paced the room, or sat on the pallet, until a soldier brought her a tray with coffee, pumpernickel bread and German sausage, and the sun went down.

The lassitude so contrary to his nature, which overtook Jacques Brunel when he realised that he was in limbo, lasted no longer than a quarter of an hour. Then he paid for the coffee an old waiter had brought him, bought a handful of *jetons* and repaired to the telephone in an evil-smelling basement by the doors marked *Toilettes*, where an old woman in a deck chair wanted to charge him two francs for a sight of the 1938 telephone directory. Jacques laughed at her. He knew the numbers he needed by heart. The trouble was, they were all engaged and didn't answer. He tried Monnier's shop, and Jean Dupont's, and Dr. Lecampion. The doctor was on his rounds, said Madame Lecampion's voice, at the sound of which Jacques hung up at once. He went back for another cup off coffee, waited for twenty minutes and tried again. Still no reply. He thought the woman at the cash desk looked at him suspiciously when he bought more *jetons*, so he went down the street to a café on the corner opposite the boys' high school where one of the teachers had been Sabre, whose murder had triggered off all this confusion. This time the thought of Pauline made him take the risk of calling his office. The phone might be tapped, as Profetti thought, but he couldn't bear the idea of her waiting at the apartment for him to come home. He could see her image on the shabby wall before him, facing into the wind, with her hand raised in that grave salute.

There was no reply from his office, and Jacques Brunel began to wonder if they were all dead or drunk in Menton. But when he tried Dupont's grocery again there was an answer, and after he said, *'C'est vous, Jean?'* there was only the slightest pause before the steady voice of his former corporal replied, 'Where are you?'

'In Nice.'

'You've got your car? I think you should get over here as fast as you can.'

'If I can,' said Jacques. 'It mightn't be too easy.'

'I'll come and meet you,' Dupont said readily, as if he had expected some objection. 'D'you remember that farm near the quarry where you had a picnic with the boys last year?'

'Perfectly.'

'Meet you there in half an hour.'

'Wait!' said Jacques, 'if I don't turn up, I rely on you to get a message to my wife.' There was no reply but a kind of croak, or some defect in the telephone line, before Dupont hung up. Jacques pictured him putting the *'Fermé'* sign on the grocery door, and getting out his truck. He walked back rapidly to the Place Masséna. His car was still there, with a policeman standing beside it. He knew the man, who was often on duty in the Place du Palais, and said *bonjour*.

'Bonjour, Maître Brunel.' The policeman let him get into the Peugeot, and then stooped to speak to him through the driver's window. 'We've been told to look out for your car,' he said in a whisper. 'Which way are you going?'

'Home to Menton.'

'Take the Grande Corniche, then, it's the safest way.' The man stood back and saluted. Jacques drove through the busy streets, feeling that he had passed the first barrier. There was no road block at the exit to the Grande Corniche.

Beyond La Turbie he took to the hill road, and saw Dupont's wagon standing in the farmyard where Victor Marcati had driven the Italian truck on one of their first raids. There was no sign of any of the farm people, and he guessed they were keeping well out of the way. Dupont drew him into the farm kitchen, and told him in one sentence that Pauline had been arrested by the Gestapo and taken to their headquarters in what had been his parents' house.

He wasn't a girl, to faint or scream, but Jacques was glad of the cup of water which Dupont pumped for him at the kitchen sink. He asked for the facts, and got them. The arrival of Miss Torrance at his office with the bad news, and her death from what Dr. Lecampion certified as a massive cerebral haemorrhage, had been followed by the removal of her body to her own house. 'They were all there,' said Dupont. 'The doctor, Julien Monnier and young Chris, along with some decent woman to lay out the body, when Monsieur Janot arrived with Madame Honorine in tow. One of her friends saw Pauline at a basement window in the Villa—what used to be the Villa Mon Bijou, so then they knew where she'd been taken and got in touch with me.'

'I'll never set foot in that damned place again!' said Jacques violently, and Dupont knew he was talking of his father's home. He shook his head. 'What do we do now, *chef*?' he asked.

'Do? We get her away, of course. You know the Boches, Jean. They're predictable. They always stick to the same pattern. When Orengo squealed they picked up Pauline after they lost my trail in Nice, and my guess is that they'll move her on tonight by the train we know goes through Menton at one o'clock. We've got to get her off the train before she ends up with Orengo at the Villa Lynwood.'

'What if she's not on it?'

'Then we take her out of the villa if I have to blow the whole place off the face of the earth.'

'Where would you plan to stop the train?'

'Just west of the Cap Martin tunnel. And get Pauline up to my old hut by the *douaniers*' path.'

'*Chef*, I don't want to make difficulties, but if you blow the train, or even if it came to a shoot-out, it might mean your poor wife's death.'

'Not if we go about it properly. Oh God, I wish I had Aletti here today!'

'You'll have to make do with the rest of us,' said Jean Dupont. 'Just tell us what you want and what to do.'

Polly's courage ebbed away as the night wore on. It grew colder, and she put the single blanket from the pallet round her shoulders, shivering as she remembered the German's sarcastic hope that she and Jacques would be able to recognise each other—after whatever horrors were waiting for the prisoners of the Villa Lynwood. She tried to say a prayer, and the words came in Russian, her almost forgotten language which her godfather, Joe Calvert, had loved so much. She remembered Joe's kind voice, in London, warning her of all the dangers which might lie ahead if she went back with Jacques to France. The one thing she hadn't been able to face was being parted from Jacques, and now she was beginning to wonder if they would ever meet again.

When midnight struck from the belfries of Menton she was taken back to the pretty drawing room and questioned by the young lieutenant who had been on duty in the hall when she was brought in. He kept saying he wanted to give her a chance, to spare her suffering, so that all she had to do was talk. When she refused to talk he struck her, twice or three times across the face, saying that was only a taste of what would happen in Nice, and laughed when the blows knocked her against the edge of the writing table and finally on to the marble floor. Her cheek was bleeding, her ribs aching, when they picked her up and half carried her to the waiting car.

At the Menton station the ticket hall and the platforms were deserted except for a German patrol, but Polly felt the presence of invisible watchers, and walked as steadily as she could between her guards. The train she'd heard described came in at ten minutes to one. Somehow she had hoped for an armed attack by the Resistance at this point, but as on the night Anne Marie Bertrand was taken from Paris, nobody came and there was no help in the world. The two coaches which made up the train were blacked out, but she could hear German spoken as the first coach drew to a halt. Polly was pushed up the high step into the second, which was little better than a cattle truck with a long bench down one side, and handed over to two strange Germans, with a warning from the sergeant that they weren't to get up to any monkey tricks with her because the captain wanted her delivered in prime condition at the Villa Lynwood.

'Scrawny little bitch,' said one of the new guards. 'Nothing to tempt us here, sergeant. What's she done?'

'Terrorist.'

'We're nursemaids to a baby terrorist, Pauli,' said the guard to his mate, and with a look from the heavy handcuffs on a peg to Polly rubbing her bruised arms he added, 'They'll be ordering us to put leg-irons on toddlers next. Just come up here, *Fräulein*, where we can keep an eye on you, and don't try to jump out of the train, because you can't.'

Jacques Brunel set the sights of his mortar and waited with it in the undergrowth beside the railway line five hundred metres west of the Cap Martin tunnel, and on the other side of the line the science teacher waited beside a mortar too. He was the most accurate of the maquisards waiting among the ilex and ivy which grew all along the line to Cabbé, although it was Julien Monnier, the most level-headed, who was to detonate the charge they had laid earlier in the night under the line itself. They had no field telephone, no device to tell them if the German train was on its way, no means of communicating with the reinforcements waiting in the bus with the Red Cross markings parked at the top of the *douaniers'* path. They only had sharp ears and the advantage of the silence in which the train could be heard coming along the permanent way from Carnolès.

The train came out of the tunnel's western portal, and in sixty seconds, counted off by Julien Monnier, the track ahead went up in a burst of explosive and flame. The driver brought his train to a halt in another split minute before he and his fireman, in their open cab, fell dead to bullets from the old Lebels. The maquisards led by Jean Dupont attacked the train with hand grenades, and the mortar fire raised a dense cloud of smoke at the back of the rear coach. Polly's guards seized their rifles and knelt to fire as the door was shot open, and when she heard her husband's voice calling her name she seized the metal handcuffs from their peg and with all her strength hit one of the Germans hard on the back of the head. She felt herself knocked backwards across the floor, had the wits to lie flat as the bullets flew, and then she was in Jacques' arms and lifted clear into the low-growing maquis by the side of the track.

'Here she is, Chris. Run both of you!'

It was amazing how fast the crippled boy could run. He dragged Polly up through the scrub pines and ivy, over the portal of the tunnel, and on to a stone staircase which presently became a cement path beside a mossy wall. Her breath was gone and her bruised side was aching when they reached a low stone hut where the door stood open, and Polly found herself in the hands of Dr. Lecampion.

He gave her a sip of brandy, told her not to talk, and made her lie down on some kind of sofa or divan covered with an old red and black spread. It was difficult to see by candlelight, but the doctor had lint and surgical spirit in his bag, and while Chris Monnier held the candle the doctor cleaned Polly's bleeding face and hands. 'That'll have to do,' he said, 'when you can walk to the top of the path they'll drive you down to the nursing home at Carnolès, and we'll have a proper look at you.'

'I'm all right,' said Polly. 'Oh doctor, where's my husband?'

'S-sh, don't worry, my dear. I'm going down to join him now, and he'll come to you later at the nursing home. You understand, don't you? Captain Jack stays with his men.'

SIXTEEN

At six o'clock on the morning of the fourteenth of July it was already very hot at Erbalunga, when Mike Marchand came back from a quick swim to have coffee and a *croissant* on the terrace of the inn. He had been awake for a couple of hours, since the bombers roused him on their way from Borga/Poretta to attack targets in Northern Italy, thinking about the mission he had to fly that morning and the unusually early start. The passage of the bombers, almost immediately overhead, never seemed to rouse Dina. In the sixth month of her pregnancy her capacity for sleep appeared to be limitless. Eight solid hours a night, a morning nap, a long siesta in the torrid afternoons, and then she was wide awake and happy in the evenings, ready to share in any entertainment her husband could devise.

Enclosed in her cocoon of sleep and physical well-being, Dina had got over the restlessness which tormented her in Cairo. Since Mike told her of his decision to return to Brazil after the war, she appeared to have no more doubts about the future, except as far as it concerned the coming child. She did keep up a steady correspondence with Senhor Rinaldo and Senhorina Lobos, the replacements for Tony and herself at the Capricorn head office, but only because she wanted to keep all the threads of the business in her hands for the planned expansion after the war, and she even spoke of the days when two cousins, Tonio da Costa and Pedro Miguel Marchand, would be running Capricorn Airways while she and Mike were celebrating their silver wedding. When Mike, to tease her, asked if Ester's children weren't to have a slice of the cake, she replied with dignity that the little da Silvas were only girls. She never hankered to fly now because it might be dangerous for Pedro Miguel.

To her brother's problems at Allied Forces Headquarters at Caserta Dina gave a good deal less than the heartfelt sympathy of the past. Tony da Costa (she said, and he said himself) should either have kept out of the whole thing or gone back to Brazil with the Moraes mission in the winter. If he wanted to play politics he should have stayed near President Vargas in Rio, without getting involved with General Dutra who obviously had presidential ambitions, or with another aspiring politician, Colonel Castello Branco, who was to be G3 in Italy. They were *all* involved with the Allied generals and jockeying for a place in the chain of command. Even de Moraes, with the Brazilian rank of Marshal, had to serve under General Willis Crittenberger of the US IV Corps, and Mascarenhas de Moraes was sixty-one, without experience of modern war. Tony, according to himself, served under everybody. He coped with the arrival of the medical officers who came from Rio by air via Natal and Dakar. He coped with the demands for accreditation of the war correspondents from *O Globo* and the *Correio da Manha*. He arranged for combat jackets and winter underclothes from the American government issue to be ready for troops on the high seas in uniforms and boots too light and too shoddy for the campaign in Italy. But through all Tony's lamentations Dina and Mike could detect the note of pride. The 1st Expeditionary Infantry Division, with its artillery, had held a grand if slightly premature parade in Brazil on March 31, and would soon embark for Europe. Twenty-five thousand men out of that vast country would rank as a token force, but to Tony da Costa, now infected by European ideas, they were the saviours of the national honour.

'Saving the national honour' had become an occupational hazard in World War II, and Mike Marchand, finishing his coffee and throwing crumbs of *croissant* to the turtle doves cooing in the bougainvillaea, hoped to hear as little about it as possible on France's national day. He had taken part in too many Fourteenth of July celebrations in too many countries to get excited about this one, with the Allied advance bogged down in Normandy and Operation Dragoon, the invasion of the south, apparently as remote as ever. Still, they were on French soil, and the exuberant citizens of Bastia wouldn't miss such a good opportunity for fireworks and a ball. He was glad their own little party was to be held at Erbalunga and wouldn't go on until the crack of dawn.

One of the hotel maids came by as he got up to go, and said madame had asked for her breakfast coffee. 'Shall I set another cup *mon capitaine*?' Mike said yes, he had just time for another cup; he was glad to hear Dina was awake, because as usual he had forgotten his lucky scarf.

When he went back to the bedroom Dina was sitting up in bed, looking rested and serene. Mike sat on the edge of the bed and took her in his arms. 'I didn't wake you, did I?' he asked.

'When did you go out? I never heard you.'

'I went down and had a swim before breakfast. The sea's like warm milk, if you can swim in milk.'

'Like Cleopatra. What time is it, darling?'

'Only half past six. Very early, for you.'

'I was in bed by half past nine. What time's your take-off?'

'Seven forty-five.'

'And your ETA?'

'About eleven o'clock.'

'If the hotel car goes in to town this morning I could go in with it and meet you for lunch in Bastia.'

'Oh, I wouldn't plan on that, darling! I might be late, and then there's the US Interrogation Report to do before I'm free. I'll grab a delicious Spam sandwich at Poretta and save my appetite for our Bastille Day dinner.'

'All right, but call me as soon as you're free.'

'Sure. Here comes Maria with your tray.'

'I'm going to get up,' said Dina. 'I hate *croissant* crumbs in bed.'

The maid had arranged the cups and saucers on a little table near the window when Dina came back from the bathroom, tying the sash of her new loose wrapper. As her figure altered her face had grown thinner, and with her high cheekbones carved in ivory she was more than ever the Aztec princess of Jacques Brunel's imagination.

'Coffee for you, Mike?'

'A quarter of a cup, and then I have to go.' He slapped the pockets of his tunic. Everything was there for once, jeep keys, I/D, wallet, money—'Oh hell,' he said, 'I nearly forgot my lucky muffler. That's what I came up to look for.'

'I saw you stuffing it in beside the baby clothes.'

Now what would a RAF psychiatrist say to that one? Mike opened the chest of drawers and there it was, with the map of Montenegro folded uppermost, on the tissue paper protecting the layette. Mike had never seen Dina sewing as much as one tiny garment, but there were local women who had fine fabrics laid by, and the skill to make them into garments fit for a royal infant. Pedro Miguel or Rose Tereza (but he hoped it would be Pedro) would be the best-dressed baby in Bastia.

He smoothed down the tissue and hung the silk scarf round his neck.

'How many people shall I tell them to expect tonight?' asked Dina, spreading wild honey on her roll.

'About twenty, unless I collect a few more bods. at the base to-day.'

'It's too bad Antoine de St. Exupéry hasn't arrived yet. Everybody says he loves a party.'

'Missed this one by three days, too bad,' said Mike. 'Still, he and his Flight will be here on the seventeenth. And some of them have rented a villa at Erbalunga, so I expect we'll see a lot of him ... Now, darling, I must run. I'll call you around noon, if not before.'

He kissed her lovingly and snatched up his cap. But Dina called him as he reached the door with one word: 'Mike!'

'Yes?'

'You're not planning to collect Lieutenant Lepage among the bods. at Poretta, are you?'

'Ask Lepage to celebrate the fourteenth of July, no thank you! We had quite enough of him on the eighteenth of June.'

'That's what I thought. Thank you, my darling.'

He came back at that and told her he loved her, there weren't any words to say how much. He told her he would bring back a sheaf of paradise-bird flowers for the party, they were her own flowers, even more than the royal tiger lilies of their wedding day. 'And if I loved you then, my darling,' he whispered, 'think how I love you now!'

The Tricolore was flying above the inn at Erbalunga when he drove off in the jeep, and he saw the flag again over the public buildings of Bastia on his way through the town. He saw the Tricolore in the distance flying side by side with the Stars and Stripes above Poretta, and was glad the American station commander had made the gesture. He made up his mind that he wasn't going to be drawn into a row or even an argument with that young hothead Blaise Lepage. The kid was only twenty, and Michel Marchand's own head had been pretty hot at that age.

He had to admit that it wasn't all that much cooler at thirty-three. Lepage was a new member of the Photographic Reconnaissance Flight, and had of course been invited to the first get-together after his arrival, this one at the Hotel des Voyageurs. It was held on a Sunday night, which happened to be the eighteenth of June, and young Lepage, who was wearing a blue enamel Cross of Lorraine on his breast pocket, had seemed to fit in with the rest of the RAF types. He sang well, and knew all the words of 'Ten Green Bottles', 'Easy Come, Easy Go' and other favourites. But at a lull in the proceedings the young Frenchman, who might have had an extra glass of wine, had boldly asked the company to drink the health of the First Resistant of France, General de Gaulle, on this the fourth anniversary of the great call whereby he had saved the national honour. The others drank good-naturedly, and it would have been easy for Mike, who was standing in the background, to put down his glass without a word. But Mike, who had certainly had a good deal of whisky, told the boy that he refused to drink to the man on whom the honour of France, *Dieu merci*! did not depend, whose Resistance began and ended in the crab-pot of Algiers. The British and the Americans were dying in the Normandy *bocage*, said Mike, while de Gaulle had had his feet on French soil for a few hours only, courtesy of Mr. Churchill, and then was taken safely back to his hideout in London.

Before he got so far, not heeding Dina's tugs at his sleeve, the noise in the room was considerable, and young Lepage was demanding satisfaction, in the style of Dumas, for the insult to his honour and his general. A good deal of calming-down had to be done by the senior men present. 'Surprised at you, Marchand,' was all his commanding officer said by way of reprimand, but Mike knew he had 'put up a black' and was pleased to see that when Lepage next appeared on duty he was not sporting the Cross of Lorraine. About ten days after the incident de Gaulle's admirer approached him and said, 'I was over at Ajaccio yesterday, Marchand. I met a Colonel Corbeau there who says he knows you.'

Biting back the words, 'He used to fly for the Nazis,' Mike said, 'I've met Colonel Corbeau several times. Is he airborne or chairborne at Ajaccio?'

'He's still flying, if that's what you mean.' Lepage moved away, and looked back over his shoulder. 'He was very interested to hear about our little—argument.'

So now Mike Marchand had confirmation of the report that Anders Lachmann, alias Corbeau, had arrived in Corsica, and was flying—what aircraft he didn't know—out of an airfield less than an hour away. Each of them could find out by a mere telephone call when and where the other man was flying, because the Americans didn't regard that sort of query as classified between air bases. Mike didn't suppose it mattered very much. He only hoped Lachmann-Corbeau wouldn't turn up as a guest at Bastia, for then the row at the Hotel des Voyageurs was likely to be repeated on a larger scale.

He left the jeep in the parking lot and went to change before the briefing for his mission. Lepage's name was not on the roster of that morning's flyers—his own name, of course was—and glad to avoid a confrontation on this emotional day he had a shower before putting on his heavy flying gear. There was sometimes a shortage of hot water at the Erbalunga inn.

They had started on Bastille Day in good time at Poretta. The powerful American amplifiers were flooding the base with music from one of the island's radio stations, which was doing a patriotic programme. The *Marseillaise* was played again and again, between '*Sambre et Meuse*' and the '*March Lorraine*'; the music, played *con brio* by a local band, drowned out the drumming of the shower. Within the steamy veil of water, claustrophobic and evocative, Mike found himself thinking of other years and other Bastille Days. Of 1940, when Lachmann attacked him outside his London flat, and Mr. Churchill's sense of drama gave de Gaulle his first chance to appear before the London public. Of 1935, when Mike Marchand was the champion pilot who set up a new record, Montreal to Bucharest, and was cheered by a Paris crowd in the Place de la Concorde. He supposed he was lucky, nine years later, to be flying still.

The *Marseillaise* was echoing across the tarmac and out to sea when the Lightning was ready to take off, and Mike emerged from the briefing session ready to be helped into his flying gear. He had a relatively short mission up the valley of the Var, but it meant nearly four hours of solo flying, most of the time at ten thousand metres altitude, for which he had prepared himself by an hour's intensive map work after Dina went to bed the night before. The heated flying suit with the Mae West above it was a burden to the pilot as the heat increased with every moment of the July day, but unlike some members of the Flight Mike never scamped on the cockpit check of instruments and equipment before the take-off. The sweat was running down his neck into his lucky muffler before the Assistant Operations Officer gave the signal to the mechanics to pull away the chocks. Mike was airborne over the lagoon, the Estang de Biguglia which had reminded Dina of Jean Mermoz's Lago do Bomfim, and flew north along the coast line towards Cap Corse.

Erbalunga came into sight, a series of land and seascapes which inspired painters, with the chapel of Our Lady of the Snows standing high on the mountainside above the Benedictine monastery. Dina wasn't always out of doors when he began his missions, but she was there today in a flowing pale blue linen dress, the colour of the plumbago which grew all over the terrace where she stood. Mike flew low enough to see her waving what looked like a blue handkerchief—Dina no longer a creature of the air, but bound to the earth by the most powerful of all ties. He dipped his wings, and began his steady climb towards the sun.

Over Cap Corse he altered his course to NNW for the mouth of the Var. That would bring him over the city of Nice, where the enemy fighters had been very aggressive lately. Mike looked in his rear view mirror every twenty or thirty seconds to make sure there was no Messerschmitt upon his tail, but the sky was empty, and beneath him the Mediterranean was wide. Two liberated islands lay to starboard, Sardinia freed at the same time as Corsica, and Elba, taken by French colonial troops on the same infernal eighteenth of June Lepage had made all the fuss about. He thought again, without wishing to, of Lachmann.

Mike Marchand had felt shame, in secret, when the sixth of June had brought nothing so unimportant as the arrival of his enemy in Corsica, but the great Allied invasion across the Channel. That made D-Day a day to remember, and in the weeks which passed since then Mike Marchand, like his cousin in the case of Pierre Orengo, had been lulled into a false sense of security where Lachmann was concerned. He had almost persuaded himself that the incident at the Pigeon Rocks was what the Lebanese authorities called it—a failed anti-government demonstration. No Lachmann was needed to add to the occupational hazards of a war pilot. Mike had had a good many adventures over the Mediterranean since he joined the Flight, and more than once came in to land at Poretta 'on a wing and a prayer', as the American song said.

Mike increased his altitude in anticipation of the flak at Nice, checked his camera, checked the mapping pad strapped to his right knee, the pencils in his pocket, and the oxygen flask fastened to his left leg. He knew well enough that a long tour of duty could cloud a pilot's better judgment, and had reached the stage of compulsive double checks, particularly where the rear mirror was concerned. He looked into it for one more time, and saw a plane coming up fast on his port wing.

At first glance he saw it was a Royal Air Force plane, a Spitfire with the red, white and blue roundels, and felt a qualm of uneasiness. There were no fighters on the ground at Borga/Poretta, and unless this fellow had made the long hop from Algiers he must have taken off from Ajaccio. He also appeared to be set on a collision course. But Mike's year in Bomber Command had given him the nerve to fly on collision courses very close to the enemy, and he pulled out under and behind the Spitfire's tail. At the next moment he heard the stutter of the Spitfires guns.

But the guy was crazy! If he'd been a German Mike would have gained height and attacked him out of the sun, but he was unarmed, and helpless except for his flying skill. He blacked out momentarily as he pulled the Lightning into a vertical climb with the throttle wide open, planning an aileron turn and a descent in a fast dive. But the crazy guy was alongside him, firing again, and as his port wing juddered to the hit he had a glimpse of the face beneath the helmet, and beside the RAF roundels on the Spitfire's fuselage the hated symbol of the Cross of Lorraine.

'Lachmann!'

Mike Marchand knew then that his luck had run out. He had been living on borrowed time for years, since he was a young test pilot in the Andes—and now the panorama of the Côte d'Azur and the white buildings of Nice was bathed in the dream-light of the Andes—and the last enemy was his old challenger, Anders Lachmann. He still had control of the Lightning, but Lachmann was coming in for the kill with his guns in action. There was blood from a ricochet on Mike Marchand's face. 'Dina!' he thought. 'The kid!' And then another primitive instinct gripped him, more urgent even than the instinct to call on his wife and child. 'I'll take him with me!' He flew the Lightning straight at Lachmann's plane.

At the airfield the Interrogation Officer had a paper cup of coffee, and was ready for Flight-Lieutenant Marchand's return at eleven o'clock. There was no sign of him by half past eleven. At twelve a call was put in to radar control, which reported no contact with the Lightning since half past eight. The station commander and the Operations Officer were watching the radar screen, hoping against hope to see the blips announcing Mike's return, when an orderly brought in a slip of paper. The senior officer read it and crumpled it in his hand.

'Marchand's wife called up,' he said briefly. 'Wants to know if he's landed okay.'

'Are you going to call her back, sir? Or shall I?'

'I'll wait for half an hour. This is the worst bloody bit of the whole business—telling the wife. Dina Marchand's expecting a baby too.'

The last half hour, when the fuel supply of even a living pilot was bound to be exhausted, dragged by in total silence. The radar screen remained blank. And at half past twelve a young man who had been invited to the Marchands' party at Erbalunga filled in the Interrogation Report Card with a sigh:

'Pilot did not return and is presumed lost. No pictures.'

SEVENTEEN

Captain Jack stays with his men. Polly had not needed Dr. Lecampion's reminder of where her husband thought his duty lay. The Resistance came first, and now that he was assured of his wife's safety Jacques Brunel gave his whole mind to the safety of the boys who had delivered her from the Villa Lynwood and the Gestapo. Eight Germans had died inside the train or on the railway line, and on the French side the science teacher and two of the Menton fishermen were severely wounded. The maquisards were far from a road of any sort, and the simplest thing was to improvise stretchers and carry their wounded along the level track to the plumber at Cabbé, whose workshop became an emergency hospital directed by Dr. Lecampion.

The other men were ordered to scatter and get as far as possible from the train before the Germans arrived. Some spent the night in the hut where Polly had been taken, some in the garage attached to Dupont's shop, while others headed for a disused quarry near Roquebrune-Bon Voyage. Wherever they went, they all had to wait until the next night for transportation to the encampment in the forest, to which they were now committed until the end of the war.

It was three o'clock in the morning when Polly was escorted by Chris Monnier, very proud of his trust, to the nursing home at Carnolès next door to the Russian church. She kept telling the matron, who was Dr. Lecampion's friend, that she wasn't hurt, and didn't need sedation because she wanted to stay awake till her husband came. It was not until she was clean and comfortable in a white hospital nightgown with strapping on the rib cracked when the Gestapo lieutenant knocked her across the table in what had once been the Villa Mon Bijou, that the matron said to the nurse who had the sleeping pill and the glass of water ready on a tray:

'The poor child doesn't need sedation, nurse, she's half asleep already. If the husband should appear before eight o'clock, he must be told not to wake her.'

He came before six on a fine summer morning, when the birds were singing among the roses of Carnolès, and listened, swaying with fatigue, to what the nurse on night duty had to tell him. She was a soft-hearted girl, whose brother was a prisoner of war in Germany, and yielding to the plea of 'Just let me look at her!' she admitted Jacques to his wife's room. When Polly woke up late in the morning he was asleep in an armchair beside the open window, with his long legs stretched out in front of him and a night's stubble mixed with the soot and dirt still smeared across his face.

She was running a temperature when the matron made her rounds, and Jacques was scolded for agitating the patient. 'I couldn't stop her from talking, madame, I never could,' he said, and she told him tartly that he should choose his subjects of conversation better. The transformation of the Villa Mon Bijou was something he didn't want to talk about himself, but the casualties of the train attack could not be kept from Polly, and she was not reassured about the wounded men until Dr. Lecampion arrived, late in the afternoon. He told her that all three had been taken by ambulance to the municipal hospital, where they had come through surgery successfully.

Polly then wanted to know when she and Jacques could start for the Jurac farm.

'Not for thirty-six hours, young lady,' said the doctor decidedly, 'and only then if you haven't a trace of fever. Matron has found a room for your husband, and if you know what's good for you you'll both keep under cover for as long as you can.'

But when Jacques, now shaved and bathed, followed the doctor into the corridor he had other ideas.

'I've got to go out tomorrow morning, Freddy. That's if you've done what you said you would, before we left for Cap Martin.'

'Arrange for that poor lady's funeral? Yes, it's done. But you're crazy to think of risking arrest at the cemetery.'

'Rachel Torrance was a brave woman,' said Jacques. 'I'm not going to be cowardly enough to stay away from her burial.'

'I'll see Père Georges again, then, and change the time to as early in the morning as possible. I'll let you know when to be at the Chappelle St. Roch.'

Miss Torrance had been a Catholic, and had purchased a grave in the Menton cemetery when she came to live in the town. A humble cortège, with only one car following the hearse, was a familiar sight in Menton, and not a German head was turned as Miss Torrance's funeral procession went up the road behind the cathedral to the ancient graveyard The only mourners were Monsieur Janot, Chris, Julien Monnier and Jacques, the last two being armed, and there was no interruption to the service. Before they drove back to town Jacques gave some instructions to his clerk which caused the good man to tremble at the latest of 'Monsieur Jacques'' innovations, in regard to the German lease of the Villa Mon Bijou. Then the innovator returned to Carnolès, and broke the news to Pauline that the old woman whom she had befriended had died of a stroke following the heat and hurry of the attempt to save her life.

That night the nurse gave Polly a sleeping pill, and late on the night after that she and Jacques went up to the Col de Castillon.

Of the seven young men whom Polly had met on her first visit to the Jurac farm, only Dany was still living with his grandparents. Marcati had been forcibly removed to Corsica, and the other five had gone down the mountain to the forest camp on the very day that they were most needed, when the bloodthirsty Bébé, now sixteen years old, at last took part in the destruction of a train. Polly was puzzled by Dany Profetti's manner. He was a fresh kid, in her own idiom, but he had always been a friendly, pleasant kid in the days when he worked alongside her at the St. Michel home. Now he almost seemed to resent her presence at the Jurac farm. She was pulling her weight there, for old Madame Jurac was failing, and spent most of her waking hours mumbling over the tarot cards, or telling long stories about some mysterious deity called the Holy Bear. Dany had done a lot of household chores before Pauline arrived to help his grandmother, with the shabby clothes and unkempt hair which caused a German patrol, investigating the dwellers on the plateau, to write her off as an ignorant peasant girl. She wondered if Dany objected to going back to his sleeping quarters in the barn after occupying the second room in the *mas* which had been hastily cleared to accommodate Polly.

After a few days she hit on another explanation, just at the time when Dany stopped sulking and seemed resigned to his fate. The second, or spare room had been cleared, certainly, but not thoroughly cleaned out. Such items as a mangle, a cheese press, a churn and a wooden cradle (the last two of which, a generation later, would be snapped up by the antique dealers of Menton) had been removed to the barn, the cobwebs brushed off the little window, and clean rough linen spread on the wooden bed. But there was a scent clinging to the blankets along with the smell of cigarettes, and it was a scent Polly could almost identify. She thought it was called *Arpège*, and some girl she knew had worn it, probably Chantal Malvy. She didn't like to think of Chantal's bedroom, with all the scent bottles on the dressing table, and the cot where poor little Patrick met his death.

Pauline hung the blankets to air in the sun and brought a bucket of water laced with *eau de Javel* to clean the cracked stone floor. The first whisk of the floorcloth brought something new to light: a Coty lipstick, hardly used, which had rolled between the head of the bed and the back wall. She put it away in a drawer and said nothing to Dany, but she told Jacques about it the next time he came up to the farm.

'Dany hasn't been wasting time on the mountain,' she said, and told him the story of the lipstick and the scent. 'It looks as if he's been having some feminine society.'

'Good for Dany,' said Jacques. 'I wonder how he managed it when the other lads were sleeping in the barn.'

'The barn's quite a long way from the house, and the old folks wouldn't know anything about it. I hear them snoring like the Seven Sleepers. What I wonder is, who wears Paris scent in Castillon? Or even in Sospel? Dany's always going to Sospel or Albaréa—'

'The Albaréa maquis!' said Jacques. 'He was talking about that! Could the young fool possibly have fallen for Fabienne Leroux?'

'What's Fabienne got to do with the maquis at Albaréa?' As soon as she spoke Polly remembered. It was Roger Malvy's mistress, not his wife, who had worn *Arpège*.

'She takes them food from the Hotel du Mont,' said Jacques. 'The trouble about Oradour put the whole thing out of my head. He said she was a great girl, but—oh no, it's impossible! Fabienne Leroux must be ten years older than young Dany.'

Ten years more experienced, ten years more fascinating than the girls he met at the 'dancings' at Menton. Just the sort of hungry, restless woman the boy might be meeting now in the Bar des Sports, if he had stayed at home in the Rue Paradis. 'I see trouble ahead for Dany,' Polly said. 'What are we going to do?'

'Us? Nothing, of course. It's no business of ours who Dany Profetti's sleeping with, or where, as long as he doesn't break security. That's what I tell them all! I'm running a *groupe franc*, not a monastery.'

'That's all very well, but I've heard you say often enough that Fabienne's bad news. What if she turns Dany over to the Germans, as she "gave" Roger Malvy to the police?'

'If you're worried about Dany I can order him down to the camp in Menton forest, but that means sending Jojo or Gigène up here. I must have somebody who knows the terrain to liaise with Sospel.'

'Dany seems to be doing *that* all right.'

They both laughed then, a little too loudly and a little too long, as they sometimes did since they both took to the maquis. They seemed to have left gravity behind them on the seashore, for even in the early days of their marriage Jacques and Polly had never been so carefree as they were now. Monsieur Janot was looking after the law practice. Norine was looking after the flat, which had a new lock on the door—the keys had been in Polly's handbag, seized by the Gestapo, along with twenty francs and a powder compact. That took care of their responsibilities in Menton. They were completely cut off from the families at Oradour and Davos, and weeks passed before Jacques learned that Michel Marchand had failed to return from his last mission.

Mike's death was and remained a mystery, and his CO at Borga/ Poretta saw no connection between his disappearance and that of another Frenchman from the Wing at Ajaccio on the same day. Lieutenant Blaise Lepage could have put him 'in the picture', as the CO was fond of saying, but Lepage had applied for a posting to Algiers, where he could wear the cross of Lorraine tattooed all over his body if he liked.

All Jacques cared about was that Polly had been saved from the Gestapo and the Villa Lynwood; it meant nothing to him that he was now an outlaw with a price on his head.

It was Jean Dupont, still driving his grocery van as far as Castillon, who brought the news of *le chef*'s value to the enemy by bringing up one of the bills the Germans had posted all over the countryside between Menton and Nice.

Wanted for Murder!

JACQUES BRUNEL

Fifty Thousand Francs Reward!

'One thousand US dollars for information leading to my arrest,' said Jacques. 'It's not much.'

'It reads better in French,' Dupont acknowledged.

'Throw the damned thing away,' said Jacques. 'I may be disbarred for my share in *l'affaire* Marcati, but I don't need a "Wanted for Murder" bill floating around.'

Polly snatched it away from him. 'Oh no you don't!' she said. 'This'll be good publicity after the war when you're running for Deputy. And when you're the prime minister, and we're living at the Hôtel Matignon, I'll have this one framed and hung up in your study.'

'Darling,' said her husband, 'how much schooling did you have in Baltimore?'

'Not very much. I only finished first grade before we came back to Paris.'

'Then how did you have time to learn all these crazy American ideas about publicity?'

'It must be in the blood,' said Polly solemnly. Dupont had no idea what they were laughing at, but he had never seen his captain so lighthearted.

Polly knew that Jacques was not only lighthearted but light-headed from the feeling that he had burned his boats behind him. She also knew that in spite of his experiences in Norway her husband, who had hankered after an army career when he was a boy, was enjoying his soldiering in the forest of Menton. She had never been invited to the camp, but she knew without seeing it that unlike some of the less disciplined groups Jacques' recruits kept everything in perfect order. Latrines had been dug at the proper distance from the huts, the cooking facilities were good, and racks had been constructed to hold the weapons brought up piecemeal from the garage and the storerooms at the *étude* Brunel. The men were taught how to strip and clean the arms dropped by the RAF, and also how to protect their food and firewood. One of the new arrivals, an electrician, had put in order the generator at the forest ranger's abandoned cottage, and they could listen to the radio news. Sometimes it was the BBC, making cryptic announcements like 'the little birds are in the woods' or 'over all the mountains there is peace', for the broadcasters talking to France could quote Goethe to their purpose. More often they had to listen to the collaborationist radio, announcing that 'Stalin's valets', as the Allies were called on those channels, were making no progress in Normandy, where Rommel would soon drive them into the sea.

It was true that after the first few days of establishing a bridgehead the invaders made slow progress. The American tanks had difficulty in advancing through the marshes and high hedgerows of seaward Normandy, and the British were bogged down in front of Caen. Even the few hours spent by Charles de Gaulle in Bayeux, where it was understood he would make no speeches but he in fact made one, had no effect on progress, and soon the invasion schedule was running twelve days late. This was one of the reasons why the invasion of the south of France had to be postponed. The other was that the French troops fighting under Juin in Italy had to be brought back from the front to embark at Naples, Taranto or Brindisi to take part in Operation Dragoon. It was not easy to keep excitable young men at the knife edge of keenness during the long delay, but the forest maquisards were given plenty of night exercises as June gave place to July. They set fire to two German ammunition dumps at Menton, blew a railway bridge between Cabbé and Monte Carlo, and mined, but not successfully, the main road into Italy. The absence of the science teacher in hospital partly accounted for the failure of the last attempt.

'I wish we'd had Maxwell along last night,' Jacques confessed to Polly when he saw her again. 'He's a better hand with explosives than any of us will ever be.'

'There's still no word of him?'

'None. Polly, do you ever get any news out of the Juracs' old wireless?'

'The only one who can make it work is Dany, and he's too busy liaising to have any time for radios.'

'He's liaising this evening, isn't he?'

'Of course.'

'Well, but you've been following what Radio Vichy says about the terrorists in the Vercors? The mountain near Grenoble?'

'Bits of it, yes.'

'I've a hunch that's where Maxwell went. I think he must have had orders from London to follow the new SOE man up to the mountains before the Vercors was sealed off. Damn the bastion theory anyway! Haven't they learned anything from that disaster at Glières?'

The defence of the Vercors bastion had received the approval of General de Gaulle. It was not his fault that the Frenchmen who shut themselves into the great natural fortress to attack the Germans in the rear were given the order to rise prematurely. It was certainly his fault, as head of the 'provisional government' and their Free French counterparts in London, that they were sent few supplies and no air support at all during the six terrible weeks before they were destroyed by the Germans. Six thousand tricolour armbands, delivered by air, were not adequate to prevent the massacre.

At the end sixty wounded men, with their doctors and nurses, who had taken refuge in a natural grotto of the Vercors, were shot dead or imprisoned when they were discovered by the enemy. Among them were an American OSS officer, who was taken to prison camp and lived, and Lieutenant Charles Maxwell, Royal Artillery, who was killed.

The partisans of the Vercors did not die in silence. Charles de Gaulle never read any blunter words than the signal sent by the maquisards on July 21:

'Those in London and Algiers understand nothing about the situation in which we find ourselves and are considered as criminals and cowards stop yes repeat criminals and cowards.'

But the Vercors was a long way from the Col de Castillon, where on a summer night there was nothing to be heard but the tinkle of cow bells from the high pastures, and the air was sweet with the scent of golden broom. Polly, lying in Jacques' arms beneath a pine tree, reminded him that he had said from the first his group of maquisards must be mobile, and now they had two vehicles in the forest: the Peugeot, brought back from the farm near the Grande Corniche, and the little bus, both carefully camouflaged beneath brushwood and foliage. None of the other maquis in the Roya valley had as much! Jacques laughed and petted her. He thought of the fantastic weight of matériel being landed in Normandy since the Americans took Cherbourg, and told her gravely that she'd forgotten to count a dozen bicycles.

He used one of the bicycles when he went up to the Jurac farm to see her, and Polly lived for those nights when he whistled outside her window, and was a boy again. Jacques was dressed like all the other maquisards in corduroy trousers and a rough shirt open at the throat; his beret was usually thrust into the front of his shirt, full of the white 'pigeon's heart' cherries he had stolen from the roadside orchards. Polly would put on a cotton dress and heavy shoes, and slip out to him as if he were a young 'Blue Devil' up from the Caserne Salel and she his girl, and then they would run across the pasture where the dew lay on the grass into the warm shelter of the trees. They would make love there, lying on the pine needles, and eat the luscious cherries, and never, not even in the first flush of their passion in the cottage in the forest of Compiègne, had Jacques and Polly known such perfect physical felicity. For Polly the pleasure was heightened by her close brush with torture and death, and for her husband by the faint glimmer of light from Fort Castillon across the plateau, the constant reminder that while the enemy held the country every day might be his last.

One other woman could have understood how Polly Brunel abandoned herself to the unbridled sexuality of those nights in early August, when the full moon rose above the singing rivers and the forests which hid the camps of fighting men. That woman was Fabienne Leroux, with whom Polly had never been in sympathy, but who was snatching in the last desperate hours of the Occupation at the unexpected passion of a boy more than ten years younger than herself. Fabienne was not in love with Dany Profetti. She was amazed when he first dared to try his luck with her, and she yielded out of curiosity and from hunger. There had been no man in her bed since Roger Malvy, for whose dreadful end she was twice responsible, and Fabienne was sick of feeling remorse and guilt. She let Dany come once to her room at the Hotel du Mont, and twice went back with him to the farm—but only in the nature of a dare, to see if they could get away with it and fool his grandparents and the boys in the barn. She wouldn't have gone back, because the ride down to Sospel before dawn on the step of Dany's bike was too uncomfortable, but she was amused to hear of Pauline's arrival, and to think of 'that little adventuress' and her Jacques sleeping in the feather bed where she had lain with Dany.

No, the place to meet her young lover, that magnificent animal of twenty, was out of doors, and Fabienne flaunted their meetings. There was no trade at the Hotel du Mont that summer, and she was free early in the evenings: she didn't care how many gossips saw Dany waiting for her on the bridge of the Bévéra, smoking and watching the surge of the water over the weir. They would walk away together down the road that led to Nice, and then turn off into the path which led to the meadows by the Merlanson, and the secret place they knew among the flowers.

She was greedy for the boy. He was a better lover than any man she had ever had, and he was mad about her too. It wouldn't last, it couldn't, she was old enough to know that, but while their passion was at fever pitch she didn't care who knew it and behaved accordingly. Until the Germans began to take an interest in them.

The German troops were growing very nervous. Since they moved in to Sospel, and discovered that their arrival had brought to birth a serious Resistance movement, they had made some spectacular arrests following swoops upon the forest maquis. They had seized one man, a noted character in the mountain country, had sent him to be dealt with by the Gestapo in Menton, and while he was on his way there under guard had seen to it that he was 'shot while trying to escape'. They had persecuted a wretched group of Polish Jews who had taken refuge in an alpine resort called Le Moulinet, and they shot and killed a band of shepherds, whom they called terrorists, in the high pastures of the Authion. In the late spring the farmers were conscripted to work on the railway, the Germans' escape route into Italy, and while the farmers were at work the Germans drove their cows and sheep away. A German detachment suffered heavy losses when attacked by Italian partisans between Fontan and Saorge, and this was followed by railway sabotage. But the real blow fell on July 28, when Allied aircraft bombed the railway at Breil, the station which, because it was the junction of the line to Ventimiglia, was the most important target on the Nice to Cunéo run. From that day forward the Occupying Power in Sospel was spoiling for a fight, and the cause for a fight presented itself in Dany.

It began with the simple words, 'Here, you!'

It began on a beautiful August evening when Dany rode down from the Col de Castillon on his bicycle, arriving at the bridge where the two arms of the Y met while Fabienne was still strolling along beneath the plane trees which bordered the upper reach of the Bévéra. She looked magnificent in her black dress, with her head bare, and when she saw Dany Profetti waiting she raised her

283

hand—once—in a languid gesture that was less a greeting than a summons.

'Here, you! What's your name, and what's your business here?'

Dany turned in surprise. The man knew quite well who he was, for Dany came to the village often, officially to buy provisions for his grandparents. He produced his identity card with a smile which annoyed the sergeant, and when Fabienne came up and slipped her arm through Dany's the man was angrier than ever. He told Dany he ought to be working on the railway, or sent to do some honest work in Germany, and he, the sergeant, would personally see him set to one job or the other if he didn't clear out of Sospel, *jetzt, sofort,* and be sure he wasn't in a hurry to come back.

The usual posse of soldiers had come up behind their sergeant, and Dany knew they were all laughing at him. He said 'Come on, Fabienne!' and turned the bike round to get away from the place, to take her in to the café of the Hotel de la Gare for a drink, maybe. He had enough money in his pocket to buy a bottle of wine.

'Where are we going?'

She didn't have to ask that, for God's sake! The old men playing *pétanque* above the banks of the Bévéra were laughing at him like the Germans, and the loafers round the Café des Platanes were craning their necks to see what was happening, and he was damned if he was going to leave her there and straddle the bike and ride away. Dany Profetti said, like a man laying down the law:

'We're going up to Albaréa. At least they'll leave us alone there!'

He knew quite well, as he led the way into the path up the pastures to the old farm where there had been a children's colony, that Captain Jack would have ordered him to get the hell back to the Jurac farm and keep away from an Italian maquis. But he had as good a right as Captain Jack to enjoy his woman, and if he'd been made to look a fool in front of her he would soon show Fabienne who was the boss. In a fury of humiliation and unsatisfied desire he strode on until they came to the outbuildings of Albaréa.

The Italian maquisards were not particularly glad to see them. Dany and Fabienne were rather a hindrance to their evening programme, especially as Fabienne had brought no food. But they were tired of the scraps from the Hotel du Mont, and of going hungry: their plan was to go down to Sospel after dark, raid the Co-operative's store and see what extra dainties they could pick up at the club house, called a hotel, beside the little golf course which there were no holidaymakers to play over now. They asked Dany Profetti to go along with them.

Even then, Fabienne could have stopped him by a show of tenderness, by a coy indication that he and she would rather be alone together. But Fabienne's pride had been injured like his own. A glass of red wine and a cigarette turned her into something like one of the gangster's molls Dany admired in the movies. With her arms akimbo, and her face flushed with excitement, Fabienne volunteered to join the raid as well.

They were picked up by a German patrol at *Le Golf*, with their arms full of stolen goods from *Le Co-op*, and taken in handcuffs to the Salel barracks where after a mass interrogation by a furious major of the *Panzergrenadieren*, the Albaréa maquisards were thrown into separate cells and interrogated further. Dany heard screaming during the night, and once he thought he heard a woman's voice. But it was certainly not Fabienne's, for she was sitting where he could see her, between two women guards, and about midnight one of them even brought her a cup of coffee. Dany was not interrogated. He wasn't able to sleep, because they had put him into a sort of open cubicle under the bright lights of the central hall where Fabienne was sitting. That proved they weren't going to be treated badly, and would be believed when they told the judge what they had told the angry major, that it was all a terrible mistake.

In his heart Dany knew that the judge would not believe him, and that all he could do now was what Captain Jack had often told them: be silent under torture as long as you can, because no man can do more. It was a shock to find out, after the guards had taken him out to a washroom, that there would be no torture and certainly no judge. The major, they said, had made up his mind overnight. There were two thousand people in Sospel and he would teach them once and for all that they couldn't go on feeding a bunch of terrorists and expect to get away with it. He was going to make an example of the Albaréa lot, and that was that.

Of this announcement, which was made partly in German and partly in ribald French, Dany Profetti understood only the sense. It was the hour of the morning when he should be having breakfast in his grandmother's kitchen before riding down to the forest to give Captain Jack the latest report from Sospel. So many more Italian partisans coming over the Col de Fende, so many more companies of *Panzergrenadieren* arriving from Turin—it was all a matter of statistics, not of human beings, and now Daniel Profetti junior was about to become a statistic too. He began to cry then, and rubbed his wet face with a dirty towel. He had to be brave for both of them—himself and Fabienne.

The prisoners were made to walk to an empty space near some warehouses behind the railway station. Everybody in Sospel who could stand had been ordered out to see the procession of the condemned go by. They were huddled in the public gardens beneath the plane trees, many of them known to Dany Profetti as Resistance sympathisers, their faces set in masks of horror. They watched the eleven Italians, four Frenchmen, Fabienne Leroux and himself. The guards let him hold her hand. She said, 'I'm sorry, Dany,' but she didn't look sorry, she looked as if she didn't care. He tried to look as if he didn't care either. He said, 'I love you, Fabienne,' and she looked at him with those wonderful dark eyes and said, 'I love you too.'

It was a bungled business at the end, because the people in the gardens were trying to sing the *Marseillaise* in several different keys, a priest was praying, and a German officer was shouting at the firing squad. Maybe what the priest said would count in the long run, but the officer's words were what the men obeyed, and they took the Albaréa maquisards out of their ranks in groups of five. They bound them to five tall posts, at the far end of the empty ground. The Italians were protesting, and there were more orders and counter-orders about bandaging their eyes. Fabienne wanted to cover her eyes too. She hid her face in Dany's shirt and the officer let him hold her for a minute while he stared over her dark head at what was going on. When he saw how easy it was, how quick, he didn't mind so much, but kissed the girl and said *adieu* to the sound of the final volley. The Germans were merciful at the last and didn't drag them to the place of execution. The officer drew his revolver and shot down Dany Profetti and Fabienne Leroux where they stood with their arms round each other, on the dusty ground, beneath the August sun.

EIGHTEEN

The Allied invasion of the south of France began in the small hours of August 15, when paratroopers of the 1st US Task Force took off from Cap Corse to drop at Le Muy in the Var. At 8 a.m. the amphibious operation started with the landing of three American infantry divisions and French II Corps on five selected beaches between Cavalaire and Anthéor, west of Cannes. It was ten weeks to the day since the invasion of Normandy, with which Operation Anvil, now called Dragoon, had been intended to coincide.

Once the beachhead was established the Americans went north up the Rhône valley to join their armies descending from Normandy, and the French went west to capture Marseille and Toulon, the two deep water ports which Eisenhower needed for the landing of men and armour. French II Corps was commanded by the dramatic General de Lattre de Tassigny, whose personality alone assured that his men would be cheered along the whole way to victory.

They were not the first French troops to be engaged in the liberation of metropolitan France. General Leclerc had had to wait a long time in Yorkshire for his Sherman tanks, but they arrived at last, and he crossed the Channel with the 2nd Armoured Division on D-Day plus 56. This was not as impressive as de Lattre's dash for the great prizes, which were soon secured along with 35,000 German prisoners of war.

In the joy of cheering a French army, 200,000 strong, returning to liberate the motherland, no civilian stopped to ask where half of them had come from. But they were Juin's men from Italy, and their transfer meant that General Alexander's denuded forces had to face a long winter war north of Florence before the Germans surrendered, with no hope of entering Austria before the Russians took Vienna.

This consequence of the invasion was still the future when de Lattre's men swept on to liberate Marseille. There was no cheering in the high country between Menton and Sospel. The execution of the maquisards had been a fearful shock, and the civic leaders of Sospel showed great courage in resisting the German orders to throw the bodies of their victims, without identification, into a common grave. The men of the town carried the dead to the cemetery chapel and the canon of the cathedral gave them Christian burial, while their names were recorded to appear later as an addition to the existing war memorial.

The one thing to be thankful for, said Jacques Brunel when he heard the news, was that the Germans hadn't run amok. 'A mass execution is quite bad enough,' he said, 'but thank God the Boches didn't turn it into a wholesale massacre, as they did at Oradour. What the hell was Dany doing at Albaréa anyway?' he asked furiously.

'I bet you Fabienne was at the bottom of it,' said Polly, who had ridden down to his command post on her bicycle to pass on the bad news brought up to Castillon that morning by a goatherd from one of the mountain pastures.

'Did you tell the Juracs that?'

'Of course not, and you mustn't either. They don't know anything about her, and it's best they should go on thinking poor Dany died a hero's death, leading a forlorn hope for the Resistance.'

'I should have ordered him down to the forest as soon as you warned me about Fabienne,' said Jacques, and Polly saw that her husband was about to indulge in the self-blame which was a defect of his character. She said briskly, 'You might as well punish yourself for sending Dany up to the Jurac farm two and a half years ago. And that was his mother's idea in the first place, wasn't it?'

'I was responsible for him, Pauline.'

Polly sighed. She felt that Dany's death marked another turning point in their always developing relationship. Their second honeymoon was over, and the ghosts of Dany and Fabienne would haunt the scented pastures where they had lain together. 'Poor Fabienne,' she said, 'I hope she had some fun with Dany before it ended for them both.'

'How am I going to break the news to that boy's parents?' said Jacques. 'He should have been killed in action, instead of being shot down like a dog.'

'His grandparents think he *was* killed in action. Talking to them's more important than breaking the news to the Profettis.'

'How are they taking it?'

'The old lady says she knew it when she read it in the cards, and saw the Holy Bear walking on the Mont Ours,' said Polly. 'She's really pretty dotty now. And so's Monsieur Jurac in another way. *He* wants to go down to Sospel and strangle the German commandant with his own hands.'

'You oughtn't to be alone there with the two of them. I'll come up first thing in the morning to see if I can persuade them to pack up and go to the Profettis at Nice.'

'The way you describe the Rue Paradis, I can't see Madame Jurac serving behind the *zinc* at the Bar des Sports. Are you going on a job tonight?'

'We've got something planned.'

The something was the cutting out of one truck from a German supply convoy unloading in the Parc de la Madone at Carnolès, and the burning of the other vehicles in what turned out to be the last of such convoys travelling east from Nice. Next morning, news of the invasion put an end to convoys as the enemy regrouped his forces and prepared his retreat.

Hitler had ordered his generals to fight for every hedge and ditch in Normandy, and while Rommel led them they very nearly boxed up the Allies during the month of June. Now it was the German 19th Army which was boxed up between Nice and the Italian border, and with no de Lattre, no General Patch to follow them up there was only a handful of Resistance men to hinder their escape.

The Occupation troops in Menton set out in the direction of Sospel.

'We'll hold our fire until they're past Monti,' said Jacques to the men around him in the forest. 'The naval guns will take care of them till they get that far.'

'Also our homes and families,' said one of the fishermen. The men had made up their minds, as the women at the doors of the Rue Longue had made up their minds already, that the new invasion would be '1940 all over again', and they were not far wrong. They had grown accustomed to shortages of food and fuel, but now there was no bread in Menton, and since Jean-Pierre, the Resistance man at Carnolès, had carried out his plan of emulating Lenin in the October Revolution, there had been no gas either. The result was to harass the Germans, but it also harassed the Mentonese, and one of the Resistance groups in the hills had cut off supplies from the reservoir. No water flowed from the taps, and the women had to go to the fountains with their jugs and buckets. Even finding the fountains took some doing since they had been covered over in the building developments of the twentieth century. An old man always known as *monsieur le fontanier* was eventually winkled out of his little cottage up the Gorbio high road and brought back to Menton, where he enjoyed a brief fame by pointing out the sites of the springs he had once kept clean and attaching emergency pumps to bring up water from the wells below. Some people feared an epidemic. Many left the town, beginning the second evacuation from Menton in four years as families locked up their homes and started westwards to Nice and the Department of the Var. All the towns between the invasion beaches and Nice had been liberated by the Americans. St. Raphaël and Fréjus were free on D-Day plus one, Nice not until two weeks later, but the Germans had not given battle there, and little material damage was done. Only Menton, the sacrifice of 1940, was sacrificed again as the naval guns fired across the city, and the Germans left a trail of destruction in their rear.

A few hours before the head of their column started up the Val du Carëi, Jacques Brunel made a hasty trip to the Jurac farm, with Julien Monnier beside him in the little bus. With Froment and Jean Dupont both out of reach, and Charles Maxwell vanished from sight, the big butcher from the Rue Trenca had become the second in command of the *groupe franc*, with as much natural talent for soldiering as Jacques himself. He had warned Jacques that his plan for the Juracs would be defeated by the old lady. 'You'll never get her away from her own bed and the black stew-pot,' he said. 'You may get Madame Pauline to move, but not the other two.'

Old Jurac was tremulously glad to see the maquisards, and to listen to all their praises of poor Dany, *mort pour la France*. 'They gave him a proper burial, *messieurs*,' he said, 'in consecrated ground. The old girl and I will soon follow, and that's the end of *la ferme Jurac*. Those filthy Boches will burn the place down round our ears ...'

'Yes, well, that's what we want to prevent, Monsieur Jurac,' said Jacques. 'We think it's not very safe for you alone up here. Pauline, I'd like to speak to you for a minute—'

In the crazy world they were living in there was nothing odd in a husband asking his wife for a few minutes' private conversation. Polly got up at once and led the way into the bedroom, where the faint scent of Fabienne's *Arpège* still clung to the blankets.

'Polly,' said Jacques abruptly, 'the road to Sospel will be a battlefield within twelve hours. The Boches are on their way, and this place is much too near the road. I want you to take the little bus and drive the Juracs down to the Profettis.'

'You'll never get her to go down to Nice.'

'That's what Julien says. He's out there now trying to persuade the old man to see reason.'

'While you try to persuade me? I'm ready to go, but I ought to take some other people along with the Juracs. If you brought the bus, there'll be room for some of the mothers and babies from Castillon village.'

'If you don't think it's too big a take-on, darling.' He knew he could count on Polly; it was exactly what he had wanted her to say.

'Can I drive straight down to Menton? If the Boches are on their way, I mean?'

'No, it's too late for that. You'll have to go by L'Escarène.'

'I don't know where that is.'

'You know the left arm of the Y, that begins at the bridge of the Bévéra?'

'Yes, but I can't go right into Sospel, even with the Red Cross on the bus!'

'You won't have to. You take the road to the left, just after you cross the plateau. It looks like an approach to Fort Castillon, but it goes right over the Col St. Jean to L'Escarène, and the Americans are there already.'

'How far is it?'

'To Nice? Not more than fifty kilometres, starting from here.'

'I hope it's not as bad a road as the Col de Brouis.' Polly tried to smile. 'The approach to Fort Castillon—I think I know the road you mean ... But won't that take me right under the guns of the fort?'

Jacques caught her in his arms. 'Pauline,' he said, 'it's the only chance for you. And for the Juracs too, and the little kids with their mothers. I know it's dangerous, but it's a damned sight less dangerous than staying here.'

'And you want to use the farm,' she said. 'Isn't that it? Isn't the Jurac farm a strong point for the maquis, on the road down to Sospel?'

'I want to divide my force, such as it is,' he said. 'The boys from Mont Ours are coming down to reinforce us at the camp.'

'The Mont Ours!' she said. 'That's an idea! I might be able to get round the old lady by invoking the Holy Bear ... What do I do when I get to Nice, and dump all the refugees on their relatives?'

'You go to the Palais Lascaris and wait for me there.'

'Oh my darling!' she said, pressing herself close to him, 'it all started at the Palais Lascaris, didn't it? I knew we'd end up there some day—'

'We'll begin there,' said Jacques. 'How are you off for money?'

'I haven't very much.'

'Here's five hundred francs. If you need more, go to Maître Pastorelli. You've got your ring?'

The diamond and sapphire ring Jacques had given her in Paris was the only thing of value left to them, and by good luck Polly had been wearing it when the Gestapo raided the apartment. She undid the button of her shirt and showed him the ring where she had worn it ever since, on a thin metal chain round her neck. Jacques stooped and kissed the hollow of her throat.

'And you—what are you going to do?' she asked in fear.

'We're going to fight the Germans, as best we can, until the Americans get here. Then I'll come to you in Nice, and after that—'

'Must there be an after?'

'Then I'll go to General Béthouart's headquarters, wherever they are, and re-enlist in the Chasseurs Alpins.'

She gave him a long look, dry-eyed, and said, 'I see you have it all mapped out. I'd better go and get started on Madame Jurac, and you'll have to drive down to the village and see who wants to leave. How are you going to get back to camp?'

'We've got our bikes in the bus.'

The prosaic words, so characteristic of the man, touched Polly as no romantic farewell, no heroic appeal could possibly have done. She caught Jacques in a strangling embrace which was their real goodbye.

In the kitchen Julien Monnier was scowling. Monsieur Jurac, he said, was all set to go to the Profettis. But as for the old lady ... Polly helped Madame Jurac out of her low chair and opened the outer door.

'See the Holy Bear,' she said coaxingly. The Mont Ours was

clear against the blue sky, a deity since prehistoric times to the people of the mountains. 'He's telling you to go to your poor daughter. She's very sad and longing for her mother. See the Bear! If he were angry you would see the clouds and hear the thunder. Come with Pauline to Nice and make the Bear happy.'

'Did you ever hear anything like that?' whispered Julien Monnier. 'The damnedest rubbish—'

'It works, though.' For Madame Jurac, quite reassured, was trotting into the *mas*, demanding her best coat and her black bonnet.

Four young mothers and five little children were picked up at Castillon, where the rest of the villagers stoutly declared that no Boches were going to make them move from their own homes. 'I've picked four that swear they've relatives to go to,' Jacques muttered to Julien. 'Otherwise the whole lot will fetch up at the Palais Lascaris. I know Pauline!'

'Pauline and the Holy Bear,' said Julien. 'We're going to need that Bear, Jack, when the Boches arrive from Menton.'

Pauline and her two old charges were ready when they got back to the Jurac farm. The farewells were short. '*A bientôt!*' cried Pauline as she drove away. 'See you soon!' And that was all.

They had to wait for hours before the enemy appeared. The Germans had decided to evacuate Menton by night, when the fire from the naval vessels had ended, and to the maquisards trained to night attacks they were an easy mark. They had brought horse-drawn transport with them, and a shower of incendiary bottles so maddened the poor animals that they broke away from the high road at Monti and careered over an old viaduct which ended in mid-air, so that the horses, the field kitchens, the field ambulances and the drivers fell headlong into the ravine of the Carëi from where there was no rescue. The vehicles on the road had their tyres burned out and, where there were better marksmen, their crews killed: nor was it possible to pursue the maquisards into the depths of the forest, for the mechanised transport coming up behind the damaged vehicles created a road block which stretched almost the whole of the five kilometres back to Menton. It was daybreak before the convoy was rolling again, and then, just beyond the shuttered village of Castillon, there was another ambush, set by Julien Monnier and twenty men. They followed the same tactics of firing from the real maquis of shrubs and scented broom, and once more the convoy was held up us bursting tyres and wounded drivers slewed the vehicles into the ditch or across the pastures, until at the last hairpin bend before Sospel a band of young boys, enraged by the deaths of the Albaréa maquisards, were waiting to copy the *groupe franc* up the hill. Three of these boys, not more than sixteen years old, died within sight of the red roofs of their homes, just as Bernard, the baby train wrecker, had died among the horses on the viaduct at Monti. These were the only lads to be killed, although there were wounds and concussions, and one fractured thigh, before by sheer force of numbers the Germans fought their way into Sospel.

Down in the valley of the Bévéra they were in a trap again. Their escape route into Italy by rail had been cut by the maquisards, and the road back to Nice by L'Ecarène, over which Polly Brunel had driven her bus, was barred to them by the Americans. Jacques and his guerillas again and again attacked the German outposts, trying to bring some relief to the little town which, since the first shells began to fall, had been without water, telephones or electricity, and where the civilian hospital was in ruins. The Hotel de Paris was manned by volunteers and used as an emergency hospital. There was machine-gunning in the streets, and Jacques Brunel lost ten men out of the one hundred maquisards who died in the Sospel fighting. He had several other men, not severely wounded, in the barn at the Jurac farm.

Meanwhile great things were happening in the outside world. General de Lattre de Tassigny's command changed its name from 'Army B' to the 1st French Army, and was preparing to drive through the Vosges into Germany. General Leclerc and his tankmen, making up for their fifty-six days' delay in going into action, were given the honour, by General Bradley, of being the first Allied troops to enter Paris and receive the German surrender. The resistants, who forced the surrender, had risen several days before. General Charles de Gaulle, alias 'Wormwood', arrived in Paris on August 25. If Leclerc came late, de Gaulle came later. It was D-Day plus 80 when he arrived in France.

Since his flight to England in June 1940 the Leader of All Free Frenchmen had spent only a few hours on French soil. This was at Bayeux in June 1944, after which, when the July fighting in Normandy was most severe, he had spent three days in Washington. Since then he had remained in the 'crab-pot' of Algiers. His activities there were negative, as in his failure to send help to the

Vercors, or boorish, as in his refusal to meet Mr. Churchill when his benefactor visited Algiers in August, but such was the power of the BBC, such was the force of his propaganda machine that he was received in Paris like a conqueror. At the Hôtel de Ville he was cheered by a crowd nearly as large as the crowd which in April was cheering for Marshal Pétain.

Echoes of these doings reached the maquisards in the south of France by way of the radio, already being purged of collaborationists, and by a new paper called *Le Patriote de Nice*, no more accurate in the spelling of proper names than *L'Eclaireur*, but free of Vichy control. Jean Dupont brought up copies of *Le Patriote* when he brought food to the maquisards in Menton forest. One copy contained the news of the death on active service of Antoine de St. Exupéry. 'The doyen of all war pilots', as the paper called him, 'a great French writer, philosopher and poet', had disappeared on July 31, while on a photographic reconnaissance out of Bastia/Poretta. No reference was made to the disappearance of Michel Marchand, which had taken place less than three weeks earlier, but at least the *Patriote*'s obituary was worthy of the man. In Algiers the disappearance of Saint Ex. was forbidden to be mentioned in the press. The followers of 'Wormwood' started a whispering campaign, saying St. Exupéry had deserted and would be heard of next in Vichy. The opponents of 'Wormwood' said the veteran pilot's aircraft had been sabotaged. The 'hate, muck and slander factory', as Saint Ex. himself had called it, was still in full production. The mystery of his death was never solved.

Jacques Brunel, who had admired him as a writer, regretted the death of Antoine de St. Exupéry, but with the newspaper Dupont gave him a letter from Polly which absorbed his whole attention. It was grimy from passing through a dozen hands, but it brought Jacques the priceless news that she had reached Nice safely with her passengers, had a roof over her head in the old flat at the Palais Lascaris, and was waiting for him there.

That day he began to think they had a future, and in the evening Jacques Brunel made his first and last speech to the men of his maquis. There were a hundred of them in the forest now, living under military discipline, but without any of the ceremonial, such as the hoisting and lowering of the Tricolore, dear to more flamboyant guerrilla leaders. The boys appreciated that, and one of the reasons they respected *le patron* was that he never indulged in the exhortations or patriotic blarney to be heard in other camps. It wasn't that he couldn't, mind you: Captain Jack could plead in court with the best of them when he was paid to do it. But he knew better than to jaw the fellows' heads off when they were all on the job together. He told you what to do, sure, and you did it, but not for the sake of *l'honneur*, God help us, and still less for *la gloire*.

It was de Gaulle, whose speeches were peppered with allusions to *l'honneur*, *la gloire* and *la France* (otherwise *moi-même*), who was uppermost in Jacques' mind when he called the men together on a September evening which had more than a hint of autumn in the air. He told them they might soon be disbanded. The war in the north was going well. 'Today the British entered Brussels,' he said, 'and the city of Lyon has been liberated No doubt the liberators will be coming our way soon. As a group we've achieved our purpose, which was to contain the enemy in Sospel, and with the help of our comrades on the other side of the Bévéra we've denied him any escape from his position. When the Americans arrive with heavy armour and air support Sospel will be set free. But our work isn't over. We all want to get back to our families or our boats or our workshops, but we're not free to go until the final defeat of Germany There's a French Army in our country now, and at the replacement depots in Nice we can enlist in the ranks under General de Lattre. General Béthouart, the victor of Narvik, is now in command of II Corps and heading for Besançon. I intend myself to make for his headquarters, and any man who fought with the 'Blue Devils' is welcome to come with me. But remember, when we leave the forest our choice is free. We've fought in the Resistance as a free group, bound to no general, bound by no oath: let's all be sure we use our freedom wisely and well.'

It was the only time Captain Jack had ever made any sort of political comment, and this one was cryptic enough to impress young minds. They all enjoyed his hint that the liberators were long in coming, for the youngsters had begun to say Menton was the forgotten town. Within a few days, however, the liberators appeared, Americans and Canadians together, fighting their way through the stiff opposition put up by the Germans left behind to hold the Côte d'Azur. The German batteries between Cap Martin and Menton kept up their fire against the naval shelling, and their minefields caused delay and destruction to the liberators. In Monaco houses and public buildings were destroyed, and at St. Roman seven people were killed by the explosion of an anti-tank mine. Two members of Jacques' original group, the Carpani brothers, were killed outside their bicycle shop by this explosion. That was bad enough, but as the worst of luck would have it, his friend and former corporal Jean Dupont was standing on the pavement talking to the Carpanis when the mine exploded and was killed outright. His death hit Jacques Brunel hard. Dupont had been one of his best men at Namsos and in the Resistance, tireless and optimistic through the years of waiting, and it was bitter to lose him at the moment when victory was so near. The only comfort remaining to Jacques was that he had got Polly safely away from the Col de Castillon.

The plateau, as he had predicted, was a battlefield. The village was caught in the crossfire between the German batteries round Sospel and the advancing Allies, and the remaining villagers were living in caverns in the mountainside. Menton was liberated on September 9, and though the much-tried citizens had been expecting *les américains* it was the First Canadian Special Service battalion who were the liberators, and the first Allied soldier to die for Menton was a lieutenant from Quebec named Paul Gatien Laporte. When the Americans arrived they brought with them a contingent of Japanese-American troops. The Mentonese had never heard of the Nisei, and when they saw Oriental faces in the Rue St. Michel they began to wonder if the war had taken an unexpected turn. But it was a detachment of Canadian sappers who first drove up the Sospel highway and made contact with Jacques Brunel.

That was a hilarious meeting in the overcrowded Jurac farm, with handshakings and backslappings and the opening of bottles hidden away for the occasion. The walking wounded hobbled in from the barn to join in the toasts, and the Canadians broke out their 'K' rations to share with the hungry men. 'We're at your orders, *mon lieutenant*,' said Jacques formally, when the celebrations ended. He didn't want to be at anybody's orders, for now that the worst strain was over he felt very tired. The Canadian officer, whose name was Bob and who appeared to be about twenty-two years old, produced a notebook. His own orders, he said, were to relieve the pressure on Sospel by reducing one of the German gun emplacements—he peered at his own handwriting—would it be right here at Castillon?

'You won't take Fort Castillon with a half-company,' said Jacques. 'That'll need bombardment from the air. Don't think we wouldn't have had a go at it ourselves, if it had been humanly possible, but it's not. They've laid a minefield along the road to the Col St. Jean, and only experienced mountaineers could get up the crags on the other side.' He remembered that he and Mike Marchand had made the climb when they were boys.

Finally, after a long discussion and study of his maps, the Canadian decided to attack a new gun emplacement near Albaréa.

'That's possible,' said Jacques. 'There used to be a maquis in that locality, and there are still kids in the forest who've kept a close watch on the German gunners. As of yesterday's report there were no mines in the area.'

The Canadian in his enthusiasm was for setting off to Albaréa immediately. Jacques advised him to bivouac in the farmhouse and give his men a few hours' sleep. It was a cold September night and the stars were shining when Monnier, who was to accompany the party, shook Captain Jack awake.

The journey through the pines and undergrowth took three hours instead of the two which Jacques had estimated, because the Canadian NCOs with the mine detectors moved forward very cautiously, and the other ranks were clearly not woodsmen, whatever else they might be. Jacques wished Mike Marchand could have seen and heard them clambering and panting while they tried to move as stealthily as Red Indians. 'I'll have a lot to tell old Michel when I see him again,' he said to himself, and touched the young officer's sleeve to let him know they were coming up to their target.

The new gun emplacement looked like a natural for dynamite. The guns had been laid on the high ground and trained on the bridge of the Bévéra and the houses along its banks, while in their rear a high overhanging crag gave shelter to the saboteurs. Jacques hoped the Canadian boy was a competent hit man, and wished Charles Maxwell, called Aletti, were with them on this sortie. The men seemed to be laying the charges smartly enough. Their officer gave the word to run and touched off the fuse.

At the last moment, when they were all running downhill, they heard the shout of a sentry on the high ground. Then there was a thunderclap of sound, and the rocks in his path seemed to rise up and rain down on Jacques Brunel. Was the fuse too short, or the timing wrong—was it Marcati's blow, or the shock of Pierre

298

Orengo's betrayal? Was it the screech of bombs falling on Namsos long ago? Was it a lock shot off a train and Polly using German handcuffs as a weapon? The images and sounds were reeling in his brain as Jacques Brunel fell into a ravine of oblivion where the accumulation of all the noise and pain which began in the snows of Norway caught up with him at last.

His fight for Sospel was over.

THE AVENUE 1944

> *I see a beautiful city and a brilliant people*
> *rising from this abyss, and, in their struggles*
> *to be truly free, in their triumphs and defeats,*
> *through long, long years to come, I see the evil*
> *of this time and of the previous time of which*
> *this is the natural birth, gradually making*
> *expiation for itself and wearing out*
>
> *Charles Dickens*

I got a good place in what was called the press tribune, but which was only a section of the pavement of the Avenue des Champs Elysées roped off and reserved for the Allied war correspondents. The tribune filled up rapidly. Everyone wanted to see the military review of the eleventh of November 1944, when Winston Churchill stood at the saluting base almost opposite the place where we were waiting, in the middle of a crowd of half a million people.

I was standing in the front row, wedged in between Irving Greenbaum of the Chicago Clarion, who had been a war correspondent in France in 1918 and let everybody know it, and a man called Ed White, who was French by birth but a British war correspondent for the London Daily Journal. I liked Ed, an older man and a knowledgeable fellow who was always willing to share his knowledge. Although his service didn't go back as far as Irv's he had been a war correspondent since 1940, when he was an eyewitness of General de Gaulle's defeat at Dakar. His little boy had been killed in the Baedeker raid on Bath.

It was bitterly cold while we stood there waiting. That year winter came early, and frost was lying on the fields and hedges as I jeeped down from the Dutch front to see the great review. In Paris the weather was dry and the skies were grey above houses etched in silverpoint; the flags of the Allies were vivid notes of colour grouped round the Place de l'Etoile. The saluting base was empty, for Mr. Churchill had gone to the Arc de Triomphe to lay a wreath on the grave of the Unknown Soldier. Just so did a Roman general, on his day of triumph, go up beneath the arches to sacrifice.

The prime minister was not alone as he came down the Avenue. He was accompanied by General Charles de Gaulle, the acknowledged President of the Provisional Government of the French Republic, whose disdainful looks and imperial gestures showed that he took at least half the triumph for himself. I once saw a picture of the Battle of Waterloo in an Amsterdam museum. It was a good painting, and from the figures on the canvas and the legend beneath it was clear that Napoleon had been vanquished by the Prince of Orange, with the assistance of an Irish lieutenant by the name of Wellington. In the same way de Gaulle had liberated France, not so much assisted as impeded by an English politician called Winston Churchill.

The French call the eleventh of November la Fête de la Victoire, meaning the victory of World War One. We were still months away from victory in the Second World War, for the enemy was resisting strongly in the Vosges, and was preparing the heavy blows of the Battle of the Bulge. But victory was in the air that day as the Parisians gave the welcome to Mr. Churchill which his long fidelity to them had deserved. The cheering was still going on when he took his place beside de Gaulle on the reviewing stand, and the parade began.

Thousands of brave men had died to make this day possible. Hundreds of those who marched down the Avenue were going out to fight new battles. There were elements of all the French Services, land, sea and air, in the procession, with units from the American, British and Canadian forces. The parade was to last for one and a half hours. The martial music played, the flags went by.

The great moment for Mr. Churchill came when the Grenadier Guards marched past. They were in battle dress with white pipe-clayed gaiters, marching as only the Guards can march, with the precision of a beautiful human machine. 'Some talk of Alexander and some of Hercules,' the bugles sang, and Mr. Churchill was ablaze with pride.

But of all the world's brave heroes, there's none that can compare
With a tow, row, row, row, row, row, for the British Grenadier

'Now watch him cry,' said Eddie White to me. Across the Champs Elysées we could see the tears rolling down Winston Churchill's face.

'I would weep too, if I had to stand beside de Gaulle,' I said, and Eddie laughed.

'How long do you give him?' he asked.

302

'In power? Eighteen months.' In that I was too generous. Only fourteen months were to pass before Charles de Gaulle, unable to command a duly elected parliament as he had commanded his Committees, gave up his office and condemned himself to twelve years in the political wilderness. 'Eighteen months too long,' I said.

'You really hate him, don't you?' said Ed, and he was right. I hated him, yes I hated him that day and always, for the monstrous campaign of bullying, broken promises and emotional blackmail which had carried him, for however short a time, to power, and for his enmity to those who had helped to raise him up. I hated him for his attempts to increase his own prestige in France by playing rough with the British and the Americans. I remembered saying to Mike Marchand in Scotland two years ago that de Gaulle would return to France like the Bourbons 'in the baggage wagons of the Allies' and it had come true. He returned in an American plane, from Algiers, a city the Americans had captured, and he was carried to Paris by the force of American tanks and British bayonets.

It was strange to think of Mike Marchand that day, in the city where I had once heard him cheered himself. His career in aviation, and his fine war record with the Royal Air Force had been mentioned briefly, along with his mysterious death, at the end of October in the Paris Herald Tribune, with the announcement of the birth of a son to his widow at Cascaís in Portugal. I was glad to think that while Marchand slept the sleep of the brave, some of his vitality had been left to the world.

I knew his cousin, Jacques Brunel, better than I knew Mike Marchand. Or rather I had seen him more often, though always in a Scottish hospital bed. I didn't recognise him when a unit of the Chasseurs Alpins marched down the Avenue with their inimitable quickstep, because my eyes were on the whole of them and not on one. There they went, the Blue Devils, and when I remembered men in that uniform hauling down their flag in a Glasgow street at the time when France surrendered, I understood why Mr. Churchill wept.

'There's Jacques Brunel,' said Ed White, who knew everybody. 'I was hearing about him last week at Besançon. They say he did a great job in the Resistance in the south, and was badly knocked about towards the end, but he's all right now. General Béthouart's given him a job on his Staff.'

I recognised him then. The thin serious face, the steady look, *made a sudden and strong impression on my mind as the blue-clad ranks went past.*

'I see a beautiful city and a brilliant people rising from this abyss and struggling to be truly free—' I didn't know I was looking at a future prime minister, but on the Champs Elysées, under the grey Paris skies, I knew that if France were to rise again it would be due not to the vain and the self-seeking, but to the work of men like Jacques Brunel.